LEE BROOK

The Shadows of Yuletide

MIDDLETON
PARK PRESS

First published by Middleton Park Press 2023

Copyright © 2023 by Lee Brook

All rights reserved. No part of this publication may be reproduced, stored or transmitted in any form or by any means, electronic, mechanical, photocopying, recording, scanning, or otherwise without written permission from the publisher. It is illegal to copy this book, post it to a website, or distribute it by any other means without permission.

This novel is entirely a work of fiction. The names, characters and incidents portrayed in it are the work of the author's imagination. Any resemblance to actual persons, living or dead, events or localities is entirely coincidental.

Lee Brook asserts the moral right to be identified as the author of this work.

Lee Brook has no responsibility for the persistence or accuracy of URLs for external or third-party Internet Websites referred to in this publication and does not guarantee that any content on such Websites is, or will remain, accurate or appropriate.

Designations used by companies to distinguish their products are often claimed as trademarks. All brand names and product names used in this book and on its cover are trade names, service marks, trademarks and registered trademarks of their respective owners. The publishers and the book are not associated with any product or vendor mentioned in this book. None of the companies referenced within the book have endorsed the book.

First edition

This book was professionally typeset on Reedsy. Find out more at reedsy.com

For Bookclub @resident—
Thank you for supporting a local author.
Merry Christmas!

Contents

Chapter One	1
Chapter Two	8
Chapter Three	17
Chapter Four	23
Chapter Five	31
Chapter Six	39
Chapter Seven	48
Chapter Eight	56
Chapter Nine	64
Chapter Ten	73
Chapter Eleven	82
Chapter Twelve	91
Chapter Thirteen	99
Chapter Fourteen	106
Chapter Fifteen	114
Chapter Sixteen	123
Chapter Seventeen	133
Chapter Eighteen	141
Chapter Nineteen	150
Chapter Twenty	159
Chapter Twenty-one	169
Chapter Twenty-two	180
Chapter Twenty-three	190
Chapter Twenty-four	200

Chapter Twenty-five	208
Chapter Twenty-six	220
Chapter Twenty-seven	228
Chapter Twenty-eight	237
Chapter Twenty-nine	245
Chapter Thirty	253
Chapter Thirty-one	261
Chapter Thirty-two	269
Chapter Thirty-three	277
Chapter Thirty-four	285
Chapter Thirty-five	295
Chapter Thirty-six	303
Chapter Thirty-seven	312
Chapter Thirty-eight	322
Chapter Thirty-nine	331
Chapter Forty	341
Chapter Forty-one	350
About the Author	358
Also by Lee Brook	359

Chapter One

The streets of Leeds lay under a heavy shroud of fog that Wednesday evening, each cobbled pathway bathed in the dim glow of streetlights. The city, usually vibrant and alive, had succumbed to an eerie desolation. The mist muffled sounds, lending an otherworldly quality to the night. Shadows clung to the corners, and the faint echo of distant footsteps seemed like whispers from another realm.

Through this misty veil, a man in his mid-forties navigated his way home. His breath formed clouds in the cold air, each exhalation a visible testament to the night's chill. Dressed in his casual post-work attire, he had just shed the jolly facade of Santa Claus, a role he played at the Merrion Centre. Now, the festive cheer of his day job felt worlds away as he trod the path to Richmond Hill.

The backstreets of Leeds City Centre, usually familiar and benign, felt unsettling under the fog's blanket. He passed by the dimly lit Aagrah restaurant, its usual bustle now just a memory. The further he walked, the more he felt a prickle of unease. It was as if the fog concealed more than just the night; it hid secrets and whispers of unseen threats.

Down St Peter's Place, his steps quickened, a subconscious response to the growing sense of anxiety. He glanced over his shoulder, a habit born of a lifetime in the city, but tonight, it was more than just routine caution. The fog rendered his surroundings obscure, shadows merging with reality. Yet, despite his heightened vigilance, he saw nothing definitive through the misty curtain.

The streets twisted and turned, a labyrinth in the night. With each step, the man felt a growing dread, an unshakeable feeling that he was not alone. His mind told him it was just the fog playing tricks, yet his instincts screamed otherwise. He pressed on, the need to reach the safety of his home driving him forward.

A solitary figure trailed behind the man, a silent spectre in the mist. Their steps were inaudible, lost in the dense fog that blanketed the city. Only the faint outline of a Santa Claus hat atop their head betrayed their presence, a chilling incongruity against the night's shroud.

From this distance, the person watched the man who turned into Brick Street, the narrower, more deserted alleyway. Here, the ambient sounds of the city, the distant hum of traffic, and the muted bustle of nightlife all faded into nothingness. His isolation was complete, his vulnerability stark in the alley's confining shadows. The person observed this with cold detachment, their anticipation heightening as the man ventured deeper into solitude.

As the victim's pace slowed, a sense of false security crept in, a dangerous lull in his vigilance. The stalker, meanwhile, maintained their steady, ghost-like pursuit. Each step was measured, patient, biding their time until the moment was ripe. The Santa hat, a grotesque symbol of merriment, bobbed gently with their movements, a dark harbinger of what was to come.

CHAPTER ONE

The victim was oblivious to the danger that stalked him, a threat as silent as the fog itself. The killer's presence was an unseen threat, a shadow moving through the mist with deadly intent. The eerie calm of the alleyway, its damp cobbles and looming walls, set the stage for the impending horror.

With its fog and shadows, the night was a perfect accomplice, cloaking the killer's movements and masking their approach. In the heart of Leeds, under a veil of mist, the killer readied for the strike, the culmination of their sinister hunt. The victim, alone and unguarded, continued unknowingly towards his fate, a fate that lurked just steps behind him in the fog.

Suddenly, the man halted, a faint sound catching his attention. He scanned the murky surroundings, the racing of his heart loud in his ears. The mist played tricks on his eyes; every shadow seemed to shift, every shape a potential threat. But the alley offered no clear danger, just the oppressive fog and his mounting anxiety.

With a deep, steadying breath, he forced himself to move on. His footsteps echoed hollowly as he ventured towards the railway bridge, the sound oddly loud in the quiet night. The weight of the fog seemed to press down on him, thick and suffocating. His mind raced, grappling with the irrational fear that clawed at his senses.

The man's steps quickened, driven by an instinctive urge to clear the open vulnerability of the underpass. The dense mist seemed to swallow him as he moved under its arches, the faint sounds of the city muffled to nothingness.

His breath misted in the air, each exhalation a visible testament to the chill that had nothing to do with the night's cold. He felt exposed under the bridge, the open space around him a stark contrast to the enclosed alleyways he had just left.

Unseen, the stalker followed. Each step was deliberate, silent on the damp cobblestones. They watched the man's every move, their patience undisturbed by his quickened pace.

The man glanced back one last time, a reflexive look born from the primal fear that now gripped him. The bridge's shadows offered no reassurance, no sign that he was indeed alone. With a shiver that ran deeper than cold, he turned back and quickened his pace, desperate to leave the bridge and its oppressive atmosphere.

But the stalker was ready. The moment was upon them, the culmination of their silent hunt. In the shadows under the railway bridge, where the fog was thickest and the night deepest, they prepared to strike. The tension that had built in the silent pursuit was about to break, the quiet about to be shattered by an act of violence that would ripple through the city of Leeds.

The mist-laden night in Leeds carried a hush, broken only by the measured footsteps of the man as he entered the gaping maw of the railway bridge, a structure that loomed as a silent sentinel in the fog. As he neared its end, his shoulders began to relax, the tension wrought by paranoia slowly unspooling.

In his mind, he chided himself for being overly cautious. "It's just the fog and the night playing tricks," he muttered, his voice barely a whisper against the whistling wind. His pace slowed the rhythmic echo of his steps on the bridge now a leisurely cadence.

Reaching into his coat pocket, he pulled out his phone, the screen's glow a stark contrast in the dim surroundings. His fingers swiped across it, a momentary escape into the digital world. He scrolled through messages, his attention now divided between the path ahead and the device in his hand.

The stalker, a shadow within the mist, observed this change. They noted the victim's slowed pace and the distraction presented by the phone. It was an opportunity, a moment of vulnerability in the otherwise cautious man. Their steps remained silent, a whisper against the cobbled path, their presence still masked by the thick fog.

In this lapse of vigilance, the man was blissfully unaware of the danger that continued to stalk him. His gaze flicked between the phone and the path, a subconscious effort to remain aware of his surroundings, but his focus was clearly compromised.

The bridge behind him was now a fading outline, its presence a mere echo in the fog. Ahead, the streets of Leeds awaited, seemingly ordinary but for the predator and prey that moved through them. The stalker's patience was unyielding, their resolve unwavering. This was their domain, a city cloaked in fog and mystery, where their grim intentions could unfold unseen.

As the man pocketed his phone and resumed his journey, a false sense of security enveloped him. He believed the imagined threat had passed, that the bridge and its eerie atmosphere were behind him. But the genuine peril was ever-present, a silent force moving inexorably closer in the shrouded night.

The attack was brutal, efficient, and utterly ruthless. The man, caught entirely off guard, gasped, a sound muffled by the fog and his assailant's grip. He struggled in a desperate fight for life, his limbs flailing in vain against the overpowering force of his attacker. His attempts to scream were stifled, his cries swallowed by the thick mist that enveloped them both.

But the struggle was futile. The killer's strength was overwhelming, their determination cold and unyielding. The man's resistance waned quickly, his energy sapped by fear and the brutal efficiency of the attack. In the end, he lay subdued under the killer's iron grasp, the fight draining from his body as he succumbed to the inevitable.

Predator and prey returned to the bridge with a silence so profound it was as if the night itself was holding its breath. The only sound was the heavy breathing of the killer, a harsh rasp that seemed too loud in the quiet that followed the vicious beating.

With a chilling precision, the killer set to work. They arranged the lifeless body in a grotesque, Christmas-themed display, a macabre twist on the festive season. The victim, once a symbol of holiday cheer, was now a pawn in a twisted game, his Santa Claus attire a jarring contrast to the horror of the scene.

The killer's actions were methodical, each movement deliberate, suggesting a mindset warped by a dark and twisted vision. The scene they created under the bridge was a scene of terror, a grim parody of the season's joy.

Once the scene was set, the killer slipped away into the night, vanishing into the fog as silently as they had arrived. The mist closed in around the gruesome spectacle, hiding it from view as if to spare the city from the horror.

Once a mere passageway, the path under the bridge was now a stage for a nightmare, a silent witness to a crime that would soon send shock waves through Leeds. The killer, a ghost in the fog, left behind a scene that would haunt the city for years to come, a chilling reminder of the evil that lurked in its

CHAPTER ONE

shadows.

A late-night worker, weary from the day's labour, strolled down the alleyway towards the railway bridge, his mind preoccupied with thoughts of home. The alley, a familiar shortcut, tonight held a sinister surprise.

As he stepped under the bridge, his foot struck something unexpected. Startled, he glanced down, and his blood froze. There, in the dim light, lay a body dressed in a Santa Claus outfit, arranged in a grotesque, holiday-themed display. His shock was palpable, a visceral punch that left him momentarily breathless.

The worker's eyes widened in horror, his heart pounding frantically. The scene before him was something out of a nightmare, a stark and twisted contrast to the festive season. He fumbled for his phone, hands shaking, and dialled emergency services. The words stumbled out in a torrent, his voice barely above a whisper, "There's a body... under the railway bridge near the BBC place... dressed as Santa."

The call set into motion an urgent response. Within minutes, the stillness of the night was shattered by the piercing wail of police sirens. Blue and red lights sliced through the fog, converging on the scene with a sense of dire purpose.

The first to arrive were uniformed officers, their expressions grim as they cordoned off the area. The cavern beneath the bridge, once a mere crossing, was now a crime scene, its dark corners to be combed for clues. The night had taken a sinister turn, the city's festive cheer now overshadowed by a chilling crime.

Chapter Two

George Beaumont wrestled with the artificial Christmas tree, attempting to set it upright. His fiancée, Isabella, handed him branches, her face etched with amusement and exasperation. On the floor, their infant daughter, Olivia, played with strands of tinsel, her giggles filling the room. "Should've gone with the real one, gorgeous," Isabella teased, handing him another branch.

George grunted, a half-smile on his face. "It's not Christmas without a bit of struggle, is it?" He finally manoeuvred the branch into its slot and stood back to assess his work. Then he froze as his phone rang. He glanced at the screen, the caller ID flashing a name that tightened his stomach. He stepped away from the festive chaos of his living room, where Isabella was untangling a mess of fairy lights, and Olivia was babbling joyously.

"DI Beaumont," he answered, his voice a low, steady contrast to the background hum of his home.

The voice on the other end, crisp and official, cut through the warmth of the family evening. "Boss, there's been a murder," Detective Constable Jay Scott reported.

George's expression hardened. The joyful noise from his family now seemed distant, incongruous with the gravity

CHAPTER TWO

of the call. He turned his back to the room, focusing on the information Jay relayed. The details were sparse but significant: a body found in the city centre not far from the BBC building, staged grotesquely in a Christmas display.

It was a chilling echo of a long-unsolved case from his early career.

"I'll be right there," George said, his decision immediate.

He ended the call and stood for a moment, gathering himself. The detective in him had swiftly taken over, the family man receding into the background. He turned to Isabella, his face set in a grim mask, instantly conveying the urgency.

"Something's come up at work. I need to go," he said, his tone leaving no room for questions.

Isabella's expression shifted from confusion to understanding, a shadow of worry crossing her features. "Be careful, George," she said softly, her gaze flickering to Olivia, who remained blissfully unaware of the change in atmosphere.

George nodded a brief touch on Isabella's shoulder, his only goodbye. He moved to the door, each step taking him further from the warmth of his family and deeper into the cold reality of his profession.

Inside the car, the warmth of the heater battled the chill that had nothing to do with the December cold. George's mind was a cyclone, thoughts swirling with the urgency of the new case and echoes of the past. Driving through the sleeping city, slicing his car through the fog that blanketed the city, George's mind was a labyrinth of thoughts, theories, and questions. The festive decorations adorning the streets seemed out of place now, their cheerfulness starkly contrasting with the darkness he was about to witness.

A decade ago, a similar case had consumed him, one that

had remained a stubborn, unresolved shadow in his career. Oliver Hughes, a man in his thirties, part of a group George had been investigating, was found dead in Leeds City Centre. The image of Hughes, dressed in a Santa Claus costume, lifeless in a cold alley, was etched into George's memory. It had been ruled an accidental death, a tragic outcome of a prank gone wrong. But George had never bought that narrative. The inconsistencies in the postmortem report, the hushed whispers, and the reluctance of witnesses to speak up—all pointed to something more sinister.

Pulling up to the scene, George's eyes were drawn to the perimeter of blue lights, cutting through the fog like beacons of truth in a sea of uncertainty. He stepped out, the chill of the air biting at his skin, yet it was the chill of realisation that ran deeper. The area was cordoned off with police tape, a stark barrier between the everyday world and the grim reality of his profession. The area was eerily quiet, the usual city sounds muted by the surrounding buildings and the dense fog that seemed to swallow everything. Under the pale glow of streetlights obscured by fog, George's footsteps echoed off the damp cobblestones.

After getting the constable to sign him in and dressing up in his Tyvek suit, mask, gloves and shoe covers, George ducked under the tape, his experienced gaze sweeping over the scene, absorbing every detail. The victim lay in the centre of the underpass, illuminated by the stark light of the forensic team's lamps, dressed in a Santa Claus costume that was now a grotesque mockery of holiday cheer.

The scene before him was eerily reminiscent of the Hughes case. The victim lay in a grotesque parody of festive cheer, his body arranged with a precision that spoke of a killer's careful planning. It wasn't just the costume or the staging; it was the air of theatricality that hung over the scene, a dreadful performance laid out for an audience of one—the West Yorkshire Police.

George's eyes narrowed as he surveyed the area, his trained gaze picking up on details like the placement of the body, the angle of the wounds, and the careful arrangement of the Christmas props. It was all too familiar. The killer was playing a game, one that George was all too eager to engage in.

"Boss?" Detective Constable Jay Scott approached, his face grim, his voice steady despite the grimness of the scene. "The victim is Ryan Baxter. Mid-forties. We found his ID on him."

George nodded, his mind already racing at the recollection of the name. George's eyes narrowed. The past was clawing back into the present. "Cause of death?" he asked.

"Severe trauma, sir," Tashan interjected, "Looks like there was a struggle. Defensive wounds on his hands and arms."

"Time of death?"

"Dr Ross estimates between eleven and midnight, boss," Jay replied.

George crouched beside the body, his eyes scanning the injuries. They were precise, the work of someone who knew exactly what they were doing. This was personal, a fact that sent a shiver down George's spine that had nothing to do with the cold.

He stood, his gaze drifting to the buildings surrounding the alley. "Any witnesses?"

Candy stepped forward, her expression serious. "No direct witnesses, sir, but some locals reported a suspicious figure. And there's CCTV footage we're pulling now."

George nodded, his brain ticking over each detail. Given

the fog and the hour, the lack of witnesses wasn't surprising, but the CCTV footage could be crucial. He turned back to the body, the macabre setting a stark contrast to the festive season. Ryan Baxter, once a name in a file, now a symbol in a killer's twisted game.

"Keep the area locked down. I want a full door-to-door in the morning and check every camera in the area," George ordered, his voice carrying the weight of experience and authority. "Oh, and keep me updated on the CCTV," George said, his voice steady despite the turmoil inside. He turned back to the scene, his eyes once again falling on the victim. Ryan Baxter was now part of a narrative that was unfolding in a way George had hoped it never would.

* * *

Amidst the sea of uniforms and flashing lights, Paige McGuiness stood on the periphery of the scene, her presence almost ethereal in the mist. Clad in a sharp, functional coat, her notebook clutched firmly, she watched with an eagle's eye, her pen moving swiftly across the pages.

Paige, a seasoned journalist known for her incisive reporting, blended into the background yet missed nothing. She absorbed every detail: the officers' movements, the snippets of conversation, the layout of the crime scene. Her demeanour was calm, her focus unyielding, betraying her years of experience covering the grimmest of stories.

Occasionally, she drifted towards the bystanders, her approach gentle but purposeful. Paige had a knack for making people talk, her questions direct yet empathetic. She listened intently, nodding, her pen never ceasing its dance. Each piece of information, no matter how small, was a thread in the larger tapestry of the story she was weaving.

The bystanders, some curious, some shocked, opened up to her. A man mentioned seeing a shadowy figure lurking near under the bridge earlier in the evening. A woman spoke of unusual noises, a commotion she couldn't place. Paige's notes grew dense with these details, each one meticulously recorded.

Her eyes flicked back to the crime scene, to the body laid out in a grotesque mockery of holiday cheer. This was no ordinary murder, and Paige sensed the story unfolding here was far more complex than it appeared. She observed Detective Inspector George Beaumont, his demeanour a blend of intense focus and underlying concern, as he surveyed the scene.

Paige had crossed paths with George plenty of times before, their interactions marked by mutual respect tinged with wariness. She knew his reputation for dogged determination, his knack for unravelling the most tangled of cases. And she was the same, she supposed.

As their eyes met briefly across the divide of the crime scene tape, a silent acknowledgement passed between them—a recognition of the gravity of what lay ahead.

As the night deepened, Paige continued her vigil, her mind already piecing together the narrative. The murder, the victim's past, the eerie staging—it all pointed to a story that would grip the city of Leeds. She knew she had to tread carefully, balancing the public's right to know with the sensitivity such a case demanded.

* * *

As the detectives dispersed to follow his orders, George stood alone for a moment, the chill of the night seeping through his coat. The ghost of the unresolved case was looming; a shadow cast long and dark over the present. George crouched beside the body, examining it. The struggle was up close and personal; the killer was strong, overpowering Baxter with alarming brutality.

Pathologist Dr Christian Ross and Crime Scene Manager Lindsey Yardley waited, their expressions solemn.

"Do you have a confirmed time of death yet, Dr Ross?" George asked, his voice cutting through the eerie silence.

Dr Ross, a seasoned professional who had seen more than his share of such scenes, replied, "Around midnight, give or take. The cold makes it a bit harder, to be precise."

George nodded, processing this information. Midnight. The city of Leeds would have been a mix of late-night revellers and quiet homes. It narrowed the window but also widened the possibilities.

Christian stood beside George, his expression grave. "I've seen this type of murder before," he remarked quietly, his eyes not leaving the body.

George turned to face him, his interest piqued. "You have?"

Dr Ross nodded, a shadow of concern crossing his features. "Yes, about a decade ago. The same meticulous binding, the same... brutal precision."

George's mind raced, connecting dots. "I remember it," he said. "Were you the pathologist on those cases?" he asked, the wheels turning in his head.

Dr Ross met George's gaze, a flicker of recognition in his eyes. "I was. But I didn't realise you were involved back then."

George's eyes narrowed slightly, his brain sifting through

memories of a decade ago, a case that had stayed with him, unresolved and haunting. "I was a Detective Constable at the time. It was one of my first major cases."

Dr Ross resumed his examination of the body, his movements deliberate and respectful. "The killer's method of display are consistent," he continued. "It suggests a level of expertise, a comfort with the act."

George absorbed this information, his thoughts darkening. The possibility that they were dealing with the same perpetrator from a decade ago was a disturbing prospect. It implied not only a serial killer but one who had evaded detection for years.

"We need to re-open the files from the previous murders," George said, his voice steady but tinged with urgency. "There could be a connection we missed."

Dr Ross nodded in agreement. "I'll go through my notes from back then. Maybe there's something we overlooked."

"Thank you."

"We found his wallet as you already know," Lindsey interjected, "but we found his mobile, too."

George's eyes flickered to the items in question. A wallet and a phone could be a treasure trove of information in a case like this. They could point to motives, connections, or even the killer.

He turned back to the body, his mind already racing with questions. Who was Ryan Baxter now compared to who he had been a decade ago? What thread connected him to the killer, and why the elaborate staging? Was it a copycat or was it the same killer?

The DI pointed towards the grotesque Christmas display. "Let's get everything back to the lab," George said finally, straightening up. "I want a full analysis of it all, including the phone and wallet. And check the surrounding area for any more clues."

Dr Ross and Lindsey nodded, each moving to carry out their part. The scene was a hive of activity, each person playing a role in the intricate dance of investigation.

George's thoughts drifted back to the Hughes case as the forensic team buzzed around him, collecting evidence and snapping photos. He remembered the frustration, the dead ends, the feeling of being so close yet so far from the truth. But this time was different; this time, he had a second chance, a chance to right a wrong that had haunted him for years.

The similarities between the two cases were more than coincidental; they were a pattern, a signature of a killer who had remained in the shadows for too long. George's jaw set in determination. This was more than just solving a murder; it was about unravelling a mystery that spanned a decade, about catching a ghost that had slipped through the cracks of the justice system. That or they had another copycat, and George wasn't sure he was up to catching another.

Chapter Three

Paige McGuiness, her reporter's instinct unerring, approached Detective Inspector George Beaumont. Her steps were measured, her eyes keenly observant.

George, standing near the police tape, turned as Paige approached. His stance was guarded, his eyes a mirror of the caution that years in the force had ingrained in him. The sight of the journalist at his crime scene was a familiar, albeit unwelcome, part of the landscape.

"Detective, can you give us any details about the investigation?" Paige asked, her voice betraying none of the urgency she felt. Her notepad was ready, her pen poised.

George regarded her, his expression unreadable. "We're in the early stages of the investigation, Miss McGuiness," he replied, his voice betraying a hint of weariness. "I can't disclose any specifics at this time."

Paige's eyes narrowed slightly, picking up on the nuances of his response. She was used to the dance, the delicate balancing act of probing for information while respecting the boundaries of the investigation.

"Is there anything you can share with the public?" she pressed, knowing her readers clamoured for any morsel of news.

George's gaze was steady, his response measured. "The public will be informed in due course. Right now, our focus is on conducting a thorough investigation."

The air between them was charged with the unspoken acknowledgement of their respective roles hanging heavy. George, the protector of the investigation's integrity, and Paige, the seeker of truths for public consumption. Their objectives were at odds, yet bound by the common goal of uncovering the truth.

Paige held his gaze for a moment longer, then nodded, her professional respect for his position evident. "Thank you, George," she said, stepping back. Her mind was already racing, piecing together the fragments of information, ready to craft her story.

As she retreated from the crime scene, her thoughts were already racing ahead. The article she would write would not only inform but evoke the deeper, darker undercurrents of the story.

George watched her retreat, a flicker of appreciation for her tenacity mixed with the constant wariness he felt towards the media. Paige McGuiness was a formidable journalist, her reputation for uncovering the heart of a story well known.

Driving through the fog-shrouded streets of Leeds towards the station, George felt the city's festive cheer clash with the darkness of the murder. Christmas lights twinkled in windows, blissfully unaware of the horror lurking in their midst.

Back at her desk, Paige's fingers flew over the keyboard, her notes transforming into sentences and paragraphs, a narrative taking shape. The story of the Santa Claus murder, as she had already begun to call it, was just beginning. And Paige McGuiness would be the one to tell it, to uncover the layers, to bring the hidden into light.

Amidst the hum of the engine and the rhythmic swipe of the wipers, George's thoughts drifted, pulling him back in time. The memory was vivid, almost tangible—a younger version of himself, fresh-faced and eager, working under the tutelage of Luke Mason. Those days were formative, the cases they worked on together shaping George into the detective he was today.

In the flashback, Luke's voice was clear, a mix of stern guidance and encouragement. "Watch and learn, George. This job's about seeing the unseen, connecting the dots that others miss." George had hung on every word, absorbing the lessons, determined to prove himself.

Snapped back to the present by the sound of his phone ringing, George refocused on the road. The present case, a chilling echo of the past, was an opportunity—a chance to right a wrong, to settle the unrest that had haunted him.

"DI Beaumont."

"Do you need us at the station, boss?" Jason Scott asked.

"What a silly question, DC Scott," George said, hanging up.

* * *

Arriving at the station, George's demeanour was all business. He strode through the corridors. The station was abuzz with activity, officers and detectives moving with purpose, the air thick with the urgency of the investigation.

The heavy door to the HMET floor at Elland Road police station swung open, admitting George into the heart of the investigative storm. The room was a hive of activity, screens flickering with data, phones ringing incessantly. George's arrival brought a momentary hush, his presence commanding an unspoken respect.

Detective Constables Jay Scott, Tashan Blackburn, and Candy Nichols converged around George, their expressions a mix of anticipation and concern. They sensed something different in this case, a gravity that was palpable in their leader's demeanour.

George scanned the room, his team's expectant faces urging him to reveal what weighed so heavily on his mind. "This isn't just another murder," he began, his voice a low rumble. The team leaned in, the intensity in George's eyes capturing their full attention. "The victim, Ryan Baxter, was part of a group we investigated a decade ago. One of them died back then, Oliver Hughes, and now Baxter. That leaves five more."

The team exchanged glances, the significance of George's words dawning on them. The past and present were colliding, the implications both ominous and urgent.

"We need to find the remaining five," George continued, his words crisp and direct. "Interview them, establish their alibis, understand their connections to Baxter. This is personal for our killer, and that's our key to unlocking this case."

Jay's eyes were sharp and analytical. "Any leads on their whereabouts, boss?"

George nodded. "We have addresses and last known contacts. Split up, cover more ground. Time is not on our side."

Tashan, his face set in determination, chimed in. "We'll get to it, sir. If there's a connection, we'll find it."

Candy, her expression thoughtful, added, "We need to tread carefully, sir. These men have been out of the spotlight for years. This will stir things up."

George acknowledged her point with a nod. "Agreed, Candy.

But we need answers, and we need them fast. This killer is making a statement, and we need to understand it before there's another victim." He paused. "Let's think about who we're dealing with," George explained, his voice cutting through the room's low hum. He moved to the Big Board, marker in hand, his movements precise and deliberate. "This killer is vicious but also methodical and calculated. The staging of the body, the thematic elements—it's theatrical, a message."

Detective Constable Jay Scott, leaning against a desk, nodded. "It's personal for them. They're reliving something, revisiting a past grievance."

"Exactly," George affirmed, his eyes scanning the room. "It suggests a deep-seated anger, a need for recognition or revenge. The Christmas theme isn't random; it's symbolic, a crucial part of their narrative."

Detective Constable Tashan Blackburn interjected, "Could it be someone from Baxter's past? Someone holding a grudge?"

George considered this, tapping the marker against the Big Board. "It's a possibility. The link to the old case, the specific target—it's too direct to be coincidental."

Detective Constable Candy Nichols, her brow furrowed in thought, added, "But why now? What's triggered this after a decade?"

"That's the key question," George said, turning to face his team. "Something has changed; something has set this in motion. We need to find that catalyst."

The room fell silent, and each member of the team lost in thought, piecing together the fragments of information. George's leadership, his ability to guide their focus and sharpen their thinking, was evident.

The team sprang into action, energised by the direction. George watched them, a sense of pride mixed with the heavy weight of responsibility. This was more than a case; it was a race against time, a battle of wits against a cunning adversary.

George remained at the centre of the room, his mind racing. The past case had been a thorn in his side, a blemish on an otherwise stellar career. The unresolved questions, the lingering doubts, had haunted him. And now, they were back, demanding attention.

Chapter Four

The Incident Room's door swung open, admitting Detective Sergeant Yolanda Williams, whose presence was immediately felt. Her striking hairstyle, a short afro mohawk adorned with red and green stripes, was not just a fashion statement—it was a symbol of her unique approach to life.

Detective Inspector George Beaumont turned, his eyes locking onto Yolanda as she approached, her confident stride cutting through the tense atmosphere. He had always admired her tenacity and her willingness to stand out in a crowd. In this room of sombre suits and serious faces, Yolanda was a splash of colour, a reminder that the world outside continued to turn, regardless of the darkness they faced within these walls.

Yolanda and George stood hunched over a bank of monitors, their eyes intently scrutinizing the grainy CCTV footage. The room was silent except for the occasional click of a mouse or a soft murmur of discussion. The footage, flickering on the screens, was a silent witness to the events of the night, holding secrets that George and Yolanda were determined to uncover.

The camera angle switched to the street outside the curry house, the neon sign casting a warm glow on the cobbled pavement. They watched as Ryan Baxter, the victim, strolled past, his gait relaxed yet slightly hurried. He glanced around, a casual observer unaware of the danger lurking just out of sight.

"Pause it there," George instructed, leaning closer to the screen. "See how he keeps looking over his shoulder? He sensed something."

Yolanda nodded, her fingers deftly controlling the playback. "He's uneasy. But did he know he was being followed, or was it just instinct?"

They watched as Baxter continued down the street, passing the familiar facade of the BBC building. The footage was clear here, but as Baxter approached the intersection leading to the railway bridge, the clarity waned, swallowed by the thick fog that had blanketed Leeds that night.

"Damn," George muttered, frustration lining his features. "We're losing him in the fog."

Yolanda adjusted the controls, attempting to enhance the image. "Wait, look there," she pointed to a figure emerging from the shadows a few paces behind Baxter.

The figure was indistinct, their features obscured by the low resolution and the fog. But one detail was unmistakably clear—the bright red of a Santa hat sitting incongruously atop their head.

"That's our killer," George said, his voice low and tense. "Just a shadow in a Santa hat, but definitely following Baxter."

Yolanda rewound the footage, playing it back frame by frame. The figure in the Santa hat moved with a deliberate, stalking gait, their attention fixed on Baxter. It was chilling to watch the predator and prey captured in this silent dance of death.

CHAPTER FOUR

"Can we enhance this?" George asked, his mind already racing through the possibilities.

"We're working on it," Yolanda answered. "But there's more. The direction they came from and where they disappeared to after... it might give us a radius to work with."

George nodded, his eyes still fixed on the screen. "Good work, Yolanda," he said, finally tearing his gaze away. "Let's get this to the team," George decided, stepping back from the monitors. "We need to canvas the area in the morning as a priority and see if anyone remembers seeing this figure. Someone must have seen something."

Yolanda nodded, her expression one of grim satisfaction.

As Yolanda sent the footage to the rest of the team and DS Josh Fry, George's mind raced with possibilities. The killer had been bold, stalking their victim in plain sight. But why the Santa hat? Was it a twisted signature or something more?

* * *

George Beaumont, amidst a sea of documents and monitors, was the calm in the storm, his mind racing through the maze of evidence and theories. In the midst of this intense concentration, his phone vibrated, a sudden reminder of the world beyond these walls.

George glanced at the caller ID, his expression softening. "Hey, beautiful," he answered, stepping away from the buzz of activity. "You should be in bed."

Isabella's voice, warm yet tinged with concern, filled his ear. "George, it's really late. Don't forget what happened with the West Yorkshire Ripper case. You promised things would be different."

George's gaze drifted to the window, the dark Leeds skyline a stark contrast to the warmth in Isabella's tone. The Ripper case had taken a toll on him, the long hours and emotional weight straining their relationship. He had vowed then to find a better balance, to not let the job consume him.

"I remember, Izzy," he said, his voice a low rumble. "I've not forgotten. I love you and Olivia. I'm just... caught up in the case already. But I promise, I've changed. I won't let it go that far again." He paused. "I promise."

In the silence that followed, George could almost feel Isabella's hesitation, her need to believe him battling her memories of past promises.

"OK," she finally said, her voice steadier. "Just remember, we're here for you. Olivia misses her dad."

A pang of guilt twisted in George's gut. He was torn between two worlds—the relentless pursuit of justice and the quiet haven of family life. "I'll be home soon, Izzy. Give Olivia a kiss for me."

Ending the call, George stood for a moment, lost in thought. The case was a siren call, its complexities and shadows pulling him in, but Isabella's words were a lifeline back to reality. He couldn't lose himself again, not like before.

With a deep breath, George returned to the task at hand, his resolve strengthened. He would solve this case, but not at the expense of his family. They were his anchor, his reason to keep fighting in a world often shrouded in darkness.

* * *

Jay was at his desk, buried in case files, when his phone rang. The caller ID flashed a familiar number, one that made his

CHAPTER FOUR

heart skip a beat. He answered, his voice steady but with an underlying hint of concern.

"Jay Scott speaking," he said, his tone professional yet expectant.

The voice on the other end was rushed, laced with urgency.

Jay's world momentarily stopped. The cornerstone of his family was in the hospital, having been picked up by an ambulance whilst Jay was at the crime scene. The details were sketchy, and the caller was equally shaken. Jay's mind raced with possibilities, fears clouding his usually sharp judgement.

Jay's gaze swept across the room, landing on his colleagues, all deeply engrossed in the Santa Claus murder case. A sense of conflict gnawed at him. He yearned to be at the hospital, yet the weight of responsibility towards his team, towards the case, anchored him in place.

He knew his family member was in the best possible hands, but the helplessness he felt was overwhelming. It was a stark contrast to his usual demeanour of confidence and control. In the world of crime-solving, Jay was used to being the one who took action and made decisions. Now, rendered powerless by circumstances, he felt adrift.

Taking a deep breath, Jay knocked and stepped into George's office. The room was steeped in the quiet intensity characteristic of late-night investigations. George, hunched over a myriad of case files, looked up, his sharp eyes softening slightly at the sight of Jay.

"Boss, I was wondering what time we're planning to wrap up tonight?" Jay asked, maintaining a composed façade.

George, ever perceptive, noted the faint lines of fatigue on Jay's face. "Soon, I think. The team's running on fumes. We need to be sharp for this, and rest is as important as persistence in a case like this."

Jay nodded, a silent wave of relief washing over him. He lingered for a moment, the words he wanted to say hovering on the tip of his tongue. But looking at George, so engrossed in the case, so dedicated, Jay couldn't bring himself to add to his load.

"Alright, boss. I'll tidy up a few things, then," Jay said, turning to leave.

George watched him go, a trace of concern etched into his features. He knew his team well, and he could sense when something was amiss. But he also respected their privacy, trusting them to share when they were ready.

Jay returned to his office, the quiet hum of the station a stark contrast to the chaos of his thoughts. He sat at his desk, his mind a tumultuous sea. The urge to be with his family, to be there for his family member, was a mighty tide, pulling at him with increasing strength. Yet the pull of his duty, his commitment to the Santa Claus murders investigation, anchored him to his desk.

* * *

In the Incident Room of the West Yorkshire Police's Homicide and Major Enquiry Team, the clock neared 3 am, casting a hush over the room bustling with activity just moments before. Detective Inspector George Beaumont stood at the head of the table, his team gathered around, their faces etched with exhaustion and determination. The weight of the Santa Claus murder case hung heavily in the air, a palpable presence in the room.

"Alright, everyone," George began, his voice firm yet infused with an understanding of the long night they'd endured. "The murder was a severe beating, consistent with kicking and stamping before the victim was tied up and decorated."

"We don't believe there's a weapon involved, boss?" asked Jay.

"No," said George, "Just a very, very severe beating." He paused. "Priority-wise, obviously, witnesses are key because I think they're going to be key to the timeline and forensics, of course."

"Forensics are still there, sir," said Tashan, "bagging everything up."

The DI nodded.

"We've made some decent progress," George said, referring to the fact that Candy and Tashan had spoken with Baxter's phone company and bank, respectively, who promised to provide the data by noon. "But we're far from done." He paused, scanning the room, meeting the gaze of each of his team members. "Thank you all for staying with me into the early hours."

Jay, Tashan and Candy all nodded.

"We've got a lead from the CCTV footage. Our killer was wearing a Santa hat, tracking our victim," George continued, his tone sharpening. "Tomorrow, we hit the ground running. Canvas the area and follow up on every possible lead. I want to know who this person is and what drove them to this."

The team nodded, their resolve mirrored in their leader's unwavering determination. They knew the stakes, knew that every hour counted in the race against a killer who had already struck with chilling brutality.

George softened his tone, his gaze lingering on each face in the room. "But tonight, you all need rest. Go home and get some sleep. We're back here at 9 am sharp."

A murmur of agreement rippled through the room, a collective exhale of tension and fatigue. They were a team, a unit, but they were also human, and George knew the importance of balance and the necessity of stepping back to recharge.

As the team dispersed, George remained behind, his eyes lingering on the maps and photos that papered the walls. The face of Ryan Baxter, the victim, stared back at him, a silent plea for justice that George felt deep in his bones.

He thought of Isabella, of Olivia, of the promises he'd made.

With a final glance at the room, George turned off the lights and locked the door behind him. The night was still, the streets of Leeds quiet as he drove home, the city unaware of the darkness that lurked in its heart.

But George knew. And as he pulled into his driveway, the warm glow of his home welcoming him, he felt a renewed sense of purpose. George would catch this killer, bring them to justice, and protect his city. But he would also protect his family and keep the promises he'd made.

As he slipped into bed beside Isabella, her soft breathing a soothing rhythm in the quiet room, George felt a peace he usually didn't feel whilst on a significant case. Tomorrow would bring new challenges and new battles, but tonight, he was home, and that was enough.

The Santa Claus killer was out there, a shadow in the night. But George Beaumont was ready, his resolve unshakable. Justice would be served.

George would ensure it.

Chapter Five

The Thursday morning light filtered through the blinds of Detective Inspector George Beaumont's office, casting elongated shadows across the room. It was a new day, but the weight of the murder case and the ghosts of the past hung heavily in the air. George sat at his desk, a dusty box before him, labelled with a date from a decade ago. His hand hovered over the lid, a moment of hesitation betraying the turmoil within.

With a steadying breath, George lifted the lid, revealing the contents of a case that had haunted his career. The files were a tangible reminder of a mystery left unsolved, a shadow that had followed him over the years, no doubt the reason for his obsession. As he sifted through the documents, old memories resurfaced, each one a piece of the puzzle he had yet to complete.

The case involved a group of young men, their lives intertwining in ways that had seemed innocuous at the time. But now, with the murder of Ryan Baxter, one of the group, the past was calling out for closure. George's eyes scanned the photographs, the reports, the witness statements, each a fragment of a story that had never found its ending.

He paused at a photograph of the group, their youthful faces smiling back at him, unaware of the dark path their lives would take. Among them was Oliver Hughes, the first victim; his death a decade ago was ruled as an accidental prank gone wrong. But George had always suspected there was more to it, a nagging doubt that had lingered through the years.

George's eyes skimmed over a report, and suddenly, he was no longer in the present. He was a younger detective again, less seasoned, his face absent the lines of experience that now marked it. The memory was vivid, a day from the past that had never faded.

He was standing in the same office, though it looked different then, less worn by the passage of time. A map of Leeds was spread out on the table in front of him, pins and strings creating a web of connections, a visual representation of the case that had consumed him.

"Young, idealistic, and relentless," his mentor, Detective Sergeant Luke Mason, had described him back then. George was poring over the files; his brow furrowed in concentration, a burning need to solve the puzzle driving him forward.

"This isn't just a random incident," he had insisted, pointing to the map. "There's a pattern here, connections we're not seeing."

Luke had watched him, a blend of admiration and concern in his eyes. "Easy, son. Don't let it consume you."

But George couldn't help it. The case, involving a group of young men, one of whom was now dead under mysterious circumstances, had gotten under his skin. He sensed there was more to it, layers of secrets and lies that were just out of reach.

Snapping back to the present, George shook off the remnants of the memory. He was different now, more experienced, the naivety of youth replaced by the wisdom of years on the force. But the determination, the drive to find the truth, was as strong as ever.

The phone on his desk rang, pulling him from his thoughts. It was Detective Constable Jay Scott, his voice urgent. "Boss, we've got something. CCTV from a shop near the crime scene. It might show our killer."

George's pulse quickened. "I'm on my way," he said.

In the Incident Room, the team gathered around the monitor, watching the grainy footage. The figure in the Santa hat was there again, moving with a purpose that sent a chill down George's spine. This was no coincidence, no random act of violence. This was personal, a message intertwined with the fabric of his own past.

"We need to identify this person," George said, his voice a command that galvanised the room into action. "Go back to the murder scene and check every angle, every lead. Someone knows something, and we're going to find out what it is."

* * *

The walls of George Beaumont's office seemed to close in on him as he rubbed his temples, the weight of frustration and confusion pressing down. The past had a way of clinging to the present, and in the quiet of his workspace, the haunting memories of a case from a decade ago resurfaced with a vengeance. He stared at the files strewn across his desk, each a fragment of a puzzle that had remained unsolved, a story that had been left incomplete.

George's thoughts drifted, unbidden, to his father, Edward. The man's influence loomed large in his life, casting a shadow that stretched far beyond familial ties. Edward's role in the investigation a decade ago, his manipulative tactics, and the mental abuse he had inflicted on George in his youth were a complex tangle of emotions that George had tried to leave behind. He hadn't spoken to his father in ten years, not since the Christmas case that had finally torn them apart.

Thinking of Edward stirred a deep, simmering anger within George. It was an anger born of betrayal and pain, a reminder of the control Edward had once wielded over him. The memories of his father's mental games were like scars, faded but permanent, marking George in ways only he could understand.

The frustration of the unsolved case, combined with the resurgence of these painful memories, left George feeling trapped in a cycle of the past. He leaned back in his chair, closing his eyes for a moment, trying to find a semblance of calm amid the storm of his thoughts.

He took a deep breath, trying to focus. The case needed him; his team needed him. He couldn't afford to be lost in the labyrinth of his past. Yet, the connections were there, undeniable and insistent. The current murder, the group of young men from a decade ago, and his father's insidious influence—they were all pieces of a larger, darker puzzle.

George stood up, pacing the room. He needed to separate the personal from the professional, yet the two were inextricably linked. His father's shadow stretched not only over his personal life but also bled into his career, affecting his decisions, his relationships, and his very perception of justice.

The anger simmered within him, a constant reminder of the battles he had fought and the ones that still lay ahead. Edward had shaped so much of his life, but George was no longer the same person he had been ten years ago. He was stronger, wiser, and more determined than ever to uncover the truth, no matter how painful it might be.

George stopped pacing and looked out the window, the city of Leeds sprawling before him. He knew that somewhere out there, the answers to the murder were waiting to be found. And with those answers, perhaps, would come a chance for George to finally step out of his father's shadow to heal the wounds of the past.

So George dialled a familiar number, one that connected him not just to a person but to a part of himself he often kept hidden. The phone rang, each tone echoing in the quiet room, amplifying the tension that had been building within him. When the call connected, the voice on the other end was a soothing balm to his frayed nerves.

"Hello?" The voice was soft, tinged with the unmistakable lilt of a Scottish accent. It was Marie, George's mother, a woman who had been his pillar of strength in a life often overshadowed by darkness.

"Hi, Mum, it's George." His voice was gentler now, the hard edges of the detective softening at the sound of his mother's voice.

"George, my boy, how are you?" Marie's voice wavered, a hint of confusion lacing her words.

George sensed something amiss in her tone but attributed it to the late hour. "I'm alright, Mum. Just... needed to hear your voice."

There was a pause, a moment of silence that spoke volumes. "Is it about your father?" Marie's question was tentative, aware of the complicated history between her son and his father.

George hesitated. He didn't want to burden her with his

turmoil, nor did he want to dredge up the painful past. "No, Mum, it's not about him. Just work... you know how it is."

Marie's sigh was audible, a sound of understanding and concern. "You work too hard, love. You need to take care of yourself."

George smiled faintly, a ghost of a smile that held a world of meaning. "I know, Mum. I'm trying."

The conversation shifted then, away from the unspoken shadows of Edward Beaumont and towards the mundane aspects of life. Marie spoke of her day, the small victories and trivial occurrences that made up her world. George listened, a son first and a detective second, cherishing the normalcy of the conversation.

But as they spoke, George's mind couldn't help but wander back to the case, to the haunting memories of the past that were now resurfacing with a vengeance. He was a man caught between two worlds, the personal and the professional, each demanding a part of him.

As the call ended, George felt a mixture of relief and unease. His mother's voice had been a comfort, yet the undercurrent of confusion, the unspoken struggle with her memory, lingered in his thoughts. He was acutely aware of the passage of time but unaware of the changes that were slowly claiming the strong, vibrant woman who had raised him.

* * *

The steely grey sky of Leeds personified Detective Inspector George Beaumont as he stepped outside the police station, his expression an unreadable mask. The mob of media personnel, like a restless sea, surged forward at his appearance. Cameras clicked, and microphones stretched towards him, eager to catch every word, every nuance of the man who stood at the heart of the city's most chilling murder case.

George's gaze swept over the crowd, a sea of expectant faces. He cleared his throat, his voice steady as he began to speak. "Thank you for coming," he said, his tone measured. "I understand the public's need for information, especially in a case as disturbing as this."

The media leaned in, hanging on his every word. George continued, his words carefully chosen. "However, I urge you not to sensationalize the killer. We've seen the consequences of such actions in the past," he said, a veiled reference to the media frenzy that had followed his previous high-profile case.

George's mind, however, was a tumult of thoughts, a whirlwind of personal and professional conflicts. The murder wasn't just another case for him. They were a grim echo of a past that refused to stay buried, a past that was now clawing its way into the present with a vengeance.

"I ask you to trust the police to do our job," George said, his voice firm. "We are doing everything in our power to bring the perpetrator to justice."

"Detective Beaumont, can you confirm the identity of the victim?" a journalist from the Leeds Gazette asked, her pen poised above her notepad.

George shook his head, maintaining his composure. "We are keeping the victim's identity from the public until next of kin has been informed," he replied.

Another journalist, a tall man from the Yorkshire Post, jumped in. "Is there any link between this murder and the so-called Santa Claus murders from ten years ago?"

George's eyes narrowed slightly, a hint of the challenge he

faced in answering. "We are exploring all possible connections. However, it's too early in the investigation to draw definitive conclusions," he responded diplomatically.

A voice from the back, a young woman George was sure wrote for a local blog, called out, "What can you tell us about the killer? Do we have a serial murderer in Leeds?"

George held up his hand, signalling for patience. "We are working tirelessly to gather evidence and understand the motive behind this heinous act. As of now, it would be premature and irresponsible to label this as the work of a serial killer."

"Detective, how is the police ensuring the safety of the public during this time?" a reporter from the BBC questioned, her tone laced with concern.

"We are increasing patrols in key areas and advising the public to remain vigilant. Safety is our top priority, and we're taking every possible measure to prevent further incidents," George assured.

A reporter from The Sun, known for his sensationalist style, asked, "Is it true that the victim was staged in a Christmas-themed display? What does this say about the killer?"

George's jaw tightened momentarily before he answered. "Yes, the victim was found in a manner that suggests the killer has a specific message or motive. We are working with our best profilers to understand the significance of this."

With that, George signalled the end of the press conference, stepping away from the microphone. The flurry of questions continued, but he remained silent, his answers already given, his mind already racing with the next steps of the investigation.

Chapter Six

After returning from interviewing friends of the victim, Ryan Baxter, Detective Constable Tashan Blackburn stood in front of the noticeboard, a flyer in his hand. The flyer, vibrant and eye-catching, announced an upcoming charity run, an event that brought together the community and the police in a shared cause. Tashan pinned it up, his movements precise, a testament to his commitment to both his work and his community.

After securing the flyer, Tashan picked up the pen attached to the registration sheet. He paused for a moment, his expression one of determination and resolve, before signing his name with a firm stroke. It was more than just a signature; it was a pledge, a symbol of his dedication to making a difference, both in and out of uniform.

The hum of activity around him continued, but Tashan's actions did not go unnoticed. Detective Constable Candy Nichols, passing by with a stack of files, paused to look at the flyer. "Running for a good cause, Tashan?" she asked, a smile playing on her lips.

Tashan turned, meeting her gaze. "Yeah, it's for the local children's hospital. Figured it's a good way to give back, you know?" His voice held a note of sincerity that resonated with

Candy.

Detective Constable Jay Scott joined them, his usual playful demeanour giving way to a look of respect. "That's cracking is that, Tashan. I'll sponsor you," Jay said.

Candy nodded, her smile widening. "I'll spread the word. And put me down for a tenner," she said, a spark of enthusiasm in her eyes. The moment was brief but significant, a glimpse into the lives of the detectives beyond the confines of their demanding profession.

Tashan looked at his colleagues, a sense of pride swelling in his chest. The charity run was more than just a physical challenge; it was a symbol of unity, of the police force's commitment to the community they served.

As colleagues passed by, some stopping to read the flyer and others adding their names, the noticeboard became a focal point, a reminder of the human aspect of their work.

Tashan stepped back, allowing others to view the flyer. His gaze lingered on the board, on the names of his colleagues who had joined the cause. It was a small gesture, but in a profession marked by tragedy and conflict, it was these small acts of kindness and community spirit that kept them going and reminded them of the good they were fighting for.

With a final glance at the flyer, Tashan turned and made his way back to his desk, his stride purposeful. The charity run was a commitment, a promise to himself and to those they served. And for Tashan Blackburn, it was another step in a journey that went far beyond his profession.

* * *

Journalist Paige McGuinness followed the shadowy trail of

CHAPTER SIX

the Santa Claus murder, her notebook in hand, a relentless pursuer of truth. Her day had been a marathon of interviews and site visits, each step bringing her closer to the heart of a mystery that had gripped the city in a vice of fear.

Paige's first stop was a small, cosy pub on the outskirts of the city centre. Here, she met with friends of the first victim, Ryan Baxter, having overheard some of the young police constables discussing the victim earlier that morning.

Their faces, etched with sorrow and disbelief, told a story beyond words. Paige listened intently, her pen moving swiftly across the pages of her notebook. Each recollection, each anecdote about Ryan, added a layer to the narrative she was piecing together. She observed their mannerisms, the flicker of fear in their eyes, the tremble in their voices. The killer was more than a news story; he was a dark cloud looming over their lives.

* * *

Detective Inspector George Beaumont's noon briefing had just concluded in the Incident Room. The atmosphere was thick with a mix of determination and the heavy burden of the case. As his team dispersed, their steps echoed the weight of the task ahead. George, standing at the head of the room, felt the familiar rush of adrenaline mixed with a pang of responsibility. He knew every decision here could be pivotal.

George's gaze lingered on the Big Board, a mosaic of photographs, notes, and leads, each piece a fragment of a larger, darker puzzle. His thoughts were interrupted by the ping of his email. He turned towards his desk, his movements a blend of practised calm and an underlying urgency.

The email was from Lindsey Yardley, the Scene of Crime Manager. Her findings were often crucial, but this time, there was an edge of something more significant. George opened the email, his eyes quickly scanning the contents. Lindsey had discovered a unique type of fibre at the crime scene—not just any fibre, but one that was rare and not commonly available. It was a lead that could point directly to the killer.

George's mind began to race. This fibre could be the break they needed, a tangible link to the person behind these chilling murders. He imagined the killer, cloaked in anonymity, leaving behind a trace so small yet so telling. It was these minor oversights that often unravelled even the most careful criminals.

He quickly typed a response, urging Lindsey to prioritize tracing the source of the fibre. Every second mattered now. If they could link the fibre to a specific source, it would narrow down their search, bringing them one step closer to the killer.

George leaned back in his chair, his mind already spinning with possibilities. The fibre could have come from a piece of clothing, a bag, or anything that the killer had brought to the crime scene. It was an unusual type, something that wouldn't just be found in any shop. This detail suggested planning, a calculated mind behind the murders.

As he pondered over the implications, George couldn't help but feel a surge of cautious optimism. It was leads like this that often unravelled cases that shifted them from endless questions to concrete answers. He knew the importance of not getting ahead of himself, but the potential of this discovery was too significant to ignore.

His thoughts were briefly interrupted by Detective Constable Tashan Blackburn, who popped his head in to update

CHAPTER SIX

George on another lead. George listened, but part of his mind remained fixed on the fibre. He thanked Tashan, his brain already working on integrating this new information into their strategy.

Once alone again, George turned his attention back to the Big Board. He added a note about the fibre, its placement a stark reminder of the complexity of the case. Every piece of evidence, no matter how small, was a piece of the puzzle they were desperately trying to solve.

Later, in the Incident Room, Detective Constables Jay Scott and Tashan Blackburn stepped forward, their expressions grave. "We've located two of the men from the case a decade ago," Jay began, his voice steady. "Ethan Turner and Daniel 'Danny' Roberts." His words hung in the air, dense with implications.

George nodded, his mind instantly conjuring images of Turner and Roberts from the past—young men then, whose lives had intersected with a case that never truly closed. Memories flickered in his mind, snapshots of interviews, interrogations, and the endless search for truth.

He reached for his phone, dialling Sergeant Greenwood, a reliable and experienced officer. "Greenwood, it's Beaumont. We need eyes on Ethan Turner and Danny Roberts," he said, his tone all business. "Keep it discreet, but I want to know if they're involved in anything... sinister."

As he hung up, George felt the weight of the past and present converging. His instincts told him there was more to the pair, layers yet to be uncovered.

The room was silent for a moment, the team absorbing the new directive. George's gaze swept over them, each face reflecting a mix of determination and the sobering reality of the task ahead.

"Alright, we keep digging," George said, his voice a firm command. "Any connection, no matter how small, could be the key. We need to understand their involvement then and now."

Jay and Tashan nodded, already turning to their next tasks. The room buzzed back to life, phones ringing, keyboards clacking, the machinery of investigation moving forward. George watched them for a moment, proud yet burdened by the responsibility they all carried.

Turner and Roberts were now central figures in a puzzle that was slowly coming together, piece by painstaking piece. George's mind raced with possibilities, scenarios playing out like scenes from a movie only he could see. The stakes were high, and the pressure was mounting, but George was no stranger to the dark and winding paths of criminal investigation.

* * *

Detective Constable Tashan Blackburn sat at his desk, pouring over Ryan Baxter's financial records. The glow of the computer screen illuminated his focused expression as he scrolled through the transactions. One detail stood out sharply: the regular use of Baxter's bank card. His eyes narrowed as he saw the most recent transaction—noon that day. But Baxter had already been dead by then.

Who was using his bank card?

Tashan stood up, his chair scraping back against the floor. He needed to share this with Detective Inspector George Beaumont immediately. Walking briskly through the bustling

CHAPTER SIX

office, he found George at his desk, surrounded by case files.

"Sir, I've got something on Baxter's financials," Tashan announced, handing over the printouts.

George took them, his eyes quickly scanning the information. "Good work, Tashan. This last transaction—it's after Baxter was killed."

Tashan nodded, "Exactly, sir. Someone else has been using his bank card."

George leaned back, pondering the implications. "There are two possibilities," he said thoughtfully. "One, the murderer stole the bank card and has foolishly used it, or two, someone else had access to Baxter's card before and after the murder."

The room buzzed with the typical sounds of a busy police station, but for Tashan and George, the focus was solely on the puzzle before them.

"I'll get DC Scott on it as you're leaving soon, right?"

Tashan nodded.

"Jay," George said, calling the other male DC over. "We need CCTV from the Skyline newsagents where the card was used," George directed.

Detective Constable Jay Scott quickly set about the task, requesting the CCTV footage from the newsagents. The urgency of their investigation was palpable.

Back at his desk, George felt a twinge of frustration. Waiting for the CCTV footage meant valuable time lost, time during which the killer could be covering their tracks. He tapped his pen against the desk, his mind racing through the various scenarios.

"Tashan, keep an eye on any other unusual activity on Baxter's accounts. It might give us more leads," George instructed his tone a mix of determination and impatience.

"Yes, sir," Tashan replied, returning to his desk to dive back into the financial records.

George stood up, stretching his legs. The case was evolving, the pieces slowly coming together, but each new revelation brought with it more questions. Who had access to Baxter's bank card? Was it the killer or someone else connected to the case?

* * *

The crisp December air was unforgiving, a chill that seeped through layers of clothing and skin. But Detective Constable Tashan Blackburn barely noticed. His breath plumed in the cold air as he ran, each stride a testament to his unwavering determination.

The streets of Leeds, adorned with festive lights, twinkled like a constellation under the night sky. The city was alive with the hum of Christmas preparations, but Tashan's world was reduced to the rhythm of his feet against the pavement, the steady beat of his heart, the focus of his mind.

He ran past shop windows displaying seasonal cheer, past families wrapped in winter coats, hands filled with shopping bags. Tashan's gaze, however, was fixed ahead, his mind locked on the goal, not just the finish line of the charity run he was training for but the more pressing race against time in the Santa Claus murder case.

For Tashan, the run was more than just physical exertion; it was a way to channel the stress of the investigation, to clear his mind and maintain his edge, and as Tashan's silhouette cut through the cold air, his form strong and unwavering, he seemed to embody the relentless pursuit of justice. His runs were a physical manifestation of the investigation's pace—persistent, enduring, unyielding.

Chapter Seven

The air was heavy with unspoken tension in the morgue as Dr Christian Ross, the seasoned pathologist, stood over the body from the latest Santa Claus murder. Detective Inspector George Beaumont, his green eyes sharp and focused, observed closely. He stood at a respectful distance as Dr Christian Ross, the experienced pathologist, prepared for the postmortem examination of Ryan Baxter, the latest victim in the Santa Claus murders.

The room was quiet, save for the subtle hum of the overhead lights and the occasional clink of metal instruments. George's mind already working through the implications of each piece of evidence that would be uncovered.

Dr Ross, clad in his scrubs, looked up at George as he began the examination. "I remember the case from a decade ago as if it happened only yesterday," he said, his voice tinged with a note of realisation. "But it still shocks me that I didn't know you were involved in the investigation back then, George."

George, his arms crossed, nodded slowly. "I was a Detective Constable at the time, so I probably didn't speak with you."

The revelation seemed to forge a new understanding between the two men. Dr Ross continued his work with renewed focus, aware now of the deeper connection George had to this case.

As Dr Ross carefully examined the body, he narrated his findings. "This was a brutal attack; the murder weapon was the killers' feet and fists."

George nodded.

"The victim was restrained in a similar manner to the previous case a decade ago," Christian observed, his fingers gently probing the ligature marks on the victim's wrists. "The knotting is identical. It's meticulous and practised. And uncommon."

"Thank you, Dr Ross," George said, his voice firm yet thoughtful. "Your insights could be crucial to this investigation."

George watched intently, every detail etching itself into his memory. The similarities to the cases from a decade ago were becoming increasingly apparent, painting a picture of a methodical and deliberate killer.

As the postmortem drew to a close, Dr Ross looked up at George, his eyes conveying a mix of professional respect and personal concern. "I'll send you the full report as soon as it's ready. Maybe this time, we can find the answers that eluded us before."

George nodded, his jaw set. "Thank you, Dr Ross."

"My pleasure, son, but bring cakes next time."

As George left the morgue, the weight of Dr Ross' observations hung heavy on him. The possibility that they were dealing with a murderer who had eluded capture for over a decade was a chilling prospect.

* * *

In the warmth of their Morley home, Isabella cradled baby Olivia, her gentle rocking a lullaby in motion. The inviting tranquillity was a world away from her role as a detective sergeant. Maternity leave had shifted her days from crime scenes to lullabies, a change she cherished, yet it brought a looming decision as her return to work neared. Her heart was torn between the thrill of her career and the love for her daughter.

The front door opened, and George stepped in, weariness etched in his posture. But upon seeing his family, a smile broke through his fatigue, softening his features. Isabella looked up, her face lighting up with a mix of affection and concern. In a few strides, George was by their side, a gentle kiss shared, a silent bond of love and understanding.

Tea time was a family affair, the table a scene of domestic bliss. Olivia, curious and playful, reached for the food with her tiny hands, her giggles filling the room. George, with a patience born of deep love, tried feeding her, each spoonful a testament to his devotion. This intimate family scene stood in sharp contrast to the detective's usual world of gritty realities.

As they ate, the conversation turned to George's work. Isabella's voice was tinged with concern as she broached the subject of his current case. "How are you holding up? This case... it seems grim." Her gaze, intense and caring, sought his.

She knew the toll it took, the shadows it cast. George, usually guarded about his work, opened up about the decade-old unresolved case. His voice was heavy with the weight of unresolved mysteries, the ghosts of cases past.

George paused, fork in mid-air, and met her gaze. The shadows of his profession often followed him home, but this time, the darkness felt deeper. He set down his fork and leaned back, the chair creaking under the shift. "It's a lot like one from ten years ago," he started, his voice a low murmur. "The Santa Claus murder... the similarities are uncanny." His eyes, usually so sharp and alert, now bore a haunted look.

Isabella listened, her heart tightening with each word. She remembered the toll the last case had taken on him, the sleepless nights, the distant stares. She reached across the table, her hand seeking his, a silent show of support. "Just remember, George, you're not alone in this."

George's eyes softened at her touch. "I know," he murmured, but his gaze drifted away, lost in memories.

Olivia's innocent giggles pierced their sombre conversation, her small hands clapping together in delight. The stark contrast between the purity of their home life and the darkness of George's work was never more apparent. In that moment, George was reminded of what truly mattered — the laughter of his daughter, the understanding in Isabella's eyes. They were his anchor in a sea of uncertainty.

The moment was a reminder of life's fragile balance, the thin line George walked every day between his duty and his family. Each case left its mark, but the love and warmth of his home were his solace, a refuge from the storm.

Isabella knew those unspoken thoughts well — the unyielding grip of the past, the fears that lurked in its shadows.

Their discussion was interrupted by Olivia's laughter, a reminder of the innocence and light that their daughter brought into their lives. The worries of the world seemed to pause in her presence, a stark reminder of what really mattered.

After tea, the ritual of Olivia's bath time unfolded. George's hands, so accustomed to dealing with the hard edges of detective work, now moved with tenderness as he bathed his daughter. The bathroom echoed with Olivia's delighted squeals and gentle splashes, a welcome respite from the burdens of his job.

He carefully lifted water with a cup, letting it trickle over Olivia's tiny toes, eliciting a chorus of giggles. Her laughter was infectious, a balm to his weary soul. Here, in this moment, he wasn't Detective Inspector George Beaumont; he was just Dad, the hero of Olivia's world. The simplicity of the act, the purity of her joy, reminded him of life's simpler pleasures, so often overshadowed by his demanding career.

Later, in Olivia's nursery, George sat beside her crib, a storybook in hand. His voice, usually firm and decisive in the line of duty, was now a soft whisper, a lullaby in words. This was a different George Beaumont, one far removed from the streets of Leeds and the dark alleys of crime.

As he turned each page, Olivia's eyes followed with wonder. Her little hands reached out occasionally, trying to touch the colourful illustrations. George watched her, a sense of peace settling over him. This was a different kind of challenge, one that required patience and tenderness, qualities that his job seldom demanded.

The story wove a tale of adventure and courage, a world away from the gritty reality of Leeds' streets. With each word, George's voice seemed to weave a protective spell around his daughter, shielding her from the complexities of the world he navigated daily.

As the story neared its end, Olivia's eyelids began to flutter shut. Her breathing slowed, falling into the rhythmic pattern of sleep. George carefully closed the book, his movements

CHAPTER SEVEN

slow and deliberate, keen not to disturb her peaceful slumber.

He lingered for a moment, watching her sleep. In the soft glow of the night light, her face was a picture of innocence. Moments like these reminded him of what was at stake, of what he fought for every day—the contrast between his role as a detective and as a father had never been more stark.

Quietly, George stood up, his gaze lingering on Olivia. In her, he saw the promise of a better world, a world he worked tirelessly to safeguard. With a final, tender look, he turned off the light and left the room, the image of his sleeping daughter etched in his mind, a reminder of his purpose and his resolve.

Once Olivia was asleep, the only sound was the soft ticking of the clock. Isabella and George sat close yet seemed worlds apart, each lost in their thoughts. Finally, Isabella broke the silence, her voice laced with concern.

"George," she said, her eyes searching his face. Isabella reached for his hand, holding it gently. "This case... I just hope it doesn't—"

"Think will be different this time, I promise," he said, squeezing her hand.

"Just please remember your therapy session this weekend." She paused. "I just hope you're not pushing yourself too hard."

George looked at her, his expression a mixture of appreciation and reassurance. "I know, Isabella. But I can handle it. It's not like last time," he replied, trying to sound convincing. But his eyes, usually so full of determination, held a shadow of doubt, betraying the turmoil brewing within.

"I understand the importance of this case, George, but please, don't let it consume you. Olivia needs you; I need you," she implored, her voice soft yet firm.

George squeezed her hand in response, a silent acknowledgement of her fears. "I won't let it get to me," he promised, his voice steady but his gaze distant. The memories of his last case, the one that had nearly broken him, loomed in the back of his mind, a ghost he was determined to outrun.

Isabella studied his face, her intuition telling her there was more he wasn't saying. She knew the signs, the subtle shifts in his mood, the way he would lose himself in his thoughts. She wanted to believe his words, to trust that he had everything under control, but the fear lingered, an unspoken question hanging in the air between them.

The room fell silent again; each lost in their thoughts, the weight of the unspoken hanging heavily. George's gaze drifted to the photographs on the mantle, reminders of happier times, of the life they had built together.

Upstairs, as he approached Olivia's crib, George's movements were gentle, a stark contrast to the harsh realities of his job. He bent down, kissing her forehead tenderly, a silent promise to protect her from the world he navigated daily.

George stood for a moment, his silhouette a mix of strength and vulnerability. The day's revelations weighed heavily on him, the lines between his professional duties and personal life blurring.

Retreating to their bedroom, George could feel the day's tension slowly receding, replaced by the comfort of family. Isabella's presence, a constant reminder of the life he fought to preserve, offered a semblance of peace amidst the turmoil.

As the couple settled into bed, the darkness of the room enveloped them, offering a temporary respite from the challenges that lay ahead. In the silence, George's thoughts lingered on the case, specifically on the mystery user of the

CHAPTER SEVEN

bank card.

Chapter Eight

In the bustling HMET shared office at Elland Road Police Station that Friday morning, Detective Constable Tashan Blackburn leaned against a desk, a pensive look on his face. He glanced at the charity run flyer pinned to the noticeboard before turning to Detective Constable Candy Nichols, who was sifting through case files.

"Candy," Tashan began, his voice lower than usual. "About the charity run... it's not just a fitness thing for me."

Candy paused, looking up with a mix of curiosity and concern. "Oh? What's the story?"

Tashan sighed, his gaze distant. "My cousin, Leo. He passed away young from cancer. This charity... they were there for him, for us, during those tough times. Running for them is my way of giving back, honouring his memory."

Candy's expression softened, her eyes reflecting understanding. "Tashan, I had no idea. That's really admirable of you."

He gave a small, sad smile. "Thanks, Candy. It means a lot, you know, keeping his spirit alive."

The moment was interrupted by the sharp ring of a phone. Tashan straightened, the professional mask sliding back into place, but Candy had seen a glimpse of the man behind the

CHAPTER EIGHT

warrant card. She nodded at him, a silent show of support, before they both returned to the task at hand, huddling around George Beaumont and a table laden with documents and photographs.

George put the phone down. "OK, we've got the CCTV footage from the Skyline shop," the DI explained. "And we've got Baxter's phone records, and they indicate nothing sinister."

Inside the Incident Room, the glow of the CCTV footage illuminated the intent faces of George, Candy, Tashan and Jay as they watched the grainy video from the Skyline newsagents played, revealing a crucial piece of evidence in the murder of Ryan Baxter.

"There," Tashan Blackburn pointed at the screen, "that's him. Same guy, both days."

The footage was clear enough. An unknown man, his features initially obscured by the angle of the camera, used the card at the till. He wore green cargo trousers and a black raincoat, conspicuous in their ordinariness. The timestamps were glaring—noon the day before Baxter's death and noon on the day of the murder.

George leaned forward, his eyes narrowing as he absorbed every detail. "He's wearing the same clothes both days. Unusual, unless he wants to be consistent for a reason."

Detective Constable Jay Scott, standing beside Tashan, chimed in, "Or he's trying not to be noticed, blending in."

George tapped his fingers on the desk, his mind racing. "We need to identify him. See if he's connected to Baxter or just a random thief using a stolen card."

Tashan was already on it, typing rapidly on his keyboard. "I'll enhance the images and see if we can get a better look at his face." He added, "Baxter didn't report the card stolen."

The room hummed with a quiet intensity as they watched the footage again. The man's movements were confident, suggesting he was either unaware of the CCTV or didn't care. He interacted briefly with the cashier, his body language relaxed, almost casual.

"What about his gait, his posture?" George mused aloud. "Anything there that could tell us more about him?"

Jay leaned closer to the screen. "He walks with a slight limp, see? Could be an old injury."

"Good catch, Jay," George acknowledged, his brain filing away every observation. "Every detail counts."

As Tashan worked on enhancing the images, George's thoughts turned to the broader implications. If this man was the murderer, using Baxter's card was risky, almost fearless. But if he wasn't the killer, then what was his connection to Baxter? Was he a red herring or a piece of the puzzle they hadn't even considered?

"Here, sir," Tashan called out, pulling up an enhanced image of the man's face.

The team crowded around Tashan's monitor. The man's features were now clearer, but he was still a stranger, his identity veiled in mystery.

"We'll circulate this to all units, see if anyone recognises him," George decided, his tone decisive. "And check Baxter's connections, anyone who matches this description."

The team nodded, already moving to carry out his orders.

Later on, and with no progress on the stranger, George called his team together and flicked on the digital display, bringing up evidence photos from the Santa Claus murder scene. "Look at this," George said, pointing to a specific detail

CHAPTER EIGHT

in one of the photos. "Notice the positioning, the symbolism. I want your thoughts."

Jay Scott, with a keen eye for behavioural patterns, observed the intensity of the crime scene. "The level of violence here, it's personal, boss," he stated firmly. "This isn't just about killing; it's about sending a message. I've seen similar patterns in cases where the perpetrator harboured deep-seated resentment towards the victim." He pulled up data on his tablet, showing past cases with similar brutality linked to revenge. "In these cases, the killer had a direct, often emotional, connection with the victim. It's not random—it's targeted." He paused, taking in his colleagues' shocked looks. "Look at the overkill," Jay continued, pointing at the crime scene photos. "It suggests a rage that's been festering. This could be the culmination of a long-standing grudge."

"Where's DC Jay Scott, and what have you done with him?" asked George with a grin.

Jason narrowed his eyes and frowned. "I'm right here, boss. It's me."

Candy Nichols, laughing, chimed in with a contrasting view. "What if we're dealing with a serial killer? The Christmas theme, it's too specific. It could be a signature."

"So consider the ritualistic element," she urged, highlighting the Christmas-themed display. "This isn't just murder; it's theatrical. It's common in serial killings where the murderer has a compulsion to follow a specific pattern or theme." She scrolled through a database of serial killers, pointing out those who left signature elements at their crime scenes. "These killers often have a need for recognition, a desire to be noticed. The staging could be a twisted way of achieving that." Candy leaned back, her eyes scanning the room. "If this is a serial killer, we might find more victims, past or future, with a similar MO. This Christmas theme could be the key to unlocking their identity."

George nodded. He'd already had a look at HOLMES 2, the Home Office Large Major Enquiry System, an administrative support system that they could use to filter MOs, victimology, and thousands of other scenarios. He looked around at the team, wanting to gauge their reactions and saw that Tashan was loaded like a spring. "You got something for us, DC Blackburn?"

Tashan Blackburn, methodical and precise, nodded and raised a cautionary hand. "These theories are compelling, but we're in the realm of speculation," he reminded the team. "We need to ground our investigation in evidence." He highlighted inconsistencies in the forensic reports. "The time of death, the nature of the injuries—there are elements that don't fully align with either theory."

Tashan scratched his chin, looking at the team. "We need to dig deeper and correlate our findings with forensic evidence, witness statements, and any other tangible data. Our approach must be comprehensive and unbiased."

Jay started to say, "Yeah, but—"

"Let's not get tunnel-visioned by a single theory," George concluded. Interrupting Jay. "We have to keep all possibilities open and let the evidence guide us."

Yolanda reminded them of the CCTV footage of the person wearing the Santa hat.

George surveyed each opinion, appreciating their diverse perspectives.

"Let's split up," George decided. "Jay, Candy, you two dig deeper into these theories. Tashan, I need you to go over the

CHAPTER EIGHT

evidence again and see if we missed anything. Yolanda, keep searching for footage of the person in the Santa hat, see if you can figure out where they come from."

The team nodded, a unified front ready to tackle the case from all angles. As they dispersed, George's phone buzzed. A text from Isabella—a simple heart emoji. A small reminder of the life waiting for him beyond these walls.

Sergeant Greenwood, invited for his insights, stood at the ready.

"Any updates on Ethan Turner and Daniel 'Danny' Roberts?" George inquired, his tone underscored by a palpable intensity.

"They're working as Santas in local shopping centres, sir," Greenwood reported, referring to his notes. "Ethan's at St John's Centre, and Danny's at White Rose. So far, they seem unconnected to Ryan Baxter's murder."

George nodded.

Meanwhile, Detective Sergeant Yolanda Williams revisited the CCTV footage. Her eyes were sharp, trained on the screen, searching for anything they might have missed. Suddenly, her fingers paused, rewinding the footage. There, on the hand of the shadowy figure lurking near the crime scene, was a distinctive tattoo.

"Look at this, sir," Yolanda called out, her voice cutting through the room's focused silence. The team gathered around her screen, their eyes following her pointing finger.

The tattoo was unmistakable—a detailed, intricate design that George recognised immediately. It belonged to Michael "Mike" Clarkson, a name from the old case that had haunted George for a decade.

"It's Mike Clarkson," George said, his voice low but carrying the weight of realisation. "If he's involved, this changes everything."

The team exchanged glances, the implications of this discovery sinking in. Mike Clarkson was a significant figure from the old case, one of the group of men George had investigated. But why would he turn on one of his own?

George's mind raced, piecing together a plan. "We need to find him, fast," he instructed, his tone laced with urgency. "But be careful. Mike was built like a bodybuilder, strong as an ox. We can't underestimate him."

Quickly, George assigned roles to each team member, ensuring they were equipped to handle the situation. Jay Scott and Tashan Blackburn were to lead the search, Candy Nichols would delve into Mike's recent activities, and Yolanda Williams would keep scouring the CCTV for any more clues.

As the team dispersed to their tasks, George stood still for a moment, his thoughts heavy. The revelation of Mike Clarkson's involvement was a crucial piece of the puzzle, but it raised more questions than answers. If Mike was the killer, what was his motive? And how deeply was he entangled in the dark web of their past case?

The revelation of Mike Clarkson's involvement tied the present to the past in a way that felt too close, too personal. He knew he needed insight, a perspective that wasn't clouded by his own history. Picking up his phone, he dialled a number he knew by heart.

"Luke, it's George. I need your advice on something," George's voice was steady, but the undercurrent of urgency was unmistakable.

Detective Inspector Luke Mason, George's old mentor, responded with his characteristic calmness, a contrast to the tension in George's voice. "Tell me what's happening, son,"

Luke said, his voice a grounding force.

George explained the situation, his words painting the picture of the investigation's latest turn. Luke listened intently, his years of experience informing his advice.

"Bring in Ethan and Danny. Talk to them directly," Luke suggested. "Sometimes, the direct approach can reveal more than surveillance."

Nodding to himself, George felt a resolve solidify within him. "Thanks, Luke. I'll do that." The call ended, but George's new determination lingered.

Turning to Yolanda Williams, who was still poring over the footage, George made his decision. "We're going to talk to Ethan and Danny. Now."

Yolanda looked up, her eyes meeting George's. She recognised the shift in him, the move from reactive to proactive. Without a word, she gathered her things, ready to follow George's lead.

Chapter Nine

In the bustling St John's Centre, amidst the festive chaos, George Beaumont and Yolanda Williams navigated their way to Ethan Turner, who was dressed as Santa Claus, a jolly facade for the shoppers. The contrast between the cheery Christmas atmosphere and the grim nature of their visit wasn't lost on George.

"Is the manager here?" George asked an elf. She was young, pretty, and blonde, with blue eyes and sharp ears.

"You're speaking with her, love," the elf said.

"I'm Detective Inspector Beaumont, and this is Detective Sergeant Williams," George said as they showed their warrant cards. "I need to talk with your Santa. Is there any chance we can prize him away from the kids for half an hour?"

She shook her head. "Not really, we're fully booked. It's Christmas in two weeks, you know."

"I do know," said George, "and whilst I phrased my words as a question, I wasn't really asking."

As they approached, Ethan's eyes darted nervously, a clear sign of discomfort. George, with a nod to Yolanda, took the lead.

"Mr Turner, I'm Detective Inspector Beaumont, and this is Detective Sergeant Williams," George introduced formally, his tone level but firm as they showed their warrant cards. "We need to ask you a few questions about Ryan Baxter. Can we talk somewhere private?"

Ethan hesitated but then nodded, leading them to a small, cluttered staff room. Once inside, George didn't waste time.

"When was the last time you saw Ryan Baxter, Ethan?" George's eyes were locked on Ethan's, searching for any flicker of deceit.

Ethan shifted uncomfortably. "It's been a while, Detective. A few years, I reckon."

"Is that so?" George probed, unrelenting. "We know that you were part of a group with Ryan a decade ago. Seems odd to lose touch with such close friends."

Ethan's hands fidgeted. "Well, we just drifted apart, you know how it is."

"Drifted apart, or was there more to it?" George pressed on. "Did something happen that led to this 'drifting apart'?"

"No, nothing like that," Ethan said quickly, too quickly. "Just life, moving on."

George leaned in, his voice low but piercing. "Ryan was murdered, Ethan. We found him dressed like this," he gestured to Ethan's Santa costume, "in a rather macabre display. You don't find that coincidental?"

Ethan's face paled. "Murdered? I... I had no idea."

George observed Ethan's reaction closely, the shock seeming genuine, but there was something else, a hidden layer of fear or guilt.

"Where were you on the night of the murder, Ethan?" Yolanda chimed in, her tone equally probing.

George's gaze never left Ethan as Yolanda questioned him. Ethan's reply came quickly, almost too quick for comfort.

"I was here, working," Ethan said, a bit of haste in his voice.

George's eyebrow arched sceptically. "Working here?" George asked, and Ethan nodded. "At midnight?"

Ethan's eyes widened slightly, realizing his slip. "No, no, not at midnight. I mean, I finished my shift earlier in the evening."

George leaned forward, his tone sharpening. "So, you finished your shift and then what? Where did you go, Ethan?"

Ethan fumbled for words, his unease growing. "I... I just went home. Straight home."

"Can anyone verify that?" George's question was pointed, his scrutiny intense.

Ethan swallowed hard. "I live alone, so no. But you can check with the security here. They'll tell you when I clocked out."

George nodded slowly, unconvinced. The pieces weren't fitting together as they should. Ethan's story had holes, gaps that begged to be filled with the truth.

"We will check," George affirmed. "Any deviation from your story, and we'll be having another chat, Ethan. A more formal one."

Ethan nodded, his Adam's apple bobbing in nervous agreement. George's instincts told him that Ethan was more than just a former friend of the victim. There was a secret here, one that Ethan was desperate to keep hidden. George made a mental note to follow up on Ethan's alibi immediately.

"Why are both you and Ryan working as shopping centre Santas?" George's tone was direct, cutting through the pleasantries.

Ethan shifted uncomfortably. "It's just a coincidence, Detective. We both needed the work."

CHAPTER NINE

George's expression remained unchanged, sceptical. "I don't believe in coincidences, Ethan. Especially not in a case like this."

Ethan's eyes darted away, avoiding George's probing gaze. "Honestly, it's just how things turned out. I didn't even know Ryan was doing the same thing until —"

"Until what?"

"OK, so I spoke to Ryan in November. We were on a training course together. I forgot."

George narrowed his eyes and studied Ethan's face, searching for any telltale sign of deception. "You expect me to believe that? Two men from the same unresolved case, both playing Santa in different shopping centres? That's quite the coincidence."

Ethan's silence spoke volumes. He looked down, his answer lost in the void of his own uncertainty.

"And there's also Danny Roberts playing Santa, too," Yolanda added.

"I know nothing about that," Ethan said.

George thought that was the first time Ethan had told them the truth, so he pushed the questioning on. "Did Ryan ever mention any trouble he was in, any enemies he might have had?"

Ethan shook his head. "No, we didn't talk about personal stuff much. Just mates hanging out, you know?"

Yolanda said, "Hanging out whilst on a course?"

Ethan nodded. "Yeah, to be Santas." He paused. "Look, I hardly knew him back then, and he's a stranger now. Or he was." Ethan looked at the clock on the wall. "I've got kids I need to see and presents to give, so if you don't mind, I'd like to go back to work now."

George nodded but placed his hand on Ethan's chest as he tried to pass the detective. "If you remember anything else, anything at all, you need to contact us immediately," George insisted, removing his hand from Ethan's chest and handing Ethan the business card he had held there.

As they left the staff room, George's mind was already racing ahead, piecing together the fragments of information abuzz with suspicion. Ethan's responses were too rehearsed, his shock a bit overplayed. The mystery of Ryan Baxter's death was deepening, and every new revelation seemed to only thicken the fog of uncertainty.

"Something's off with him," George muttered to Yolanda as they walked away. "He knows more than he's letting on."

Yolanda nodded in agreement, her experienced eyes having picked up on the same subtleties. "We'll dig deeper into his story. He's hiding something, for sure."

The interview with Ethan raised more questions than answers. George's instincts were rarely wrong, and right now, they were screaming that Ethan Turner was a key to unravelling the mystery surrounding Ryan Baxter's death. The challenge now was to uncover the truth.

* * *

At the White Rose Shopping Centre, the festive atmosphere contrasted sharply with the purpose of George's visit. He and Yolanda found Danny, dressed in his Santa suit, taking a break in a quiet corner of the break room.

"Mr Roberts, I'm Detective Inspector Beaumont, and this is Detective Sergeant Williams," George introduced themselves as they both showed warrant cards. "We need to ask you a few

CHAPTER NINE

questions about Ryan Baxter."

Danny nodded, his expression guarded. He removed his hat and beard and said, "Sure, what do you need to know?"

"Where were you on the night Ryan was killed?" George asked, scrutinizing Danny's reactions closely.

"Here, working the late shift," Danny responded, his voice steady but his fingers twitching.

"Till midnight?" George pressed, his gaze unwavering.

Danny hesitated, then shook his head. "No, I finished at ten. But I was here all evening." He paused. "I was walking up and down the centre with a charity bucket. You can ask anyone."

"And after your shift?" Yolanda interjected, watching Danny closely.

"I went straight home. Alone," Danny added quickly, too quickly for George's liking.

George leaned forward. "Did you keep in touch with Ryan after what happened a decade ago?"

"We'd run into each other now and then, but we weren't close. Not really," Danny answered, avoiding eye contact.

George raised an eyebrow. "Yet you both end up as Santas in different shopping centres. That's a curious coincidence, don't you think?"

Danny shrugged. "It's just a job, Detective. It pays the bills."

"But why this job? And why now?" George pressed, sensing there was more beneath the surface.

Danny shifted uncomfortably. "It's seasonal work. Lots of people do it."

George noted the defensiveness in Danny's tone. "It seems too convenient, Danny. Two men connected to an old case, both playing Santa. That's not just a coincidence."

Danny's gaze finally met George's. "Look, I needed the job.

I didn't know about Ryan until after... after it happened."

George nodded. "We spoke with Ethan Turner earlier, Danny. He said he was on a Santa course with Ryan." He paused and looked Danny in the eye. "Were you on that same course? And don't lie," he added, "because we will check."

Danny's expression shifted, his eyes widening slightly at George's mention of Ethan. "No, it was Eddie." He paused and pondered the name. "Yeah, Eddie got me this gig," he admitted, a hint of unease creeping into his voice. "It was just a job, nothing more."

George's interest was piqued at the mention of 'Eddie'.

His mind was awash with thoughts, the gears turning relentlessly. Edward Beaumont—his father—had been a figure of significant influence, a man whose shadow had loomed large over George's life and career. That same man had been tangentially involved in the case a decade ago, a fact that George had never fully reconciled within himself.

"Eddie..." George mused silently. The possibility that his father could be connected to the current case, even in the most peripheral way, sent a ripple of unease through him. Was it a mere coincidence, or was there a deeper, more sinister link?

George knew all too well the power his father wielded, the ease with which he navigated the corridors of influence and authority. Edward Beaumont was a man who moved pieces on a chessboard few even knew existed. The thought that one of those pieces could be tied to the Santa Claus murders was a troubling prospect.

It was a link, however tenuous, that George could not afford to ignore. His father's involvement in the case a decade ago had been a point of contention, a complication in an already complex investigation. Now, it resurfaced, a ghostly hand

CHAPTER NINE

reaching out from the shadows of history.

On one hand, it could be a simple case of mistaken identity, a red herring that led nowhere. But on the other, it could be a thread, one that, if pulled, might unravel a tapestry of deception and secrets long buried.

The detective in him, trained to follow the evidence wherever it led, knew that this lead warranted investigation, irrespective of his personal connections. Yet, the son in him, the part of him that had spent a lifetime in the orbit of Edward Beaumont's formidable presence, felt a pang of apprehension.

George's mind drifted to the past case, to the unresolved threads that had frayed at the edges of his consciousness for years. Could his father have been more than just a peripheral figure in those investigations? Was there more to Edward Beaumont's involvement than he had dared to consider?

The DI leaned in. "And this course with Ryan, you were all there?"

Danny's gaze flickered away for a moment before returning to meet George's. "Nope." Then, recognition dawned in Danny's eyes. "Wait a minute," he said, pointing at George. "I remember you now. You were much younger back then. And you know that Ed—"

George cut him off, keen to stay on topic. "Did you know of anyone who might have wanted to hurt Ryan?" he asked, his tone firm.

Danny shook his head, his expression sombre. "No, as I said, we didn't speak much. I had no reason to think anyone would want to harm him."

George studied Danny's face, searching for any hint of deceit. There was a complexity to Danny's answers that intrigued him. The mention of 'Eddie' and the recognition of

George added new layers to the investigation, layers that were becoming increasingly personal for George. He said, "You're sure?"

"Yep. One hundred per cent."

George studied Danny, his instinct telling him there was something Danny wasn't saying, but clearly Edward Beaumont was involved somewhere. "If you think of anything else, anything at all, you'll let us know, right?"

"Of course," Danny replied, but his voice lacked conviction.

As they left the shopping centre, George shared a glance with Yolanda. They both felt it—the nagging suspicion that Danny was holding something back. The coincidences were piling up, and George knew they were vital to unravelling the mystery.

Chapter Ten

George's fingers hesitated over the phone before he dialled. The number was as familiar as the apprehension that knotted in his stomach. The call connected, and Marie's voice, warm but laced with caution, filled his ear.

"Hello, love," Marie greeted, her Scottish accent as pronounced as ever.

"Hi, Mum," George replied, his voice betraying a hint of the turmoil within. "I need to know where Dad is."

There was a pause on the other end, a silence that spoke volumes of the unspoken tensions and secrets that lay buried in their family history. Marie's voice, once steady, now wavered slightly, a symptom of her hidden struggle with Alzheimer's that George was yet to discover.

"Why do you need to find Eddie now, George?" Marie asked, her tone wary.

"It's important, Mum. It's about the case I'm working on," George pressed, trying to mask the urgency in his voice.

Marie sighed a sound that carried the weight of years of complex emotions. "He's at the old mansion in Cookridge. Why?"

George's heart raced. The mansion in Cookridge—a place he hadn't been to since he was a boy, a place that held as many shadows as secrets, a place he was sure Edward had sold.

So why was Edward living there?

He knew this meeting with his father was inevitable, yet he dreaded what truths might come to light.

"Thanks, Mum. I will," he said.

As he ended the call, George sat back, bracing himself for what was to come.

* * *

George Beaumont drove through the rain-slicked streets of Leeds, his thoughts clouded by the complexities of the Santa Claus murders. The rhythmic swipe of the windscreen wipers matched the cadence of his contemplation. The investigation had reached a crucial juncture, but clarity remained elusive.

George's phone rang, breaking the monotony of the drive. He glanced at the caller ID—Dr Christian Ross, the pathologist. Expectation tightened in his chest. Perhaps Ross had unearthed something pivotal from the postmortem.

"DI Beaumont," George answered, his voice a blend of hope and weariness.

"George, it's Christian," came the pathologist's voice, tinged with a note of regret.

"What have you got for me, Dr Ross?"

"I wish I had more for you, son, but the postmortem hasn't revealed much beyond what we already knew."

George's grip on the steering wheel tightened. He had been clinging to the hope that the postmortem would provide a breakthrough. "Understood, Christian. I appreciate the update."

There was a brief pause before Christian spoke again, his

CHAPTER TEN

tone tentative. "Are you making any progress on your end?"

George exhaled slowly, staring out at the blurry city lights. "We're hitting walls, doctor. It's like we're chasing a ghost."

The admission hung heavy in the air, a stark acknowledgement of their frustrating reality.

"I wish I could offer more," Christian said, his voice a mirror of George's frustration.

"It's not your fault. This case is... unconventional," George replied, the understatement a small attempt to lighten the weight of their conversation.

The call ended with mutual assurances of continued collaboration, but George felt a familiar sense of isolation as he disconnected.

George's car cut through the wind blasting at him as he took winding roads at speed leading to Cookridge, each turn drawing him closer to a confrontation he'd spent a decade avoiding. The mansion loomed ahead, its grandeur stark against the twilight sky, a testament to Edward Beaumont's affluence and influence.

As George parked his car, he took a moment to steel himself, his jaw set with determination, eyes reflecting the complex storm of emotions brewing within. Exiting the vehicle, he approached the house, his strides measured but resolute.

The door opened before George could knock. Edward Beaumont stood in the doorway, his stature as imposing as the house behind him. Age had touched him, but his eyes still held that familiar icy detachment. The air between them was charged, heavy with years of unsaid words and unhealed wounds.

"George," Edward greeted, his voice devoid of warmth. "This is unexpected."

George met his father's gaze, an unspoken challenge passing between them. "We need to talk. It's about a murder case." He paused. "Two murder cases."

Edward's expression remained unreadable, but there was a flicker in his eyes, a brief hint of something that George couldn't quite place. Resignation? Guilt? It was gone as quickly as it had appeared.

"Very well," Edward said, stepping aside to let George in. "Come into my study."

As George followed Edward through the opulent hallways of the mansion, memories of his childhood, both bitter and sweet, echoed in his mind. The house hadn't changed much, still bearing the mark of Edward's impeccable taste and need for control.

Entering the study, a room lined with bookshelves and dominated by an enormous mahogany desk, George felt as though he'd stepped into a part of Edward's mind—organised, imposing, and slightly intimidating.

Edward took a seat behind his desk, the familiar fortress from which he'd orchestrated both his business and family life. George remained standing, not willing to concede any ground in this subtle battle of wills.

"It's about the Santa Claus murder," George began, his voice steady despite the turmoil within.

"That occurred a decade ago, George." He grinned. "They've put you on cold cases now?"

"No, but there's been another murder."

"Ryan Baxter," Edward said. His expression didn't change, but his fingers steepled in front of him, a telltale sign of his mind working behind the façade.

"Yes."

CHAPTER TEN

"And what does that have to do with me?" Edward asked, his tone casual, almost disinterested.

George leaned forward slightly, his gaze never leaving his father. "I've come across a lead that might connect you to these murders, both past and present."

For a moment, the air in the room felt charged, as if a storm was about to break. Edward's gaze hardened, a flicker of something dangerous passing through his eyes.

"Be careful, George," Edward warned, his voice low. "Digging up the past can have unforeseen consequences."

George straightened, his resolve firm. "I'm not afraid of the past any more. I need the truth."

Edward leaned back in his chair, a mask of indifference settling on his face. "Then seek your truth, George. But remember, not all truths set you free."

George turned to leave, his heart pounding with a mixture of fear, anger, and a burning need for answers.

But he wanted to confront the man who had loomed like a shadow over much of his life. The air was thick with unspoken tension, a testament to the years of unresolved conflict and emotional turmoil between father and son.

"Your social circle," George began, his voice edged with a mix of accusation and desperation. "The murders, past and present, they're connected to you somehow."

Edward Beaumont, seated behind his grand desk, let out a derisive chuckle. He leaned back in his chair, regarding George with a mixture of disdain and amusement. "Oh, George, you always were one for dramatics."

George's hands clenched at his sides, his jaw tightening. The old dynamic of dismissal and superiority was playing out again, but this time, he was determined not to back down.

"I'm not here for your games. People are dead, and there's a link to your world. I need answers."

Edward's eyes narrowed slightly, a glint of something unreadable flashing in their depths. He steepled his fingers; his posture relaxed yet calculated. "Accusations require evidence, Detective Inspector. And from what I can see, you have none."

George stepped closer, leaning forward. "I'm not blind to the connections, nor to the past. I know there's more to this, and I intend to find out what it is."

The tension in the room spiked as Edward's expression hardened. "You're chasing shadows, George. And you'd do well to remember the consequences of overstepping."

The underlying threat in Edward's tone was clear, but George was undeterred. He'd come too far to be intimidated. "I'll uncover the truth. No matter where it leads."

Edward's smile was cold, devoid of warmth. "Then be prepared for what you might find. Truth, as you should know, can be a double-edged sword."

"If you visit me again, ring me so I can have my solicitor present." With that, Edward waved a hand dismissively, signalling the end of their conversation. George, filled with a tumultuous mix of anger and determination, turned on his heel and left the room. As he walked through the opulent corridors of the mansion, the weight of the encounter hung heavy on his shoulders.

George Beaumont stepped out of his father's mansion, the cold night air doing little to quell the heat of his anger. His eyes, hard with resolve, scanned the darkening sky as he made his way to his car. The encounter with Edward had been as fruitless as it was frustrating. Yet, it had ignited something

CHAPTER TEN

within him—a fierce determination to uncover the truth, no matter how unsavoury it might be.

Settling into the driver's seat, George allowed himself a rare moment of vulnerability. His mind replayed the conversation, each of Edward's dismissive remarks stinging as sharply as ever. But it was more than just the clash of wills with his father; it was the gnawing realisation that this investigation could unearth secrets about Edward Beaumont that George was not sure he was ready to face.

George's fingers gripped the steering wheel, the leather cool and smooth under his touch. He took a deep breath, releasing it slowly, feeling the weight of the case press upon him. The silence of the car was a stark contrast to the turmoil of his thoughts. This was not just another case; it was a journey into his family's darkness, a path that he knew would test him in ways he couldn't yet fathom.

As he started the car, the engine's hum was a reminder of the world moving on outside the confines of his family's drama. George glanced one last time at the mansion, a symbol of wealth and influence but now also a reminder of the secrets that lay hidden within.

With a determined set to his jaw, George put the car into gear and drove away into the night. The streets of Leeds stretched out before him, each turn taking him further from his father's house but closer to the truth he sought. His mind was already racing, plotting the next steps in the investigation, each one a potential step closer to exposing the reality of Edward Beaumont.

* * *

Back at the police station, George entered the bustling shared office, the noise of ringing phones and hurried footsteps filling the air. He needed an update on the case, any lead, no matter how faint, that could bring them closer to solving the Santa Claus murders.

Lindsey Yardley was waiting for him outside his office, her eyes reflecting the weariness of a long day's work. She held a small evidence bag containing a delicate strand of fabric.

"The fibre we found on Baxter's body, DI Beaumont," she began, her voice tinged with a mix of anticipation and fatigue. "It's a luxury cashmere-silk blend. I'm going to dig deeper into it, see if we can trace its origin."

George's gratitude shone through his tired eyes. "Thanks, Lindsey. Let me know as soon as you have anything."

As Lindsey turned away to continue her work, George's mind raced. Luxury cashmere-silk. The mere mention of it sent a ripple of unease down his spine. He knew that such a fabric was reserved for the most exclusive of garments, the finest quality men's suiting fabric in the world.

And there was one man who came to mind immediately— his father, Edward Beaumont.

The web of connections, both familial and professional, was a tangled one. George had grown up in a world where his father's influence was vast.

But now, with the spectre of luxury fabric hanging over the case, the past threatened to resurface. George couldn't ignore the possibility that his father, or those connected to him, might hold the key to unlocking the mystery of the Santa Claus murders.

Hell, he could even be the killer.

As he leaned against his desk, the weight of his decisions

CHAPTER TEN

pressing upon him, George knew that the path ahead was fraught with peril.

Chapter Eleven

The shrill ring of his phone shattered George Beaumont's sleep. He squinted at the clock—6 am. Grasping the phone, he listened, his face hardening with each word: another murder, the killer striking again in the early morning hours. The urgency in the caller's voice was unmistakable.

Without a word, he swung his legs out of bed, his mind already racing. The room was still dark, Isabella and Olivia asleep, oblivious to the night's grim turn. He tiptoed, collecting his coat and warrant card, the familiar weight of responsibility settling on his shoulders.

The drive to the crime scene was a blur, Leeds' streets empty in the early morning chill. George's thoughts were a whirlwind, piecing together what little he knew. The same eerie Christmas theme, another victim, the killer's audacity growing with each passing day.

Detective Inspector George Beaumont's car pulled up to the cordoned area in the quiet suburb of Rodley, Leeds. The street, usually vibrant with Christmas decorations, was now tainted with the grimness of a crime scene. The flashing lights of police cars pierced the dawn's darkness.

The air was crisp and biting as George stepped out of his car, his expression steely. He pulled his coat tighter around him,

CHAPTER ELEVEN

the festive decorations on the suburban houses standing in stark contrast to the grim task ahead.

Detective Constable Jay Scott approached, his face grim. "Boss, it's bad," he said, his voice low. "Same MO as the first. It's definitely our guy."

Yellow tape fluttered in the cold breeze, marking the boundary of a nightmare. The second Santa Claus victim lay in a macabre display, a twisted echo of the festive season.

George nodded, his jaw set. The killer was bold, almost taunting them. He crossed the outer cordon, his eyes scanning the area, absorbing every detail.

Then, after getting the PC to sign him in, George, dressed in his Tyvek suit, mask, gloves, and shoe covers, ducked under the police tape, his eyes immediately taking in the scene. The contrast was stark: festive lights and decorations in the gardens, a backdrop to the horror that unfolded on the pavement. From a nearby house, the sound of Christmas music played, a haunting juxtaposition to the scene before him.

Dr Christian Ross, the pathologist, arrived with his kit, and his greeting to George was brief and professional. "George," he nodded, turning his attention to the body.

Lindsey Yardley, the Scene of Crime Manager, was already coordinating her team. "We're documenting everything before moving him," she informed George, her voice steady despite the grim task.

George's gaze fell upon the victim, another man in his forties, the scene hauntingly similar to the first murder but with a chilling new detail—the complete Santa attire. The killer had struck again, leaving behind a chillingly familiar display. He noticed the way the body was positioned, the grotesque arrangement of the limbs, the killer's signature growing more apparent with each murder.

"Any ID on him?" George asked, his voice low.

"Not yet," Lindsey replied. "We'll need to go through his pockets once we've processed the scene."

Jay Scott approached, his face grim. "Neighbours reported hearing some commotion around 2 am," he said. "But no one saw anything. The fog was too thick." He paused. "They're all moaning about being woken up because it's Saturday."

George nodded, his mind racing. The killer was brazen yet careful. No witnesses, no immediate clues, just the eerie aftermath. He turned to Dr Ross, who was bent over the lifeless body of the latest Santa Claus murder victim. "Cause and time of death?"

Dr Ross looked up, pushing his glasses up the bridge of his nose. The frost-laden morning air in the quiet suburb of Rodley was pierced by Christian's voice. "The cause of death is similar to the first one," he began, his voice low. "Severe trauma to the head, chest, and neck as before." He paused. "As for a time, it's hard to say with the cold, but I'd estimate between midnight and 2 am," Dr Ross replied, frowning as he worked.

"Thank you." George then watched as Lindsey and her team meticulously collected evidence, photographing the scene and bagging potential clues. Every piece could be the key to unlocking the killer's identity.

His phone vibrated in his pocket, a reminder of the world beyond the tape. He glanced at the screen—Isabella. He'd have to call her back. Right now, every second at the crime scene mattered.

CHAPTER ELEVEN

* * *

The living room was silent except for the low hum of the television. On the screen, Paige McGuinness appeared, her expression sombre as she delivered the news to the Leeds community. "A second Santa Claus murder has been discovered early this morning in the Rodley suburb," she announced, her voice steady but tinged with concern. "This chilling development has intensified fears that a serial killer may be at large in our city."

In homes across Leeds, people gathered in front of their televisions, their faces reflecting the shock and fear that Paige's words invoked. Neighbours exchanged worried glances, their festive cheer dampened by the unfolding news.

The camera panned to a live feed of the crime scene, showing police activity around the cordoned area. Paige continued, "The police have not yet released details about the victim or the circumstances of the murder, but sources close to the investigation have confirmed similarities to the first Santa Claus murder."

In a small flat, an elderly couple watched in silence. The woman clutched her husband's hand, her eyes wide with fear. "It's happening again, just like ten years ago," she whispered.

On the other side of town, a group of young men paused their video game to watch the news. One of them shook his head in disbelief. "This is messed up. Right before Christmas."

Paige's voice broke through the growing anxiety. "Residents are advised to remain vigilant and report any suspicious activity to the police. The identity of the killer remains unknown, and the motives behind these horrifying crimes are still a mystery."

The camera returned to Paige, standing outside the police cordon, her face illuminated by the flashing blue lights of the police cars. "We'll continue to bring you updates as this story develops. For now, the city of Leeds is left reeling from another shocking murder as the hunt for the killer intensifies."

As the news segment ended, families sat in stunned silence, the gravity of the situation sinking in. The festive lights that adorned their homes seemed dimmer, the joy of the season overshadowed by a growing sense of dread.

In a quiet room, Isabella Wood watched the news, her jaw set in a firm line. She knew the fear that gripped the city all too well, just as she knew the responsibility weighed heavily on George, a constant reminder of the stakes at hand.

Turning off the television, Isabella stood up, her mind already worrying about her fiancé.

The killer was out there, hidden in the shadows of the city George vowed to protect. And she knew her George, with his unwavering resolve and sharp instincts, would be determined to bring the murderer to justice, restoring peace to the frightened community of Leeds.

The clock was ticking, and for George, failure was not an option.

But Isabella wondered about the cost of solving such a case.

* * *

As the morning sun struggled to pierce the dense fog enveloping the Leeds suburb of Rodley, the flash of media cameras added an unsettling strobe effect to the grim scene. Detective Inspector George Beaumont, standing within the police tape, could feel the weight of every flash, every click, intensifying

CHAPTER ELEVEN

the pressure mounting around the second Santa Claus murder.

Onlookers gathered at a respectful distance, their expressions a mix of fear and morbid fascination. The community's sense of safety was crumbling under the shadow of a killer who had struck twice, cloaked in the deceptive cheer of Christmas.

George crouched beside the body, his eyes scanning every inch. He noted the precise arrangement of the Christmas-themed elements around the victim. A sense of Déjà vu washed over him, the eerie familiarity of the killer's pattern sending a shiver down his spine.

Detective Constable Jay Scott approached his expression sombre. "Boss, I think it's Alex Green," he said quietly. "He lived in Rodley, and we've been unable to reach him."

George nodded slowly, his mind racing. The location, the victim's identity—it couldn't be a coincidence. He gazed around the scene, searching for anything that might lead them to the killer.

The CSI team worked in silence, collecting evidence, photographing the scene, and taking notes.

Beaumont's team moved with urgency, aware of the prying eyes and the need for discretion. The media's presence wasn't just a distraction; it was a reminder of the public's demand for answers, answers that Beaumont was still grappling to find.

Detective Constable Jay Scott glanced towards the gathering crowd, his expression one of frustration. "This is turning into a circus, boss," he muttered, stepping closer to Beaumont. "The last thing we need is panic."

Beaumont nodded, his gaze fixed on the scene. "Let's keep focused," he said, his voice steady despite the chaos around them. "We need to find something concrete before this killer becomes bolder."

Detective Constable Jay Scott and Scene of Crime Manager Lindsey Yardley joined Beaumont, their expressions grim. Lindsey held up a bagged item. "Found this in his pocket," she said. "Wallet with ID. It's Alex Green, 42 years old."

Beaumont exhaled slowly, a mix of frustration and determination in his gaze. "Another link to the past case," he muttered, and then he turned to Jay. "You were right."

"Cheers, boss."

Lindsey interjected, "We need to comb through every detail, find something we're missing. This killer whilst meticulous, are human. They'll slip up."

Beaumont turned to his team, his voice firm. "We keep this close to the chest. No leaks. We can't afford to tip off our killer or cause more panic."

Jay's expression hardened. "Understood, boss. We'll dig deeper and cross-reference everything. There has to be a pattern we're not seeing."

Lindsey nodded in agreement. "I'll get my team on the forensic analysis right away. Every fibre, every print could lead us to him."

George's thoughts were interrupted by a call from Yolanda Williams. "We've got something from the CCTV footage near Alex's house," she said urgently. "You need to see this."

George thanked her and ended the call. He turned to Jay. "Gather the team. We're heading back to the station. We might have another lead."

The relentless clamour of journalists as George Beaumont left the crime scene left a sour taste in his mouth. Camera flashes flickered like distress signals in the dim light of dawn, each journalist vying for his attention.

"Detective Beaumont!" one reporter called out, shoving

CHAPTER ELEVEN

a recorder forward. "Can you give us any details about the murder?"

George paused, his face betraying nothing of the turmoil inside. He turned, facing the sea of expectant faces, their eyes hungry for information. "We are investigating a serious incident," he began, his voice steady, "and we ask anyone with information to come forward."

"Is this related to the previous Santa Claus murder?" another reporter shouted, trying to edge closer.

George remained impassive. "We are exploring all avenues and cannot disclose specifics at this stage. Our priority is to ensure public safety."

He stepped back, signalling an end to the impromptu press conference. The questions continued, a cacophony of voices, but George walked away, his pace measured and resolute.

Inside his car, George finally allowed himself a moment of vulnerability. He leaned back against the seat, closing his eyes, the images from the crime scene replaying in his mind. The killer was meticulous, leaving a trail of horror dressed in the garb of festive cheer. And now, another life lost, another family shattered.

The weight of the case pressed down on him, a tangible burden. The city of Leeds, his city, was gripped by fear. People were looking to him for answers, for safety, for justice. He opened his eyes, staring at the busy crime scene now fading in his rear-view mirror.

George knew he was racing against time. The killer was out there, possibly planning their next move, and he had to be one step ahead. The pattern was emerging, but it was like grasping at shadows, each clue leading to more questions.

As he started the engine, a determined look settled over

his features. This wasn't just another case; it was a personal challenge, a battle of wits against an unseen adversary. He couldn't let the killer continue their macabre spree.

Driving away from the chaos, George's mind was a tornado of thoughts and strategies. He needed to delve deeper into the past, into the connections that seemed to tie the murders together. Every detail mattered; every piece of evidence was a step closer to the killer. The only problem was they had very little evidence to go by.

The streets of Leeds passed by in a blur as George headed back to the station. His team would be waiting, ready to dissect the latest developments. There was no room for error, no chance to let personal feelings cloud his judgment.

The city depended on him, on his ability to solve this puzzle. George Beaumont, the seasoned detective, the man who had seen the darkest corners of human nature, was once again at the forefront of a battle against the shadows.

As the police station came into view, George's grip on the steering wheel tightened. This was more than a case; it was a fight for justice, a fight against the darkness that threatened to engulf his city. And George Beaumont was ready to face it head-on.

Chapter Twelve

The dim light of the surveillance room flickered across George Beaumont's face, casting shadows that mirrored the dark thoughts swirling in his mind. Beside him, Detective Constable Jay Scott leaned in closer to the monitor, his brow furrowed in concentration.

"There," Jay pointed at the screen, "Clarkson, near the first murder scene. Look at his movements."

The grainy footage showed Michael Clarkson moving erratically, his body language tense, almost frantic. It was a stark contrast to the controlled aggression they knew him for. George's eyes narrowed, analysing every frame.

"Rewind that," George said, his voice a low growl. "Stop... there." He tapped the screen where Clarkson seemed to pause, looking over his shoulder, a gesture of paranoia or guilt.

Jay nodded, "He looks like he's trying to avoid being seen, boss. It's suspicious, to say the least."

George leaned back, his mind racing. Clarkson's presence near the murder scene was no coincidence. The erratic behaviour suggested he knew he was doing something he shouldn't. Something sinister.

"This could be the break we need," George mused aloud, his voice carrying a mixture of hope and grim determination.

Jay looked over at him, "We should bring him in, question him. His reaction might tell us more."

George considered this, weighing the risks. Clarkson was a volatile element; confronting him could escalate things. But they needed answers.

"Agreed," George finally said, his decision made. "But we'll do it carefully. Clarkson's dangerous."

The Incident Room at Elland Road Police Station hummed with a palpable tension. George Beaumont stood at the head of the room; his team arrayed before him. On the screen behind him, the image of Michael 'Mike' Clarkson glowed ominously.

"This is our suspect," George began, his voice carrying a note of grim determination. "Michael Clarkson. An acquaintance of our first victim and a known figure from a case a decade ago." He paused. "Clarkson was near the first murder scene. We're bringing him in for questioning."

The team leaned forward, absorbing every detail. The image on the screen shifted to a map of Leeds city centre, pinpointing a high-end gym exclusive to the city's elite.

"He's been working here," George continued, indicating the gym's location. "It's private, mainly for the penthouse renters. That means limited access and possibly limited witnesses."

Jay Scott raised his hand. "Do we know his schedule, boss? When he's most likely to be there?"

George nodded. "Yolanda's working on that. We need to move quickly but carefully. Clarkson is no stranger to violence."

The room buzzed with a newfound urgency. Tashan Blackburn was already on his phone, coordinating with surveillance teams, while Candy Nichols scribbled notes, her face etched with concentration.

George's gaze lingered on the screen. Clarkson's face, a mixture of brute strength and cunning, seemed to mock them from the digital display. There was something there, a clue perhaps, lurking in the depths of those cold eyes.

"We'll approach this with a two-pronged strategy," he said. "Surveillance to monitor his movements and an interview team to gauge his reaction. I want no mistakes."

The team nodded in unison, each member keenly aware of the stakes. George's expression hardened, his eyes reflecting the weight of the responsibility he carried.

"Jay, you're with me. We'll handle the interview. DCs Blackburn and Nichols," George said, his voice firm, "you're on discrete observation. We need eyes on Clarkson's known haunts. Keep it low-key."

Tashan nodded a determined glint in his eyes. Candy, ever meticulous, jotted down notes, her mind already racing through surveillance strategies.

As they prepared to leave, Detective Chief Inspector Alistair Atkinson approached, his steps measured, a sealed envelope in hand. He extended it to Tashan, his expression unreadable.

"This came for you," Atkinson said, his tone neutral.

Tashan took the envelope, a mix of curiosity and apprehension on his face. He carefully opened it, his eyes scanning the contents. The room fell silent, all eyes on him.

It was an opportunity for promotion, a leap forward in his career. But it came with a catch—he'd have to leave George's team. Tashan's face was a canvas of conflicting emotions—pride, uncertainty, loyalty—all warring within him.

As the team dispersed, George lingered for a moment, his thoughts racing. This was more than just tracking down a suspect. Clarkson's link to the past case, to the shadows that had haunted George for years, added layers of complexity to the investigation.

Detective Constable Tashan Blackburn sat, hunched over his desk. The letter, now a folded crease in his pocket, weighed on his mind like a stone. Beside him, Detective Constable Candy Nichols outlined their surveillance strategy, her voice a steady stream of logistical details. But Tashan's thoughts were elsewhere, adrift in a sea of what-ifs and might-bes.

His fingers drummed a restless beat on the desk, echoing the tumult within. The offer of promotion, a coveted step up the career ladder, now felt like a crossroads, each path leading to vastly different futures. On the one hand, there was the opportunity for advancement, recognition, and a new challenge. On the other, the camaraderie of George's team, the familiar rhythm of their daily grind, the shared purpose that had become a cornerstone of his professional life.

Candy glanced at him, her sharp eyes catching the distant look on his face. "You alright, Tashan?" she asked, her tone laced with concern.

Tashan blinked, pulling himself back to the present. "Yeah, just... thinking," he replied, attempting a nonchalant shrug.

Candy leaned in, lowering her voice. "It's about the letter, isn't it?"

Tashan only nodded.

Candy said nothing more.

Tashan sighed, the internal battle evident.

"I'm here if you need to talk, Tashan," Candy said.

"It's a promotion offer," he eventually whispered. "It's a big decision. I mean, it's what I've been working towards, but..." His voice trailed off, the unspoken but hanging between them.

"But this team, what we have here, it's not just about solving cases. It's more than that," Candy finished for him, her understanding clear.

Tashan nodded, grateful for her insight. "Exactly. I don't know if I'm ready to leave that behind."

Candy's hand rested briefly on his shoulder, a gesture of solidarity. "Whatever you decide, Tashan, we've got your back. Just know that."

A small smile cracked Tashan's thoughtful expression. "Thanks, Candy. That means a lot."

Their moment of connection was interrupted by the buzz of activity around them, the team gearing up for the stakeout. Tashan stood, the letter's weight now a tangible presence, a decision looming on the horizon.

He looked around the room at the faces of his colleagues, each absorbed in their tasks, each a thread in the fabric of the team. The bond they shared, forged in the fires of countless cases, was not something he could easily walk away from.

Tashan's gaze settled on George, the man who had been both mentor and guide through the maze of police work. The respect and loyalty he felt for George ran deep, another factor in the complex equation of his decision.

With a deep breath, Tashan focused on the task at hand, pushing the decision to the back of his mind. Now was not the time for introspection; now was the time for action. The killer was still out there, and they had a job to do.

As Tashan and Candy finalised their surveillance plan, the letter remained unaddressed, its implications hanging in the balance. But for now, Tashan Blackburn, the dedicated detective, set his personal crossroads aside, his commitment to the case unwavering.

* * *

Night had fallen over Bramley, casting shadows that deepened the sense of anticipation. Tashan Blackburn and Candy Nichols, hidden in the unmarked car, kept their eyes fixed on the suspect's council residence. The stakeout was a waiting game, a test of patience and vigilance. They communicated in hushed tones over the radio, each movement outside the residence scrutinised under their watchful gaze.

The suspect, Michael 'Mike' Clarkson, emerged from the building. He paused, his head swivelling as if sensing the air for danger. His nervous energy was palpable even from a distance. Mike, dressed in a dark jacket, glanced around furtively before hurrying down the street, his steps quick and purposeful.

"Target on the move," Tashan whispered into the radio, his voice steady but charged with adrenaline. Candy, her eyes sharp, nodded in silent agreement.

They waited a beat longer before exiting the car, blending seamlessly into the night. Their footsteps were soft, their presence barely noticeable as they tailed Mike, keeping a safe distance. Tashan's senses were heightened, his training kicking in, every nerve attuned to the task at hand.

Mike's pace quickened, his glances over his shoulder growing more frequent. The duo matched his speed, adept at tailing without drawing attention. Candy's eyes never left the suspect, her focus unwavering.

As they moved through the dimly lit streets, the quiet of the night was their ally. The soft rustle of leaves and the distant

CHAPTER TWELVE

hum of the city all melded into the background. Their target was oblivious to the shadows that trailed him.

Mike turned into an alley, a shortcut known only to those familiar with the area. Tashan signalled to Candy, and they picked up their pace. The alley was narrow, the walls close, a perfect spot for confrontation.

But Mike didn't stop. He continued, his stride breaking into a near run. Tashan and Candy exchanged a look, a silent agreement passing between them. This was it. They quickened their pace, closing the distance.

Suddenly, Mike stopped his back to them. He seemed to sense something amiss. Tashan and Candy froze, their training taking over. They were close, too close to back down now.

Mike turned, his face a mask of surprise and fear as he saw them. Tashan stepped forward, his voice authoritative, warrant card displayed. "Michael Clarkson, it's the police; we need to talk."

Mike's eyes darted around, looking for an escape route. But the alley offered no reprieve. He was cornered, his options dwindling.

The chase erupted suddenly, tearing through the quiet streets of Bramley. Tashan Blackburn, his instincts honed, responded instantly, his body surging forward in pursuit. The suspect had bolted, panic lending speed to his steps. The streets blurred into a mosaic of lights and shadows as Tashan closed the gap, his training driving him onward.

George Beaumont, limping slightly, was a step behind. He signalled Jay Scott, who was positioned further down the street. Jay, understanding immediately, joined the pursuit, his own pace matching Tashan's.

The suspect weaved through the network of narrow streets and ginnels, a labyrinth only known to those familiar with Bramley. His desperation was palpable, a wild animal caught in a trap. But Tashan and Jay were relentless, their determination fuelled by the urgency of the chase.

The suspect made a sudden turn into an alley, a dead-end he hadn't anticipated. Tashan and Jay, right on his heels, saw the moment of realisation dawn on the suspect's face. They closed in, their presence an inescapable net.

Cornered, the suspect turned, his back against the wall, his breath ragged. Tashan approached, his voice steady, "You have nowhere to go. It's over."

Jay moved in from the other side, ensuring there was no escape. The suspect defeated, slumped slightly, the fight draining out of him.

George arrived moments later, his expression a mix of relief and resolve. He took in the scene, his experienced eyes assessing the suspect. "Good work," he nodded to Tashan and Jay.

Chapter Thirteen

It was overly hot in the interrogation room, Michael sweating profusely as he sat across from George, his demeanour a mix of defiance and nervousness. George, his eyes sharp and analytical, observed Michael's erratic behaviour, noting every twitch and shift. The tension in the room was palpable, a tangible presence that seemed to feed Michael's growing unease.

George began the interrogation, his questions probing, designed to unravel the web of lies and deceit. "Talk to me about your relationship with the victims. What were your recent activities?" His tone was direct, leaving no room for evasiveness.

Michael, now composed, met George's gaze. "I knew them, yes. But I had nothing to do with what happened to them." His voice was steady, but George's trained ear picked up a slight quiver.

George leaned forward, his presence dominating the room. "Your actions say otherwise. Why run if you're innocent?" He watched Michael closely, every shift, every flicker of the eyes.

"Because you were following me," he explained. "Or your lackeys were, Detective."

George leaned forward, placing his elbows on the table.

"You have a distinctive tattoo on your hand, Mike. The same tattoo was seen on the person following Ryan on CCTV footage. How do you explain that?"

Mike's hands trembled slightly. "Lots of people have tattoos, Detective. Doesn't mean anything."

"But yours is unique, Michael," George countered sharply.

"It was when I got it, but I show it off a lot. Check my Insta."

George's questions became precise like a surgeon's scalpel cutting to the heart of the matter. "Where were you on the nights of the murders?" he asked, his voice steady and unwavering, elaborating on the dates and times.

Michael's response was jittery, his words tumbling out in a rush. "I was at home both nights," he said, his eyes darting away from George's piercing gaze. "I have proof."

George leaned forward, his interest piqued. "Proof?" he echoed, scepticism etching his voice.

Michael produced a ticket stub from a local cinema, time-stamped for the night in question. "I was watching a film last night," he explained, a hint of relief in his voice.

George examined the ticket, his mind working rapidly. The evidence was unexpected, a curveball that threatened to derail their theory. Frustration flickered across his features, a brief moment of vulnerability in the face of this new challenge.

"And on the night of Ryan Baxter's murder?"

"I was out with my mates from the gym, having a curry," Mike responded a bit more confidently.

"Can anyone verify that?" George questioned, his tone implying scepticism.

"Yeah, my friends can. All of them, especially Grant. He'll tell you the same because we stayed in the bar and had more drinks after the others left."

CHAPTER THIRTEEN

George slid his PNB across the table and said, "Write his full name and address down." He paused. "And add his mobile number."

George noted Mike's response, his eyes analysing every movement, every twitch that might indicate deceit. "And your recent activities? Anything that would connect you to the crimes?"

"I told you, I haven't done anything!" Mike's voice rose slightly, a hint of panic creeping in. "I don't know anything about these murders."

George closed the file and stood up. His stare was unwavering, piercing through Mike's defences. "If that's the case, then you have nothing to worry about. But if you're hiding something, we will find out, Michael."

Mike remained silent, his eyes finally meeting George's. There was a mixture of fear and defiance in his gaze.

George turned and walked towards the door of the interview room. Before exiting, he paused, looking back at Mike. "Before I go, Michael, one last thing," George said, his eyes fixed on Mike. "Can you think of any reason why anyone would want to hurt the victims? Any grudge, any conflict that comes to mind?"

Mike hesitated, his eyes briefly flickering with something unidentifiable before settling back into a guarded expression. "No, I... I can't think of anything," he replied, his voice laced with uncertainty. "Like I said, I wasn't close to Ryan or the others. I don't know what their business was."

George studied Mike's face for a moment longer, searching for any hint of deception or hidden knowledge. "Alright, Michael. If you do remember anything, anything at all, you know how to reach us."

With those final words, George left the room, leaving Mike alone with his thoughts and the weight of the investigation bearing down on him. The tension in the room was palpable, a clear indication of the complex web of truths and lies that George was determined to unravel.

After the interview, the team gathered for a debrief in the Incident Room. The atmosphere was heavy with disappointment, the weight of the unsolved case bearing down on them.

George stood at the head of the room, his posture resolute despite the setback. "This isn't over," he said firmly. "We need to explore every possible alibi for chinks. We can't afford to miss anything."

Detective Constable Jay Scott nodded, his expression serious. "We'll double-check the alibis, boss," he suggested, ready to dive back into the investigation. "Hell, I'll even triple-check them, boss."

Detective Constable Tashan Blackburn, his mind always analytical, added, "Let's also revisit the CCTV footage. There might be something we overlooked."

George's eyes moved across his team, each member eager to contribute to finding the missing piece of the puzzle. "Good," he said, a note of determination in his voice. "Let's keep pushing. We owe it to the victims."

* * *

The bustling shared office contradicted the relative quiet of George Beaumont's office as Detective Constable Tashan Blackburn stood hesitantly by the door, clutching the envelope that had arrived earlier. George, preoccupied with case files sprawled across his desk, looked up and gestured for Tashan to come in.

"Sir, I need to talk to you about something," Tashan began, his voice betraying his inner turmoil.

George nodded, setting aside the files. "What's on your mind, Tashan?"

Tashan took a deep breath, holding out the envelope. "I've been offered a promotion, sir. It's a great opportunity, but it means leaving the team."

George's expression softened with understanding. He knew all too well the weight of such decisions. "Promotions are a sign of your hard work, Tashan. But they also bring new challenges and responsibilities."

Tashan nodded, his gaze fixed on the floor. "I know, sir. But I'm not sure if I'm ready to leave the team, especially with this case ongoing."

George leaned back in his chair, his eyes thoughtful. "You have to consider what's best for you and your career, Tashan. Opportunities like this don't come around often."

"But what about loyalty, sir? To the team, to the case?" Tashan's voice was laced with uncertainty.

"Loyalty is important, but so is growth," George replied. "You have to think about where you see yourself in the future. What path will lead you to where you want to be?"

Tashan mulled over George's words, a mix of relief and confusion on his face. "I appreciate your guidance, sir. It's just... a lot to think about."

George nodded sympathetically. "Take your time, Tashan. Whatever decision you make, make sure it's the right one for you. You're a valuable member of this team, but your future is ultimately in your hands."

Tashan gave a small, grateful smile. "Thank you, sir. I'll

think it over."

As Tashan left the office, George's gaze lingered on the young detective's retreating figure. He remembered his own crossroads moments, the choices that had shaped his career and life. It was never easy, but it was a part of growth, a part of life.

Turning back to his desk, George's mind refocused on the case at hand, the faces of the victims haunting his thoughts. The road ahead was uncertain, but like Tashan, he too had decisions to make, choices that would impact not just the case but his own life.

The dim light of the desk lamp cast long shadows across the room, mirroring the dark intricacies of the case that consumed his thoughts.

The clock on the wall ticked away, its sound a constant reminder of the urgency pressing upon him. The images of the murder victims stared back at him, their silent pleas for justice resonating in the hollow space. With each passing moment, George felt the weight of responsibility tightening its grip.

He leaned back in his chair, rubbing his temples in a futile attempt to ease the tension that had built up over the hours. The case was a tangled web, its threads stretching into the past, intertwining with personal demons he had long fought to keep at bay.

The potential involvement of his father, Edward Beaumont, was a twist he hadn't anticipated. It was a connection that brought forth a tumult of emotions he struggled to suppress.

George's mind raced, piecing together the fragments of evidence, seeking patterns in the chaos. The killer's method, the Christmas-themed displays, the possible motives—all these elements formed a puzzle that he was determined to solve. But with each new lead, the path seemed to grow more convoluted, leading him deeper into a maze of uncertainty.

He glanced at the photo of his family, a stark contrast to the grim images surrounding it. The sight of Isabella and Olivia, their smiles frozen in time, was a bittersweet reminder of the life he was fighting to protect. And then there was Jack, George's double. It was for them, as much as for the victims, that he pushed himself to the brink.

Chapter Fourteen

Detective Constable Jay Scott stood in the stairwell outside the Homicide and Major Enquiry Team floor, his phone pressed against his ear. The usual light-heartedness that danced in his eyes had vanished, replaced by a deep, consuming concern. His colleagues continued their tasks, unaware of the personal storm brewing in Jay's world.

As he listened, Jay's hand tightened around his phone, his knuckles whitening. His gaze drifted to the floor, lost in the weight of the words pouring through the receiver. The call, brief yet heavy, ended with a sigh from Jay, a sound that carried the burden of worlds.

He pocketed his phone, taking a moment to gather his thoughts. The usually cheerful detective now wore a mask of solemnity. He made his way through the maze of desks and paperwork, each step measured, his mind clearly elsewhere.

Reaching Detective Inspector George Beaumont's office, Jay paused at the door. He took a deep breath, steeling himself. The door creaked open, and he stepped inside, closing it softly behind him.

George looked up from his desk, his face etched with the fatigue of the ongoing investigation. He noticed the unusual seriousness in Jay's demeanour and gestured for him to sit.

CHAPTER FOURTEEN

"Everything OK, Jay?" he asked, his tone laced with genuine concern.

"It's my mum, boss," Jay began, his voice barely above a whisper. He paused, struggling to find the words. "She's... she's not doing well. The doctors, they say it's serious." His voice cracked, revealing the emotional turmoil beneath his composed exterior.

George leaned back, his expression softening. He knew Jay's mother had been battling illness, but the gravity of the situation seemed to have deepened. "I'm sorry to hear that, Jay. If there's anything I can do—"

Jay shook his head slightly. "Thanks, boss, but there's not much anyone can do right now." He ran a hand through his hair, a gesture of frustration and helplessness. "It's just hard, you know? Trying to focus on work when this is hanging over my head."

George nodded, understanding the conflict all too well. "Take whatever time you need, Jay. Your family comes first. We'll manage here." His words were firm, an unwavering assurance of support.

"I appreciate that, boss. Really, I do. It's just that I don't want to let the team down, especially now," Jay replied, torn between his duty and his family.

"You're not letting anyone down. We're a team, and we look out for each other. That's how it works." George's tone was resolute, leaving no room for doubt.

Jay managed a weak smile, grateful for George's understanding. "Thanks, boss. It means a lot."

As Jay stood to leave, George added, "Jay, keep me updated, alright? We're all here for you."

Jay nodded a silent acknowledgement of the bond they

shared, not just as colleagues but as people navigating the complexities of life and duty.

The door closed softly behind Jay, leaving George alone with his thoughts. He stared at the closed door, pondering the delicate balance between professional obligations and personal challenges. In the world of crime solving, the lines were often blurred, the weight of their work spilling over into their private lives.

* * *

Leeds General Infirmary was ghostly quiet as Detective Constable Jay Scott walked with a measured pace, his footsteps echoing against the linoleum floor. His usually bright and confident demeanour was replaced by a look of solemnity as he navigated through the maze of hallways, passing by doctors and nurses who moved with an urgency that mirrored the gravity of their profession.

Jay arrived at a door marked with a room number and a name—his mother's name. Taking a deep breath, he pushed the door open and stepped into the room, the smell of antiseptics and medicine permeating the air. The room was stark in contrast to the bustling life outside, with only the beeping of the heart monitor breaking the silence.

At the bedside, Jay's mother lay, looking fragile amidst the white sheets and hospital equipment. Her face, usually so full of life and expression, now appeared tired and drawn, the illness taking its toll. Jay's heart clenched at the sight, a mix of pain and resolve settling within him.

He pulled a chair close to the bed and sat down, taking his mother's hand gently in his. Her skin was cold to the touch,

CHAPTER FOURTEEN

but Jay's grip was warm and reassuring. He leaned forward, speaking in soft, comforting tones that filled the room with a sense of warmth and familiarity.

"Hey, it's me, Jay. I'm here now," he said, giving her hand a gentle squeeze.

His mother stirred, her eyes fluttering open. A faint smile appeared on her face upon seeing Jay. It was a small gesture, but it spoke volumes of the bond they shared, a bond not even illness could diminish.

"How are you feeling?" Jay asked, his voice laced with concern.

"Been better," came the weak reply, tinged with the mother's characteristic humour.

Jay chuckled softly. "You always were the tough one," he said, his smile bittersweet.

They talked for a while, Jay keeping the conversation light and cheerful, recounting stories from work and the antics of his colleagues. His mother listened, her occasional laughter a sound Jay treasured in these moments. Despite the setting, there was a sense of normalcy in their interaction, a momentary escape from the reality of the situation.

As the visit continued, Jay's expression grew more contemplative. He looked at his mother, seeing not just the person in the hospital bed but the memories they shared and the strength and resilience she had always shown. It was this strength that Jay drew upon now in the face of his own challenges.

"I'm here for you, you know that, right?" Jay said, his voice steady. "Whatever you need, I'm here."

His mother nodded, her grip on Jay's hand tightening slightly. "I know, Jay. And I'm proud of you for all you're doing."

Those words, simple yet powerful, filled Jay with a renewed sense of purpose. He was a detective, yes, but he was also a son. His role extended beyond the confines of his job into the lives of those he cared about.

As the visit came to an end, Jay stood up, reluctant to leave but knowing duty called. He leaned down and kissed his mother's forehead, a silent promise of his return.

"Take care of yourself," he said softly. "I'll be back soon."

With one last look, Jay left the room, the weight of his responsibilities heavy on his shoulders. But within him burned a fire, a determination to fight, to protect, to serve—not just as a detective, but as a son. The hospital room, with its beeping monitors and sterile environment, had witnessed a moment of human connection, love and resilience, a testament to the strength of the human spirit.

* * *

In their home in Morley, Isabella watched George, who sat hunched over a sea of case files spread across the dining table. The evening lamplight filtered through the curtains, casting shadows that danced across the room, reflecting the turmoil within George. His eyes scurried across the pages, absorbing every detail, every nuance. He was a man lost in his world, a world of grim realities and haunting questions. The furrow in his brow deepened with each passing moment, a testament to the weight of the investigation bearing down on him.

Isabella observed him silently, a mixture of admiration and concern etched on her face. She knew this side of George well—the relentless detective whose dedication to his work often blurred the lines between his professional and personal life. It was a duality she had come to accept, yet it never ceased to worry her.

"George," she called out softly, her voice barely rising above a whisper.

He didn't respond, his focus unbreakable.

Isabella approached him, her steps gentle yet determined. She placed a hand on his shoulder, a gesture meant to anchor him back to the present, to their home, away from the dark alleys and cold crime scenes.

"George," she repeated, a little firmer this time.

He looked up as if emerging from a deep dive into the abyss. "Sorry, love," he murmured, his voice laced with fatigue. "Did you say something?"

Isabella sighed, a small smile gracing her lips. "I asked if you wanted some tea. You've been at this for hours."

George glanced at the clock, surprised by how much time had elapsed. "Tea sounds good, thanks."

As Isabella retreated to the kitchen, George's gaze drifted back to the files. His mind raced with theories, connections, and possibilities. Each document, each piece of evidence, was a puzzle piece in a larger, more complex picture. He knew the killer was methodical, leaving behind a trail of clues that were both deliberate and cryptic.

A sudden realization struck him, a connection he hadn't seen before. It was subtle, almost imperceptible, but it was there. His hand reached for his notebook, scribbling down the thought before it could slip away. It was a lead, albeit a small one, but in the world of criminal investigations, even the slightest lead could be the key to unravelling the mystery.

The sound of a kettle whistling in the background pulled

him out of his thoughts. Isabella returned, placing a steaming cup of tea beside him.

* * *

Back at Elland Road Police Station, Jay Scott sat amidst a sea of files, his focus flickering like a faulty light. He scrolled through case details, but his attention was repeatedly drawn to his phone, the screen illuminating his face in the dim light. Each vibration, each ring, sent a jolt of apprehension through him, a constant reminder of his mother's plight. He managed to keep his professional facade, but beneath it, the strain of balancing duty and personal worries was taking its toll.

Later, Detective Constable Jay Scott sat alone in his car, the engine idling softly in the quiet of the late night. The dim glow of the dashboard illuminated his face, revealing a furrow of deep thought etched across his brow. The streets of Leeds lay still outside, cloaked in the darkness of the night, mirroring the sombre mood inside the car.

His shift had ended, but the weight of the day's events lingered, clinging to him like a shadow. The hospital visit to his ill mother earlier in the day played in his mind on a continuous loop, a vivid reminder of the fragile line between his professional responsibilities and his personal life.

Jay's gaze shifted to the rear-view mirror, his reflection staring back at him, a symbol of the duality of his life. The confident, resourceful detective was there, but so was the concerned, weary family man. In the solitude of his car, away from the prying eyes of his colleagues and the demands of his job, he allowed himself a moment of vulnerability.

The phone call he received earlier echoed in his mind, the

words of the doctor both reassuring and alarming. His mother was stable, yet the road to recovery was uncertain, a path fraught with challenges and unknowns. Jay exhaled slowly, his breath fogging up the window momentarily, a transient mark of his presence in the still night.

He glanced at the clock on the dashboard. The time seemed to crawl, each second a reminder of the delicate balance he was trying to maintain. The cases at work demanded his attention, each one a complex puzzle needing to be solved, but his heart was elsewhere, with his family, in the sterile corridors of the hospital.

Chapter Fifteen

The Sunday morning air was crisp and filled with the buzz of excitement as Tashan Blackburn geared up for the charity run. It was the week before Christmas Eve and all around him, the atmosphere was festive, a sea of runners adorned in holiday-themed costumes, their laughter and chatter creating a backdrop of cheerfulness. Tashan, however, stood apart, his expression focused, his mind clear of everything but the task ahead.

The starting line was a riot of colours and energy, with participants snapping photos and sharing jokes. Yet, Tashan remained in his bubble of concentration, stretching his muscles, his eyes scanning the course ahead. The contrast was stark; amid the joviality of the event, his seriousness was a reminder of the purpose that drove him.

As the starting signal blared, the runners surged forward, a wave of holiday spirits in motion. Tashan moved with them, his strides steady and strong. The crowd of spectators lining the route erupted in cheers, their voices a vibrant chorus encouraging the runners. Among them, Tashan's colleagues, their faces bright with pride, shouted words of support. There, slightly removed from the others, stood Jason Scott, his clap firm, his eyes tracking Tashan's progress with a mixture of

CHAPTER FIFTEEN

respect and concern.

The run wound through the streets of Leeds, the city adorned with festive decorations, its usual hustle paused to celebrate the spirit of giving and community. Runners in Santa hats, reindeer antlers, and elf costumes added a whimsical touch to the scene. Tashan, however, was a blur of focus and determination, his costume minimal, his mind on the finish line.

As Tashan rounded a corner, the energy of the event seemed to envelop him. The cheering of the crowd, the smiles on the faces of the spectators, the shared sense of purpose—it all fused into a powerful motivator. He pushed forward, his pace unwavering, his breath steady in the chilly air.

The final stretch of the run was in sight now, the finish line beckoning like a beacon. Tashan's colleagues, led by Jay, had gathered there, their anticipation palpable. As Tashan approached, the cheers grew louder, more insistent, urging him on.

The morning sun cast a soft glow on the streets of Leeds as Tashan Blackburn crossed the finish line of the charity run. He did so with a look of sheer accomplishment etched across his face. For a moment, he stood there, chest heaving, drawing in deep breaths of the crisp winter air. The crowd's cheers and applause rang in his ears, a symphony of appreciation and encouragement. It was a moment of unity, of shared goals, of a community coming together to make a difference.

As the runners dispersed, Tashan stood for a moment, catching his breath, his eyes scanning the crowd. There was a sense of fulfilment in his gaze, a recognition of the impact of his actions, not just in the race but in the larger context of his life and career.

As Tashan regained his breath, representatives from the charity approached him, their faces beaming with gratitude. They extended their hands, shaking his warmly. "Thank you, Tashan," one of them said, her voice filled with sincerity. "Your participation means so much to us and those we help."

Tashan nodded, a humble smile curving his lips. "It's my pleasure. I'm just glad to help in any way I can," he replied, his voice steady despite the physical exertion.

The charity workers shared stories of the people they assisted, painting vivid pictures of lives changed and hopes renewed. Tashan listened intently, his eyes reflecting the depth of his empathy and understanding. The cause he ran for was no longer a distant concept; it was real, tangible, and profoundly moving.

As the representatives left, Tashan turned his gaze to the festive celebration around him. The city was alive with energy—runners in colourful costumes mingled with spectators, sharing stories and laughter. There was a sense of unity and purpose in the air, a collective spirit of giving and compassion that transcended the race itself.

Tashan's eyes roamed over the scene—children laughing as they played, families gathered in small groups, sharing food and conversation, volunteers handing out medals and refreshments. It was a tapestry of community and celebration, a vivid reminder of the good that comes from people coming together for a common cause.

A sense of pride swelled within Tashan. He had not just run a race; he had been a part of something much more significant, a force for positive change. He had connected with his community in a way that went beyond his role as a detective, touching lives in a different yet equally significant

CHAPTER FIFTEEN

way.

He glanced down at the medal around his neck, a small but meaningful symbol of his contribution. It was more than just a token; it was a reminder of the impact one person could make.

As Tashan left the event, walking back through the streets of Leeds, his stride was confident, his thoughts clear. The experience had rekindled a sense of hope and determination within him, a reminder of why he chose to serve and protect.

* * *

Detective Inspector George Beaumont stood at the head of the Incident Room at Elland Road Police Station. His team, already assembled, watched him with a mixture of respect and anticipation. George, with a determined expression etched on his face, began the day's briefing.

"Right, team," George started, his voice commanding the room's attention. "We've got leads to follow up on. I want everyone on their toes. This killer is meticulous, and we can't afford any oversights."

The team nodded in agreement; the mood focused yet undeniably tense. Detective Constable Jay Scott, standing by the digital display, was already flipping through the case files, his eyes scanning each page with precision.

An hour later, George and Jay found themselves navigating the quiet streets of Rodley. They were on their way to meet a witness who reportedly saw the suspect on the night of the last murder.

The witness, a middle-aged man named Martin Fletcher, lived in a modest semi-detached house. He answered the door, his expression wary as he recognised the detectives.

"Mr Fletcher, we need to talk about what you saw the night of the city centre murder," George said, his tone direct yet empathetic.

Martin led them into a sparsely furnished living room. He seemed hesitant, his hands fidgeting as he sat across from the detectives. Jay, observing Martin's body language, exchanged a glance with George.

"Mr Fletcher, any detail, no matter how small, could be crucial," Jay urged gently.

Martin's eyes darted around the room, avoiding direct contact. "I... I'm not sure what I saw," he stammered. "It was late, and... well, it was dark."

George leaned forward, his gaze steady. "Mr Fletcher, did you see anyone near the murder scene in Rodley that night? Anyone unusual?"

Martin hesitated, his voice barely above a whisper. "There was a man, I think. Wearing a hoodie... but I couldn't see his face."

"Can you remember anything else? Anything distinctive about him?" George probed.

Martin shook his head, his voice growing more evasive. "No, I... I don't remember. I'm sorry."

George studied Martin carefully, sensing there was more he wasn't saying. But it was clear that pushing further would yield no results. He exchanged a knowing look with Jay, signalling it was time to leave.

Back in their car, George's expression was thoughtful, his mind racing with possibilities. "He's holding back," George murmured.

Jay nodded his eyes on the road. "Agreed, boss. But why? Fear, or something else?"

CHAPTER FIFTEEN

George sighed, his gaze fixed on the passing scenery. "We need to keep digging. None of this is adding up."

* * *

In Rodley, the day was unfolding with the usual rhythm of urban life. Shops were opening, people bustled on the paths, and cars lined the streets. Yet amidst this ordinary scene, Detective Constable Candy Nichols and Detective Constable Tashan Blackburn moved with a purpose that set them apart from the everyday crowd.

Candy, her sharp eyes scanning the faces around her, approached a local shopkeeper, her badge conspicuous against her plain clothes. She introduced herself with a professional ease, her voice steady but friendly. "Good morning, I'm Detective Nichols. We're investigating an incident that occurred nearby. May I ask you a few questions?"

The shopkeeper, a middle-aged man with a friendly demeanour, nodded, wiping his hands on his apron. "Of course, love. How can I help?"

Candy produced a photo of the crime scene area. "Did you notice any unusual activity or unfamiliar faces around here in the past few days?"

The man furrowed his brow, thinking hard. "Well, you know, it's been busy with the holidays. But nothing unusual that I can remember." His response, while polite, held no valuable leads.

A few streets over, Tashan was experiencing a similar lack of progress. He stood outside a café, speaking with a young couple who frequented the area. "We're just trying to piece together anything out of the ordinary. Even the smallest detail could help," he explained, his tone earnest.

The couple exchanged glances, their expressions apologetic. "Sorry, we haven't seen anything strange. It's been the usual hustle and bustle," the woman replied, her voice tinged with regret.

Tashan thanked them and moved on, his strides long and focused. He glanced at his notepad, the pages still mostly blank, his frustration growing but contained. He knew the importance of patience in cases like these, yet the lack of progress weighed on him.

Meanwhile, Candy continued her inquiries at a local bakery; her questions met with similar responses. The people were cooperative but had little to offer. She made notes, her handwriting neat and precise, but the information was disappointingly scarce.

The morning wore on, and the detectives' efforts persisted, each interaction a blend of hope and routine. They methodically covered the area, speaking with residents, shop owners, and people in the area, their questions thorough but unobtrusive.

As the afternoon approached, Candy and Tashan reconvened, their expressions mirroring their shared sentiment. "It's like looking for a needle in a haystack," Candy remarked, her voice laced with a mix of determination and weariness.

Tashan nodded, his eyes scanning their notes. "We need a break, something concrete to go on," he said, his analytical mind working through the puzzle.

They stood there for a moment, the sounds of the city around them, each lost in their thoughts. The case was proving to be as challenging as it was critical, and the lack of tangible progress was a silent adversary in their quest for answers.

CHAPTER FIFTEEN

* * *

George Beaumont sat across from his mentor, a steaming cup of coffee in his hand.

Their conversation drifted to the current case that weighed heavily on George. Luke's eyes, sharp and perceptive, caught the subtle signs of stress in George's demeanour. "This case, it's taking its toll on you, isn't it?" Luke inquired, his tone gentle yet probing.

George hesitated, then nodded. "It's... complicated. More than just the murders. There are personal aspects that I can't shake off." He paused, the weight of his thoughts evident. "It's like chasing shadows, Luke. And with every turn, I find pieces of my own past staring back at me."

Luke leaned forward, his expression serious. "You've always had the knack for seeing the bigger picture, son. Trust that instinct. But don't let it consume you. You're more than this case, more than your rank, too."

George's eyes flickered with a mixture of gratitude and conflict. "Thanks, Luke. It's just hard, you know? Every clue, every lead feels like it's tangled in my own history."

Luke reached across the table, placing a reassuring hand on George's shoulder. "You're a brilliant detective, George. But remember, you're also human. Don't lose sight of that. Don't lose yourself in the darkness of this case."

The room fell into a comfortable silence, the two men lost in their thoughts. George looked up, his eyes meeting Luke's. "I won't, Luke. I promise." His voice was steady, resolute.

Luke nodded, a sense of pride evident in his gaze. "I believe you. Just remember, no case is worth sacrificing your well-being. You've got a family, a life outside this madness. Hold onto that."

As they finished their coffee, the bond between the mentor and protégé was palpable. They stood up, sharing a moment of mutual respect and understanding. George felt a renewed sense of purpose, a clarity that he hadn't realised he needed.

"Thanks, Luke. For everything," George said as he headed for the door.

"Anytime, son. You know where to find me," Luke replied.

George left the office, and his mobile rang. "DI Beaumont."

"We've found your bank card thief," said PS Greenwood.

"Bring him in."

Chapter Sixteen

Police Sergeant Greenwood stood in the early morning chill, his breath forming misty clouds in the air. Around him, a team of Armed Firearms Officers were poised, ready for the raid on Simon Clarke's property. The grey light cast long shadows across the street, an ominous prelude to the task at hand.

"Check your gear. Remember, we need him unharmed for questioning," Greenwood instructed, his voice low and steady. The AFOs, clad in tactical gear, nodded silently, their expressions a blend of focus and intensity.

Greenwood glanced at his watch. It was time. He signalled to the team, and they moved towards the shabby flat where Simon Clarke, a potential lead in the Santa Claus murders, resided.

The street was eerily quiet; the only sound was the muffled footsteps of the officers as they approached. Greenwood's hand signalled a halt, and he surveyed the property. No lights, no movement. It was as if the house itself was holding its breath.

"Go," Greenwood whispered.

The team sprang into action. Two officers moved to the back of the house while the rest followed Greenwood to the front door. He nodded to an officer equipped with a battering ram.

With a swift, practised movement, the door was forced open.

"Police! Down on the ground!" Greenwood barked as they entered.

The interior was dark, the air stale. They moved swiftly, clearing each room. In the small, cluttered bedroom, they found Simon Clarke, jolted awake by the commotion.

"What's going on?" Clarke stammered, his voice laced with confusion and fear.

"For a prompt investigation and to prevent disappearance, you're being arrested in connection with the Santa Claus murders. You do not have to say anything. But it may harm your defence if you do not mention when questioned something which you later rely on in court. Anything you do say may be given in evidence," Greenwood recited, his tone authoritative yet devoid of emotion.

Clarke's confusion turned to shock. "Wait, what? I didn't—"

"Save it for the station," Greenwood cut him off, signalling to the officers to handcuff Clarke.

They escorted him outside, the scene now illuminated by the flashing blue lights of the police vehicles. Greenwood watched as Clarke was led into the back of a van, his mind already on the interrogation that awaited.

The drive to Elland Road Police Station was tense. Greenwood sat in the front passenger seat, his thoughts on the case. Simon Clarke, a friend of the victim, using his bank card—it was a lead that couldn't be ignored, yet Greenwood couldn't shake the feeling that there was more to this than met the eye.

At the station, Clarke was processed by the desk sergeant and taken to an interview room. Greenwood watched through the one-way glass as Detective Inspector George Beaumont

CHAPTER SIXTEEN

entered the room. The exchange that followed would be crucial, a dance of questions and answers that could either propel the investigation forward or send them back to square one.

* * *

Paige McGuiness moved with purpose. Her notebook was open, pen ready, as she approached the residents and shop owners. There was a determined look in her eyes, one that bespoke of a journalist's tenacity mixed with a human touch that was hard to miss.

Paige stopped first at a small grocery store, the bell jingling as she entered. The owner, a stout man in his fifties, looked up, his face etched with worry. "Afternoon," Paige greeted, offering a warm yet professional smile. "I'm Paige McGuiness from Leeds Live. May I ask you a few questions about the recent incidents?"

The man nodded, his voice tinged with a mix of fear and anger. "It's terrible, just terrible. We've never had anything like this before. People are scared to step out after dark now," he said, his hands fidgeting with a piece of cloth.

Paige jotted down his words, her brow furrowed. "Have you noticed anything unusual or any strangers around lately?" she asked, her voice gentle yet probing.

"No, nothing. That's what's so frightening. It could be anyone, couldn't it?" The shopkeeper's eyes darted around as if expecting the killer to walk through the door at any moment.

Thanking him, Paige moved on, her steps leading her to a group of residents gathered near a park, their conversation filled with hushed tones and anxious glances. As she approached, they quieted, their eyes turning towards her with a mixture of curiosity and suspicion.

"I'm Paige McGuiness," she introduced herself again, showing her press ID. "I'm collecting community reactions for a piece on the murders. Would any of you be willing to share your thoughts?"

A woman in her thirties stepped forward, her face a portrait of concern. "It's just awful. I've lived here all my life, and nothing like this has ever happened. We're all on edge. My kids are scared to go outside," she said, her voice trembling slightly.

Paige's pen flew across her notebook, capturing every word. Her expression softened as she listened, her role as a journalist momentarily taking a backseat to her empathy. "Thank you for sharing. It's important that your voices are heard," she reassured the woman, who nodded gratefully.

As the early afternoon progressed, Paige continued her rounds, speaking with more locals. Each conversation added layers to the story—not just of a crime but of a community grappling with a terror that had disrupted their peaceful lives. Anger, fear, disbelief—the emotions were raw and honest, painting a vivid picture of the impact of the crimes.

As she wrapped up her interviews, Paige found a quiet bench and sat down, her notes spread out before her. The sun cast long shadows on the pavement, mirroring the dark undercurrent that now ran through the suburb. She looked around, seeing the place not just through the eyes of a journalist seeking a story but as a member of the community touched by the same fear and uncertainty.

Paige's story would not just be about the facts of the crime; it would be about the people it affected, their fears, and their

CHAPTER SIXTEEN

resilience. With a deep breath, she gathered her notes and stood up, ready to weave the myriad threads into a narrative that would bring to light not just the darkness of the crimes but the enduring spirit of the community.

* * *

Detective Inspector George Beaumont and Detective Constable Jay Scott sat across from Simon Clarke. The air was thick with tension, and the room was charged with unspoken questions and fears.

Simon, his hands fidgeting nervously on the table, appeared on the edge of panic. Beside him sat his duty solicitor, a middle-aged woman with a stern face, whispering last-minute advice. "Remember, Simon, 'no comment' to any questions you don't want to answer."

George opened the folder in front of him, his gaze steady and assessing. "Simon Clarke, you were found using a bank card belonging to Ryan Baxter, the victim in the Santa Claus murders. Can you explain why?"

Simon's eyes darted between George and Jay, then to his solicitor. He opened his mouth, closed it, and then blurted out, "I was in debt, OK? Ryan... he was generous. He helped me before."

The solicitor's hand shot up. "No comment," she interjected firmly. She scowled at Simon, and he sheepishly retreated.

George leaned forward slightly, his voice calm but authoritative. "Simon, how did you come into possession of Mr Baxter's bank card?"

Simon's gaze fell to his hands. "I... I took it from him about a week ago. I didn't mean any harm. I was desperate."

Again, the solicitor cut in, "Simon, no comment. Please."

Jay, who had been silently observing, spoke up. "Simon, were you aware that Ryan Baxter was murdered?"

Simon's head snapped up, his eyes wide with a mix of fear and surprise. "What? No, I... I didn't know." A tear fell from his left eye. "When?"

George watched Simon closely, reading the play of emotions on his face. "You used the card on the day of Baxter's murder. Can you account for your whereabouts?"

Simon wrung his hands, glancing at his solicitor, who was shaking her head subtly. "I was just buying essentials, that's all. I didn't know he was dead. You've got to believe me."

The solicitor leaned in, whispering harshly, but Simon seemed unable to stop the flow of words. "I was going to pay him back, I swear. Ryan was a good guy. He wouldn't have minded. He knew I was struggling."

George took note of Simon's admissions, his demeanour remaining neutral. "Simon, we need to establish the facts. Your actions have implications in an ongoing murder investigation."

Simon's shoulders slumped, defeat etched in his posture. The solicitor, recognising the futility of further intervention, sat back with a resigned sigh.

"Simon," George began, his voice measured, "you admitted to taking Ryan Baxter's card. Did you ever discuss this with him? Did he know you had his card?"

Simon shifted uncomfortably in his chair, his eyes darting to his duty solicitor before answering. "No, he didn't know. I... I just took it. I was planning to tell him, eventually."

George noted his response, then continued, "And on the day

CHAPTER SIXTEEN

of the murder, what exactly were your movements? Can you walk us through your day?"

Simon's hands trembled slightly. "I... I was at home most of the morning. Then I went out to get some essentials, that's when I used the card. I swear, I didn't know anything about... about him being dead."

George leaned forward, his tone firm. "You understand how this looks, Simon—using the card of a murder victim on the day of his death. It's suspicious. You need to be very clear with us."

Simon's face was a picture of anxiety. "I know how it looks, but I didn't have anything to do with Ryan's death. He was my friend."

"Did you have any recent arguments or disagreements with Ryan?" George asked, watching Simon's reactions closely.

Simon shook his head vigorously. "No, nothing like that. We were friends, good friends. I just needed help, that's all."

George paused, allowing the weight of his questions to sink in. "Simon, think carefully. Was there anyone else in Ryan's life who might have wanted to harm him? Any strange behaviours or encounters he mentioned?"

Simon bit his lip, thinking. "I... I don't know. Ryan never said anything to me about being in trouble or anything. He was just a normal guy, as far as I knew."

George nodded slowly, jotting down notes. "One last question, Simon. Have you ever heard Ryan mention someone named 'Eddie'?"

At this, Simon's brow furrowed in confusion. "Eddie? No, I don't think so. Should I have?"

George's gaze remained steady. "Just covering all bases. Thank you, Simon."

"So I can go?" asked Simon, relieved.

"No," said George.

The duty solicitor was about to interfere when George put up his hand. "We need to go through his phone and take swabs before we release him, OK?"

"OK."

As the interview concluded, George and Jay stood up, their expressions unreadable.

Leaving the interview room, George and Jay walked down the corridor, their footsteps echoing in the quiet. "What do you think?" Jay asked.

George considered for a moment. "He's scared and in over his head. But I don't think he's our killer. Still, we'll need to verify his alibi."

"And who the hell is Eddie, boss?"

George stood still. "Somebody Danny Roberts mentioned."

* * *

Tashan Blackburn, his face a play of emotions—the furrowed brow of contemplation, the brief flicker of resolve in his eyes, the slight quiver of his lips as he battled with his internal conflict—found himself in the small, seldom-used break room at the back of the station. He sat at the far end of the room, his back against the wall, the letter of promotion clutched in his hands. The room was silent, save for the distant hum of activity from the main office. It was a rare moment of solitude in the otherwise bustling environment of the police station.

Tashan's gaze drifted over the letter, his eyes tracing the words he had read countless times since receiving it. The offer was more than just a step up the career ladder; it was a recognition of his hard work and his dedication. Yet, as he sat there, a tumult of emotions churned within him

Ambition, a driving force in his career, flickered in his eyes. This promotion was an opportunity to advance and make a difference on a larger scale. He had always aspired to rise through the ranks, to prove his worth, to be a role model, especially for the younger officers who looked up to him.

But along with ambition, there was doubt. The letter in his hand was also a ticket away from the team he had grown to respect and trust. He pondered the dynamics of his current team—the camaraderie, the collective passion for justice, the shared triumphs and setbacks. Could he leave that behind? Was the allure of promotion worth the trade?

A sense of responsibility weighed on him. His role in the current team was crucial, his insights invaluable. They were in the midst of a challenging case, one that demanded every ounce of their collective skill and experience. Could he step away at such a critical juncture?

The room around him felt constricting, the walls inching closer as he delved deeper into his thoughts. Tashan leaned forward, resting his elbows on his knees, his head bowed. The letter rustled softly as his grip tightened.

He thought about the conversations he had had with George, the mentorship and guidance he had received. He remembered the moments of doubt and how George had steered him through them, instilling confidence and resilience.

Tashan exhaled slowly and realised that this decision was not just about his career trajectory; it was about defining who he was as a detective and as a person.

After a long moment, Tashan stood up, the letter still in his hand. He looked at it once more, then folded it carefully and slipped it into his pocket. His decision wasn't clear yet, but he knew that whatever he chose, it would be a decision that honoured both his ambition and his loyalty to his team.

Chapter Seventeen

Detective Inspector George Beaumont sat across from the witness, a middle-aged man with a nervous demeanour, in one of the interview rooms at Elland Road police station. The room was small, the walls bare except for a clock ticking steadily. George's gaze was steady; his posture relaxed yet attentive.

The man, named Robert Matthews, had come forward claiming to have seen someone suspicious near the crime scene in Rodley on the night of the second Santa Claus murder. Robert fidgeted with his hands, his eyes darting around the room, not quite meeting George's.

"So, Mr Matthews, can you describe what you saw that night?" George's voice was calm, his tone even, designed to put the witness at ease.

Robert cleared his throat, "Yes, Detective. It was around midnight. I was walking my dog, and I saw this figure..."

"A figure?" George interjected gently, encouraging more details.

"Yes, a person in a dark coat, tall, walking hurriedly. They had something in their hand, but I couldn't see it clearly... It was quite dark."

George nodded, making notes. "And this was near where Mr Green's body was found?"

"That's right. It was odd because it's usually quiet around there. This person seemed... I don't know... hurried, anxious."

George observed Robert's body language. There was something off in his narrative, a hesitance that didn't fit. "Did you see which direction they went?"

Robert hesitated, his brow furrowing. "Uh, towards the main road, I think. Yes, towards the main road."

George leaned forward slightly, his tone remaining soft. "Mr Matthews, it's crucial you remember as accurately as possible. Are you sure about the direction?"

Robert's eyes flicked to George's, then away. "Yes, I... I am pretty sure."

"Pretty sure or certain, Mr Matthews? This is important."

Robert's hands twisted in his lap. "I... I might be mixing it up. It was dark, and I was a bit far..."

George's expression didn't change, but internally, he was reassessing the reliability of Robert's account. "Anything about the figure that stood out? Any distinctive features?"

Robert shook his head. "No, nothing specific. Just the hurried walk and the dark coat."

George sat back, his mind racing. This testimony was too vague, too inconclusive. Was Robert holding back, or was it just a case of a confused witness? "Thank you for coming in, Mr Matthews. If you remember anything else, no matter how small, please let us know immediately."

As Robert left the room, George remained seated, pondering. He knew from experience that eyewitness accounts could be tricky, but something about Robert's demeanour suggested there was more to his story. George's intuition, honed by years on the force, was buzzing with suspicion.

He stood up, his mind already shifting gears. They needed

more concrete leads, something substantial to move the investigation forward. The clock on the wall ticked on, a reminder of the urgency of their task.

* * *

Detective Constable Tashan Blackburn leaned against the wall outside the Incident Room, his eyes distant, lost in thought. The corridor was quiet, save for the occasional footsteps of colleagues passing by. He clutched the envelope in his hand—the offer of promotion, a pivotal moment in his career.

Jay Scott approached him, his usual easygoing demeanour replaced by a look of concern. "Hey, Tashan, you alright? You've been out here a while."

Tashan looked up, a faint smile crossing his face. "Yeah, just... thinking."

Jay leaned beside him, sensing the gravity of the moment. "Want to talk about it?"

Tashan hesitated, then handed Jay the envelope. "I got offered a promotion, Jay. It's a big step, but it means leaving the team."

Jay read the letter and nodded, handing it back. "That's a big deal, Tashan. Congratulations. But I can see it's not an easy decision for you."

Tashan sighed, "It's what I've worked towards, but... I don't know. This team, working with George, it's more than just a job."

Jay nodded, understanding. "I get it. We've been through a lot together. It's hard to leave something like that behind."

Tashan looked at Jay, his expression conflicted. "How do you deal with it, Jay? Making these kinds of decisions?"

Jay took a moment before answering. "I think about what matters most to me. It's not just about the job or the title. It's about where you feel you can make the most impact, where you belong."

Tashan mulled over Jay's words. "I've always wanted to climb the ranks, to make a difference. But I wonder if I'm ready to step away from the front line."

"It's a tough call," Jay agreed. "But sometimes, growth means stepping out of your comfort zone. You're a great detective, Tashan. You'll be great wherever you go."

Tashan's gaze drifted back to the envelope. "Did you ever face a decision like this?"

Jay thought about his mother and the big decisions he would soon be forced to make. "A few times. But what I learned is that no matter where you go, you carry your experiences with you. They shape you. This team, the boss, they've been a big part of that for you."

Tashan nodded slowly, absorbing Jay's words. "Yeah, they have. And I guess part of me worries about leaving that behind."

Jay placed a reassuring hand on Tashan's shoulder. "Whatever you decide, Tashan, it's the right decision for you. And you won't be leaving it all behind. You'll be taking it with you, in a way."

Tashan looked at Jay, gratitude evident in his eyes. "Thanks, Jay. It helps, talking it out."

Jay smiled. "Anytime, mate. We're a team, after all."

* * *

Detective Inspector George Beaumont stood over the shoulder

of Detective Sergeant Joshua Fry, their tech expert, in the Incident Room, who was busily analysing data on his screen.

"Got anything, Josh?" George asked, his voice a mix of hope and impatience.

Joshua tapped a few keys, bringing up a map with a series of dots and lines. "Simon's phone GPS for the day of the murder, sir. He was nowhere near the crime scene."

George exhaled, a mix of relief and frustration. "So his alibi checks out."

"Seems so, sir," Joshua confirmed, glancing up at George.

Nodding, George turned and quickly headed downstairs. He approached the desk sergeant, his stride purposeful. "Release Simon Clarke. His alibi's solid."

Back upstairs in the Incident Room, George gathered his team. The relief of clearing an innocent man was overshadowed by the stark reality that they were no closer to catching the killer.

"We've cleared Simon Clarke," George announced to the team. "Which puts us back at square one, with two dead bodies and no leads."

The frustration in his voice was palpable. The team exchanged looks of concern and determination.

Detective Constable Tashan Blackburn spoke up, "What about the cashmere-silk fibre? Any leads on that?"

George shook his head. "It's a dead end so far. It's a luxury item; it could be from anywhere," he said, thinking about his father. He made a mental note to ring Lindsey Yardley and see if she had anything else for him.

Jay Scott, leaning against a desk, added, "And no one else in Baxter's circle seems to fit the profile or have a motive."

George's hands clenched into fists at his sides. "We're

missing something. There's a piece of this puzzle that's eluding us."

The room was silent for a moment, everyone deep in thought. The case was a labyrinth, and they were in the thick of it with no clear way out.

George looked around at his team, their faces a mirror of his own frustration. "We need to go over everything again. Re-interview witnesses and re-examine evidence. Anything that can give us a new angle."

The team nodded, ready to dive back into the investigation. They knew the road ahead would be challenging, but they were determined.

"Head back to the crime scenes, interview people you see, and probe and probe and probe." George paused. "I'll speak with PS Greenwood and see if he can spare some uniforms."

* * *

Back at Elland Road Police Station, Detective Inspector George Beaumont was yet again sat across from a Mr Matthews whose earlier testimony had promised a breakthrough in the Santa Claus murder case. Mr Matthews had initially seemed cooperative, providing details that could lead them to the killer.

However, now that Mr Matthews was back, a change came over the witness. His initial certainty began to waver, his answers growing more hesitant. George, sensing the shift, leaned in closer, his voice calm yet insistent. "You seemed sure earlier about what you saw. What's changed?"

The witness fidgeted in his chair, avoiding George's steady gaze. "I... I might have been mistaken," he stammered, his

CHAPTER SEVENTEEN

voice barely above a whisper.

George's brow furrowed in confusion. "Mistaken? You were very specific about the time and the person you saw near the scene."

"I don't know... I think I got confused. It was dark, and I... I don't want to be involved in this," Mr Matthews replied, his agitation growing.

George pushed back his chair and stood up, his frustration barely contained. "Your statement could be key to catching a murderer. Think carefully about what you're saying."

Mr Matthews shook his head, panic rising in his eyes. "I can't... I'm sorry. I didn't see anything. I was wrong to come here."

"If somebody is threatening you, we can help you."

Mr Matthews stopped, his eyes roaming, clearly trying to find an excuse. "Nobody is threatening me."

With that, Mr Matthews hurriedly stood up and left the room, leaving George in shock. They had been close, so close to a lead, only for it to slip away.

In the Incident Room, the atmosphere was tense, the team's frustration palpable. Detective Constable Jay Scott reported first. "Every door we knocked on, every person we talked to... nothing. It's like we're chasing shadows."

Detective Constable Candy Nichols chimed in, her usual optimism dimmed. "The community's scared, but no one's seen anything useful. It's like the killer's a ghost."

Detective Constable Tashan Blackburn, his eyes reflecting his exhaustion, added, "The CCTV footage around the area didn't give us anything new either. It's all dead ends."

George listened to each report, a growing sense of helplessness settling in. They were running out of leads, and the killer was still out there, potentially planning their next move. The weight of responsibility pressed down on him; he knew the community was counting on them to bring the murderer to justice.

Finally, George spoke his voice firm despite the frustration. "We can't let this break us. We're dealing with someone clever and careful. But they'll slip up, and we need to be ready."

He stood up, addressing the room. "I know it's tough, and we're all feeling the pressure. But we can't lose hope. Let's go back over everything and look at it with fresh eyes. There's something we're missing, and we're going to find it."

The team nodded a silent agreement to keep pushing, to keep searching for the elusive truth hidden in the shadows of this complex case. As they filed out of the room, George stayed behind, his gaze lingering on the empty chairs. The challenges were mounting, but so was his resolve. The killer had evaded them so far, but George Beaumont was not one to give up easily. The game of cat and mouse continued, and he was more determined than ever to win.

Chapter Eighteen

Paige McGuiness waited patiently in the bustling press room of the Elland Road Police Station for the briefing to begin. The air was thick with tension, the weight of unanswered questions pressing heavily on everyone in the room. Detective Inspector George Beaumont stepped up to the podium, his face a mask of controlled professionalism.

Paige, her notebook at the ready, scrutinised George as he addressed the gathering. She knew her role was more than just a journalist; she was a conduit for the fears and concerns of the Leeds community.

"As many of you are aware, we are investigating two murders, both with a disturbing Christmas theme," George began, his voice steady. "We understand the public's concern and assure you that we are doing everything in our power to apprehend the perpetrator."

Paige raised her hand, waiting to be acknowledged. George nodded in her direction. "Paige McGuiness, Leeds Live. Detective Inspector Beaumont, can you share any significant leads or developments in the case?"

George hesitated for a moment, choosing his words carefully. "While we can't divulge specific details of the investigation, I can assure you that we are following up on several leads."

"But is there any connection between the victims?" Paige pressed, undeterred by his vague response. "The public needs to know if there's a pattern or a specific target group."

George's gaze met Paige's, a hint of respect in his eyes for her direct approach. "Both victims were middle-aged men, and there appears to be a connection to their past. However, it's too early to confirm a definitive pattern."

Paige noted the careful phrasing, her instincts telling her there was more to the story. "Has the police increased patrols or taken any specific measures to prevent another such incident?"

"Yes, we have increased our presence in key areas and are working closely with the community to gather information," George replied. "We urge the public to remain vigilant and report any suspicious activity."

Paige scribbled down his responses, her mind racing. She knew George was holding back the necessity of confidentiality in a police investigation clashing with the public's right to know. She decided to shift her approach.

"Detective Inspector, what message do you have for the residents of Leeds during this time of fear and uncertainty?" she asked, her tone softer, more personal.

George paused, looking out at the sea of expectant faces. "We understand the anxiety and fear that these crimes have caused. I want to assure everyone that we are committed to bringing the perpetrator to justice. We ask for your cooperation and patience as we continue our work. Please, keep your loved ones close and stay safe this holiday season."

* * *

CHAPTER EIGHTEEN

The air was thick with frustration and fatigue in the Incident Room of Elland Road Police Station as Detective Inspector George Beaumont stood before his team, his eyes scanning the faces of his dedicated team. They all showed signs of the toll the investigation was taking. Detective Constable Jay Scott's usually bright demeanour was dimmed by worry, no doubt because his mother was in hospital. Detective Constable Tashan Blackburn appeared deep in thought, probably obsessing over the promotion. Detective Constable Candy Nichols' usual energy seemed subdued, which was unusual.

George cleared his throat, ready to address his team. "I know this case is challenging," he began, his voice firm yet empathetic. "We're dealing with a clever and elusive perpetrator. But I need each of you to stay focused and determined."

His gaze settled on Jay. "Jay, I know you're struggling, but we need your sharp mind on this. Anything you can find on the victims' backgrounds could be crucial."

Jay nodded a determined glint in his eye despite the underlying exhaustion. "Understood, boss. I'll dig deeper into their pasts."

George turned to Tashan. "Tashan, your analytical skills are invaluable. Review the crime scenes again. Look for anything we might have missed."

Tashan straightened up, his face set in a mask of concentration. "I'll go over everything with a fine-tooth comb, sir."

Candy spoke up, her voice steady. "What about community leads? People are scared, but they might have seen something important."

George nodded approvingly. "Exactly, Candy. Keep canvassing. Talk to everyone. Fear might loosen some tongues."

The team members exchanged glances, a silent agreement passing between them. They were a unit bound by the common goal of bringing a murderer to justice.

George's expression softened slightly. "I know we're all feeling the pressure. This case is personal for me too. But I believe in this team. We've cracked tough cases before. We can do it again."

As he finished speaking, there was a renewed sense of purpose in the room. The team members began to disperse, each returning to their task with a little more determination than before.

As George watched them, a mix of pride and responsibility washed over him. This was more than just a job; it was a mission to protect the community and bring closure to the victims' families. He knew the road ahead would be difficult, but he also knew his team was up for the challenge. They had to be. There was a killer on the loose, and time was running out.

* * *

Tashan Blackburn, immersed in the postmortem reports in the quiet of the Incident Room, felt a growing sense of unease. Something was off. The reports from Dr Christian Ross, usually meticulous and thorough, seemed lacking in their usual depth of detail. Frowning, Tashan pulled out a stack of previous assault case reports that Dr Ross had worked on, seeking a comparison.

As he pored over the older files, the disparity became clear. Dr Ross had consistently provided detailed light source results in past cases, crucial in cases like theirs where the murder

CHAPTER EIGHTEEN

weapon was unknown. These results often offered insights into bruising patterns, potential weapon types, and even assailant profiles. But in the current Santa Claus murder reports, this critical information was missing.

With this realisation, Tashan headed straight to George Beaumont's office. He found George at his desk, surrounded by case files, his expression a study in concentration.

"Sir," Tashan began, "I've been reviewing the crime scenes and files again as you requested, specifically the postmortem reports and noticed something odd."

"Go on," said George, not looking up from a report he was reading.

"Dr Ross hasn't provided the light source results. It's unusual for him, especially considering the significance of the bruising on the bodies."

George looked up, his attention immediately piqued. "No light source results? That's not like Christian. That's critical in a case like this, especially for identifying shoe prints or any other marks made by the assailant."

Tashan nodded. "Exactly. It could give us the physical evidence we've been missing."

George's brow furrowed in thought. "This could be an oversight, or..." His voice trailed off, the implication hanging in the air.

Tashan understood the unspoken suspicion. In a case as complex and fraught as the Santa Claus murders, every anomaly had to be considered.

"I'll follow up with Dr Ross," George said, standing up. "Good catch, Tashan. This could be important."

Tashan left George's office, feeling a renewed sense of purpose. Every piece of information, no matter how small, was a potential key to unlocking the mystery.

George, now alone in his office, felt a twinge of concern. Dr Ross was a seasoned pathologist known for his precision and attention to detail. The omission of the light source results was out of character. Was it a simple mistake, or was there more to it?

He reached for his phone, intent on calling Dr Ross. The bruising on the victims' bodies could tell a story and offer a glimpse into the violence they had endured. If the light source results could reveal the pattern or type of weapon used, it might lead them to the killer.

The room was quiet, save for the faint sounds of the bustling station beyond the door. George dialled Dr Ross' number, his mind racing with possibilities.

* * *

Paige McGuiness sat in her own world of concentration in her booth at the Leeds Live office. Around her, the cacophony of ringing phones, chattering journalists, and the occasional roar of the printer created a symphony of the daily grind, but she was unfazed, her focus unwavering.

Her fingers danced across the keyboard, each click echoing her determination to tell the story that had gripped the city—the Santa Claus murders. The glow of her computer screen cast a soft light on her face, highlighting her furrowed brow and the intensity of her gaze.

The words on the screen told a tale of fear, uncertainty, and a community on edge. Paige weaved the hard facts of the case with the personal stories of those affected, creating a narrative that was both informative and emotionally resonant.

CHAPTER EIGHTEEN

"Two Murders, One Killer: Leeds Gripped by Christmas Horror," read the headline. Paige paused, rereading her opening paragraph. It detailed the discovery of the second body in Rodley, dressed in a full Santa outfit, mirroring the chilling modus operandi of the first murder.

She typed with a sense of purpose, aware of the weight of her words on the public psyche. She recounted the details known to the public: the locations, the eerie Christmas-themed staging of the bodies, and the fear that had begun to spread through the streets of Leeds.

Paige's article wasn't just a recitation of facts; it was a canvas where the human element of the tragedy was painted vividly. She included quotes from local residents, their voices a mixture of fear and defiance. A shop owner in Rodley expressed his disbelief and grief, a mother spoke of her anxiety for her children's safety, and a retired policeman shared his insights into the investigation's progress.

The newsroom around her buzzed with activity, but Paige was in her zone, oblivious to the world around her. Her journalistic instincts drove her to uncover the truth, to provide clarity amidst the chaos, and to hold those in power accountable.

Paige took a moment to glance at the photos accompanying the article—the cordoned-off crime scenes, the solemn faces of the police officers, and the worried looks of the public. Each image was a piece of the puzzle she was trying to solve through her writing.

She scrolled through her notes, double-checking her sources and facts. Accuracy was paramount, and she prided herself on her integrity as a journalist. The last thing she wanted was to contribute to the hysteria or spread misinformation.

As she crafted her closing paragraphs, Paige reflected on the impact of her work. She had a responsibility to inform but also to empathise and to convey the stories of those affected with sensitivity and respect.

It was a piece that went beyond mere reporting; it wove a narrative that captured the raw emotion and palpable tension simmering in Leeds. Her words painted a vivid picture of a community shaken but resilient, a police force under pressure but unwavering in their pursuit.

Paige leaned forward, her fingers hovering over the 'Publish' button. This wasn't just another article; it felt like a culmination of her relentless pursuit of the truth, her empathy for the community, and her commitment to journalism. She clicked the button, sending the article out into the world.

As the article went live, Paige exhaled deeply, a mix of relief and apprehension filling her chest. This story was personal. It wasn't just about reporting facts; it was about giving a voice to a city's fear and hope. Her reflection in the monitor looked back at her, eyes tired but resolute.

The immediate response was overwhelming. Her phone started buzzing relentlessly, a cascade of emails and calls flooding in. Some were from colleagues offering congratulations or critiques, but many were from members of the Leeds community. Her article had struck a chord.

One email, in particular, caught her eye. It was from a local Leeds resident, someone who claimed to have seen something on the night of the latest murder. The message was brief, but the implications were enormous. Paige leaned in, her journalistic instincts kicking into high gear. This could be the lead she had been waiting for.

CHAPTER EIGHTEEN

Her fingers flew over the keyboard, responding to the email, asking for more details, and setting up a meeting. She couldn't let this opportunity slip. This was what journalism was about—not just telling stories but uncovering truths.

The phone rang again, snapping her back to the present. She answered, her voice steady, professional. It was a local radio station requesting an interview about her article. She agreed, knowing that this was more than just another interview. It was a chance to amplify her findings, to keep the conversation going, to keep the pressure on.

As she hung up, Paige looked back at her screen, her article now being shared and commented on across various platforms. Her words were out there, shaping perceptions, sparking discussions, and keeping the story alive. It was a weighty responsibility but one she carried with a sense of purpose.

Paige stood up, stretching her tired muscles. The newsroom was still bustling, the energy palpable. She grabbed her notepad and camera, ready to follow up on the new lead. Her article was just the beginning. The real work—the relentless pursuit of truth—was still ahead.

And so she walked out of the office, her stride confident, her mind already racing with possibilities. This was more than a job; it was a calling. And Paige McGuiness was ready to answer it, whatever it took.

Chapter Nineteen

Detective Inspector George Beaumont dialled Dr Christian Ross' number, his fingers tapping a steady rhythm on his desk. The omission of the light source results from the postmortem reports had set off alarm bells in his mind. The phone rang twice before Dr Ross' familiar voice came on the line.

"Dr Ross, it's George Beaumont. I have a query about the postmortem reports for the Santa Claus murders."

"Ah, George," Dr Ross' voice carried a hint of weariness. "What can I do for you?"

George didn't waste time. "The light source results are missing from both reports. It's not like you to overlook such details."

There was a brief pause on the other end. "Missing? That's... highly unusual. I used the process extensively on both bodies. It must have been an error by my assistant. I apologize, George."

George's brows knitted together. "Can you ensure it doesn't happen again? Those results could be key in our investigation."

"Of course, I'll speak with my assistant immediately. I'll make sure the results are sent over as soon as possible," Dr Ross replied, his tone apologetic yet firm.

CHAPTER NINETEEN

"Before you send them, could you give me a brief outline of what you found?" George asked, hoping for some immediate insight.

There was a momentary hesitation. "I... uh, I don't have the notes in front of me, George. I'm not as young as I used to be, and the details escape me at the moment. I'll ensure everything is in the report."

George sensed something amiss in the pathologist's tone, a subtle shift that didn't quite fit the seasoned professional he knew Dr Ross to be.

"Are you sure everything's alright, Christian?" George's voice carried a note of concern mixed with suspicion.

"Yes, yes, just the usual old age catching up with me," Dr Ross said, a forced lightness in his voice. "I'll send those results as soon as I can."

Before George could press further, Dr Ross ended the call abruptly, leaving a thread of unease hanging in the air.

George set down the phone, his mind churning. The conversation had taken an odd turn, and Dr Ross' abruptness was out of character. He had known the pathologist for years, and this sudden evasion was unlike him.

He leaned back in his chair, his gaze distant. The missing light source results were a crucial piece of the puzzle, and Dr Ross' oversight, whether genuine or not, was a concerning development.

Detective Inspector George Beaumont gathered his team for an impromptu briefing. The room fell silent as he began to speak about the missing light source results from Dr Christian Ross' postmortem reports.

"We've had a significant oversight in the Santa Claus murders case," George started, his tone serious. "The light source results were missing from Dr Ross' initial reports."

Detective Constable Tashan Blackburn and Detective Sergeant Candy Morton quickly came to Dr Ross' defence. "He's always been thorough before," Tashan pointed out. "Maybe it was just an oversight?"

Candy nodded in agreement. "Dr Ross has been under a lot of pressure with these cases. It could be an honest mistake."

Before George could respond, Detective Constable Jay Scott, who had been tapping away on his tablet, looked up. "The reports have just landed in the shared inbox," he announced.

Immediately, Tashan pulled up the report on the smart whiteboard, and the team crowded around to read the details and examine the images.

One of the images showed a detailed imprint on the left side of the first victim's chest. "This is one of our best marks here," George pointed out, examining the clear lines. "These patterns—they're similar to what you'd find on shoes. These could potentially be our murder weapon."

The team absorbed the information, understanding the gravity of the finding. A shoe print, used with enough force, could be as lethal as any knife in a murder.

Next, they reviewed the second victim's light source results. A similar, distinct pattern was visible on the man's thigh, matching the print found on the first victim.

"This is a breakthrough," George said, his voice firm. "It's the same pattern on both victims. We're looking for a very specific type of shoe."

The mood in the room shifted from frustration to a focused determination. "I want everyone to cross-reference this pattern against all known shoes," George instructed. "We need to narrow down what kind of shoe we're looking for.

CHAPTER NINETEEN

This could lead us to our killer."

The team sprang into action, the Incident Room buzzing with renewed energy. As they dispersed, George remained by the whiteboard, his gaze fixed on the images. The discovery of the shoe prints was a crucial lead, one that could change the course of their investigation.

* * *

In his office, Detective Inspector George Beaumont was meticulously poring over the postmortem reports once again. The dim light from his desk lamp cast long shadows across the room, mirroring the deep lines of concentration etched on his face. Despite the breakthrough with the shoe prints, George was still visibly agitated by Dr. Christian Ross' earlier oversight. It was unlike the seasoned pathologist to miss such crucial details.

As he flipped through the pages, filled with clinical descriptions and forensic findings, his office phone rang, cutting through the silence. George glanced at the caller ID before answering.

"DI Beaumont," he said, his tone a mixture of curiosity and lingering frustration.

George straightened in his chair as he recognized the voice on the other end of the line. It was Lindsey Yardley, the Scene of Crime Manager.

"Lindsey, what have you got for me?" George's tone was a blend of urgency and expectancy.

"We've traced the cashmere-silk blend fibre," Lindsey's voice crackled through the line, tinged with excitement. "It's from a charcoal-coloured Kiton suit. High-end stuff."

"Kiton, you say?" George repeated a flicker of recognition in his voice. He thanked Lindsey quickly before hanging up and turned to his computer.

As he typed in 'Kiton,' his mind raced. He was sure he had heard of the brand before, but the context eluded him. The search results came up swiftly, revealing that Kiton was an Italian luxury brand known for its fine tailoring and exquisite fabrics.

George's eyes narrowed as he read on. The brand had three boutiques in London and, notably, one in Leeds that had opened on December 1st.

He leaned back in his chair, deep in thought. The connection was too significant to ignore. A high-end brand like Kiton wouldn't have many customers; it catered to a specific clientele. And now, the discovery of its fabric on the murder victims linked the brand directly to the case.

George grabbed his phone and dialled Tashan Blackburn. "Tashan, get down here. We've got a lead on the Kiton suit fibre. There's a boutique in Leeds. We need to check it out."

As he set down the phone, George's mind was already several steps ahead. He knew that luxury brands like Kiton kept meticulous records of their clients, especially for such high-priced items. This could be the break they needed in the case.

But only if the company would provide details of their clients.

* * *

At the Kiton boutique in Leeds, George Beaumont and Tashan Blackburn arrived with a sense of purposeful urgency. The

CHAPTER NINETEEN

store, with its sleek design and exclusive aura, was a stark contrast to the gritty reality of their investigation.

As they entered, a well-dressed sales assistant approached them, her expression changing from one of welcome to curiosity upon seeing their badges.

"Detective Inspector Beaumont and Detective Constable Blackburn," George introduced them as both revealed their warrant cards. "We're here about an ongoing investigation and need some information on your clientele."

The assistant's eyes widened slightly, a mix of surprise and concern. "Of course, how can I assist you, Detectives?"

George took the lead. "We're looking for information on any recent purchases of charcoal-coloured Kiton suits."

The assistant nodded, her professionalism kicking in. "Let me check our records. Please, this way."

They were led to a sleek computer terminal where the assistant quickly began scrolling through the digital records. George and Tashan exchanged a look, both aware that they were potentially on the brink of a significant breakthrough.

After a few moments, the assistant turned the screen towards them. "Here we are. There was one purchase of a charcoal Kiton suit in early December. It's quite a rare item, so it stands out."

George leaned in, scrutinising the details. "Can you give us the name of the purchaser?"

The assistant hesitated, a flicker of apprehension crossing her face. "I'm afraid customer confidentiality—"

George cut her off, his tone firm but polite. "This is crucial for a murder investigation. Any information you provide will be handled with the utmost discretion."

"I'm sorry, but without a warrant, I cannot provide that

information to you."

George Beaumont's Mercedes sped through the streets of Leeds, urgency propelling them forward. In the passenger seat, Tashan Blackburn was on his mobile, speaking rapidly.

"Sir, it's Tashan. We're at the Kiton boutique. They've got a record of a suit purchase that could be vital, but they're insisting on a warrant for the details," Tashan explained, his voice a mix of urgency and frustration.

Detective Chief Inspector Alistair Atkinson's voice, gruff and authoritative, came through the phone. "Understood. I'll get the legal team on it right away. Hold tight, Tashan."

George's grip on the steering wheel tightened as he navigated the busy roads. "What did Atkinson say?"

"He's on it. They're pushing for the warrant now," Tashan replied, ending the call and looking out the window, his expression pensive.

George's mind was racing with the possibilities this new lead presented. The boutique's insistence on a warrant was a setback, but it also underscored the potential importance of the information they were guarding.

As they pulled up at the station, George was already out of the car and heading towards the building, Tashan hurrying to keep up.

In the Incident Room, the team looked up as George and Tashan entered. "We may have a significant lead," George announced to the room. "A purchase at the Kiton boutique that links directly to our case. We're waiting on a warrant for the details."

The team, sensing the urgency, nodded in understanding. They knew the importance of following every lead, especially in a case as complex as the Santa Claus murders.

CHAPTER NINETEEN

In his office, George paced, waiting for the call to come through. The wait was agonising, each minute stretching out interminably. Finally, his phone rang. It was DCI Atkinson.

"We've got it, George. The warrant's been approved. You can collect the details from the boutique."

A wave of relief washed over George. "Thank you, sir. We're on it."

George and Tashan wasted no time. Within minutes, they were back in the Mercedes, racing towards the Kiton boutique. The city passed in a blur, the urgency of their mission lending speed to their journey.

Upon arriving at the boutique, the warrant in hand, the assistant's demeanour changed from reluctance to cooperation. She pulled up the record of the suit purchase, revealing the name of the purchaser.

As the name appeared on the screen, George felt a chill run down his spine. It was a name they knew, a name that brought a new dimension to the case and potentially a direct link to the murderer.

George straightened up, a mix of shock and determination on his face. "Thank you. This has been incredibly helpful."

Back in the car, George and Tashan sat in silence for a moment, processing the revelation. "This changes everything, sir," Tashan said, the weight of the discovery evident in his voice.

"It does," George agreed, starting the engine. "Let's get back and figure out our next move."

Tashan nodded, fully aware of the implications. "What's our next move, sir?"

"We verify this information, establish a timeline, and then we bring them in for questioning," George replied, his mind already formulating the next steps.

The drive back to the station was filled with a tense anticipation. The discovery at the boutique had opened up a new avenue in the investigation, one that could lead them directly to the killer.

For George Beaumont, the case was becoming increasingly personal, the lines between professional duty and personal connections blurring. But one thing was clear—they were closer than ever to solving the Santa Claus murders, and George was determined to see it through to the end.

Chapter Twenty

In the Incident Room of Elland Road Police Station, Detective Sergeant Yolanda Williams and Detective Constable Tashan Blackburn were deeply engrossed in their analysis. Spread out before them were high-resolution images of the shoe prints found on the bodies in the Santa Claus murders. The attention to detail in their work was meticulous, reflecting the gravity of their task.

Yolanda, with years of experience in pattern analysis, was the first to break the silence. "Tashan, look at this tread pattern," she said, pointing to the magnified image on the screen. "It's distinct, very high-end. I think we've seen this pattern before."

Tashan leaned in closer, his eyes scanning the intricate design. "You're right. Let me cross-check it with our database."

After a few moments of intense searching, Tashan's face lit up with recognition. "Got it! These are from a pair of Testoni Camolgi Leather Derby shoes, size 10.5. These are not your average shoes; they're incredibly expensive, much like the Kiton suit we found fibres from."

Yolanda nodded her expression a mix of satisfaction and concern. "This can't be a coincidence. The same high-end brand for both the suit and the shoes? There's a connection here."

Tashan was already on his feet, energized by the discovery. "I'll get this information to DI Beaumont right away. He needs to see this."

They hurried to George Beaumont's office, where they found him deep in thought, poring over the case files. George looked up as they entered, his expression shifting to one of keen interest.

"Sir, we've made a significant find," Tashan began, his tone urgent. "The shoe prints on both victims—they're from Testoni Camolgi Leather Derby shoes, size 10.5. High-end, expensive, just like the Kiton suit."

George's eyes narrowed as he processed the information. "Testoni shoes and a Kiton suit... This is more than just a coincidence. It suggests a certain lifestyle, a specific social stratum."

Yolanda added, "The perpetrator is either affluent or has access to these luxury items. This could be a crucial lead in profiling our suspect."

George leaned back in his chair, the wheels in his mind turning rapidly. "Excellent work, both of you. This narrows down our search significantly. We're looking for someone who not only has a taste for luxury but also the means to afford it."

As Yolanda and Tashan left the office, George's gaze returned to the case files spread out before him. The discovery of the Testoni shoes added a new dimension to the case, a thread that, if pulled, could unravel the mystery surrounding the Santa Claus murders.

Later, George's office was steeped in a tense silence, punctuated only by the occasional rustling of papers and the soft hum of a computer. Detective Inspector George Beaumont

CHAPTER TWENTY

and Detective Constable Jay Scott were hunched over a table, their focus unwavering on the evidence sprawled before them. Hours had passed in their meticulous scrutiny, each clue a potential key to unravelling the chaotic mystery of the Santa Claus murders.

George's intense gaze was locked onto a set of photographs and documents. His brow was furrowed, his mind deep in the throes of analysis, piecing together the increasingly intricate puzzle. Beside him, Jay was absorbed in cross-referencing the evidence against the database, his fingers a blur over the keyboard.

Then, a breakthrough. George's eyes landed on a specific document, and his heartbeat quickened. A seemingly innocuous detail now demanded urgent attention. It was a list of names, and among them was one indelibly linked to the inner circle of Edward Beaumont, George's estranged father. A cold shiver ran down George's spine as the realization dawned: his father was undeniably entangled in this sordid affair.

Jay, attuned to the shift in George's demeanour, glanced up. "Anything significant, boss?" he inquired, leaning in closer.

George hesitated, the weight of the revelation momentarily overwhelming. His voice, though strained, held a semblance of steadiness. "It's... it's a lead," he uttered, grappling with the internal storm the discovery had sparked.

Jay, perceptive of George's sudden reticence, probed gently, "Is it someone you know, boss?"

George averted Jay's curious gaze, the turmoil within him coiling tighter. "No, it's... let's just say it's complicated," he responded, a deliberate evasion of the truth. The implication of his father's involvement was a bitter pill, too complex to disclose without further introspection.

Jay nodded, his curiosity piqued yet respectful of George's evident discomfort. He knew better than to pry when George was like this.

Abruptly, George stood, the need to distance himself from the damning evidence compelling him to move. The notion that his own father, from whom he had deliberately estranged himself, was now a pivotal figure in his investigation was laden with irony and conflict, especially if you considered the Kiton suit and the Testoni shoes.

How deep was his father's involvement? Was he a mere accomplice or the puppeteer of these atrocities? The questions swirled chaotically in George's mind, each more unnerving than the last.

After Jay left, George sat motionless, staring at the wall adorned with maps and timelines of the case. The dim light from his desk lamp cast long shadows, mirroring the dark thoughts that plagued his mind. The discovery of a connection between the murders and his father, Edward Beaumont's inner circle, was a revelation that threatened to shatter the fragile balance between his personal and professional life.

The room was silent, but for George, it was as if a storm was raging within. His thoughts were a tumultuous mix of duty, betrayal, and a deep-seated animosity towards his father. Edward, the man who had cast a long shadow over his life, was now a part of his most challenging case.

A heavy sigh escaped George's lips as he leaned back in his chair, closing his eyes. The past, which he had tried so hard to distance himself from, was now intruding into his present with a vengeance. A brief flashback took hold of him, transporting him back to a time when he was just a young man, standing in the shadow of his father.

CHAPTER TWENTY

The memory was vivid—a young George, full of ambition and idealism, standing beside Edward, a figure of authority and influence. They were in Edward's study, a room filled with the trappings of success and power. Edward's voice was stern, his words sharp, instilling in George a sense of inadequacy that he had struggled to overcome all his life.

"You need to understand, George, this world is not for the weak," Edward had said, his gaze piercing. "You have to be ruthless to survive, to succeed."

Young George had bristled at the words, feeling a chasm growing between him and his father. Edward's world was one of manipulation and control, a world that George had vowed never to be a part of. Yet, here he was, years later, dealing with the consequences of Edward's actions.

The flashback faded, and George opened his eyes, finding himself back in the reality of his office. The revelation about his father's connection to the murders was a bitter pill to swallow. It brought to the surface the resentment and anger he had harboured for years, emotions that he had tried to bury under the weight of his badge.

George stood up, pacing the room. He needed to approach this case like any other, with objectivity and detachment. But how could he when every clue seemed to lead back to Edward? His father's influence, once a source of frustration, was now a critical element of the investigation.

In Luke Mason's office, George stood by the window, gazing out but not really seeing the bustling streets of Leeds below. He was there for advice, but the true depth of his turmoil remained locked away within him.

Luke Mason, seated behind his desk, watched George with a keen, understanding eye. Despite the years of experience etched on his face, Luke's demeanour was one of calm reassurance.

"Luke, I need your perspective," George began, his voice betraying a hint of the internal struggle he was facing. "What do you do when a case... starts to become personal?"

Luke regarded him thoughtfully. "George, in our line of work, it's a thin line between personal and professional. But we must always follow the evidence, no matter where it leads. No case is worth compromising our principles."

George nodded slowly, the words resonating with him, yet the turmoil inside him twisted tighter. He couldn't disclose the full extent of his father Edward's potential involvement in the case. It was a shadow he had long tried to outrun, a part of his past that threatened to derail his present.

Luke's voice brought him back. "You've always had a strong moral compass, George. Trust that. And remember, a detective's first duty is to the truth, however difficult it might be to face."

George's expression softened slightly, gratitude mixed with the complexity of his thoughts. "Thanks, Luke. I'll keep that in mind."

As George left the office, Luke's advice echoed in his mind. Follow the evidence wherever it leads. It was a simple directive, yet in George's case, it was like walking through a minefield blindfolded. Every step could unearth a buried truth about his father that he wasn't sure he was ready to face.

When George arrived at his office, Detective Constables Candy Nichols and Tashan Blackburn were immersed in their work in the Incident Room, poring over a cluttered desk strewn with witness statements and tips. The murmur of their discussions mingled with the steady hum of activity around

CHAPTER TWENTY

them.

Tashan, his brow furrowed, sifted through a stack of papers, his mind a whirlpool of thoughts. The recent offer of promotion still weighed heavily on him, a decision that tugged at his conscience and ambition in equal measure.

Candy, ever perceptive, glanced at Tashan. "Anything useful there?" she asked, nodding towards the pile of papers.

Tashan shook his head, a trace of frustration in his voice. "Nothing concrete. It's like grasping at shadows." He paused, looking up. "I've got a lot on my plate, Candy. Not just this case."

Candy offered a sympathetic smile, understanding the unspoken context of his words. "You'll figure it out, Tashan. You always do."

Their moment was interrupted by the arrival of Detective Chief Inspector Alistair Atkinson. His presence filled the room, an air of authority and expectation surrounding him.

Atkinson's gaze swept over the room before settling on Tashan. "DC Blackburn, I need a decision from you. We can't have this hanging over us indefinitely."

Tashan straightened, meeting Atkinson's gaze. "I understand, sir. I'll have an answer soon."

Atkinson nodded, seemingly satisfied, then turned his attention to the rest of the team. "I expect results, people. This killer isn't going to catch themselves."

The team members exchanged glances, a silent acknowledgement of the pressure they were under. As Atkinson left, the room returned to its former buzz of activity, but the weight of his words lingered in the air.

Candy turned back to her work, her mind racing with theories and possibilities. She picked up a photograph from the crime scene, her eyes narrowing as she noticed a small, overlooked detail in the background.

"George needs to see this," she muttered, rising from her desk with the photograph in hand.

Across the room, Tashan watched her leave, his thoughts drifting back to his own dilemma. The offer of promotion was tempting, a chance to advance his career, but it meant leaving the team, leaving behind the camaraderie and the sense of purpose he found in his current role.

His gaze drifted to the bustling room, his colleagues immersed in their work, a team united in their quest for justice. It was more than just a job; it was a calling, a commitment to something greater than themselves.

Tashan's fingers drummed on the desk, a rhythm of indecision and resolve. He knew he had to make a choice, one that would define his path forward. But for now, there was work to be done, leads to follow, and a killer to catch.

With a deep breath, Tashan pushed aside his personal turmoil, refocusing on the task at hand. The case demanded his full attention, and he wouldn't let his team down. The decision about his future would have to wait. Right now, there were lives at stake and a city on edge.

In the solitude of his office, Detective Inspector George Beaumont sat hunched over his desk, the weight of the world seemingly resting on his shoulders. The dim light from the desk lamp cast long shadows across his face, accentuating the deep lines of conflict and determination etched there.

His gaze was fixed on a photo of his father, Edward Beaumont, a man whose influence had cast a long, dark shadow over George's life and career. The revelation that his father might be implicated in the Santa Claus murders had shaken him to his core.

George's mind was a storm of emotions and thoughts. He owed his father nothing; that much was clear. The years of manipulation, the overshadowing presence in his life, and the emotional turmoil he had endured were more than enough to sever any filial bonds. Yet, the prospect of implicating his own father in a murder investigation was daunting, fraught with personal and professional ramifications that he could scarcely begin to untangle.

He considered stepping away from the case, the idea tempting in its simplicity. But George knew himself too well. He was a detective to the core, driven by a relentless pursuit of justice. To walk away now would be to betray everything he stood for, everything he had fought so hard to achieve in his career.

The silence of the room was oppressive, punctuated only by the ticking of the clock on the wall. Time was moving forward, unrelenting, and George knew he had to make a decision.

Slowly, he leaned back in his chair, his eyes never leaving the photo of his father. The conflict within him was palpable, a fierce battle between duty and blood. But deep down, George knew there was only one choice he could make, one path he could follow.

With a deep breath, he reached a resolution. He would not reveal his father's potential involvement to the team, not yet. The risk of bias, of clouding their judgment with his personal history, was too great. He would carry this burden alone, for now.

George stood up, his movements deliberate and resolute. He tucked the photo into a drawer, a symbolic gesture of his decision to continue with the investigation, no matter the personal cost. He was a detective, first and foremost, bound by his duty to seek the truth, even if that truth threatened to unravel the very fabric of his life.

As he stepped out of his office, his expression was one of quiet resolve. The decision had been made, and there was no turning back. The investigation would continue, with George at the helm, steering the course through the treacherous waters of a case that had become deeply personal.

Chapter Twenty-one

In Middleton, a suburb where affluence whispered rather than shouted, Detective Inspector George Beaumont and Detective Constable Jay Scott arrived at New Lane. Here stood the residence of Jürgen Schmidt. The house, decent-sized and subtly extended, melded seamlessly with its surroundings, its presence unassuming yet unmistakably prosperous.

As they parked the car, George noted the tall, thick hedges that ringed the property, a green fortress obscuring the house from prying eyes. The drive hosted a couple of expensive SUVs, their polished surfaces reflecting the muted light of the overcast sky.

"Discreet, isn't he?" Jay remarked, eyeing the high hedges.

"You know what he's like," George replied, stepping out of the car. His eyes caught the security camera mounted above the oversized garage, its lens following their movements. It was a silent sentinel, recording their arrival.

They approached the front door, their footsteps echoing slightly on the well-kept path. George rang the bell. As they waited, the front door swung open, revealing Jürgen Schmidt. His initial frown of surprise quickly morphed into a knowing smirk as he recognized George.

"You again," Schmidt said, his voice tinged with a mix of

disdain and amusement. "Not interested. Come back with a warrant."

George, unfazed by the reception, maintained his professional demeanour. "Mr. Schmidt, we're investigating a series of serious crimes. Your cooperation could be vital."

Schmidt crossed his arms, his stance unyielding. "I have nothing to say without legal representation. You know the drill, Inspector. No warrant, no entry."

Jay, standing a step behind George, exchanged a glance with his superior. They had anticipated resistance, but Schmidt's outright dismissal was a clear sign that he was more than just a reluctant witness.

George, still calm, tried a different approach. "This isn't just a routine inquiry, Mr. Schmidt. There's evidence linking a purchase you made to the crimes. It's in your best interest to clarify things."

Schmidt's smirk faded slightly, replaced by a guarded expression. "I've already told you, Inspector."

The air was thick with tension, the unspoken implications hanging heavily between them. George knew they were on the right track, but without a warrant, their hands were tied.

"We'll be in touch, Mr. Schmidt," George said finally, stepping back from the doorstep. "Expect a follow-up."

As they walked back to their car, the sound of the door clicking shut behind them, Jay spoke up, "He's hiding something, isn't he?"

George nodded, his gaze fixed on the rear-view mirror as they drove away. "Yes, and he knows we're onto him. We need to move fast. Let's get that warrant."

* * *

CHAPTER TWENTY-ONE

An hour later, with persistence and a detailed presentation of their findings, Detective Inspector George Beaumont had managed to secure a warrant, albeit from a seriously annoyed judge. The urgency of the Santa Claus murders case had warranted the interruption of the judge's evening, and George's compelling argument had tipped the scales.

Now, as evening cast long shadows over the quiet streets of Middleton, George and Detective Constable Jay Scott stood once again at the threshold of Jürgen Schmidt's property. This time, they held the legal authority to search his residence. The air was thick with anticipation.

George rang the doorbell, the sound echoing slightly in the cool evening air. The door opened, and Jürgen Schmidt appeared, his earlier smugness replaced with a look of surprise and irritation.

"Back so soon, Inspector? And with a warrant, I presume?" Schmidt's tone was acidic, his eyes flickering to the document in George's hand.

"Yes, Mr Schmidt," George replied calmly, holding up the warrant. "We're investigating a series of murders in Leeds, and we've found a connection to a purchase you made—a Kiton suit." George paused as he enjoyed the look on Schmidt's face. "We need to search your property in connection to the Santa Claus murders."

Schmidt's demeanour shifted subtly, a hint of unease betraying his composed facade. "Yes, I have a Kiton suit. But I fail to see how this relates to any criminal activity."

"We found fibres from a suit of that make on the victims," Jay added, watching Schmidt closely.

Jürgen stepped aside, gesturing them in with a resigned air as he said, "I see," Schmidt said, his voice measured. "But I assure you, I've had no involvement in any such matters."

As they entered, George motioned to Jay to start the search. They methodically began to comb through the house, looking for any evidence that could link Schmidt to the murders. The team worked efficiently, opening drawers, examining documents, and scrutinising every corner of the lavish home.

In the study, George's attention was drawn to a series of photographs on the wall. Among them was a picture of Schmidt at a social event, his arm around a figure George recognised from the investigation. He made a mental note to cross-reference the event with their timeline of the murders.

Meanwhile, Jay called out from the living room. "Sir, you might want to see this." He was standing over an open briefcase, its contents revealing stacks of financial documents and several mobile phones.

George joined him, his eyes quickly scanning the papers. "Looks like we've got more than just a simple purchase here," he muttered, his mind piecing together the potential implications.

As they continued their search, Schmidt watched from a distance, his expression unreadable. The detectives could feel his gaze on them, heavy with unspoken thoughts.

As Detective Inspector George Beaumont and Detective Constable Jay Scott combed through Schmidt's well-organised wardrobe, they came across a significant piece of evidence: the charcoal-coloured Kiton suit.

George held the suit out, examining it closely under the light. The luxurious fabric and the distinct style matched the description they had. This was more than just a coincidence; it was a tangible link between Schmidt and the crimes.

"Looks like we've found our missing piece," George said,

his voice tinged with a mix of triumph and gravity.

Jay, who had been methodically documenting the search, added, "This could be the breakthrough we needed. It could tie Schmidt directly to the evidence found on the victims."

Carefully bagging the suit as evidence, George couldn't help but feel the weight of this discovery. It was a significant leap forward in the case, yet he was aware that the journey to proving Schmidt's guilt if he indeed was guilty, was far from over.

Schmidt, who had been observing the search from a distance, maintained his composure, but his eyes lingered on the suit as it was being bagged. His body language was controlled, yet there was a barely perceptible tightening of his jaw.

After thorough searching, they gathered a collection of items that could potentially serve as evidence—financial records, phones, and a few personal items that seemed out of place.

"Thank you for your cooperation, Mr Schmidt," George said as they prepared to leave, the evidence bagged and ready to be examined back at the station. "We'll be in touch regarding our findings."

Schmidt said nothing, his silence speaking volumes as he escorted them to the door.

Back in the car, George and Jay sat in silence for a moment, processing the evening's events. "We're getting closer," George finally said, starting the car. "Let's see what the suit, the documents and the phones reveal."

* * *

Detective Constable Candy Nichols sifted through the dusty

archives, her eyes scanning the yellowed pages and faded photographs from an old case file. Her search was meticulous, driven by the nagging feeling that the key to unravelling the Santa Claus murders lay buried in the past. And then, like a beacon in the darkness, she found it – a photograph that could potentially connect the dots in their complex investigation.

The photo was slightly curled at the edges, the colours faded, but the faces were unmistakable. It showed a group of young men – Oliver Hughes, Ethan Turner, Daniel 'Danny' Roberts, Liam O'Sullivan, Alex Green, Michael 'Mike' Clarkson, and Ryan Baxter – the same names that were now central to their current case. But what made this photo particularly intriguing was the company these young men kept.

Standing alongside them were figures of considerable influence and power within Leeds: Elias Marston, a solicitor to the wealthy; Sir Charles Denning, a bastion of high society; Fiona Appleton, a local politician with her fingers on the city's pulse; Graham Norton-Hughes, a renowned barrister; Catherine Devereux, a fashion industry magnate; and Margaret Vane, a prominent philanthropist.

The setting of the photo appeared to be a high-end event, the kind of place where deals were made and futures were decided. The young men looked out of place amidst this elite gathering, their expressions a mix of excitement and nervous anticipation.

Candy felt a surge of adrenaline as she pondered the implications of this discovery. This wasn't just a gathering of acquaintances; this was a nexus of the young and the influential, a convergence of paths that had now led to a series of brutal murders.

Clutching the photograph, Candy hurried to find George

CHAPTER TWENTY-ONE

Beaumont. The information held in this single image could unravel the tightly wound threads of their investigation, shedding light on connections that were previously shrouded in darkness.

Candy Nichols approached her boss' office, her steps hesitant yet purposeful.

There was a soft knock on the door, and Candy stepped in. In her hand was the photograph she had unearthed from the archives, a picture that had added a new dimension to their investigation.

"Sir, I thought you should take a look at this," Candy said. In her hand, she clutched a photograph, its edges slightly crumpled from her tight grip. George looked up, his eyes meeting hers. There was an urgency in her expression that immediately piqued his interest.

"It's from a decade ago, sir," Candy said, laying the photograph on his desk.

George looked at it, his eyes immediately drawn to the faces in the photograph—the victims alongside a group of Leeds' most influential figures.

"This photo..." George began, his voice trailing off as he absorbed the implications. "It suggests the victims were involved in circles we didn't know about. They had connections to some of the city's elite."

Candy nodded, her expression serious. "It raises more questions than answers. Why were they at an event with these people? What was their relationship?"

George leaned back in his chair, his mind racing. "Each of these individuals—Denning, Appleton, Norton-Hughes, Devereux, Vane—they could hold the key to understanding the motive behind these murders."

"And there's Elias Marston," Candy added, observing George closely. "He seems to be a common link here."

George felt a pang at the mention of Marston, a name he knew was tied to his estranged father, though this was a fact he had kept to himself. "Yes, Marston..." he said thoughtfully. "He's a pivotal figure. We need to know more about his connection to the victims."

Candy sensed George's hesitation but didn't press further. "What's our next step?"

"We need to discreetly look into these individuals' backgrounds and their connections to the victims," George replied, his tone resolute. "But we must tread carefully. We're dealing with some of the most powerful people in Leeds."

Candy understood the delicacy of the situation. "I'll start digging into their pasts, see what I can find. Maybe there's something there that ties them to the murders."

"Be discreet," George interjected. "The last thing we need is to tip off the wrong person."

Candy left, her mind already formulating a plan of action. George remained at his desk, staring at the photograph. The pendant was more than just a clue; it was a symbol of the tangled web he was unravelling, one that entwined his professional duty with the shadows of his family's past.

* * *

Detective Inspector George Beaumont watched as Detective Sergeant Yolanda Williams and Detective Constable Tashan Blackburn sifted through stacks of files and rapidly populated spreadsheets on their computers. The task at hand was a meticulous background check on the influential figures from

CHAPTER TWENTY-ONE

the photograph—a picture that had become the linchpin of the Santa Claus murders investigation.

"Yolanda, Tashan, I need everything you can find," George instructed, his tone firm. "Past interactions, financial ties, anything that links them to our victims."

Yolanda, her eyes scanning a financial report, nodded without looking up. "We're on it, sir. If there's a connection, we'll find it."

Meanwhile, Tashan was cross-referencing names against police databases. "Some of these figures have minor records or past inquiries," he reported. "Nothing major, but it's a start."

George leaned over Tashan's shoulder, observing the data. "Keep digging. These kinds of connections can be subtle."

Their first stop for George and Candy was the opulent office of Sir Charles Denning, a man whose name commanded respect and whose influence was felt across the city. As they were ushered into his office, George noted the luxurious decor, a testament to Sir Charles' wealth and status.

"Sir Charles, thank you for agreeing to speak with us," George began, his tone respectful yet firm.

Denning, a tall figure with a commanding presence, nodded curtly. "Detective Inspector, I understand this is about the unfortunate series of events that have occurred recently."

"Yes," George replied. "We found this photograph." He slid the picture across the desk. "It was taken at an event you attended ten years ago. We're interested in understanding your relationship with the individuals in this picture, particularly the victims."

Denning studied the photo, his expression unreadable. "Ah, yes, the charity gala. I attend many such events, Detective.

I'm afraid I don't recall any specific interactions." He paused. "And it was a decade ago."

Candy, observing closely, chimed in. "Did you notice anything unusual about the victims that evening or any interactions they might have had with others?"

Denning leaned back, considering. "Nothing out of the ordinary. It was a typical gathering—fundraising, networking, the usual."

The detectives exchanged a glance. George probed further. "Were you familiar with any of the victims personally?"

"There's always a crowd at these events," Denning replied, his tone neutral. "One meets so many people. It's hard to remember everyone."

Thanking Denning, George and Candy left, feeling the weight of unspoken truths lingering in the air. Each interview was a dance around delicacies, extracting information from individuals unaccustomed to being questioned.

Their next visit was to Fiona Appleton, a local politician whose name had surfaced repeatedly in their investigation. Her office was less ostentatious but no less intimidating.

"Miss Appleton," George began after introductions and production of the photo, "we're investigating the connections between several murder victims and certain prominent individuals."

Appleton's response was swift and rehearsed. "The tragedy deeply saddens me, but I assure you, my interactions with them were purely incidental."

Candy, taking a different tack, asked, "Did you notice any unusual behaviour or interactions at the event a decade ago?"

Appleton paused, a flicker of hesitation crossing her face. "Not that I recall. It was a large event. I spoke to many people."

CHAPTER TWENTY-ONE

She paused. "And it was so long ago."

As the interview concluded, George sensed a pattern emerging. Each individual they spoke to provided minimal information, careful not to reveal too much or implicate themselves in any way.

The day wore on, and with each interview, the puzzle grew more intricate. Wealth and reputation formed a shield that was hard to penetrate. Yet, George knew that behind the polite deflections and rehearsed responses, there were secrets waiting to be uncovered.

Chapter Twenty-two

Back at the station, George and Candy debriefed, their minds heavy with the day's revelations.

The Incident Room buzzed with the sound of focused activity. Phone calls were made, databases queried, and social media profiles scrutinized. Yolanda and Tashan worked in tandem, piecing together a complex jigsaw of relationships and events.

Yolanda looked up from her screen, a trace of excitement in her voice. "Sir, several of these individuals were on the board of a charity event last year. The same event our victims attended."

George's interest was piqued. "Can we get a list of all attendees?"

"On it," Tashan replied, already pulling up the relevant information.

The atmosphere in the room was electric, the team sensing they were on the brink of a significant breakthrough. The connection between the city's elite and the victims of the Santa Claus murders was becoming clearer, the lines of their investigation crossing in unexpected ways.

George, standing amidst the flurry of activity, felt the tension mounting. This investigation was leading them into uncharted territory, where the affluent and influential mingled with the dark underbelly of crime.

As Yolanda and Tashan continued their work, George pondered their next move. They needed to approach these influential figures with caution. Any misstep could send potential suspects into hiding or close off valuable sources of information.

Detective Constable Jay Scott sat hunched over his computer in the corner of the Incident Room, his eyes scanning through the digital labyrinth of the victims' lives.

His screen was a mosaic of financial records, social media timelines, and personal correspondences. Jay's focus was unwavering as he sifted through the data, searching for the elusive thread that might connect the victims - Oliver Hughes, Ethan Turner, Daniel Roberts, Liam O'Sullivan, Alex Green, Michael Clarkson, and Ryan Baxter - to the influential figures in the photograph.

"Come on," Jay muttered under his breath, clicking through another series of emails. "There's got to be something here."

He paused, zooming in on a series of transactions that seemed out of place. The amounts were significant, and they were all linked to an exclusive social club known for its affluent membership. Jay's pulse quickened. This could be the link they were looking for.

At that moment, George walked over, her eyes questioning. "Anything?"

Jay nodded, pointing to the screen. "Look at these transactions, boss. They're significant, and they all tie back to this club."

George leaned in, his eyes scanning the information. "Could be our connection. These guys were living way beyond their means."

"Exactly, boss," Jay said. "And guess who frequents this club? Some of the names from our elite photograph."

The day wore on, and the pieces of the puzzle slowly began to fit together. Financial records revealed substantial donations to the charity event by some of the individuals in the photo. At the same time, social media posts and pictures provided hints of deeper social connections with the victims.

"It's like a network," Yolanda observed, leaning back in her chair. "These people, our victims, they were all connected in ways we didn't see before."

Tashan nodded in agreement, his eyes still on his screen. "There are patterns here. Financial ties, shared interests, and recurring names in event guest lists. It's intricate, but it's there."

George listened, his mind working through the implications. "We need to map out these connections, find the common threads. There's a story here we're not seeing yet."

Jay's attention returned to the screen as he delved deeper into the social media accounts of the victims. Amidst the usual array of posts and photos, he found a series of messages that hinted at an invitation to an exclusive event—the same event where the photograph was taken.

"They were invited," Jay said, his voice a mix of excitement and dread. "Look at these messages. It wasn't just a chance encounter. They were brought into that world deliberately."

George's brow furrowed. "But why? What was the purpose?"

"That's what we need to find out, boss," Jay replied, his fingers flying over the keyboard as he followed the new trail of breadcrumbs they had uncovered.

CHAPTER TWENTY-TWO

* * *

Detective Sergeant Joshua Fry and his team were engrossed in a deep digital drive. Screens flickered with streams of data—bank records, phone logs, and email correspondences. The Santa Claus murders had plunged them into a world of high-stakes analysis, where every byte of data could be the key to unlocking the mystery.

Fry, a veteran in digital forensics, was methodical in his approach. "Focus on the weeks leading up to the murders," he instructed his team. "Look for anything that stands out—large transactions, unusual communication patterns, anything."

His team, a group of skilled tech analysts, worked in silence, their fingers dancing across keyboards. The room was a symphony of soft clicks and the low hum of computer processors.

One of the analysts, a young woman named Lisa, called out, "DS Fry, I've got something here. A series of large payments from one of the victim's accounts to a private account. The transactions are coded, but they're substantial."

Fry leaned over her shoulder, studying the screen. "Trace the receiving account. Let's see where this leads."

Lisa's fingers flew over the keyboard, her concentration palpable. After a few moments, she looked up, a trace of surprise in her eyes. "The account belongs to a shell company, but I've managed to trace it back to one of the influential figures from the photo."

Fry's brow furrowed. "Which one?"

"Sir Charles Denning," she replied.

Fry's mind raced. Denning was a significant player in Leeds, a man whose influence was felt in both the business and social spheres. What was his connection to the victim?

"Keep digging," Fry said, turning to another analyst. "Steve, cross-reference these transactions with the phone logs. I want to know if there were any corresponding communications."

Steve nodded, his focus already back on his screen. The room was alive with activity, each team member a vital cog in the investigative machine.

As Fry surveyed the room, his phone buzzed. He glanced at the caller ID—it was DI Beaumont.

"DI Fry here," he answered.

"Josh, it's George. How's the data analysis coming along?"

"We may have a lead, sir," Fry replied. "A series of payments from one of the victims to a company linked to Sir Charles Denning. We're looking into it now."

There was a pause on the other end of the line. "Good work. Keep me updated. This could be significant."

"Will do, sir," Fry said before ending the call.

Downstairs in their new forensics lab, Detective Inspector George Beaumont stood alongside a team of forensic experts; their focus centred on a set of physical evidence that could potentially pivot the direction of the Santa Claus murders investigation. The items in question—a pair of Testoni Camolgi Leather Derby shoes and fibres from a Kiton suit—lay meticulously out on the examination table.

George, his expression a mask of concentration, watched as the lead forensic expert, Dr Helen Cartwright, peered through a microscope at the fibres. "We're looking to see if there's anything unique about these fibres that can tie them to a specific individual," she explained, her voice steady and precise.

CHAPTER TWENTY-TWO

"And the shoes?" George asked, gesturing towards the Testoni Derbies.

Dr Cartwright glanced up, removing her glasses. "Shoe prints can be as distinctive as fingerprints in some cases. We're comparing the wear patterns, looking for any oddities that might match our suspects."

The atmosphere in the lab was charged, each expert acutely aware of the stakes. George's gaze shifted between the team members, his mind racing through the possibilities.

A younger forensic analyst, Mark, spoke up. "We've run the fibres through our database. The composition is consistent with high-end Kiton suits, but there's something else. We found traces of a rare dye, one that's not commonly used."

George leaned in, intrigued. "Could that help us narrow down the purchase to a specific batch or store?"

"Possibly," Mark replied. "It's a lead worth exploring."

The team then turned their attention to the shoes. Another analyst, Sarah, was examining them closely. "The wear pattern is unique," she observed. "See here," she pointed to a slight unevenness on the sole, "it suggests the wearer has a particular gait. It could help us match them to one of our suspects."

"Any DNA?"

Helen shook her head. "Not yet, but we're doing what we can."

George absorbed the information, his mind already piecing together the new leads. "Good work. Let's get this information over to the tech team. They might be able to cross-reference it with our suspects' purchase histories."

As the consultation wrapped up, George stepped aside, dialling Jay Scott. "Jay, it's George. We've got something from forensics. I need you to cross-reference a specific dye used in a Kiton suit with our list of suspects. And check for any purchases of Testoni shoes that match a unique wear pattern."

"On it, boss," came Jay's immediate response.

Exiting the lab, George felt a renewed sense of direction. The forensic evidence was providing tangible leads, pulling back the veil on a case that had seemed impenetrable.

Walking through the corridors of the police station, George's thoughts were a whirlwind of strategy and anticipation. Every new piece of evidence brought them closer to the killer, and with the forensic team's findings, they were now one step closer to unravelling the mystery that had gripped Leeds.

In the Incident Room, the team was assembled, ready for George's briefing. He looked around at the expectant faces, each member poised for action.

"We're making progress," George announced, his voice imbued with a quiet determination. "Forensics has given us new leads. It's up to us to follow them to their end."

The team nodded, their resolve evident.

As night fell, the Incident Room remained a hive of activity. The team, fuelled by coffee and determination, continued their work, aware that with each new discovery, they were unravelling a web of deception and power that spanned the upper echelons of Leeds society.

That was until George called his team together and dismissed them for the night.

* * *

In the common area of the Elland Road Police Station, a rare

CHAPTER TWENTY-TWO

moment of levity had descended upon the team. A Santa hat sat at the centre of the table, filled with folded pieces of paper. The team, usually tangled in the grim realities of their work, found themselves momentarily distracted by a simple game: a Secret Santa draw.

George stood leaning against a wall, his arms folded. His gaze flitted over his team–Jay Scott, Candy Nichols, and Tashan Blackburn among them–their faces alight with a mixture of curiosity and amusement. It was a welcome reprieve from the intensity of their investigation.

Jay, ever the cheerful one, reached into the hat first, his hand theatrically rummaging before pulling out a slip. He flashed a wide grin as he unfolded it, his eyes twinkling with mischief. "Ah, now, who's the lucky one?" he mused aloud, tucking the paper into his pocket with an exaggerated flourish.

Candy, smiling, was next. She plucked a name with a graceful movement, her eyes scanning the paper quickly. A smirk danced on her lips as she looked up, her gaze sweeping the room as if trying to guess who she had picked.

Tashan, still carrying the weight of his decision about the promotion, approached the hat with a more subdued demeanour. His hand hesitated for a moment before drawing a name. He glanced at the paper, a faint smile breaking through his contemplative expression. The exercise seemed to momentarily lighten his burden.

Yolanda snuck in quickly and took a name out of the hat, apologising to each member as she headed back outside. Working between teams had been DCI Atkinson's idea, and when George had Isabella and Luke on his team, that was fine. But now he was without a DS.

Finally, it was George's turn. He pushed off from the wall

and approached the hat with a thoughtful look. His hand delved in, and he withdrew a slip, unfolding it discreetly. A flicker of surprise crossed his features, quickly masked by a neutral expression. He pocketed the paper without a word, but a hint of a smile hinted at his involvement in the festive spirit.

The atmosphere was infectious, with team members laughing and speculating about who had drawn whom. The usual barriers of rank and professionalism momentarily dissolved in the shared camaraderie of the moment.

"Alright, remember, the limit is fifteen pounds," George announced, his voice carrying a lightness rarely heard in the midst of their demanding work. "Let's see who can be the most creative."

The group dispersed, chuckles and whispers of conspiracy echoing as they returned to their desks. For a brief moment, the weight of their work had lifted, replaced by the simple joy of a shared holiday tradition.

As they each pondered over their Secret Santa gifts, the task provided a much-needed distraction, a small island of normalcy in the turbulent sea of their work.

* * *

Detective Sergeant Fry's team worked into the night, the glow from their screens casting an eerie light in the room. The data was a puzzle, and each piece they uncovered brought them closer to the truth.

Steve suddenly spoke up. "DS Fry, I've got something. Phone logs show a series of calls between the victim and Denning's office around the time of the transactions."

CHAPTER TWENTY-TWO

Fry's expression hardened. "We need to know the nature of those calls. Can we get any content?"

"I'm on it," Steve replied, already working on accessing the call records.

The room was a hive of focused energy, each discovery a potential breakthrough.

Chapter Twenty-three

The streets of Leeds were still shrouded in darkness, the city quietly slumbering. But Detective Inspector George Beaumont was already awake, his mind racing with thoughts of the case that had consumed him. He arrived at Elland Road Police Station while the city slept, his car's headlights cutting through the morning fog.

The Incident Room, usually bustling with activity, was eerily silent at this early hour. George stood alone amidst walls plastered with evidence—photographs, maps, timelines—each piece a fragment of the complex puzzle he was determined to solve. The dim light from his desk lamp cast long shadows across the room, adding to the solemn atmosphere.

George moved methodically from one board to another, his eyes scanning every detail. He revisited the photos of the crime scenes, the reports from the pathologist, the witness statements—each element critical to his quest for the truth. His expression was one of intense concentration, a testament to his deepening obsession with the case.

He shuffled through the old files, his fingers brushing over photographs of the crime scene from ten years prior, his younger self looking back at him from the images, full of determination and yet unaware of the complexities that would

CHAPTER TWENTY-THREE

unravel over time.

Having returned from Jürgen Schmidt's residence with the Kiton suit but without finding the Testoni shoes, George knew their work was far from over. In the tech room, he briefed Detective Sergeant Joshua Fry, head of the tech team, on their next crucial task.

"Josh, we didn't find the Testoni shoes at Schmidt's, but we need to keep pushing on this lead," George said, his tone underscored by the urgency of their mission.

Fry nodded, his eyes already scanning through the database on his computer. "We'll cross-reference the unique dye in the Kiton suit fibres and the wear pattern of the Testoni shoes with purchase records. I'll also reach out to luxury retailers for any sales data."

"Focus on our list of suspects and those influential figures we've identified," George added. "If there's a match, it could be the break we need."

The tech room buzzed into action as Fry and his team began their meticulous work. Cross-referencing such specific details required both precision and creativity, sifting through mountains of data to find the needle in the haystack.

Meanwhile, George stepped aside to make a call. "Keep me updated, Josh. Every bit of information could be critical," he said before leaving the room and returning to the Incident Room.

The clock on the wall ticked steadily, marking the passing of time, but for George, it seemed to stand still. He was lost in a world of connections, theories, and haunting memories. The room around him was a testament to his dedication—coffee cups littered his desk, case notes were strewn about, and the glow from his computer screen cast a pale light on his face.

***

In the bustling Leeds city centre, the festive spirit was in full swing. With there being only seven shopping days until the big day, the Christmas market was a hive of activity, with twinkling lights and the aroma of mulled wine and roasted chestnuts filling the air.

Detective Constable Candy Nichols walked through the crowded aisles of a quaint book shop, her eyes scanning the shelves lined with an array of novels. Her task was to choose the perfect book for a team member who cherished literature. Her brow furrowed in concentration, and she carefully considered each title, reflecting the thoughtfulness she put into her Secret Santa gift.

Elsewhere, Detective Constable Jay Scott found himself in a modern gadget shop, a stark contrast to the old-world charm of the book shop. The shelves were filled with the latest tech wonders—quirky gadgets, innovative tools, and electronic gizmos. Jay's face lit up with excitement as he explored each section, his mind working to pick a gift that was both fun and functional. He wanted to find something that would bring a smile to his colleague's face, something that spoke of his understanding of their personality.

In another part of the city, Detective Constable Tashan Blackburn browsed through a sports store. He moved with purpose, his eyes searching for something special. Tashan knew his Secret Santa recipient was a fitness enthusiast, and he was determined to find a gift that would be both practical and appreciated. He paused at a display of high-quality running accessories, weighing his options, his choice reflective of his thoughtful nature.

CHAPTER TWENTY-THREE

Back at the police station, Detective Sergeant Yolanda Williams was in her element, crafting a handmade gift in the break room. Her fingers moved skilfully as she assembled materials, creating something unique and personal. It was a testament to her creativity and the care she put into her gift, a reflection of the camaraderie and respect within the team.

As the team members went about their Secret Santa preparations, there was an air of light-heartedness, a welcome respite from the intensity of their work. Each gift was chosen with care and consideration, a small but meaningful gesture of appreciation and understanding among colleagues.

* * *

In the Incident Room of Elland Road Police Station, the team gathered around as Detective Inspector George Beaumont prepared to brief them on the latest development in the Santa Claus murders case. The room was filled with a mix of anticipation and focus, each member ready to play their part in the intricate dance of investigation.

"Alright, everyone, listen up," George began, his tone commanding the room's attention. "We've made some headway, but there's still a lot of ground to cover."

He paused, ensuring he had everyone's full attention. "I've tasked Sergeant Joshua Fry and his tech team with a crucial job. They're cross-referencing the unique dye found in the Kiton suit fibres and the distinct wear pattern of the Testoni shoes with purchase records. This is a meticulous task involving liaising with luxury retailers and cross-checking these details against our list of suspects and influential individuals."

The team nodded, understanding the significance of this

task. Forensic evidence had narrowed their search, and now it was a matter of connecting the dots.

George continued, "We're focusing on transactions that match the criteria we've established from the forensic analysis. This is a delicate thread, but if we follow it carefully, it could lead us directly to our killer."

Detective Sergeant Yolanda Williams, a seasoned member of the team, spoke up. "Are we looking at any specific time frame for these transactions, sir?"

"Focus on the months leading up to the first murder," George replied. "Any purchase made during that period could be crucial."

Detective Constable Jay Scott, who had been part of the team that discovered the Kiton suit at Jürgen Schmidt's residence, added, "And we're cross-referencing these details with the suspects' financial records and known whereabouts, right?"

"Exactly, Jay," George confirmed. "We need to establish a clear connection between our suspects and the evidence. Every piece of information is vital."

The room buzzed with renewed determination. This was the kind of lead they had been waiting for—tangible, actionable, and potentially pivotal.

"As always, discretion is key," George reminded them. "We're dealing with influential figures, so we need to tread carefully. But remember, no one is above the law, and our priority is to bring the killer to justice."

The briefing concluded with a clear sense of purpose. Each team member knew their role and the part they played in the larger scheme of the investigation.

***

CHAPTER TWENTY-THREE

As the hours passed, Fry and his team worked tirelessly. The screens in the tech room glowed with streams of data – bank transactions, purchase histories, and customer profiles from luxury retailers. The team methodically checked each detail against their list of suspects and influential individuals.

Fry's eyes were fixed on his screen when a pattern started to emerge. "Got something here," he called out, his voice cutting through the focused silence. "There's a purchase of Testoni shoes that matches our criteria, and it's linked to one of the individuals from our list."

The team gathered around Fry's desk, their attention riveted on the screen. The evidence was compelling but not conclusive – yet it was a significant lead that warranted further investigation.

"Good work, Josh," George's voice came through the phone. Fry relayed the information to him, explaining the intricacies of the match they had found.

"We're on it, sir," Fry concluded, his team already diving back into their work, energised by the lead.

* * *

With the identity of the individual linked to the purchase of the Testoni shoes now revealed as Elias Marston, Detective Inspector George Beaumont called his team together for an urgent briefing. The atmosphere was thick with anticipation as George revealed the latest breakthrough.

"We've had a significant development," George announced, his voice steady but charged with the gravity of the news. "The Testoni shoes we've been tracking have been linked to Elias Marston."

A murmur of surprise rippled through the room. Elias Marston, a name that carried weight and complexity in the context of their investigation, was now at the forefront.

Detective Constable Jay Scott spoke up, his expression a mix of intrigue and concern. "Elias Marston? That's a major lead. What's our next move?"

George looked around the room, his gaze meeting each team member's eyes. "We proceed with caution. Marston is influential and well-connected. This requires a strategic approach."

Detective Sergeant Yolanda Williams, her experience evident in her composed demeanour, added, "We'll need to re-examine his background, look for any connections to the victims or the events we've been investigating."

George nodded in agreement. "Exactly, Yolanda. We also need to verify his alibi for the dates of the murders. If there's a crack in his story, we need to find it."

"I'll start with Marston's financial records, affiliations, and social calendar," Yolanda said. "We need to map out where he was and who he was with, especially on the dates of the murders."

The team sprang into action, diving into databases, financial records, and social media accounts. They traced Marston's movements, pieced together his interactions, and scrutinized his connections.

Meanwhile, Detective Constable Jay Scott focused on verifying Marston's alibi for the murder dates. He liaised with officers who had initially taken Marston's statements, cross-checking them against other sources. "We're looking for inconsistencies, overlaps, anything that doesn't add up," Jay explained as he poured over the records.

CHAPTER TWENTY-THREE

George observed his team, his mind racing with the implications of their findings. Marston's world was a tapestry of influence and affluence, each thread weaving a complex narrative. As the team sifted through the data, patterns began to emerge.

Yolanda called out from her workstation, "Sir, Marston's financials are revealing. There are large, unexplained transactions around the dates of the murders. And his social calendar places him at events with several of our victims."

Jay looked up from his notes. "His alibi for two of the murder dates is shaky. Witnesses place him in locations different from what he claimed."

George leaned in, examining the evidence. "Good work. This is what we need. We're building a picture here, and it's not looking good for Marston."

The hours ticked by as the team continued their meticulous work. They mapped out Marston's life in the weeks and months leading up to the murders, constructing a timeline that began to align ominously with the sequence of events they were investigating.

As the night deepened, George remained at his desk, piecing together the emerging picture of Elias Marston. His connections to the victims, his presence at key events, and the cracks in his alibi—all pointed towards something sinister.

"Sir," Yolanda approached George's desk, her expression serious. "Marston's world intersects with our victims more than we initially thought. And there are rumours, whispers of something darker beneath his polished surface."

George nodded, his thoughts aligning with Yolanda's findings. "We're on the right track. Marston is at the heart of this; I can feel it. But we need concrete evidence."

Later and in the seclusion of his office, George sat alone, the room illuminated only by the glow of his desk lamp. The case files of the Santa Claus murders lay spread out before him, a tangible representation of the complexity and weight of the investigation.

George leaned back in his chair, his eyes drifting over the documents, but his mind was elsewhere. The potential involvement of Elias Marston, an associate of his estranged father, Edward Beaumont, added a deeply personal dimension to the case. It was a connection that could not be ignored, yet it put George in an incredibly precarious position.

With a heavy sigh, George contemplated the dilemma that faced him. He knew that disclosing this connection to DCI Alistair Atkinson was the right thing to do, the procedural approach that any diligent officer would follow. Yet, he also knew it would likely lead to his removal from the case. His personal ties to Marston, however indirect, could be seen as a conflict of interest.

George's sense of duty warred with his desire to see the investigation through to the end. He had led the team this far, unravelling threads of deceit and corruption, and the thought of stepping back now, just as they were closing in on the truth, was almost unbearable.

He thought about the victims and their families, their lives forever altered by the heinous acts of an elusive murderer. They deserved justice, and George had promised himself that he would be the one to deliver it. But could he continue to lead this case with the shadow of his father looming over him?

The clock on his wall ticked steadily, marking the passage of time and the urgency of the decision before him. George knew that every moment of hesitation was a moment lost in

CHAPTER TWENTY-THREE

the pursuit of the killer.

With a deep breath, George stood up and walked over to the window, gazing out into the night. The city of Leeds lay before him, its streets a maze of light and shadow. He thought about his career, built on the principles of integrity and justice, and the sacrifices he had made along the way.

Finally, with the weight of the decision heavy on his shoulders, George turned back to his desk.

Chapter Twenty-four

In the shared office, the mood was a stark contrast to the usual high-tension environment. Christmas decorations adorned the walls and desks, and a tree decked with twinkling lights and tinsel stood proudly in the corner. The atmosphere was warm and inviting—a rare moment of respite for the hard-working team.

Detective Inspector George Beaumont found himself among his colleagues, including Jay Scott and Candy Nichols, who were in high spirits. Their laughter filled the room, mixing with the soft strains of Christmas music playing in the background. George, usually reserved and focused, seemed more relaxed, his demeanour softened by the festive cheer.

As the evening wore on, the group began sharing stories from past cases and personal experiences. Each tale was met with laughter or gasps of surprise, adding to the camaraderie that had been forged through years of working together. Jay's recounting of a peculiar case involving a runaway parrot had everyone in stitches, while Candy's story of her first day on the job reminded them of the lighter side of police work.

George listened intently, his eyes twinkling with amusement at the anecdotes. He occasionally chimed in with a comment, his dry wit eliciting chuckles from his colleagues.

CHAPTER TWENTY-FOUR

It was rare to see him so at ease, a side of him that few got to witness.

The atmosphere was a pleasant change from the daily grind and the current case that weighed heavily on their minds. For a few hours, they could forget the stress and dangers of their job, basking in the joy of the holiday season and the comfort of good company.

George looked around at his team, a sense of pride filling him. They were more than just colleagues; they were a family, each with their own quirks and strengths. In that room, they were united not just by their profession but by the shared experiences that had bonded them.

He smiled as Jay launched into another story, this one about a misadventure during a stakeout. The laughter that followed was genuine, a sound that filled George with a sense of belonging. It was moments like these that reminded him why he did what he did—why they all did. Amidst the laughter and storytelling, there was a sense of purpose and a commitment to making a difference.

In the midst of the festive atmosphere, an innocuous phrase uttered by one of his colleagues jokingly about someone's hidden talent—"You know, it's always the one you least suspect."—snagged George's attention, tugging him back to a memory he'd long buried. The laughter around him dimmed as the gears in his mind clicked, retracing steps down a path he had not walked in years. His expression, usually so guarded and controlled, wavered, revealing a fleeting glimpse of nostalgia mixed with a deeper, more complex emotion— perhaps a touch of regret or unresolved pain.

George's eyes lost their focus on the present, staring into a distance only he could see. The room's joviality continued unabated around him, but he was no longer part of it. He leaned back in his chair, his fingers tapping a silent rhythm on the table as he delved into the recesses of his mind.

There was a subtle shift of emotion. There was a softening around George's eyes as he revisited a particular case from his past, a case that had left an indelible mark on him, both professionally and personally. It was a case that had taught him hard lessons, shaped his approach to detective work, and perhaps even altered the course of his life.

In his mind's eye, George was back on those rain-drenched streets, the neon lights of Leeds flickering in the night, casting long shadows. He remembered the weight of the responsibility he had felt then, young and eager to prove himself. The case had been complex, fraught with moral ambiguities and difficult decisions. It had been his first brush with the darker undercurrents of the city and the human psyche.

There was a particular moment that stood out, a turning point where his decision had set the trajectory for the rest of the investigation. He recalled the faces of the people involved, the victims and the suspects, their lives intertwining with his in ways he hadn't foreseen. There was one decision, one critical choice, that had stayed with him all these years. It was a moment of moral compromise, a grey area where the lines between right and wrong had blurred.

As he sat there, lost in his thoughts, the laughter and chatter around him became a distant murmur. He was grappling with the ghosts of the past, the what-ifs, and the consequences of his actions. It was a rare glimpse into the inner workings of George Beaumont, a man who had built his career on logic and evidence yet was not immune to the emotional toll of his work.

CHAPTER TWENTY-FOUR

Candy Nichols was the first to notice the subtle shift in George's demeanour. The others caught up in the festive cheer, hadn't picked up on the fleeting shadow that had crossed his face, but Candy had. She moved towards him, her approach quiet and unobtrusive.

"Sir," she said softly, drawing him away from the group into a quieter corner of the room. Her voice was low, laced with genuine concern. "Is everything alright?"

George looked at her, a momentary hesitation in his eyes before he nodded slowly. It wasn't his usual assertive, confident nod, but one filled with a quiet introspection. He seemed to weigh his words, a rarity for a man who usually had a firm grip on his thoughts and emotions.

"It's just old memories," George finally admitted, his voice a mere whisper, almost lost in the hum of the celebration around them. "Sometimes they come back uninvited."

Candy, who had always admired George for his stoicism and professionalism, saw a different side of him in that instant. It was a glimpse into the vulnerability that he kept so well guarded.

"Is it about the case from a decade ago?" Candy ventured, recalling the snippets of overheard conversations and pieced-together information. George had always been tight-lipped about his past cases, especially the ones that had left a deeper mark.

George hesitated but nodded his head. Ten years ago, a young George Beaumont, fresh-faced and eager, had been told something strikingly similar during that complex case. "In our line of work, George, it's always the one you least suspect. Remember that."

The memory sparked a train of thought, a thread in the

complex tapestry of the current investigation. Dr Ross, a figure so integral to their process, so trusted and respected, had subtly steered the conversation about the murders on more than one occasion. George had taken it as professional insight, but now, he wondered if there was more to it.

Could the man who had taught him to look beyond the obvious be himself the one they should have been scrutinising all along? The irony of the situation was not lost on George. The pathologist he had looked up to might be the key to unlocking the case.

The festive atmosphere in the room continued, but George was no longer present in the celebrations. His mind was racing, piecing together conversations, revisiting crime scenes, and re-evaluating evidence with a new perspective.

Candy watched her expression, a mixture of surprise and understanding. She had always known there was more to George than met the eye, layers and complexities that he seldom revealed.

George's thoughts circled back to Dr Ross. The idea seemed almost ludicrous at first. Dr Ross, the pathologist who had been a fixture in their investigations for years, was old and meagre, a far cry from the profile they had constructed for the Santa Claus murderer. They were looking for someone middle-aged, strong, and capable of committing violent acts. Dr Ross didn't fit that description; he was an academic, a man of science, not brute force.

But George's training as a detective had taught him that appearances could be deceptive, and assumptions often led to dead ends. He pondered the possibility, no matter how improbable it seemed. Could Dr Ross have orchestrated these crimes? Was it possible that they had overlooked him simply because he didn't fit their preconceived notions of a killer?

George pulled out the autopsy reports and crime scene photos once more, scanning them with a fresh perspective. He considered Dr Ross' access to the victims, his knowledge of forensic science, and how that could be exploited to mislead an investigation. The more George thought about it, the more he realized that physical strength wasn't the only way to overpower someone – intellectual cunning and manipulation could be just as potent.

After a while, George shook off the remnants of the memory, returning his focus to the present. The emotional journey was hidden away once more behind his professional façade. He forced a smile, rejoining the conversation, but the echo of Dr Ross possibly being the killer lingered in his mind.

And try as he might, he couldn't keep his mind off the pathologist, despite DC Scott's continued attempts at telling ridiculous stories of his time on the beat.

Finally, as the night came to a close, George stood for a moment, looking at the team he had come to respect and care for. This was more than just a Christmas celebration; it was a reminder of the humanity and warmth that existed even in the toughest of professions.

The festive lights of the HMET's Christmas tree cast a soft, warm glow across the room, but the laughter and chatter that had filled the space only moments ago had dwindled to a serene quiet. One by one, Detective Inspector George Beaumont's team members had left, their cheerful "Merry Christmas" greetings still echoing faintly in the air.

George stood there for a moment longer, his gaze lingering on the now-empty chairs and the remnants of the evening's celebration. The festive decorations seemed to contrast starkly with the pensive expression on his face. In the silence, the weight of the case, the burdens of his past, and the complexities of his present converged, leaving him enveloped in a cocoon of thought.

As he turned off the lights, the room plunged into semi-darkness, the shadows seeming to stretch and dance in the dim light from the corridor. George paused at the door, his silhouette framed against the backdrop of the festive lights. He glanced back, his eyes tracing the room's familiar contours, each corner holding memories of cases solved, challenges faced, and the relentless pursuit of justice that had defined his career.

Stepping out of the office, George walked through the empty shared office space and into the Incident Room, his footsteps echoing in the stillness. The station, usually abuzz with activity, was quiet as if respecting his need for solitude. Each step he took seemed to carry the weight of his thoughts, his mind obsessing over the Dr Ross.

He remembered the moment Detective Constable Tashan Blackburn had brought to his attention the missing light source results from the postmortem reports. It was an anomaly that had seemed minor at the time, easily dismissed as an oversight.

But now, in the context of his growing suspicions about Dr Ross, this detail assumed a new significance. Dr Ross had deflected the blame onto his assistant when confronted about the omission. At the time, George had accepted the explanation; such errors were not unheard of in the high-pressure environment of forensic pathology. But the memory now nagged at him, a piece of a puzzle he hadn't realized he was assembling.

CHAPTER TWENTY-FOUR

Why would light source results, typically standard in autopsies, especially in murder cases, be missing? And why was Dr Ross so quick to blame his assistant? Was it a genuine mistake or something more calculated? The more George pondered these questions, the more he felt a sense of unease.

He thought about Dr Ross' demeanour during their interactions. The pathologist had always been professional, yet there was an air of detachment about him, a sense that he was always holding something back. Could it be that Dr Ross had purposefully omitted the light source results to manipulate the investigation's direction?

George knew the implications of what he was considering. Accusing a respected pathologist of tampering with evidence and possibly being involved in the murders was a serious allegation. He needed to be absolutely sure before taking any action.

Chapter Twenty-five

Lindsey Yardley, the Scene of Crime Manager, sat in the forensic lab, her eyes fixed on the results displayed on the computer screen. The late hours of the night had given way to the early hues of dawn, but the lab was still a hive of activity. She had been meticulously re-examining the evidence collected from the bindings used on the Santa Claus murder victims, determined to find something the killer might have overlooked.

Then, there it was—a breakthrough. A tiny trace of DNA, almost imperceptible, yet significant enough to alter the course of the investigation. Lindsey's heart raced as the DNA analysis revealed a match to evidence left behind a decade ago in a case that had haunted the West Yorkshire Police for years.

Without hesitation, she picked up the phone to call Detective Inspector George Beaumont. It was critical information that couldn't wait.

Meanwhile, in the cluttered, festive ambience of Leeds city centre gift shop that Tuesday, Detective Inspector George Beaumont stood, his tall frame slightly hunched as he contemplated two items in his hands. One was a sleek, modern-looking pen, its surface glinting under the shop's bright lights. The other, a book of classic detective stories, its cover worn

CHAPTER TWENTY-FIVE

with a vintage charm. Each object seemed to tell a story, and George was caught in the midst of deciding which story he wanted to share.

His brow furrowed in concentration, and George turned each item over in his hands. It wasn't just a gift; it was a symbol, a small gesture that spoke volumes in the language of unspoken police camaraderie. He wanted it to be perfect, to reflect his understanding and appreciation for his colleague, someone who had become more than just a part of his team.

As he weighed his options, his phone vibrated in his pocket, breaking his concentration. He glanced at the screen, seeing Lindsey Yardley's name flashing. His heart rate quickened slightly; calls from Lindsey were rarely without urgency.

"Hi, Lindsey," he answered, his voice steady despite the sudden shift in his focus.

"Hi, George," she said as soon as he answered, her voice a blend of excitement and gravity. "I've found something you need to see. There's a DNA match on the bindings from our current victims. It matches evidence from the unsolved cases a decade ago."

George's response was immediate, a mix of urgency and shock. "Are you sure, Lindsey?"

"Absolutely," she affirmed. "This isn't a coincidence. It links the current murders to those unsolved cases. We're looking at the same perpetrator, George."

The implications of Lindsey's discovery were profound. This DNA link provided a tangible connection between the past and present, suggesting that the Santa Claus murderer had been operating for far longer than they had realized.

George's gaze shifted from the items in his hand to a distant point, his detective instincts kicking in. "Great work, Lindsey.

I'll be right over," George said, his mind already racing with the new possibilities this revelation opened up.

As he placed the book of detective stories on the counter, a shop assistant approached him with a polite smile. "Just this?"

George offered a small, absent smile. "Aye," he said, his mind already racing with the possibilities of what Lindsey had discovered.

The assistant put through the purchase, and George tapped his card, his movements automatic. He thanked the assistant, his thoughts already miles away, at the lab with Lindsey, piecing together the new evidence.

As he left the shop, the festive lights and holiday cheer faded into the background, replaced by the weight of the case that was consuming his every waking moment. He clutched the small, neatly wrapped package in his hand, a tangible representation of the care he held for his team amidst the chaos of their work.

In his car, George's thoughts were a whirlwind of possibilities and connections. What had Lindsey found? How would it alter the course of their investigation? The streets of Leeds passed by in a blur as he drove, his mind focused, his determination renewed.

* * *

In the early hours of a chilly Leeds morning, Detective Inspector George Beaumont entered the forensic lab, a place where cold facts often revealed chilling realities. The lab, awash in the harsh light of fluorescents, felt more like an antechamber to hidden truths. Lindsey Yardley, the Scene of

CHAPTER TWENTY-FIVE

Crime Manager, stood amidst a sea of reports and screens, her expression a blend of professionalism and urgency.

"George," Lindsey greeted, her voice tinged with the gravitas of their grim task. She handed him the DNA reports, her eyes betraying the significance of what they contained.

George took the reports, his fingers brushing against the crisp paper as if touching the very essence of the investigation. The DNA results stared back at him, stark against the white background. Three tiny but definitive DNA profiles were found on each victim—a silent yet screaming testament to the killer's presence.

"It's a match across all the victims," Lindsey said, breaking the heavy silence. "But the DNA isn't in the national database. We have no direct match for a suspect."

George's jaw tightened. This was both a breakthrough and a setback. The matching DNA confirmed a crucial piece of the puzzle, yet the lack of a database match meant the killer remained a ghost in the system.

"This confirms it, though," George mused, his mind racing. "The killer from a decade ago is the same as now. We're dealing with someone who's been evading us for years."

Lindsey nodded, her demeanour reflecting the mix of frustration and determination that gripped them both.

George's eyes scanned the reports again, each line of data a potential clue, each finding a possible key to unlocking the murderer's identity. "We need to widen our net," he declared. "Re-examine old leads and cross-check with any partials we have on other databases. Someone, somewhere, must know something."

The room around them felt charged with the tension of their findings. This was a critical junction in their investigation, one that could either propel them forward or leave them grappling in the dark.

"I'll have my team go over everything again, see if we missed anything in the initial analyses," Lindsey affirmed, her resolve mirroring George's.

George gave a curt nod, his mind already outlining their next steps. As he left the lab, the corridors of the police station seemed to echo with the weight of their discovery. The same killer, a decade apart—it was a revelation that cast a long, ominous shadow over the case.

As Detective Inspector George Beaumont ascended the stairs to the Incident Room, his mind churned with the implications of the DNA breakthrough.

The revelation of the DNA link to the decade-old cases had been a seismic shift in the investigation. Still, as he walked, a realisation dawned on him, offering a moment of unexpected clarity. The DNA profile they had uncovered—it couldn't belong to Dr Christian Ross, the pathologist who had been under a cloud of suspicion in George's mind.

A sigh of relief escaped George's lips, unbidden. He remembered the Contamination Elimination Database (CED), a crucial tool in forensic science used to prevent and identify contamination in DNA evidence. As a pathologist, Dr Ross' DNA profile would undoubtedly be registered in the CED. Any accidental contamination he might have caused at a crime scene would have been flagged during the forensic analysis.

This realisation was a weight off George's shoulders. The prospect of suspecting Dr Ross, a colleague and mentor, had been a deeply uncomfortable one. George had always valued the camaraderie and trust within their ranks, and the thought of pointing fingers at one of their own was disheartening.

CHAPTER TWENTY-FIVE

With this new perspective, George reached the top of the stairs, feeling a renewed sense of focus. The true perpetrator was still out there, but at least he could cross Dr Ross off the list of suspects. This was more than just a professional relief; it was a personal one as well.

But then he remembered that being on the CED was voluntary, and it was possible Dr Ross had been on it when it was compulsory but asked to be removed when it became voluntary.

He pulled out his phone, wanting to be sure.

The phone rang twice before Dr Ross' familiar, calm voice answered. "George, my boy, how are you?"

"I'm well, Christian. Hope I'm not interrupting anything."

"Not at all, son. What can I do for you?"

"I just wanted to clear the air about something. I've been thinking about the DNA evidence from the recent cases and its link to the old ones."

There was a brief pause on the line, an unspoken understanding of the delicate topic. "Go on," Dr Ross encouraged.

"Well, we have some unknown DNA, and I was wondering about the Contamination Elimination Database," George began. "Officers and pathologists, a decade ago, would have been on it, right?" He paused. "Mine is on it, and it occurred to me that your DNA would be on, considering your role as a pathologist," George said, his tone respectful yet straightforward.

"Ah, yes, the CED," Dr Ross replied, a hint of relief in his voice. "That's correct. My DNA, along with that of all pathologists and forensic personnel, is registered to prevent misinterpretation of evidence. It's a crucial safeguard in our line of work."

"I thought as much," said George. "I wasn't sure whether it was voluntary or compulsory."

"It's very much voluntary, my boy, but I wouldn't be able to do my job as effectively if I weren't on the database," Dr Ross replied, his tone warm yet professional.

"Indeed," George agreed, then shifted the topic. "Actually, while I have you on the line, there's something else. We're organizing a charity event at Elland Road next month. It's a small gathering, but it's for a good cause, supporting local youth programs. I thought you might like to join us."

Dr Ross' response was immediate and enthusiastic. "That sounds wonderful, George. Count me in. It's always good to step away from the lab and contribute to the community in other ways."

"Christian, before I let you go, do you need me to add a plus one to the guest list? A partner or a girlfriend, perhaps?" George asked, his tone casual yet considerate.

There was a momentary pause on the other end of the line. When Dr Ross spoke, his voice carried a hint of something George couldn't quite place—was it hesitation? Regret?

"No, no need for that, George," Dr Ross responded, his voice slightly lower than before. "I haven't had a girlfriend for quite some time. My work tends to consume most of my time, and well, at my age, such prospects seem increasingly distant."

George sensed the subtle change in Dr Ross' demeanour. The pathologist's words were tinged with an inevitable resignation, a hint of personal revelation that they seldom shared in their professional interactions.

"I understand, Christian. Work does have a way of taking over," George replied, his tone empathetic. "But who knows, these kinds of events can be surprising. It's always good to

CHAPTER TWENTY-FIVE

mingle and meet new people."

"Yes, you're quite right, George. And I do look forward to the event. It's important to step away from the lab and engage with the community," Dr Ross replied, a hint of warmth returning to his voice.

"Absolutely. I'll send the details over soon. And Christian, thank you again for the chat," George said, preparing to end the call.

"It was my pleasure, George. And thank you for the invitation. I'll see you there," Dr Ross replied.

As George rang off, he continued towards the stairwell, lost in thought for a moment. The brief conversation had offered a glimpse into Dr Ross' personal life, a side of the pathologist that rarely came to light amidst the demands of their rigorous work. It was a reminder that behind the professional facades they all maintained, there were personal stories, struggles, and sacrifices.

The conversation with Dr Ross had not only reaffirmed his exclusion from the suspect list but also reinforced the bonds of trust and respect within their professional community.

Arriving at the Incident Room with a skip in his step, George found his team weary but unwavering. They looked up as he entered, their expressions a mix of expectation and apprehension.

"We have a match on the DNA from the murder scenes," he announced, his voice carrying the burden of their task. "But there's no match in the National DNA Database. But it's clear we're dealing with the same killer from ten years ago."

A murmur rippled through the room. This was the moment they had been both dreading and anticipating. The realisation that their adversary was not a newcomer but a seasoned predator added a new layer of complexity to their hunt.

"We revisit everything," George continued, his tone commanding. "Old case files, witness statements, anything that can give us a lead. We're not just solving a series of murders; we're ending a decade of terror."

The team nodded, their fatigue momentarily forgotten in the face of renewed purpose. They understood the magnitude of their mission. It was more than a case; it was a quest for closure, for justice.

A knock on the Incident Room door distracted the detectives from their work. Desk Sergeant Samantha Green entered and handed Detective Constable Tashan Blackburn a package that was wrapped neatly with a touch of personal care.

His name was scrawled across it in familiar handwriting, bringing an unexpected smile to his usually composed face. His colleagues, busy with their tasks, paused to observe the unusual scene.

"Looks like someone's got a fan," quipped Detective Constable Jay Scott, casting a teasing glance towards Tashan.

Tashan, usually stoic and focused, blushed slightly, a rare occurrence that didn't go unnoticed. "It's just something from home," he replied, trying to downplay his obvious curiosity and excitement.

Detective Inspector George Beaumont, who had been deeply engrossed in case files, looked up with a hint of amusement in his eyes. "Well, don't keep us in suspense, Tashan. Let's see what's got you all flustered."

Encouraged by his colleagues' interest, Tashan carefully opened the package. Inside, he found a collection of personal items: his favourite snack—a bag of home-made trail mix, a heartfelt note scribbled in his partner's distinctive handwriting, and a small keepsake—a key ring they had bought together on a holiday.

As Tashan read the note, a soft smile played on his lips. The words were simple but full of affection, a reminder of the life outside the demanding world of police work. The note spoke of support and understanding, acknowledging the challenges Tashan faced and the strength he showed.

The atmosphere in the room shifted as Tashan's colleagues witnessed this personal moment. There was a collective softening, a shared understanding of the importance of having someone in your corner, especially in a job as demanding as theirs.

George, observing the scene, felt a pang of nostalgia. It reminded him of the early days of his career, the simple joys and support that helped him through tough times. "Looks like you've got a good one there, Tashan," he said, a genuine warmth in his voice.

Tashan looked up, meeting George's gaze. "Yeah, I do," he replied, his voice tinged with gratitude. "Makes all the difference."

The moment was brief but meaningful. It was a rare glimpse into the personal lives of the team, a reminder that behind the warrant cards and titles were individuals with lives, loves, and connections that kept them grounded.

The teasing resumed, light and good-natured, as Tashan's colleagues ribbed him about his partner's thoughtfulness. Tashan took it in stride, his earlier reserve replaced by a sense of belonging and camaraderie.

As they returned to their tasks, the mood in the room was lighter, a brief respite from the gravity of their work. Tashan carefully placed the note and the keepsake on his desk, a tangible reminder of the support waiting for him at home.

George watched his team resume their work and saw that for Tashan, the care package was a source of renewed energy and motivation. But George also felt buoyed by his own personal anchor, reminding him of why he did what he did.

It also reminded him of what he had to lose.

* * *

George continued to pour over the old case files. Years of dust and memories clung to these pages, each one a reminder of a case that had haunted him for a decade. His eyes, sharpened by years of experience, scanned the documents with a renewed intensity, searching for the elusive thread that might connect the past to the present.

As the clock ticked away, the silence of the night was his only companion, save for the occasional rustle of paper. George's mind, a labyrinth of facts and theories, worked tirelessly, piecing together fragments of information that had once seemed irrelevant. It was a painstaking process, but George was undeterred, driven by a deep-seated need for justice and closure.

Then, amidst the sea of data, something caught his eye—a minor detail in the old case files that he had never given much thought. It was small and seemingly insignificant.

George's heart quickened as he realised the significance of this discovery. He looked at Oliver Hughes' victimology report, which reported no next of kin, meaning no parents or siblings.

Yet there, in black and white, was a reference to Jonathan Hughes, or Jonny as Ethan Turner had referred to him in his original statement a decade ago. It was a clue that had been

CHAPTER TWENTY-FIVE

hiding in plain sight, overlooked in the chaos of the initial investigation.

For a moment, George sat frozen, the weight of this revelation sinking in. This discovery didn't just bring him closer to solving the case; it also meant that he was treading dangerous ground. Oliver having a brother was more than just a clue; they now had a solid motive.

The realisation sent a chill down George's spine.

As he grappled with the implications of his discovery, George's mind raced with possibilities. Could finding Jonny Hughes mean finding the killer? Or by finding Jonny, could they find something more, a clue to a larger, more sinister plot?

George's thoughts were interrupted by a sudden noise outside his office—a reminder that he was not alone in the building. The sound was a jarring contrast to the quiet contemplation of the last few hours, pulling him back to the present.

And when the DI saw the time, he panicked.

With a deep breath, George gathered the files, his resolve hardening. He knew what he had to do next. The discovery was too significant to ignore, and he couldn't let personal fears stand in the way of justice.

But he had something else to do, something more important.

Chapter Twenty-six

George raced through the streets of Leeds, his heart pounding in his chest as he made his way towards Middleton St Mary's Church. The sharp mid-afternoon chill bit through his coat as he exited his car, but he barely noticed, his mind consumed by a singular goal. He could hear the distant toll of church bells, a melancholy melody that seemed to quicken his steps.

As he approached the church, his breaths came in short, sharp bursts, visible in the cold air. The old stone building stood majestically against the darkening sky, its windows glowing warmly. But George's expression was one of trepidation, a stark contrast to the serenity of the scene before him.

The sound of the final bell chimed, resonating through the quiet street, and George felt a pang of urgency. He had to make it in time. The importance of this evening wasn't lost on him; it was more than just an event; it was a promise, a commitment he'd made.

Bursting through the church doors, George's eyes scanned the interior, searching for the one face he hoped to see. But what greeted him was a scene of dispersing families, children in colourful costumes chattering excitedly about their performances, parents offering congratulations and snapping pictures. The play had concluded, and the actors were taking their final bows.

George's gaze swept over the dispersing crowd at Middleton St Mary's Church, a sense of urgency etching lines across his forehead. He was looking for two specific faces in the sea of people—Mia, his ex, and Jack, his son. The festive lights of the church hall cast a warm glow on the faces around him, but George's eyes were clouded with a growing sense of frustration and guilt.

He moved through the crowd, his tall frame weaving past families wrapped in the joy of the evening. Each step he took was heavy, laden with the weight of his own shortcomings. Every face that wasn't Mia's or Jack's deepened the furrow in his brow. They were nowhere to be found.

With a growing sense of helplessness, George stepped outside into the cold evening air. He pulled out his phone, his fingers fumbling slightly as he dialled Mia's number. The phone rang, each tone echoing in his ear, amplifying his anxiety. But there was no answer, just the hollow sound of the call diverting to voicemail.

He hesitated for a moment before speaking, his voice strained with emotion. "Mia, it's George. I... I'm sorry I missed the play. Something came up at work, and I couldn't get away." He paused, searching for the right words. "I know it's not the first time, and I'm sorry. I really wanted to be there for Jack."

His words felt inadequate, even to his own ears. Hanging up, George leaned against the cold stone wall of the church, the festive lights from within casting long shadows around him. He closed his eyes, a mix of regret and exhaustion washing over him.

The sounds of the evening—the laughter of children, the chatter of families—seemed distant, as if he were removed from the world around him. His mind drifted to Jack, the son he loved but too often failed to show up for. He thought of the milestones missed, the promises broken, the growing gap between them that his job had widened.

George's steps echoed on the pavement as he walked away from Middleton St Mary's Church, the lively sounds of the play's aftermath gradually fading into the background. He moved slowly, each step measured and heavy, a physical manifestation of the weight of his thoughts. There was sadness etched in the lines around his eyes and the downward turn of his mouth.

The festive atmosphere, usually a source of joy and celebration, only served to highlight the stark contrast between George's inner world and the world around him. He felt like an outsider looking in, caught in a life that demanded too much and gave back too little in the moments that truly mattered.

His eyes, usually so keen and observant, now seemed distant, lost in thought. The cases he worked on and the crimes he solved were more than just a job; they were a calling. Yet, in pursuing that calling, George recognised the sacrifices he'd made, the moments missed, the time he could never reclaim with his son, Jack.

As he stood there, lost in his thoughts, a sense of determination slowly began to build within him. He couldn't change the past, but he could shape the future. It was a realisation that came with its own set of challenges, but George knew it was time to start making amends, to be there for Jack in ways he hadn't been before.

And not just for Jack, but for Olivia and Isabella, too.

CHAPTER TWENTY-SIX

As George walked towards his car, his pace steady but unhurried, the quiet of the evening enveloped him. The streets of Leeds, usually a source of constant stimulation for his detective's mind, now offered a backdrop for his introspection. He pondered the decisions he'd made, the roads taken and those left untravelled, each choice leading him to this moment of solitude.

He thought about Mia, her frustration and disappointment a mirror to his own, reflecting a shared history of broken promises and unmet expectations. And Jack, his son, who deserved a father present not just in duty but in love and attention. George's heart ached at the thought, a silent acknowledgement of his failings.

George Beaumont made a silent promise to himself. It was a promise to be present, to prioritise the things that truly mattered. It was a promise to find a balance, however difficult that might be. And with each step, the weight of his decision settled firmly on his shoulders, a reminder of the path he had chosen to take.

* * *

The evening was still and silent as Tashan Blackburn prepared for the video call, the glow of the laptop screen casting a soft light in the dim room. The clock on the wall showed it was evening in Leeds, but for his partner, it was just the beginning of the afternoon. This time difference, a reminder of the physical distance between them, had become a routine part of their lives.

Tashan positioned himself in front of the laptop, adjusting the angle to catch the best light. His face, usually so serious and focused at work, transformed as he pressed his mouse. There was an anticipation, a softening of his features, as he waited for the call to connect.

The moment the screen flickered to life, showing his partner's face, Tashan's expression brightened. A genuine smile spread across his face, reaching his eyes and lighting them up with a warmth rarely seen. This was a different Tashan, one who allowed himself to relax and be vulnerable, far from the composed detective at the Elland Road Police Station.

"Hey, Amara," Tashan greeted, his voice warm with affection.

"Hi, Tashan! How's Leeds tonight?" Amara asked, her face lighting up with a smile that mirrored his.

"Cold and quiet," Tashan replied, relaxing into his chair. "It's been a long day, but it's better now."

They slipped into their familiar routine, sharing stories of their day. Tashan spoke first, carefully choosing his words as he described the latest developments in the case. He avoided specifics, mindful of the confidentiality of his work, but Amara could read between the lines.

"It sounds like it's getting intense over there," Amara observed, concern evident in her voice.

Tashan nodded, running a hand through his hair. "Yeah, it's complicated. But we're making progress. Just wish I could tell you more."

"I understand, Tashan. Just take care of yourself, OK?" Amara's eyes conveyed the depth of her worry and affection. "I miss you, Tashan. This distance... it's not easy."

"I will, I promise," Tashan assured her, offering a reassuring smile. "And I know," he said softly. "I miss you too. More than you can imagine."

CHAPTER TWENTY-SIX

There was a pause, a moment of shared longing that transcended the digital divide. Then Tashan added, "But we're making it work, aren't we? And soon, we'll be together again."

Amara nodded, a small smile returning. "Yes, we are. You're doing important work there. I'm proud of you, Tashan."

The conversation shifted as Amara began sharing updates from back home. She spoke about her work, the small triumphs, and the everyday frustrations, her animated expressions bringing her stories to life. Tashan listened intently, laughing at her anecdotes and offering his own insights.

The ease and comfort between them were palpable, bridging the physical distance with a connection that was as strong as ever. They talked about mutual friends, the latest news, and the small, mundane details that formed the tapestry of their shared life.

As they spoke, the distance seemed to shrink, the digital divide rendered insignificant by the strength of their bond. They shared dreams and plans for the future, the conversation filled with hope and longing.

As the call neared its end, Amara held up a small object to the camera. "Look what arrived today," she said, showing a ticket. "I've booked my flight. I'll be there in a week."

Tashan's face broke into a wide grin, a look of pure joy that transformed his entire demeanour. "That's the best news I've heard in weeks," he said, his voice filled with excitement.

Tashan glanced at the clock, noting the hour. "I should let you go. It's—"

"Just a few more minutes," Amara pleaded, her smile coaxing.

Tashan couldn't resist. "OK, a few more minutes."

They continued talking, savouring these moments together,

until finally, Tashan sighed. "I really need to go; I've got that charity event at the station soon."

"I know. Good luck with everything, Tashan. And remember, I'm always here for you," Amara said, her voice soft but firm.

"Thanks, Amara. That means a lot," Tashan replied, his voice tinged with gratitude.

They said their goodbyes, promising to talk again soon. As the screen went dark, Tashan sat back, a contented sigh escaping him. The loneliness of his flat didn't seem so oppressive now; the promise of reunion filled the space with a soft glow of anticipation.

* * *

George Beaumont walked through the door to his home, his face etched with the day's burdens. Isabella looked up from where she was setting the table, her expression a mix of relief and concern.

"Hiya, handsome," she greeted, trying to infuse warmth into her voice. George offered a weary nod, his eyes distant.

"Dada!" Olivia's little voice rang out as she ran towards George, her arms wide for an embrace.

George's features softened momentarily as he bent down to scoop Olivia into his arms. "Hey, princess," he murmured, but the flicker of affection quickly faded, replaced by the faraway look that had become all too familiar.

Dinner was a silent affair. George picked at his food, his mind visibly elsewhere. Isabella watched him, her heart sinking at the sight. Olivia, sensing the tension, ate quietly, occasionally glancing at her father with a puzzled expression.

CHAPTER TWENTY-SIX

"George, you haven't said a word about your day," Isabella ventured, trying to pierce through his shell of concentration.

George looked up as if snapping out of a trance. "I'm sorry. I've just figured out something important, and I'm mulling it around."

Isabella reached across the table, placing her hand over his. "I know it's important, George, but you're missing out here... with us."

A pang of guilt hit him. "I know. And I'm going to do better. I promise."

Chapter Twenty-seven

In the quiet of their living room, with Olivia now asleep and the festive lights outside casting a soft glow, the atmosphere was ripe for an earnest conversation.

"George, talk to me," she began, her voice steady but laced with emotion.

George, his features haggard from the day's toll, sighed deeply. "Isabella, I really don't want to talk about the case right now." He paused. "Plus, I need to get ready for the charity event."

She shook her head gently. "It's not just the case, George. It's about us, our family. I'm worried about you... about us."

George reached out, covering her hands with his. "I'm sorry I've been shit recently." His eyes flickered with pain.

"Just tell me what's bothering you then," she pleaded.

"I missed Jack's play earlier," he admitted.

Isabella's heart ached at his admission. "Oh, I had no idea, I'm so sorry."

George looked up, his eyes meeting hers. "It's this addiction with work, and it's stopping. Right now!"

Isabella nodded. "George, how are the therapy sessions going?" she asked, her voice gentle yet laden with concern.

George shifted uncomfortably in his seat, avoiding her gaze.

CHAPTER TWENTY-SEVEN

"I... I stopped going, Isabella."

Isabella's heart sank. "Why? George, it would help if you talked to someone to manage all this stress and obsession. What you're doing to yourself is not healthy."

George shook his head, his jaw set. "I only had enough time to concentrate on work and family or do therapy." He paused. "And going to therapy won't help me find the killer."

"George, listen to yourself."

"I can handle it, Isabella. I've always handled it," George retorted, his voice firm, but there was a hint of desperation beneath the surface. "Trust me."

Isabella sighed, her heart heavy. "You said that the last time and the time before. When will it end, George? When will you realise that you're more than just this job?"

George paused, his expression softening for a moment, but then his resolve returned. "This is who I am, Isabella. This is what I do."

Isabella watched him, her eyes filled with a mixture of love and sadness. "Then maybe you need to change what you do."

"I think you're right."

Isabella felt a tear slip down her cheek. "So you'll go back to therapy?"

"If that's what you want."

"This isn't anything to do with me, George," Isabella said, her voice low. "This is all about you and what you need." She paused. "I just need my fiancé. And Olivia needs her dad."

George looked at her, torn. He knew she was right. "I'll do whatever's necessary."

Isabella nodded. "I love you."

"I love you more," he replied.

***

George sat alone on the sofa, dressed in his best suit, the only sound the steady ticking of the clock. He stared into the empty space, his thoughts swirling in a tumultuous sea of duty, obsession, and personal conflict. Isabella's words echoed in his mind, a poignant reminder of the rift his dedication to the job had caused in their family.

His gaze fell upon a photograph on the table—a candid shot of him, Isabella, Jack, and Olivia, taken in happier times. A shadow of regret crossed his face. He knew Isabella was right. He had been consumed by the job, letting it overshadow everything else in his life. But how could he step back now, especially with the revelation that his father, Edward, might be involved?

George's mind replayed the recent discoveries, the connection to his father's inner circle, a clue that had hit too close to home. This case was not just another challenge in his career; it had become a personal vendetta, a chance to unravel the complex relationship with his father and maybe, just maybe, to reconcile with the demons of his past.

He leaned back in his chair, closing his eyes for a moment. The memories of his father, Edward, filled his mind—a man of influence and power, yet distant and cold. George had always sought his approval, yet he had always felt like he had fallen short. Now, as he delved deeper into the case, he feared what he might uncover about his father. Would it change everything he thought he knew?

Opening his eyes, George's gaze hardened. He couldn't let his personal feelings interfere with the case. He was a detective, first and foremost. His duty was to the victims, to

CHAPTER TWENTY-SEVEN

bring justice to those who had been wronged. He couldn't allow his father's possible involvement to cloud his judgment.

Nor could he allow this to cloud his love for his family. And the ones who loved him.

George stood up, walking over to the window. He looked out into the night, the city lights flickering in the distance. He felt torn between two worlds—the world of his family, warm and inviting, and the dark world of his work, filled with secrets and danger.

He made a silent vow to himself. Once this case was over, he would make things right with Isabella, Jack and Olivia. He would find a way to balance his career with his family life.

George turned away from the window, his expression one of determination. No. He would start right away before it was too late.

* * *

In the festively decorated lobby of the police station, Detective Inspector George Beaumont stepped in, carrying a bag brimming with toys. The twinkling lights and a towering Christmas tree set a cheerful atmosphere, but George's expression held a deeper, more personal significance.

Earlier that week, in Mia's house in East Ardsley, George had shared a moment of connection with his nearly-two-year-old son, Jack. The living room was scattered with toys, each holding memories of Jack's young life. With serious contemplation, Jack had picked out toys, carefully considering what other children would love.

"That one, Daddy," Jack had said, pointing to a bright red fire truck.

Mia, watching from the doorway, had smiled at the scene. George caught her eye, and for a moment, they shared a silent acknowledgement of their son's growing empathy and kindness.

"Thank you, Jack," George had said, ruffling his son's hair. "You're making other kids very happy this Christmas."

In the foyer, as George placed the toys on the designated table, he couldn't help but feel a swell of pride for his son. Despite the chaos of his own life, the moments with Jack grounded him, reminding him of the simpler joys in life.

The station was bustling with activity, colleagues greeting each other, laughter mingling with the sound of Christmas carols. George moved through the crowd, his eyes briefly scanning the room. He noticed Detective Constable Candy Nichols arranging gifts on a table, her laughter infectious.

Detective Constable Jay Scott approached George, clapping him on the shoulder. "Good to see you, boss. Jack did a great job with the toys."

George nodded, a small smile breaking through. "Yeah, he's growing up fast. It's important to him, giving to others."

Jay's expression softened. "It's a good lesson for all of us."

The flashback to earlier that day lingered in George's mind as he watched his colleagues. The simplicity of Jack's gesture, choosing toys for other children, starkly contrasted with the complexity of the case he was embroiled in. It was a reminder of what mattered most—the innocence of childhood, the importance of empathy, and the spirit of giving.

* * *

The charity Christmas event at Elland Road Police Station

was in full swing, with decorations adorning the walls, music filling the air, and laughter echoing through the hall. Detective Chief Inspector Alistair Atkinson stepped in, momentarily pausing at the threshold. The festive atmosphere softened the edges of his usually stern demeanour.

Atkinson, known for his no-nonsense approach and sharp leadership, appeared slightly out of his element in this more casual setting. His eyes scanned the room, taking in the sight of his colleagues and their families enjoying the celebrations. Slowly, a rare smile crept onto his face, revealing a seldom-seen side of the seasoned detective.

As he made his way through the crowd, Atkinson's attention was caught by Eleanor, a volunteer coordinating the event. She approached him with a warm smile, extending a hand in greeting. "Welcome! I'm Eleanor, one of the organisers. It's great to see so many joining in the festivities."

Atkinson took her hand, his smile widening. "Thank you. It's a wonderful event. I'm Alistair."

Eleanor, unaware of Atkinson's rank in the police force, continued the conversation with a casual ease. "I hope you find some good gifts for the charity raffle. We've got quite a collection this year."

The usual rigidity in Atkinson's posture relaxed as they strolled towards the raffle table. Their conversation flowed effortlessly, with Eleanor's charm and wit drawing out a side of Atkinson rarely witnessed by his colleagues.

"So, Alistair, do you have any kids?" Eleanor asked, her tone light.

Atkinson chuckled, a sound that surprised even him. "Yes, two. They're both grown up now, though."

"You don't look old enough," Eleanor remarked, her eyes

sparkling with curiosity. "That must be a different kind of challenge, though."

"You could say that," Atkinson replied, his voice tinged with a mix of pride and nostalgia. "Parenthood never really ends, does it?"

Their banter continued, with Eleanor's genuine interest in his life outside of work and Atkinson's candid responses creating an easy rapport between them. The usually reserved detective found himself enjoying the conversation, his guarded professional facade melting away in the warmth of Eleanor's presence.

As they talked, colleagues passing by did double-takes, surprised to see him in such a relaxed and cheerful mood. It was as if the festive spirit of the event had cast a spell, allowing Atkinson to step away from his duties and just be himself.

Their interaction was marked by subtle glances and smiles, a mutual interest that was both surprising and refreshing. For Atkinson, it was a reminder that there was more to life than work, a realisation that came as a gentle revelation amidst the joyous chaos of the charity event.

* * *

In one corner, Jay Scott, dressed as Santa Claus, was the centre of attention. His booming laughter and playful antics with the children brought smiles to everyone's faces, including George's. Watching Jay, who usually maintained a composed facade, embrace the role of Santa with such enthusiasm was a delightful sight.

Nearby, Candy Nichols and Tashan Blackburn staffed a gift-wrapping booth. Their banter and laughter as they wrapped presents added to the event's festive atmosphere. George approached, watching them deftly twist ribbons and fold paper.

"Never knew you had such a talent for gift wrapping, Candy," George joked, his tone lighter than usual.

Candy looked up, a smile spreading across her face. "It's all in the wrist, sir," she replied playfully.

"I know all about that," remarked Santa Claus, making the adults laugh and leaving the children wondering what was so funny.

Tashan, meticulously adjusting a bow, added, "We might have a second career in this, Candy."

As he mingled, George's interactions with the locals revealed a side of him that was often overshadowed by his professional duties. His laughter was genuine, his smile more frequent, and his conversations peppered with personal anecdotes. It was a reminder that beneath the detective's exterior was a man deeply connected to his community.

In these moments, George was more than just a detective inspector; he was a figure of trust and respect. The positive impact of his work and that of his team was evident in the community's response. They didn't just see him as an officer but as a pillar of their society.

George's stroll through the event was interrupted by the enthusiastic greetings of children excited to show him their newly wrapped gifts. He crouched down to their level, listening with interest and joining in their excitement. These interactions, simple yet profound, highlighted a softer side of George, a stark contrast to his usual intensity.

The evening continued with laughter, music, and the clinking of glasses. George, watching his team and the community come together, felt a sense of pride and contentment. It was moments like these that reminded him of the reasons behind his tireless work—not just to solve cases, but to protect and serve the community he had grown to love.

Chapter Twenty-eight

The festive spirit of the Christmas charity event had transformed the usually sombre Elland Road Police Station into a lively, vibrant scene. Alistair Atkinson was still talking to Eleanor, a charming volunteer coordinating the event. Their conversation had begun with the formalities typical of such interactions, but a comical incident involving a mix-up with a raffle prize had sparked a surprising connection. They found themselves laughing together, the humour of the situation breaking down barriers.

As the noise of the festivities buzzed around them, they instinctively moved towards a quieter corner, where their conversation turned to more personal topics. They talked about holiday traditions, each sharing fond memories of Christmases past.

Atkinson, who seldom spoke of his personal life, surprised Eleanor with tales of his childhood holidays, recounting tales of family traditions and festive mishaps. His stories were infused with warmth and nostalgia, offering a glimpse into a side of him that few colleagues ever saw.

Eleanor listened, her expression a mix of amusement and interest. She shared her own memories, creating a bond over shared experiences and the universal magic of the holiday season.

Their conversation flowed effortlessly, bridging the gap between professional and personal. Atkinson, who had always kept a firm line between his work and private life, found himself enjoying the rare opportunity to just be himself without the weight of his rank and responsibilities.

As they talked, Atkinson's usual reserve melted away, revealing a man with a rich tapestry of life experiences and a depth of character that went far beyond his role as a police officer. He spoke of his love for classical music, his interest in history, and his secret talent for cooking, each revelation bringing a surprised and delighted smile to Eleanor's face.

The conversation was a revelation for Atkinson as well. He was reminded of the joys of connecting with someone on a human level without the constraints of his professional persona. Eleanor's easy-going nature and genuine interest in his stories allowed him to open up in ways he hadn't in years.

As the evening progressed, their conversation became a haven of shared laughter and meaningful exchange, a stark contrast to the usual dynamics of Atkinson's life. For a few precious hours, he wasn't the Detective Chief Inspector; he was just Alistair, a man with a rich past and a wealth of stories to tell.

* * *

In the midst of the Christmas charity event, George found himself momentarily alone, his gaze drifting across the lively scene unfolding in the lobby of Elland Road Police Station. The twinkling lights, laughter, and festive decorations formed a stark contrast to the grim realities he faced daily in his work.

For a brief moment, the weight of the Santa Claus murders seemed to lift from his shoulders, replaced by a rare sense of connection to the world around him.

George stood somewhat apart, a silent observer in the sea of joy and celebration. His eyes lingered on families gathered around the Christmas tree, on children's faces lit up with excitement, and on his colleagues, who, for once, were not weighed down by the demands of police work. In this moment, the station was more than just a workplace; it was a hub of community, a place where people came together to share in the spirit of giving and camaraderie.

His thoughts wandered to the recent string of murders, to the fear and uncertainty they had instilled in the community he had sworn to protect. The contrast between the warmth of the event and the cold brutality of the crimes was stark. Yet, it was in these moments of shared joy and togetherness that George found a renewed sense of purpose. It was a reminder of what he was fighting for—not just justice but the safety and well-being of the community.

As George's gaze swept the room, he saw more than just a festive gathering; he saw resilience, the unspoken strength of people coming together in the face of adversity. He saw the importance of these moments of light and hope and how vital they were in counteracting the darkness of the crimes he investigated.

Lost in his thoughts, George barely noticed Santa Claus making his way over to him. Jay's cheery voice broke through his contemplation. "Not getting into the spirit, boss?" he asked, a teasing smile on his face.

George offered a small, wistful smile in return. "Just thinking about how important all of this is," he replied, gesturing to the room. "How it's these moments that keep a community strong, especially when times are tough."

Jay nodded in understanding, the merriment in his eyes giving way to a more serious, reflective look. "It's more than just a party, isn't it? It's about showing that we're here, not just as police officers but as part of the community."

"Exactly," George agreed. "It's easy to get lost in the details of the cases, in the pursuit of justice. But nights like this, they remind us of the bigger picture, of the lives and the people we're working to protect."

Their conversation was interrupted as a group of children, laughing and chattering excitedly, approached Santa Jay for a photo. George stepped back, allowing Jay to slip back into his role with ease. Watching the scene, George's thoughts turned once again to the community and the role he played within it. It was moments like these, he realised, that grounded him, that reminded him of the humanity at the heart of his work.

* * *

The Christmas charity event at Elland Road Police Station was drawing to a close. The once-bustling lobby, filled with laughter, music, and festive decorations, was slowly emptying, leaving behind a warm, lingering sense of community spirit. Detective Chief Inspector Alistair Atkinson, who had spent most of the evening in the delightful company of Eleanor, the charming event volunteer, found himself lingering by the exit, not quite ready to leave the comforting ambience of the evening.

Eleanor, with her vibrant personality and easy laughter, had managed to draw out a side of Atkinson rarely seen by

CHAPTER TWENTY-EIGHT

his colleagues. Their conversation had flowed effortlessly, covering everything from trivial holiday anecdotes to more personal topics. Now, as they stood somewhat apart from the dwindling crowd, there was a palpable sense of connection between them.

With a gentle smile, Eleanor reached into her purse and pulled out a small card. "I don't usually do this," she admitted, her cheeks tinged with a hint of colour, "but I'd really like to see you again, Alistair." She handed him the card, her fingers brushing against his as she did so.

Atkinson, usually so composed and stoic, felt a flutter of anticipation. He took the card, his eyes meeting hers. "I'd like that, Eleanor," Alistair said, his voice revealing a hint of vulnerability that was new to him. He glanced at the card, noting her number and the name of the charity she worked for. "I'll call you."

Their eyes held for a moment longer, each silently acknowledging the potential of what lay ahead. Then, with a final warm smile, Eleanor turned to help with the clean-up, leaving Atkinson standing by the door, her card securely in his hand.

As Atkinson stepped outside, the cold night air hit him, but it did little to dampen the warmth he felt inside. He paused for a moment, looking back at the police station. The festive lights from inside cast a soft glow into the night, symbolizing the joy and community spirit that had defined the evening.

Atkinson allowed himself a rare, genuine smile. The evening had been a welcome respite from the demands of his professional life, a reminder that there was more to life than work. The encounter with Eleanor had been unexpected, a pleasant surprise that had stirred something within him he hadn't felt in a long time.

He began to walk away, his usual brisk, purposeful stride now replaced with a more relaxed, almost jaunty step. His thoughts were on Eleanor, on the possibility of what might come from their chance meeting. It was a new beginning, a chance to explore something personal, something just for himself, amidst the responsibilities and pressures of his demanding career.

* * *

The Christmas tree stood tall and proud in the HMET's shared office, its branches waiting to be adorned with the warm glow of festive lights. The charity event had been a resounding success, and now, as it drew to a close, George Beaumont and his team gathered upstairs and around the tree for the final act of the evening.

George stood slightly apart from his team, his eyes fixed on the tree. Despite the challenges of the Santa Claus murder case, which weighed heavily on his mind, he allowed himself this moment of respite. Around him, his colleagues chatted and laughed, the strains of a festive tune playing softly in the background.

Jay Scott, still in his Santa costume, was the centre of attention, cracking jokes and eliciting laughter from the team. Candy Nichols and Tashan Blackburn, who had been wrapping gifts at a booth earlier, now stood side by side, their faces alight with the joy of the season.

As the team prepared to light the tree, George's thoughts briefly drifted to his father, Edward, and the recent confrontation they had. But he pushed those thoughts aside, focusing instead on the present moment, on the camaraderie

CHAPTER TWENTY-EIGHT

and warmth that surrounded him.

"All right, everyone, let's light this up!" Jay announced, his voice booming with festive cheer. The team cheered in response, their faces expectant and bright.

A hush fell over the group as the lights were switched on. The tree burst into life, its lights twinkling and shimmering, casting a warm, inviting glow over the lobby. The sight was mesmerizing, a beacon of hope and joy in the midst of winter's chill.

George's expression softened. For a moment, the weight of his responsibilities, the darkness of the case he was working on, all seemed to lift. He was here, among friends and colleagues, sharing in a simple yet profound moment of joy.

His gaze moved from the tree to his team. He saw the smiles on their faces, the genuine delight in their eyes, and he felt a surge of gratitude. These were the people who stood by him, who worked tirelessly to bring justice and safety to their community. They were more than just colleagues; they were a part of his extended family.

As the group began to disperse, George lingered by the tree, taking in the scene. He thought about his son, Jack, and the moment they had shared earlier in the day, selecting toys to donate, rather than the disappointment he'd caused by missing the nativity play. George thought about Isabella and the challenges they faced, yet their love remained strong. He thought about Olivia and how he needed to be there for her. And he thought about his father, the unresolved tensions that loomed large.

But for now, he allowed himself to just be in the moment, to feel the peace and hope that the season brought. The tree, with its bright lights, stood as a testament to the spirit of Christmas, to the possibility of joy and light even in the darkest of times.

George turned away from the tree, ready to face whatever challenges lay ahead, but for now, buoyed by the warmth and camaraderie of the evening. The chapter closed with George walking away from the tree, its lights a soft glow behind him, a symbol of the light that he and his team brought into the world.

Chapter Twenty-nine

The HMET Incident Room was charged with tense energy as Detective Inspector George Beaumont led the team meeting. It was early Wednesday morning, and the team looked weary, evidence of the long, gruelling hours they'd been pouring into the Santa Claus murder case over the last week. Every face around the table bore the mark of sleepless nights and relentless pursuit of justice.

George stood at the head of the table, his gaze sweeping over his team. "Alright, let's get to the point," he began, his voice steady but tinged with urgency. "We need to talk about Jonathan Hughes."

A collective focus sharpened around the table. Jonny Hughes, the newly uncovered piece of the puzzle, had everyone's attention.

"Has anyone found out why this crucial information was hidden or overlooked?" George asked, his eyes locking on Detective Constable Tashan Blackburn.

Tashan, looking more composed than most in the room, nodded slightly. "Yes, sir," he began, "the initial investigation into Oliver Hughes' background didn't turn up a sibling because Jonny was estranged from the family. He changed his surname after a falling out. It seems he wanted nothing to do with the Hughes family, so there was no link made at the time."

George processed the information, his mind already racing with implications. "So, he effectively vanished from Oliver's life and, therefore, from our radar," he mused aloud, his expression hardening. "Could this estrangement be the motive we've been missing?"

"It's possible, sir," Tashan replied. "Estrangement doesn't always lead to murder, but given the nature of these crimes, we can't rule out a personal vendetta."

The room buzzed with murmurs as the team considered this new angle. George raised his hand, silencing the room. "We need to find Jonny Hughes. He could be our key to unravelling this entire case."

Detective Constable Jason Scott spoke up, his voice carrying a mix of certainty and curiosity. "Jonny Hughes could be the key to understanding these murders," he stated. "If there were hidden family dynamics, conflicts, or secrets involving Oliver, it could provide a strong motive."

George nodded thoughtfully. The revelation about Jonny Hughes had opened up a new avenue in the investigation, one that delved deep into the murky waters of family history, inheritance issues, and long-standing grudges.

Just then, Detective Sergeant Yolanda Williams entered the room, her presence immediately drawing attention. She noticed the intense focus and realised she had walked into a crucial discussion.

"Yolanda, we need to revisit the past case files," George said, his tone indicating the urgency of the matter. "We might have overlooked details or misinterpreted evidence a decade ago."

Yolanda's expression hardened with determination. "Understood, sir. I'll re-evaluate the entire investigation and its conclusions."

George watched as Yolanda swiftly left to begin her task. Turning back to his team, he said, "We're looking at this case with fresh eyes. Everything we thought we knew, every conclusion we reached back then, is now up for question."

Jason Scott leaned forward. "Boss, considering the brutality, it could be personal, revenge perhaps?" He referenced similar cases he'd studied, drawing parallels.

Candy Nichols chimed in with a contrasting view. "What if we're dealing with a serial killer? The Christmas theme, it's too specific. It could be a signature."

Tashan Blackburn, ever the analytical thinker, interjected. "Both theories have merit, but let's not jump to conclusions without solid evidence." He gestured to the photos. "There are inconsistencies here we can't ignore."

George absorbed their input, his mind working at a rapid pace. "Good points, all of them. We need to consider every angle. But our immediate focus is on Jonny Hughes. He might just be the thread that unravels this entire case."

Tashan's words cut through the tense atmosphere like a sharp blade. "This new lead on Jonny Hughes changes everything. It injects an urgency we can't ignore," he said, his voice laced with a mix of tension and determination. The room, already buzzing with a sense of heightened stakes, seemed to absorb his words, echoing the gravity of their situation.

Detective Constable Jason Scott, leaning against the wall with arms folded, chimed in, his frustration palpable. "So, what? We go back to basics? Door-to-door, talking to people, collecting physical evidence?" He sounded almost incredulous, his patience wearing thin under the relentless pressure.

Tashan nodded, undeterred by the scepticism. "Exactly. Traditional methods have their place, even in a case as convoluted as this. We need eyes and ears on the ground, Jason."

Jason pushed off the wall, stepping closer. "And if he's planning another move? We might not have the luxury of time for old-school policing, Tashan."

The debate escalated, voices rising, echoing the growing strain on the team. Every member felt the unspoken weight of expectation, the unyielding demand for results.

George Beaumont, observing the exchange, saw it as a reflection of their collective strain. He interjected, his voice commanding yet calm. "Both of you have valid points. We need to cover all our bases. Time might be against us, but thoroughness can't be compromised."

He turned to Tashan. "Coordinate the neighbourhood canvassing. We need to know if anyone's seen Hughes recently." Then, addressing Jason, "And keep digging into his digital footprint. There might be something we've missed."

The directives from George, clear and decisive, diffused some of the tension. The team, recognizing the importance of unity in the face of their daunting task, refocused their efforts.

Detective Chief Inspector Alistair Atkinson strode into the Incident Room, his entrance sudden and commanding. The energy shifted palpably, the team's focus snapping towards him. In his wake lingered the tense residue of his earlier meeting with the senior officials.

George, standing by the evidence board, turned to face Atkinson. The weight of the recent directives was evident in Atkinson's posture, his usually impeccable suit seeming to

CHAPTER TWENTY-NINE

bear down on him.

"George," Atkinson began, his tone carrying an uncharacteristic blend of curt authority and veiled apology. "I've just come from the top brass. They're clamping down, demanding faster results, more definitive answers."

George, his green eyes meeting Atkinson's steely gaze, nodded, a mix of understanding and concern etching his features. "I understand the pressure, sir, but rushing can compromise the case's integrity."

Atkinson's frustration, barely contained, seeped into his voice. "Integrity doesn't quell public fear, Beaumont. We need progress, and we need it now."

The room, already a cauldron of stress, simmered with added tension. George remained composed, his mind racing to balance the urgency with the need for meticulous investigation.

Atkinson's gaze then shifted to Detective Constable Tashan Blackburn. "Tashan, have you made your decision yet?" His tone, expectant and demanding, hung heavily in the air.

Tashan, taken aback, replied with careful consideration. "Sir, I'm close to a conclusion. Just need a bit more time."

Atkinson's response was a curt nod, his impatience barely masked. "Time is a luxury we don't have. Wrap it up, Blackburn."

As Atkinson exited the room, the pressure he left in his wake was almost tangible. George refocused his team, his leadership more crucial than ever in the face of escalating demands.

"Let's stay sharp," George said, his voice firm yet encouraging. "We're on the right track. Just need to push a little harder."

The team nodded, their resolve fortified by George's steady presence, but the air in the Incident Room was thick with a mix of determination and concern as the team absorbed the weight of DCI Atkinson's demands. The team exchanged glances, their expressions hardened by the reality of their situation. The urgency was not just a whisper but a shout now, reverberating through the room.

Cutting through the tense atmosphere, George's voice was calm yet authoritative, "Let's focus and get to work. We've got a murderer to catch." His leadership qualities, always apparent, now shone like a beacon in these trying times.

In one corner of the room, Detective Constable Jason Scott was hunched over his computer, his eyes scanning through social media trends. His fingers flew across the keyboard as he searched for any digital footprint that Jonny Hughes might have left behind. Every post, every tweet, every shared image was scrutinised for clues, for anything that might lead them to Hughes.

Across the room, Detective Constable Tashan Blackburn was gearing up to hit the streets. His approach was different— personal, direct. He was preparing to interview locals, to knock on doors and look into the eyes of those who might have seen something, anything. Tashan knew the value of human interaction, the tiny details that only surfaced in face-to-face conversations.

Meanwhile, other team members were absorbed in processing forensic evidence. They pored over every item with meticulous attention, understanding that even the smallest piece of evidence could be the key to unlocking the mystery of the Santa Claus murders.

Through it all, George moved among his team members,

CHAPTER TWENTY-NINE

offering guidance and support. He studied the social media analysis over Jason's shoulder, offering insights and suggestions. His presence was reassuring, a steadying force amidst the storm of activity.

Then, standing beside Tashan, George clapped a hand on his shoulder. "You've got a good instinct, Tashan. Trust it out there," he said, his tone imbued with confidence in his detective's abilities.

The team worked diligently, each member playing their part in the intricate dance of investigation. The clock was ticking, and with each passing minute, the urgency ramped up. They were a well-oiled machine driven by a common goal—to bring a murderer to justice.

George stood back for a moment, observing the concerted efforts of his team. The determination etched on their faces was a mirror of his own. He knew they were pushing their limits, but he also knew they wouldn't have it any other way. This was more than a job; it was a calling.

Later, in his office, Detective Inspector George Beaumont sat absorbed in thought. The revelation about Jonny Hughes had cast a long shadow over the investigation, temporarily eclipsing other significant leads. But it was the image of Elias Marston, cosied up with Jürgen Schmidt in a photograph, that gnawed at George's mind.

The photograph, discovered in Schmidt's study, hinted at a complex web of connections tying together key figures in the case. George needed to delve deeper, to untangle these threads. He powered up his computer, the Police National Database and the National DNA Database loading onto the screen.

Methodically, George began cross-referencing names. First,

Jürgen Schmidt. His fingers danced over the keyboard, entering the details. The system churned for a moment before returning a result—Schmidt's DNA was not on file—a dead end, but not a surprising one. Schmidt had always been careful to stay under the radar.

Next, Elias Marston. George held a faint hope here. Marston's social and business dealings had placed him at the periphery of the murders, a shadowy figure with unclear motives. The computer hummed, processing the inquiry. Again, no match. Marston's DNA was not on the system—a growing sense of frustration knotted in George's stomach.

One name remained—a name George had hoped to avoid. Edward Beaumont. His father. Entering his father's details felt like crossing an invisible line, but the investigation demanded thoroughness, unhampered by personal ties. The database returned its verdict—no match. Edward Beaumont's DNA was not on the National DNA Database. George leaned back, his mind racing. This opened a Pandora's box of possibilities, each more unsettling than the last.

Yet, amidst the whirlwind of suspicion, George's instincts told him the killer was not Edward, Elias, or Schmidt. There was still one more person to consider—Jonny Hughes. The estranged brother whose sudden emergence in the case had sparked a new line of inquiry.

Determined, George stood up, his decision made. He needed to find Jonny Hughes. If Jonny's DNA matched the evidence found by Lindsey, it could be the breakthrough they needed. If not, it was another suspect they could rule out.

Chapter Thirty

Detective Sergeant Yolanda Williams knocked and entered George's office with an air of purpose. She approached George, a folder clutched tightly in her hand.

"Sir, I've got something on Jonny Hughes," she announced, her voice carrying a mix of urgency and revelation.

George turned to her, his attention immediate. "What have you found?"

Yolanda opened the folder, laying out the documents she had meticulously gathered. "Firstly, his DNA is on the database, but it was from a minor crime twenty years ago. It doesn't match the DNA on the fibres or ropes used on the victims."

George's brow furrowed, processing this new information. "So, Jonny isn't our man, but he's still a key piece in this puzzle."

"Yes, and there's more," Yolanda continued, her tone indicating the importance of her following words. "As you know, Jonny has been living a hidden life, off the radar, which is why we missed him a decade ago. But I've found a connection between him and three of our victims: Ethan, Danny, and Mike."

George leaned in, his interest piqued. "What kind of connection?"

Yolanda flipped through her notes. "They were all part of a community project twenty years ago. It was run by a local charity, one that a man named Edward Beaumont was heavily involved in."

The mention of Edward Beaumont caused a subtle shift in George's expression, a mix of personal conflict and professional curiosity. "Do we know the nature of their involvement?"

"It's not clear yet, sir," Yolanda admitted. "But it's more than a coincidence. These men, now victims, were connected in their youth, and Jonny was part of that circle." She paused. "He's not a relation of yours, is he, sir? Only, Beaumont isn't a popular name."

"We need to dig deeper into this charity and their activities. There might be something we're missing, something from the past that's influencing the present," George said, ignoring her question, his mind already racing with the implications.

Yolanda agreed, her eyes reflecting the same determination that George felt. "I'll get on it. There's more to Jonny Hughes than meets the eye."

As Yolanda went to continue her investigation, George took a moment to reflect on the new information. The pieces of the puzzle were slowly coming together, but with each revelation came more questions. The connection between Jonny Hughes and the victims was a significant lead, yet it deepened the mystery surrounding the Santa Claus murders.

In the back of his mind, George couldn't shake the feeling that they were on the brink of a major breakthrough, one that could potentially unravel the entire case. The hidden life of Jonny Hughes and his past connection with the victims

CHAPTER THIRTY

pointed to secrets long buried, secrets that were now clawing their way to the surface.

* * *

"Attention all," George said, grouping his team together. "We've got a new angle, and we're going to pursue it with everything we have," George declared his voice firm, commanding the room's attention. He scanned his team, their faces reflecting a spectrum of anticipation and resolve.

"Tashan, Jay," George continued, pointing to the two detectives, "I want you two to interview Danny and Ethan. Dive deep. We need to understand their connection to Jonny Hughes."

Detective Constable Tashan Blackburn nodded, his expression set in a mask of seriousness. Detective Constable Jason Scott, beside him, mirrored the resolve, a silent agreement between them evident in their swift departure.

George then turned to Detective Constable Candy Nichols, her youthful energy a stark contrast to the weight of the case. "Candy, you're with me. We're going to pay a visit to Mike. It's time we got some answers straight from the horse's mouth."

Candy nodded, her readiness clear in her brisk nod. There was a glimmer of eagerness in her eyes, a hunger for the truth that matched George's own.

George's gaze then found Detective Sergeant Yolanda Williams, her experience and keen insight invaluable in this intricate web of connections and secrets. "Yolanda, keep digging into the charity and its activities. Anything you find could be the key to unlocking Jonny's motives."

Yolanda acknowledged with a sharp, determined nod, already flipping through her notes to resume her investigation.

With the team dispatched on their respective missions, George felt a familiar thrill, the adrenaline of the chase. He knew they were on the cusp of something significant. The hidden connections, the shadows of the past now coming to light, were pieces of a puzzle that, once solved, would reveal the truth behind the Santa Claus murders.

As George and Candy prepared to leave for Mike's place, the Incident Room buzzed with activity, a hive of dedicated professionals, each playing their part in the pursuit of justice. The air was electric with possibility, with the sense that they were on the verge of a breakthrough.

In the car, George's mind raced through the possible scenarios, the questions he needed to ask Mike. Beside him, Candy was a silent presence, her focus evident in her steady gaze.

* * *

Detective Constables Jay Scott and Tashan Blackburn stood at Danny's front door, the chill of the evening air biting at their skin. When the door opened, Danny's wary eyes met theirs.

"Danny, we need to ask you a few questions about Jonny Hughes," Tashan stated, his tone direct.

Danny shrugged, a puzzled frown creasing his forehead. "Jonny? That's a name I haven't heard in years."

"What is his relation to Oliver?" asked Jay.

"Oliver's cousin, I think." Danny shrugged. "Haven't seen him in years."

Jay noted the response, his instincts tingling. "Are you sure about that, Danny? It's crucial we get this right."

"Yeah, pretty sure. Why? What's this about?" Danny asked,

CHAPTER THIRTY

a hint of suspicion in his voice.

"We're investigating the murders of two of your old friends," Tashan replied, watching Danny's reaction closely.

Danny's eyes widened slightly, but he quickly regained composure. "Sorry, I can't help you there."

Jay exchanged a quick, knowing glance with Tashan. Something didn't quite add up, but they moved on.

The night was growing older.

Their next stop was Ethan's house. The detectives received a similar response, almost echoing Danny's words.

"Ethan, when was the last time you saw Jonny Hughes?" Tashan asked, his gaze steady.

"Jonny Hughes?" he pondered. "Oliver's cousin, you mean?"

"You tell us," said Jay.

"I'm sure he was just a distant cousin of Oliver's. It's been years, really," Ethan responded, his tone nonchalant.

Jay's brow furrowed. The similarity in their statements was too uncanny, too rehearsed. "You haven't had any contact with him since then?"

Ethan shook his head. "No, none at all." He shrugged. "We weren't really friends; he was just a family member of Olivers."

"A brother instead of a cousin, perhaps?"

Ethan shrugged again. "Dunno, mate."

As they left Ethan's house, Tashan voiced his thoughts. "Their stories are too aligned. It feels rehearsed."

Jay nodded in agreement. "Yeah, there's more to this than they're letting on."

Meanwhile, at the penthouse gym in the centre of Leeds, George Beaumont and Candy Nichols sat across from Mike in his plush office. George's eyes were sharp and analytical.

"Mike, we're trying to locate Jonny Hughes. What can you tell us about him?" George asked, his voice calm yet probing.

Mike leaned back, his expression one of genuine confusion. "Jonny Hughes? I don't know anyone by that name. Never heard of him."

Candy watched Mike closely, trying to read any sign of deceit. "Are you sure about that, Mike? This is important."

Mike spread his hands, a picture of innocence. "I'm telling you, I've never met the guy. I don't know what you want me to say."

George's gaze lingered on Mike a moment longer before he stood up. "Thank you for your time, Mike. If you remember anything, please let us know."

As they left the gym, the air between George and Candy was thick with unspoken thoughts. The pieces were not fitting together, and every new piece of information only seemed to deepen the mystery.

Back in the car, George broke the silence. "What do you think, Candy?"

Candy sighed, her mind racing. "It's hard to tell."

George nodded, his eyes on the dark streets ahead. "We need to keep digging. There's a piece we're missing, and it's key to understanding this whole puzzle."

The night wrapped around them, the city a maze of shadows and secrets. In the heart of it all, George and his team were the seekers of truth, unwavering in their pursuit, no matter how elusive the answers seemed to be.

The evening had deepened into night as Detective Inspector George Beaumont drove towards Elland Road Station, the quiet hum of the car a stark contrast to the day's events. Beside

CHAPTER THIRTY

him, Detective Constable Candy Nichols sat in contemplation, both reflecting on the day's interviews.

Reaching the station, George turned to Candy. "That's it for tonight. Get some rest; tomorrow's another day." His voice was steady, the weariness of the day masked by a veneer of resolve.

Candy nodded, her eyes tired yet determined. "Thanks, sir. See you tomorrow." She stepped out of the car, disappearing into the station.

George then headed home, his thoughts drifting to the promise he made to his family. Balancing the demands of his career with his personal life was a tightrope walk he navigated every day. The Santa Claus murders, however, had stretched him thinner than usual.

His phone rang, breaking the silence of the car. Glancing at the screen, he saw Jay's name. He answered, Jay's voice booming through the car speaker.

"Boss, the interviews with Ethan and Danny were a bust," Jay reported a tinge of frustration in his voice. "Both of them thought Jonny was Oliver's cousin, not his brother. It's like they're reading from the same script."

George's grip on the steering wheel tightened slightly. "Interesting. Mike gave me the same line. He claimed he had no idea Oliver had a brother and that he's never heard of Jonny Hughes."

Jay's sigh was audible over the speaker. "What do you make of it, boss?"

George navigated the car through the dark streets, his mind working through the possibilities. "Either they're all telling the truth, or they're all lying. But why? What's to gain?"

Jay was silent for a moment before responding. "Maybe

259

somebody is paying them to lie?" He paused. "Or threatening them."

"True," the DI said, thinking of his father. "Keep me posted," George said before ending the call.

The rest of the drive was a quiet one, with George lost in his thoughts. The pieces of the puzzle didn't fit together, and the elusive nature of Jonny Hughes added another layer of complexity to the case.

Chapter Thirty-one

As George turned onto his street, the glow of Christmas lights bathed the street in a festive hue. The entire area was abuzz with the spirit of the season, a stark contrast to the dark case that occupied George's mind. Houses lined the street, each adorned with an array of decorations, competing in the street's annual decorating contest. A banner announcing the contest fluttered in the gentle evening breeze.

George parked his car, the tension of the day's investigations temporarily receding as he took in the sight. It was a reminder of the world outside his work, a world filled with simple joys and community spirit.

Stepping out of the car, George's attention was drawn to his son, Jack, who came bounding towards him with unrestrained excitement. Isabella had clearly planned this surprise, conspiring with Mia in secret. Jack's eyes sparkled with the same intensity as the Christmas lights around them.

"Daddy, look!" Jack exclaimed, tugging at George's hand and pulling him towards a neighbour's house. The display was elaborate, a dazzling array of lights and festive figures that captured the magic of the season.

George couldn't help but smile at his son's enthusiasm. "It's incredible, Jack. Jane's outdone herself this year," he said, his voice warm with affection.

Jack's face lit up with an idea. "We do it, Daddy!"

George chuckled, ruffling Jack's blond hair. "Maybe we should. What do you think, champ? Got any ideas?"

Jack's mind raced with possibilities, his excitement infectious. George found himself drawn into the idea, the childlike joy of the season momentarily pushing away the shadows of his work.

Nearby, Isabella stood holding their daughter Olivia, who was cooing and reaching out towards the twinkling lights. Isabella's eyes met George's, a knowing smile on her lips. She had orchestrated this evening to give him a break from the intensity of the investigation, a chance to reconnect with the lighter side of life.

He blew her a kiss and fought the tears that were trying to break through.

George walked over to them, taking Olivia into his arms. The baby's laughter filled the air, a sound of pure joy that resonated deep within him. In that moment, surrounded by his family and the festive atmosphere of the neighbourhood, George felt a sense of peace.

The warmth of the Beaumont household contrasted sharply with the chilly December air outside. Inside, George, Isabella, and their son Jack gathered around the dinner table, a cosy scene of domesticity. The chatter revolved around the neighbourhood's Christmas decorating contest, a topic that brought an animated sparkle to Jack's eyes.

"Daddy, we best lights!" Jack exclaimed, his excitement infectious.

Isabella smiled at her soon-to-be stepson's enthusiasm, then turned to George. "It could be fun, a nice break for you.

CHAPTER THIRTY-ONE

We could all do it together." Her voice was encouraging, a gentle nudge for George to step away from the shadows of his work.

George hesitated, his mind momentarily drifting to the unsolved case that awaited him. The Santa Claus murders, with their web of mysteries and dark revelations, were never far from his thoughts. But as he looked at his family's expectant faces, their excitement palpable, he felt a shift within him.

"You know, maybe you're right," George conceded, a rare smile tugging at the corners of his mouth. "It might be nice to do something... normal for a change."

Jack's cheer erupted, his plans for their decorations already spilling out in a rapid, excited stream. Isabella's eyes met George's, her smile warm and appreciative, acknowledging the effort it took for him to step away from the demands of his job.

As tea progressed, the conversation was light, filled with ideas and plans for their festive display. George found himself drawn into the simple joy of the moment, his detective instincts and the looming case momentarily pushed to the background.

Isabella's suggestions were creative yet practical, balancing Jack's more extravagant ideas. George listened, occasionally chiming in, his contributions thoughtful. It was a side of him that rarely saw the light of day, overshadowed as it often was by the grim realities of his work.

The laughter and chatter around the table were a balm to George's often weary soul. Here, in the warmth of his home, surrounded by his family, he could be just a husband and father, not Detective Inspector Beaumont, the man tasked with solving a series of heinous crimes.

After tea, as they cleared the table together, George's thoughts briefly wandered to the case. The interviews with Danny and Ethan, Mike's denial of knowing Jonny Hughes, and the pieces of the puzzle were slowly coming together, yet the complete picture eluded him.

But tonight, he allowed himself to be fully present with his family. The case would be there tomorrow, waiting for him, its shadows lurking just beneath the surface of his consciousness.

As they discussed where to place the lights and which decorations to use, George's participation became more active, his own creativity coming to the fore. It was a rare glimpse into a different aspect of his character, one not defined by his badge or the weight of his responsibilities.

The crisp evening air was filled with the sounds of laughter and chatter as George Beaumont and his family set up their Christmas decorations. The neighbourhood was alive with a festive spirit, each household contributing to the communal display of holiday cheer.

George, usually stoic and composed, was perched precariously on a ladder, stringing lights along the edge of the roof. His movements were cautious, a hint of tension in his posture. It was a little-known fact, even to those close to him, that George was acutely afraid of heights. Each stretch to clip a light in place was a battle against his instinctive discomfort.

Below him, Isabella was arranging figures on the front lawn, her hands deftly placing each decoration with an artist's touch. She occasionally glanced up at George, a playful yet concerned smile on her face. She knew of his fear and admired the way he pushed through it for the sake of their family tradition.

Nearby, Jack was busy helping with the ornaments, his

CHAPTER THIRTY-ONE

youthful energy adding to the light-hearted atmosphere. He darted around with a box of decorations, carefully choosing where each piece should go, his laughter echoing down the street.

In her pram, little Olivia gurgled and cooed, her tiny hands reaching out towards the twinkling lights. Onlookers stopped to admire her and the display; their coos and smiles were a testament to the tight-knit community they were a part of.

"Looking great, Beaumonts!" called Mr Henderson, a neighbour, as he walked his dog. "Can't wait to see it all lit up!"

George, managing a smile while gripping the ladder, called back, "Thanks, Mr Henderson! Just trying not to fall off here."

Isabella chuckled, calling out to their neighbour, "We're giving it our best shot this year!"

As the evening wore on, the Beaumonts' front garden transformed into a festive spectacle, a dazzling array of lights and decorations that captured the essence of the holiday spirit. George, finally descending from the ladder, felt a sense of accomplishment, not just in the decorations, but in overcoming his personal discomfort for the joy of his family.

Jack ran up to him, his eyes shining with excitement. "Daddy, best Christmas ever!"

George ruffled his son's hair, his heart swelling with love and pride. "It sure is, buddy."

George reached for the switch. A hush fell over them, a moment of anticipation. But when he flicked the switch, nothing happened. The lights remained stubbornly off, the Beaumont house dark amidst a sea of festive illumination.

A frown creased George's forehead. "That's odd," he muttered, checking the connections. Isabella and Jack watched, their expressions a mix of disappointment and curiosity.

"Maybe the bulbs are faulty?" Isabella suggested, trying to sound helpful.

George peered up at the lights. "Or maybe the Christmas light gremlins got them," he joked, trying to lighten the mood despite his frustration. He went back to check the switch, his detective instincts kicking in, examining every possible cause for the failure.

"Let me check the socket inside," George said, more to himself than anyone else. He stepped back into the house, his family following.

In the living room, George bent down to inspect the socket. A moment later, he straightened up, a sheepish grin spreading across his face. "Well, that would explain it," he said, turning to Isabella and Jack. "The socket wasn't turned on."

Isabella burst into laughter, joined by Jack. "The great Detective Inspector foiled by a plug switch!" she teased.

George joined in the laughter, the tension of the moment dissolving into a family joke. "I'll stick to solving crimes rather than handling Christmas lights," he quipped, flipping the socket switch on.

They hurried back outside, the air crisp against their skin. This time, when George flicked the switch, the house came alive with light. Brilliant colours danced across their lawn, the Beaumont house now a beacon of festive cheer.

Jack whooped with delight, jumping up and down. "It's amazing, Daddy!"

Isabella wrapped an arm around George, her eyes shining in the glow of the lights. "You did it despite the gremlins," she said, her voice warm with affection.

George looked at his family, their faces illuminated by the

twinkling lights. This was what mattered—these moments of joy, of togetherness.

With Olivia in his arms and Isabella and Jack standing next to him, George stepped back to admire their collective effort. Their home, now beautifully lit with an array of Christmas lights, stood out in the street, a testament to their family's teamwork and holiday spirit.

The house, bathed in a warm, festive glow, seemed almost magical. Strings of lights twinkled along the roofline and around the windows while the lawn was adorned with figures of reindeer and snowmen, glowing softly in the evening light.

George, usually so caught up in the complexities of his detective work, found himself captivated by the simple beauty of the scene. It was a reminder of the world outside his investigations, a world filled with moments of joy and togetherness.

Isabella, standing beside him, wrapped an arm around his waist. "We did good, didn't we?" she said, her voice tinged with pride. "Now we just need a decorated tree."

"We did, and we do," George agreed, a rare smile gracing his features. He looked down at Jack, who was beaming, his face illuminated by the colourful lights.

"Best Christmas ever!" Jack declared, his youthful enthusiasm infectious.

With Olivia in her pram, Isabella handed George a cup of hot chocolate, the steam rising into the cool evening air. He took a sip, the warmth of the drink seeping through him, a comforting contrast to the chill of the night.

They stood there, a family wrapped in scarves and gloves, sipping hot chocolate and soaking in the festive atmosphere. The street was quiet, the only sound the gentle hum of the Christmas lights and the distant laughter of neighbours.

In that moment, the worries and stresses of George's work seemed to melt away, replaced by a sense of peace and contentment. It was these moments, he realised, that made all the challenges worthwhile. The simple pleasure of being with his family, of creating something beautiful together, was a solace to his often weary soul.

As they stood together, the scene held a sense of completion, a perfect picture of holiday cheer. But for George, there was an undercurrent of something else—a reminder of the fleeting nature of such moments, of the delicate balance between light and darkness.

His eyes lingered on the lights, their cheerful twinkling belying the depth of his thoughts. In the world of crime and justice, moments like these were rare and precious. They were a reminder of what he fought for, of the peace and safety he sought to preserve.

As they eventually turned to go inside, the festive lights continued to twinkle behind them, a beacon of holiday spirit in the quiet night. And while the scene was one of complete and joyful closure, there remained an unspoken understanding that, come morning, the realities of George's work would return, the complexities of his cases awaiting him.

But for now, they were just a family, united in the warmth of their holiday creation, a small island of light in the vast sea of the world.

Chapter Thirty-two

The morning light barely filtered through the blinds of the Incident Room at Elland Road Police Station, casting a sombre mood over the team gathered within. Detective Inspector George Beaumont stood at the helm, surrounded by his team, their faces etched with the weariness of the long and gruelling investigation into the Santa Claus murders.

The room, usually a hub of controlled chaos and strategy, fell into a tense silence as a police constable hurried in, his face grave. "Sir, there's been another murder," he announced, his voice betraying the urgency of the situation.

George's head snapped up, his expression shifting from focused concentration to shock. "Details," he demanded, his voice a sharp command.

"It's a homeless man in his late forties, found near some bushes in Pudsey Park. He's been... it's the Santa Claus Killer's MO," the constable replied, handing over a folder containing the preliminary report.

The news hit the room like a physical force, a tangible wave of dismay and resolve. George's expression hardened, his initial shock morphing into a steely determination. "OK, we've got work to do," George said, his tone leaving no room for doubt about the gravity of their task. "We need to be at the scene now. This killer is escalating, and we need to catch up."

He quickly began assigning roles and responsibilities, his orders crisp and clear. "Jay, Candy, you're with me. We need to scour the scene for any evidence before it's contaminated. Tashan, stay here. We'll need you to search for information for us."

The team sprang into action, galvanized by the urgency in George's voice. They knew what was at stake—another life lost, another family shattered. The pattern of the murders was evolving, becoming more unpredictable and more dangerous.

As they prepared to leave, George took a moment to gather his thoughts. The image of the homeless man, a victim of a ruthless killer, haunted him. It was a stark reminder of the brutality they were up against.

In the car, the drive to the crime scene was tense; the team was focused and silent. George's mind raced with possibilities and theories, each one darker than the last.

The morning air was bitingly cold as Detective Inspector George Beaumont and his team pulled up to Pudsey Park, the site of the latest Santa Claus murder. The flashing blue lights of police vehicles sliced through the fog, casting an eerie glow on the gathering crowd. Onlookers, drawn by the commotion, pressed against the barriers, their faces a mix of curiosity and horror.

George stepped out of the car, his eyes immediately scanning the scene. Detective Constable Jay Scott and Detective Constable Candy Nichols were right behind him, their expressions set in grim determination. The media, like vultures circling their prey, had already descended upon the scene, cameras rolling, capturing every movement, every expression.

Paige McGuiness, a persistent reporter George had encoun-

CHAPTER THIRTY-TWO

tered more times than he cared to remember, approached him with her microphone poised. "Detective Inspector Beaumont, with only five days left until Christmas, and three dead bodies in the morgue, can you give us any hope that you'll find the killer before the big day?"

"Not now, Paige," George replied tersely, his focus elsewhere. "Please, let us do our work."

He quickly donned his Tyvek suit, gloves, mask, and shoe covers, the familiar ritual grounding him as he prepared to step into the chaos of the crime scene. Crossing the police tape, he entered a world that had become all too familiar in recent weeks.

The body lay in the shrubbery, a grotesque parody of a festive display. The victim, a man in his late forties, was dressed in a Santa Claus costume, the red suit a stark contrast to the pallor of death. Christmas lights were wound around his body, some still faintly twinkling, adding a macabre touch to the grisly scene.

George's eyes moved methodically over the body, noting the positioning, the bindings, and the way the lights were strung. It was consistent with the previous murders but with a chilling escalation. The killer was becoming bolder, more theatrical.

"Looks like our killer is sticking to the theme but upping the ante, sir," Candy observed, her voice steady despite the grim spectacle.

Jay nodded in agreement, his gaze sharp and searching. "It's like he's taunting us, boss, becoming more audacious with each kill."

George crouched beside the body, his mind processing every detail. The killer's pattern was clear, but the message behind it remained elusive, a riddle wrapped in brutality.

As the Crime Scene Investigators began their work, George stood back, giving them space to collect evidence. His mind raced with questions. Why Pudsey Park? Was there a significance to the location, or was it just another stage for the killer's morbid performance?

He glanced around, noting the position of CCTV cameras, the layout of the park, and the proximity of escape routes. Each piece of information was a thread in a larger tapestry they were slowly unravelling.

"This isn't just about killing any more," George said, more to himself than to his team. "It's a statement, a performance. Our killer is evolving, becoming more confident."

Dr Christian Ross approached him, his face grave under the grey Leeds sky.

"George, it's the same MO," Dr Ross stated, his voice low. "This murder is definitely linked to the others."

George nodded, his jaw set. The pattern was unmistakable, a haunting echo from a decade ago. Around them, Lindsey Yardley and her forensic team moved with meticulous precision, collecting evidence, their every movement under George's watchful eye.

Detective Constables Jay Scott and Candy Nichols were huddled nearby, poring over a file. "We think it's Liam O'Sullivan," Jay said, looking up at George. "The last of the group from those unsolved cases."

George's expression tightened at the mention of the name. George's eyes were drawn to the victim's face, frozen in a final expression of fear. It was a face he recognised from the files, a face that had haunted the periphery of their investigation.

Lindsey approached him, holding an evidence bag. "We found something," she said, her tone cautious. "A piece of

CHAPTER THIRTY-TWO

fabric caught on the shrubbery. It's not from the Santa suit."

George took the bag, examining the fabric. A clue, possibly a significant one. "Good work, Lindsey. Get this analysed immediately."

He stood up, his gaze sweeping over the park. The media was still there, cameras trained on them, the eyes of the city upon their every move. The pressure was mounting, the need for answers growing more urgent with each passing moment.

"We need to dig deeper," George said, addressing his team. "Re-examine the connections between the victims, especially Liam O'Sullivan. There's a pattern here we're missing."

Jay and Candy nodded, their expressions determined. They understood the stakes better than anybody.

George looked at the body once more and was transported back to a decade ago when an interview room at Leeds Police Station had been a battleground of wills. Detective Inspector George Beaumont, then a Detective Constable, sat across from Liam O'Sullivan, a key figure in a case that had remained stubbornly unresolved. O'Sullivan, a man whose presence dominated the room, was all sharp edges and hard stares.

Tall and broad, with a physique that spoke of both strength and intimidation, O'Sullivan's dark hair was slicked back, giving him a sleek, almost predatory appearance. His beard, neatly trimmed, framed a face that was accustomed to being in control. He wore dark colours as if to accentuate his imposing nature, and his voice, when he spoke to George, was laced with aggression.

"Why am I even here, Detective?" O'Sullivan had barked, his tone dismissive, confrontational. "You think you've got something on me? You're clutching at straws."

George, younger, less seasoned, but equally determined,

had met O'Sullivan's gaze unflinchingly. "It's not about what I think, Mr O'Sullivan," he'd replied. "It's about putting together pieces of a puzzle. And right now, you're a piece."

The memory faded, bringing George back to the present. He stood in Pudsey Park, looking down at the latest victim of the Santa Claus killer. The contrast between the man he had interviewed a decade ago and the victim before him was stark.

Liam O'Sullivan, once a figure of authority and defiance, lay before him, a shadow of his former self. Dressed in the garb of Santa Claus, strung up with Christmas lights, he was a grotesque caricature of the festive symbol. The man who had once exuded aggression and control was now a display of the killer's macabre handiwork.

George felt a pang of something—not quite sadness, but a recognition of the cruel passage of time. Ten years had transformed O'Sullivan from an imposing figure into a victim, a pawn in a game played by a murderer with a penchant for dramatic flair.

He crouched beside the body, his mind working methodically. The killer had a message, a purpose behind each murder, each staging. What was the connection? Why Liam O'Sullivan, and why now?

"Boss?" Jay's voice cut through George's thoughts. "We've got to get back. The lab might have something on that fabric Lindsey found."

George nodded, standing up. The urgency of the investigation pulled him back from the past, focusing him on the task at hand. They needed to catch the killer before another life was lost to this decade-long nightmare.

As they left the park, George cast one last glance at the crime scene. The flashing blue lights of police cars threw unsettling shadows, reflecting the growing unease in the crowd that had gathered. The press, always hungry for a story, had descended like hawks, their cameras pointed at the grim spectacle.

A reporter pushed through, microphone in hand, her eyes fixed on George. "Detective Beaumont, can you give us any details? Is there a message you wish to share with the public?"

George turned his face a mask of controlled professionalism. "We are doing everything we can to resolve this situation," he said, his voice firm, deliberate. "I urge the public to remain vigilant and report anything they might deem suspicious. Your cooperation is crucial."

His brief statement delivered, he turned back to the crime scene, leaving the reporters with no more than they had come with. Behind the police tape, Lindsey Yardley and her forensic team were still meticulously collecting evidence. Each item was bagged with precision, including several Christmas-themed items the killer had left behind, a macabre signature of sorts.

George watched as Lindsey held up a piece of evidence, her expression one of focused concentration. It was a Christmas ornament, twisted and distorted—much like the scene before them. He made a mental note to review everything collected, knowing even the smallest detail could be the key they were looking for.

As he surveyed the area, George's gaze fell on the faces in the crowd. There was fear and concern—a community grappling with the reality of a killer in their midst. Whispered conversations filled the air, a mix of rumours and fear, reflecting the growing anxiety gripping the city.

Each face told a story—parents holding their children a little tighter, elderly couples watching with worried eyes, young people whispering in hushed tones. This wasn't just another case for George; it was personal. He felt a responsibility not just to catch the killer but to calm the fears of the community he had sworn to protect.

"We'll get him, boss," Jay's voice broke through George's thoughts. The young detective's eyes were steady, echoing the resolve George felt.

"We have to," George replied, his voice low. "Too many lives have been shattered."

Chapter Thirty-three

The atmosphere in the Incident Room was palpable, with a mix of determination and sombreness as Detective Inspector George Beaumont convened an impromptu meeting in the wake of Liam O'Sullivan's death. The team, a tight-knit group honed through countless hours of investigation, gathered around the incident room, their expressions mirroring the gravity of the situation.

George stood at the head of the room, his posture firm despite the turmoil brewing within. The news of Liam's death had hit hard, not just as another tragic twist in the already complex case but as a stark reminder of the human cost of their pursuit of justice.

"We are dealing with a perpetrator who is not only meticulous but also callously indifferent to human life," he said, his gaze sweeping across the room, meeting the eyes of his team members. "This changes our approach. We need to be even more thorough, leave no stone unturned."

Detective Sergeant Yolanda Williams, her face a mask of focused resolve, spoke up. "We'll need to comb through Liam's history. There might be connections or details we previously missed."

"Exactly," George acknowledged with a nod. "Yolanda,

I want you and Tashan to lead on this. Go through his communications, financial transactions, anything that could give us a lead."

Tashan Blackburn, his usual stoic self, added, "I'll also cross-reference his known associates against recent activities. We need to map out his last known movements in detail."

George then turned his attention to Jay Scott. "Jay, coordinate with forensics. I want a thorough analysis of the crime scene. We can't afford to overlook even the smallest detail."

Jay, his expression grim, nodded in understanding. "I'm on it, boss. I'll make sure we get everything the scene can offer."

The room was a hive of activity as the team sprang into action, each member acutely aware of the heightened stakes. George watched them for a moment, pride mingling with a heavy sense of responsibility. This team, his team, was his greatest asset in the unrelenting quest for truth.

Taking a deep breath, George stepped out of the room, needing a moment of solitude to gather his thoughts. The case had taken a toll on him, pushing him to his limits both as a detective and as a human being. Yet, amidst this maelstrom of emotions, his resolve only strengthened.

Later, Yolanda and Tashan, amidst a sea of financial records and communications, uncovered a series of transactions that stood out starkly. "Look at this," Yolanda said, her voice low but edged with a discovery's excitement. "Regular payments going into Liam's account from a Jonathan Hughson."

George, leaning over the desk, scrutinized the bank statements. "Hughson... that's not a common name. Could he be Jonny Hughes?" he mused, the gears in his mind turning rapidly. "Keep digging. This could be the link we've been missing."

CHAPTER THIRTY-THREE

The two detectives nodded, their determination mirroring George's. They set to work, piecing together the connection between Liam and this mysterious benefactor, their investigation branching out into a new, unexpected direction.

Meanwhile, in another part of the station, Jay Scott and the forensic team pored over evidence from the crime scene. The room buzzed with the sound of analysis equipment and hushed conversations. Jay, donning latex gloves, carefully handled a piece of evidence, his focus absolute.

"Sir, look at this," one of the forensic analysts called out, holding up a bagged item for Jay to see. Inside was a piece of fabric, unique in its texture and colour, clearly not belonging to Liam.

Jay examined the fabric, a frown forming on his brow. "This doesn't match anything we've found before. Maybe the killer made a mistake," he mused, his voice a mix of cautious optimism and professional rigour.

The discovery of the unique fibre and the partially obscured footprints at the crime scene added a new dimension to the investigation. The team worked methodically, comparing the fibre to their existing evidence pool and enhancing the images of the footprints, hoping to find a match that would lead them closer to the perpetrator.

In the pursuit of Jonathan Hughson, identified through the financial breadcrumbs leading back to Liam O'Sullivan, George Beaumont had swiftly secured a warrant. This was a critical step forward, allowing Detective Sergeant Yolanda Williams and Detective Constable Tashan Blackburn access to Hughson's bank records. The urgency of the situation was palpable; they were on the cusp of uncovering a potentially vital piece of the puzzle.

In the Incident Room, Yolanda and Tashan, with the warrant in hand, delved into the labyrinth of Hughson's financial activities. The bank's cooperation was prompt, a testament to the gravity of the case. They sifted through pages of transactions, tracing the flow of money, until they hit a crucial lead — contact information for Jonathan Hughson.

"Got something," Tashan announced his voice a blend of triumph and intensity. "Here's his contact info — phone numbers, an address. It's all here."

Yolanda leaned over to glance at the screen. "Let's not waste any time. We need to find this man and see what he knows about Liam."

* * *

With the news of Jonathan Hughson, George Beaumont sat hunched over his computer, his eyes scanning the screen with a focused intensity. The clock ticked steadily in the background, marking the passage of time in the quiet room.

Beside him stood Detective Sergeant Josh Fry, equally absorbed in the task at hand. They were searching the deed poll records for any trace of a Jonathan Hughes. The theory was that Jonathan Hughes might have altered his identity to Jonathan Hughson, a possibility that, if proven true, could be a significant breakthrough.

"Anything yet, Josh?" George asked, his voice tinged with a mix of hope and urgency.

"Not yet, sir," Josh replied, his fingers flying over the keyboard. "If Hughes changed his name officially, it has to be here."

Minutes turned into an hour, yet the records yielded no

CHAPTER THIRTY-THREE

confirmation of a name change for Jonathan Hughes. The absence of such evidence was both frustrating and enlightening. It suggested that if Hughes had assumed a new identity, he had done so without leaving the usual legal trails.

"Looks like there's no deed poll record for a Jonathan Hughes changing his name," Josh finally said, leaning back with a sigh. "If he's now Hughson, he's managed to cover his tracks well."

George rubbed his chin thoughtfully, his mind racing with the implications of this new information. It meant he had to have contacts within an OCG, an organised crime group, which was never good news. "Keep digging, Josh. There has to be something we're missing," he said, the wheels in his mind already turning with alternative strategies.

As Josh continued his search, George's phone rang, breaking the concentration in the room. It was DCI Atkinson asking George if he was ready for the warrant to be signed off. Police Sergeant Greenwood was already in Garforth with a team, where they were about to raid Hughson's apartment.

"PS Greenwood is in position, ready to move on your command, George," Atkinson said.

"Thank you, sir, let's proceed with the raid."

Atkinson hung up, and George called PS Greenwood. "Do we have confirmation, sir?" Greenwood asked, his voice crackling through the speaker.

George straightened in his chair, a surge of adrenaline coursing through him. "Proceed with the raid. Keep me updated," he instructed, his voice firm and authoritative.

With the call ended, George stood up, his stature reflecting the gravity of the situation. He knew that the raid on Hughson's apartment was a crucial step. If Hughson was indeed their man or at least a significant piece of the puzzle, the raid could yield vital evidence. But George's thoughts were a mix of anticipation and apprehension. The outcome of this raid could either propel the investigation forward or send them back to the drawing board.

* * *

The early afternoon air in Garforth, an affluent area of Leeds, was pierced by the swift and precise movements of Police Sergeant Greenwood and his team of Authorised Firearms Officers (AFOs). They had one clear objective: raid the apartment of Jonathan Hughson, a man now pivotal in Detective Inspector George Beaumont's investigation.

Garforth, usually tranquil and untroubled, was about to become the centre of a significant police operation. The team, clad in tactical gear, moved stealthily towards Hughson's apartment, a sense of urgency evident in their every step.

PS Greenwood led the charge, his mind razor-sharp, focused entirely on the task at hand. The warrant for this raid was hard-earned, and there was no room for error. Greenwood communicated with his team through hand signals, a silent language that spoke volumes of their training and experience.

The team positioned themselves strategically outside Hughson's door. Greenwood gave a curt nod, the signal they had been waiting for. In one fluid motion, the door was breached, the sound resonating through the quiet halls of the apartment building.

"Police! We have a search warrant!" Greenwood bellowed as they entered, his voice echoing off the walls. The team flooded into the apartment, swiftly clearing each room with

CHAPTER THIRTY-THREE

practised efficiency.

Hughson, working on a laptop on his sofa in his pyjamas, was caught by surprise and was quickly apprehended. His expression, a mix of shock and confusion, told Greenwood this was not a man expecting to be arrested by a team of AFOs.

As Greenwood secured Hughson, his team meticulously searched the apartment. Every drawer, every cupboard was opened, every piece of paper scrutinized. They were searching for any piece of evidence that could link Hughson to Liam O'Sullivan and, ultimately, to the string of murders that had Leeds in a chokehold.

The apartment, a neat and modest dwelling, seemed at odds with the nature of their investigation. It was a stark reminder that appearances could be deceiving and that the truth often lay hidden beneath layers of normalcy.

Meanwhile, back at the station, George Beaumont waited anxiously for news of the raid. Every second that ticked by was a second closer to a potential breakthrough or a disheartening dead end. The weight of the case rested heavily on his shoulders, a burden he carried with a steadfast resolve.

Back at the apartment, Greenwood's team concluded their search. They bagged various items – documents, a laptop, a phone, and several other pieces that could potentially be of significance. Hughson was escorted out of the building, his future uncertain, his connection to the case yet to be determined.

As the team departed from Garforth, the sun began to set, casting a soft light over the city. The raid was over, but the investigation was far from it. In the coming hours, the evidence collected would be scrutinized, and Hughson would be interrogated. The pieces of the puzzle were slowly coming together, each step bringing George Beaumont and his team closer to the truth.

Chapter Thirty-four

Inside an interview room at Elland Road Police Station, the air was thick with tension. Detective Inspector George Beaumont and Detective Constable Jay Scott sat across from Jonathan Hughson. The fluorescent lights hummed overhead, casting stark shadows on the walls. Jonathan, a man in his forties with an aura of worn resilience, met George's steady gaze. There was a sense of resignation about him, a man seemingly burdened by years of untold stories.

George, his demeanour calm yet authoritative, leaned slightly forward. "Jonny, why the change in identity? What prompted you to become Jonathan Hughson?"

Jonny shifted uncomfortably in his seat, a man burdened by a past he had long tried to escape. His eyes, reflecting a mix of regret and resignation, met George's steady gaze.

"After Oliver's murder a decade ago, things got complicated. I was scared," Jonny began, his voice barely above a whisper. "I knew too much about Oliver's dealings, the kind of people he was involved with. After his death, I felt like I was being watched, followed."

Jay, observing closely, interjected. "So, you changed your identity to protect yourself?"

Jonny nodded. "Yes. I couldn't just disappear; I had to

become someone else entirely. Jonathan Hughson was a clean slate, a nobody. It was the only way I could think of to start over, to stay safe."

George's expression remained impassive, but his mind was racing. Jonny's fear and drastic decision to alter his identity spoke volumes about the dangers Oliver was entangled in.

"Did you have contact with Oliver before his death?" George pressed, keen to understand the whole picture.

Jonny hesitated, then slowly shook his head. "No, we had a falling out years before. I tried to convince him to leave that world, but he wouldn't listen. After that, we barely spoke. His death... it hit me hard, even though we were estranged." Jonny sniffed and then continued, "I did come back to Leeds once I found out he was murdered, though."

The detectives exchanged a glance, acknowledging the complexity of the brothers' relationship. It was a tangle of familial bonds, unheeded warnings, and tragic outcomes.

"And the people Oliver was involved with, do you know who they were?" Jay asked, delving deeper into the heart of the mystery.

Jonny's eyes darted away, fear flickering across his face. "I never knew names, just rumours, whispers of dangerous men with far-reaching influence. After Oliver's death, I didn't stick around to find out more."

George leaned forward, his eyes never leaving Jonny. "Did you have any part in the murders? Oliver's, a decade ago, or the recent ones?"

Jonny shook his head vehemently. "No, I didn't kill anyone. I've been hiding, not hunting."

George believed the man. They'd taken his prints and shoe size, which was a size 13, and forensics had gone over the

CHAPTER THIRTY-FOUR

clothes he wore. The team at Jonny's apartment also found nothing.

Jay, watching intently, chimed in. "Tell us about Oliver, Jonny. What kind of person was he? Why would someone want him dead?"

Jonny sighed a deep, weary exhalation. "Oliver... he got involved in some bad stuff. Dangerous people, dangerous deals. I tried to pull him out, but he was too deep in."

As Jonny spoke, George listened intently, analysing every word, every inflexion. This was more than just gathering information; it was about understanding the victim, the environment he thrived in, and the potential motives for his murder.

"And these dangerous people, could they be behind his murder?" George pressed his detective instincts on high alert.

Jonny hesitated, his gaze shifting to the table before locking eyes with George again. "It's possible. Oliver crossed paths with some people you wouldn't want to cross."

The room fell silent, the gravity of Jonny's words hanging in the air. George and Jay exchanged a glance, both recognizing the significance of this admission.

Before George could delve deeper, Jonny leaned in a sense of urgency in his eyes. "There's something else you should know. Something about why Oliver might have been killed..."

* * *

The interview room was steeped in a profound silence after Jonny Hughes dropped the revelation about his brother Oliver. Detective Inspector George Beaumont and Detective Constable Jay Scott sat across from him, digesting the information that shifted the entire landscape of the decade-old case.

George's expression was one of shock, a rare loss of composure for the seasoned detective. "Oliver was gay?" he asked, his voice tinged with disbelief. "In all the time we spent on the initial investigation, not once did this come up."

Jonny nodded solemnly, his eyes reflecting a mixture of sadness and resignation. "Oliver kept that part of his life very private. Even a decade ago, being openly gay wasn't as accepted as it is now. He feared the repercussions, both personally and professionally."

George leaned in, his detective instincts piqued. "You mentioned Oliver was involved with someone influential. Someone connected to an Organized Crime Group or the police?"

Jonny's gaze faltered, and he sighed. "I can't remember exactly who. It's been ten years, and Oliver was discreet about his relationships. But I know the person had a significant influence. And they desperately wanted to keep their relationship with Oliver a secret."

The weight of Jonny's words hung heavily in the room. George processed the information, realising the potential implications. An influential figure, desperate to hide their sexuality, could indeed have the motive to silence Oliver permanently.

George, with a look of disbelief, leaned in closer. "Are you certain, Jonny? You believe Oliver's partner, or someone under their influence, was responsible for his murder?"

Jonny's face was a canvas of fear and certainty. "I'm sure of it," he replied, his voice unwavering. "That's why I had to leave Leeds, to hide away in London. Whoever was involved had enough power to silence Oliver, to keep their own secrets

CHAPTER THIRTY-FOUR

safe. I couldn't take that risk."

Jay, his expression a mix of shock and contemplation, added, "So, your disappearance, changing your identity... it was all to protect yourself from whoever silenced Oliver?"

"Exactly," Jonny said, a tinge of sadness in his eyes. "I loved my brother despite our differences. But after his death, I knew that whoever he was involved with wouldn't hesitate to come after me."

The detectives exchanged a glance, both understanding the magnitude of what Jonny had just revealed. This was no longer just a search for a murderer; it was a delve into a world where personal secrets intersected with powerful, possibly dangerous entities.

"Why didn't you come forward with this information sooner?" Jay asked, his voice steady but probing.

Jonny's face was a mask of fear and frustration. "Because I was scared. After Oliver's death, I realised his partner had a lot to lose if their relationship came out. I knew they'd go to great lengths to keep it hidden. I had to disappear, change my identity, just to stay safe."

George sat back, his mind racing. This new angle brought a dramatic twist to the investigation. It wasn't just a case of unearthing a killer; it was about unravelling a web of secrets, power, and hidden identities.

George, his mind racing with the implications, stood up. "Thank you, Jonny. Your testimony has shed new light on this case. We'll do everything we can to get to the bottom of this."

As Jonny was escorted out of the room by a police constable to be released, George turned to Jay. "We need to tread carefully. This case has just taken a turn into very deep waters. If what Jonny says is true, we're dealing with someone who has the means to influence or even control the outcome of this investigation."

Jay nodded in agreement, his usual composed demeanour tinged with concern. "I'll start looking into Oliver's past again, see if we can find any connections to someone with that level of influence."

And for the first time during the investigation, George was relieved. He was sure his father wasn't gay, but he knew that Elias Marston was.

* * *

The White Rose Shopping Centre, bustling with festive cheer, was a stark contrast to the world Detective Inspector George Beaumont had inhabited these past weeks. The bright lights, the jingles, the laughter of shoppers—it all seemed surreal, a world away from the grim realities of his investigation.

George moved through the throng of people, his tall figure cutting a solitary path amidst the holiday revellers. The festive stalls, adorned with glittering decorations, seemed to mock the darkness he felt inside. He stopped briefly, his eyes scanning a display of jewellery. Each piece sparkled under the artificial lighting, but George's gaze was distant and thoughtful.

His mind wasn't on the jewellery, though. It was on Isabella, his rock through the tumultuous times. He wanted to find something perfect for her, a token of his appreciation and love. But nothing seemed right. How could he express everything she meant to him through a mere object?

He moved on, passing a stall stacked with books. He paused, picking up a novel, then placing it back down. It felt like

CHAPTER THIRTY-FOUR

an inadequate gesture, too impersonal. George's expression revealed his inner turmoil; a man used to making tough decisions is now uncertain in the face of a simple gift.

Crafts, ornaments, gourmet foods—he examined them all, but nothing seemed to fit. Each item he considered and discarded only added to his growing sense of frustration. He wasn't just looking for a gift; he was trying to bridge the gap that the case had created in his personal life.

George's phone buzzed, pulling him from his reverie. It was a message from Isabella, simple and loving, a beacon in his sea of thoughts. He typed a quick reply, a small smile playing on his lips. It was then he realised that the perfect gift wasn't something he could buy in a shop. It was his presence, his time, his commitment to their life together.

In his Merc, parked just outside the bustling White Rose Shopping Centre, George sat with a furrowed brow. Beside him, a bag lay unopened, its contents—an unchosen gift— a testament to his indecision. The festive cheer inside the shopping centre had only amplified his sense of disconnection, a stark reminder of the chasm the recent case had created between his professional and personal lives.

His phone was pressed against his ear, the familiar voice of Detective Inspector Luke Mason providing a much-needed distraction. "I just couldn't find anything, Luke," George confessed, his frustration evident. "It feels trivial, considering everything that's happened."

Luke's response crackled through the speaker, tinged with his characteristic humour. "Come on, son. You've faced down killers and solved crimes that had us all stumped. Surely, picking a gift for Isabella can't be that hard."

A faint smile tugged at the corner of George's lips despite

the turmoil inside. Luke, always the voice of reason, had a way of cutting through the noise. "It's not just about the gift," George replied. "It's finding a way to... to reconnect. To show her she's still the most important part of my life."

"You've always been rubbish at this sentimental stuff," Luke chided gently. "But you're overthinking it, son. It's not about the gift. It's about the thought, the effort. Isabella knows what you've been through. She understands."

George let out a sigh, the tension easing from his shoulders. Luke was right. Isabella had been his pillar, unwavering and understanding, through the tumultuous waves of the investigation.

"You know, sometimes I think you missed your calling as a counsellor," George said, a hint of lightness in his voice for the first time in weeks.

Luke laughed. "And miss out on all the action? Not a chance. Listen, just spend some time with her. That's what she'll value the most. And maybe cook her dinner or something. Can't go wrong with a bit of effort in the kitchen."

George chuckled, the sound foreign yet comforting to his ears. "Thanks, Luke. I'll give it a shot. And hey, thanks for having my back through all of this."

The call ended, but the warmth of the conversation lingered. George glanced at the unopened bag again, a decision forming in his mind. Luke was right; it wasn't about grand gestures or perfect gifts. It was about being there, about showing Isabella in his own way that she was his world.

With newfound resolve, George started the car and pulled out of the car park. The streets of Leeds, adorned with festive lights, no longer seemed as jarring. He had a plan, a simple one, but it felt right.

CHAPTER THIRTY-FOUR

George arrived home, the weight of unresolved thoughts from the White Rose Shopping Centre still clinging to him. Stepping inside, he was greeted by a scene that contrasted sharply with the turmoil in his mind. Isabella was on the living room floor, playing with their daughter Olivia, her laughter filling the room with a warmth that seemed foreign to George after the chilling weeks he'd endured.

He paused in the doorway, observing them. Isabella's face was alight with joy, her attention entirely devoted to Olivia, who was babbling excitedly. The simplicity and purity of the scene struck a chord in George's heart. Here, in this ordinary yet precious moment, lay the essence of what truly mattered.

As he watched them, an idea began to take shape in his mind, growing clearer with each passing second. The perfect gift for Isabella wasn't something that could be bought in a shop. It was something far more personal, more heartfelt.

A plan formed in George's mind, and a genuine smile, the first in what felt like an age, spread across his face. He imagined creating a collection of moments, snapshots of everyday life with Isabella and Olivia—a scrapbook of memories that celebrated their family, their love, and their journey together.

He pictured himself, camera in hand, capturing the laughter, the play, the quiet moments of contentment. Photos of Isabella reading to Olivia, the three of them on a walk in the park, cosy evenings spent in each other's company. Each image would be a testament to the life they shared, to the resilience of their love amidst the chaos of his career.

This gift would be a promise, too—a promise to be present, to cherish and to make more such memories. It was a vow to balance the scales between his duty as a detective and his role as a husband and father.

Quietly, George retreated from the doorway, his heart lighter than it had been in weeks. He went to an old drawer, rummaging through it until he found what he was looking for—his old camera, slightly dusty but still functional. It was perfect for his purpose, lending a touch of authenticity and nostalgia to his project.

As he inspected the camera, ensuring it still worked, George's mind was already framing shots, visualizing the pages of the scrapbook he would create. This wasn't just a gift for Isabella; it was a gift for himself, too, a reminder of the beauty and love that existed in his life outside the demands of his job.

Later that evening, as Isabella put Olivia to bed, George began his project. He started with simple photographs around the house—Olivia's toys scattered in the living room, Isabella's favourite mug on the kitchen counter, and the cosy nook where they often sat together. Each photo was a piece of their shared story, a story that continued to unfold day by day.

Chapter Thirty-five

The Friday morning air was crisp as Detective Inspector George Beaumont and Detective Constable Jay Scott made their way through the bustling streets of Leeds City Centre. Their destination was a high-rise that housed some of the city's most prominent financial firms, among them the workplace of Elias Marston.

As they entered the sleek, modern lobby, George adjusted his coat, aware of the stark contrast between the world of the police and the polished corporate environment they were stepping into. Jay, following closely, scanned their surroundings, his detective's instincts alert to every detail.

They approached the reception desk, where George introduced themselves. "Detective Inspector Beaumont and Detective Constable Scott. We're here to see Elias Marston."

The receptionist, a young woman with a practised professional smile, nodded and made a quick call. "Mr Marston will be with you shortly. Please have a seat."

The detectives took a seat in the plush waiting area, surveying the steady flow of well-dressed professionals moving through the lobby. Jay leaned in, speaking in a low tone. "What's the play here, boss?"

George, his gaze fixed on the elevators, replied, "We need

to tread carefully. Marston's influential, and we can't afford to spook him. Let's stick to the facts and gauge his reactions."

Before long, Elias Marston emerged from the elevator. He was a man in his early sixties with a commanding presence and an air of self-assuredness. His tailored suit spoke of success and power. He extended a hand to George as he approached. "Detective Inspector Beaumont, Detective Constable Scott. To what do I owe the pleasure?"

George shook his hand firmly. "Thank you for seeing us, Mr Marston. We have a few questions about your connection to the recent murder investigations."

Elias' expression remained composed, but there was a flicker of something in his eyes—a hint of wariness. "Of course, let's talk in my office," he said, leading them to the elevator.

Once in Elias' office, a room with a view of the city skyline, George watched the morning sun as it streamed through the floor-to-ceiling windows, casting long shadows across the room, mirroring the gravity of their conversation. The two detectives faced Elias Marston across his polished desk and got down to business. George began methodically, outlining the connections they had uncovered, watching Elias' reactions closely.

Elias listened intently, his face a mask of calm, but George noted the subtle shifts in his body language, the occasional tightening of his jaw.

When questioned about his whereabouts during the murders, Elias provided alibis, his answers smooth and rehearsed. "As you can see, Detective, I have no involvement in these tragic events. My work and reputation speak for themselves."

George and Jay exchanged a look, both aware that while

CHAPTER THIRTY-FIVE

Elias' responses were polished, they lacked the ring of absolute truth.

George, his expression unreadable, decided to cut straight to the heart of the matter. "Mr Marston, were you ever romantically involved with Oliver Hughes?"

The question hung in the air like a charged cloud. Elias Marston, a picture of composure until now, visibly stiffened. His eyes, confident and steady a moment ago, flickered with a trace of something undefinable.

"I beg your pardon?" Elias responded, his voice a mix of surprise and anger. "That's a rather personal and, frankly, inappropriate question, Detective."

George held Elias' gaze, unfazed. "It's relevant to our investigation, Mr Marston. Oliver Hughes' death a decade ago, and the recent related murders, have led us to explore all possible connections."

Elias leaned back in his chair, a thin veneer of control masking his discomfort. "My personal life has no bearing on this investigation, Detective Beaumont. I assure you, I had no such relationship with Mr Hughes." He frowned. "I'm two decades older than him, for one!"

Jay, observing the exchange, noted the subtle shift in Elias' demeanour. The mention of Oliver Hughes had unsettled him, however briefly.

"Understood, Mr Marston. But you can see how important it is for us to investigate every angle. Oliver's private life is becoming a significant factor in our case," George continued, his tone firm yet diplomatic.

Elias sighed a momentary lapse revealing his irritation. "I've been a respectable member of the financial community for decades. My reputation is beyond reproach. These insinuations are not only unfounded but offensive."

"These are not insinuations, Mr Marston," George stated firmly, locking eyes with Elias. "We have reliable information that Oliver Hughes was gay and involved with a man who may have had a hand in his death. Understanding his relationships is crucial to our investigation."

Elias' facade of control wavered slightly under George's steady gaze. The mention of Oliver Hughes being gay and the implications of his death seemed to have struck a nerve.

"I... I find this line of questioning highly irregular and deeply personal," Elias replied, his voice strained. "Oliver Hughes' private life should have no bearing on your investigation."

George leaned forward slightly, his tone resolute yet measured. "Mr Marston, any relationship Oliver Hughes had, especially one that could provide a motive for his murder, is of utmost importance to us. It's our responsibility to explore every possible angle."

Elias sat back in his chair, a sheen of perspiration visible on his forehead. The mention of Oliver's sexuality and the potential involvement of a romantic partner seemed to unsettle him more than he cared to show.

Jay watched the exchange closely, noting the undercurrents of tension. The mention of Oliver's secret life had introduced an element of unpredictability into the conversation.

"Detective, I assure you, my personal life has nothing to do with Oliver Hughes or any criminal activities," Elias said, attempting to regain his composure. "I've built my reputation on integrity and professionalism," he repeated.

Jay, taking a calculated risk, addressed Elias Marston with a direct challenge. "If it's not you, Mr Marston, then prove it. Give us a DNA sample so we can exclude you from our

CHAPTER THIRTY-FIVE

investigation."

Elias Marston, who had maintained a composed demeanour until now, suddenly erupted in anger. He stood abruptly, his chair scraping back against the floor, and pointed an accusatory finger at George Beaumont. "How dare you treat me this way, George? After all, I've been such a good friend of your father, Edward," he shouted, his voice laced with indignation and betrayal.

This mention of Edward Beaumont was a jolt to the conversation, introducing an unexpected and personal element to the discourse. Jay, who had been observing the exchange, reacted subtly to the mention of George's father, a flicker of surprise crossing his features.

George, taken aback by the sudden outburst and the mention of his estranged father, remained outwardly calm. Inside, however, his thoughts raced. Elias' reaction, particularly his reference to Edward Beaumont, added a new layer of complexity to the investigation.

"Mr Marston, please understand that our request is a standard procedure in an investigation of this nature," George responded, his voice steady despite the charged atmosphere. "It's not meant as a personal affront."

Elias, now pacing the room, was visibly agitated. "A standard procedure? You barge into my office, make insinuations about my personal life, and now you want my DNA? This is outrageous!"

Jay, watching the unfolding scene, noted the shift in Elias' behaviour. The calm, controlled financier had given way to a man clearly rattled by the detectives' inquiries.

George stood, ready to de-escalate the situation. "Mr Marston, we appreciate your cooperation thus far. Please understand that any information you provide will be crucial in helping us solve this case."

Elias, however, seemed beyond consolation. "I'll have you know, George, that I've been nothing but supportive of your father and his endeavours. For you to come here and accuse me in this manner is a betrayal of the highest order."

The mention of Edward Beaumont again caught George's attention. The connection between Elias and his father was something he hadn't anticipated and added an unexpected personal dimension to the case.

"Are you sure you won't give us a voluntary sample?" asked George.

"No, I will not!"

George nodded, acknowledging Elias' response. "We appreciate your cooperation, Mr Marston. If there's nothing further you can add, we'll conclude our visit."

As they stood to leave, Elias' posture remained rigid, a clear sign that the detectives' questions had hit a nerve. "I trust this will be the end of such unfounded inquiries," he said, a note of finality in his voice.

Once outside, George and Jay walked in silence, each lost in thought. The reaction they had witnessed from Elias Marston, though carefully controlled, had added a layer of complexity to their investigation.

"Boss, do you think he's telling the truth?" Jay finally asked, breaking the silence.

George pondered for a moment before replying. "Hard to say, Jay. But one thing's clear – we've rattled him. And in cases like this, that reaction alone can be very telling."

* * *

CHAPTER THIRTY-FIVE

Back at the Incident Room, the air was charged with anticipation. Detective Inspector George Beaumont gathered his key team members – Jay, Tashan, Candy, and Yolanda – for a candid meeting. The room was abuzz with the usual hum of police activity, but within this circle, a more serious tone prevailed.

George, standing at the front, took a deep breath. The weight of the revelation he was about to share hung heavily on his shoulders. "I need to tell you all something important," he began, his voice steady but laced with a hint of apprehension. "Edward Beaumont, the man whose name has come up in connection with Elias Marston... he's my father."

He paused, bracing himself for a wave of shocked stares and uncomfortable silences. But the reaction he received was different from what he expected.

Instead of surprise or judgment, his team exchanged knowing looks before turning back to George with smiles of solidarity. It was Jay who spoke first, his tone supportive. "Boss, we already knew."

George was taken aback. "You did?"

Tashan nodded, a wry smile on his face. "It's not exactly a secret, George. Your father's a well-known figure in Leeds. And when his name started surfacing in the investigation, we put two and two together."

Candy stepped forward, her expression one of empathy. "We understand it's a difficult position for you, being caught between your duty and your personal connections. But we've got your back, George."

Yolanda, usually reserved, added her reassurance. "Your integrity's never been in question, George. You've led us with nothing but professionalism. We trust you, regardless of your family ties."

George felt a wave of relief wash over him, mingled with gratitude. He had expected tension and perhaps even distrust, but instead, he found unwavering support from his team.

"Thank you," he said, his voice thick with emotion. "I've been wrestling with this, wondering how it might affect our work, our investigation. Your support means a lot."

Jay grinned. "We're a team, boss. We tackle cases together, no matter how complex or personal they may get."

George looked around at the faces of his team, each showing a mix of determination and loyalty. This moment solidified their bond, reinforcing the trust and camaraderie that was the foundation of their unit.

With renewed vigour, George addressed the team. "Alright, then. Let's get back to work. We have a case to solve, and I couldn't ask for a better team to do it with."

As they dispersed to their respective tasks, the Incident Room buzzed with a renewed sense of purpose. George, feeling a weight lifted off his chest, returned to his desk, ready to dive back into the investigation with the full support of his team behind him.

Chapter Thirty-six

Detective Inspector George Beaumont was deep in thought at his desk, strategising his next move regarding his father, when the call came through. The desk sergeant's voice echoed through the receiver, informing him of an unexpected visitor waiting in reception. Curious and slightly apprehensive, George made his way downstairs.

As he entered the bustling reception area of Elland Road Police Station, George spotted the last person he expected to see – Elias Marston. The change in setting – from the polished corporate world to the pragmatic confines of the police station – added a layer of contradiction to Elias' presence.

"What can I do for you, Mr Marston?" George asked, masking his surprise with professional courtesy.

Elias, standing tall yet with a less imposing demeanour than before, replied firmly, "I will not have my reputation sullied by baseless accusations, Detective. So, I've come to give a voluntary DNA sample."

George, taken aback by this voluntary cooperation, nodded in appreciation. "Thank you, Mr Marston. That's very cooperative of you. I'll book you in with one of our forensic scientists."

As they walked through the corridors towards the forensic

lab, the atmosphere between them was markedly different from their last encounter. Elias, previously defensive and agitated, now appeared more relaxed, even chatty. He engaged in small talk with George, discussing benign topics like the weather and local sports, a stark contrast to the tense exchange they had in his office.

George, while appreciative of Elias' cooperation, remained cautious and alert. He was aware that Elias' change in demeanour could be strategic, an attempt to sway the investigation or to preserve his image.

Upon reaching the lab, George introduced Elias to the forensic scientist, who promptly began the process of collecting DNA swabs. George observed the procedure, ensuring everything was conducted by the book.

Throughout the process, Elias maintained his composure, showing no signs of discomfort or reluctance. Once the swabs were taken, Elias turned to George, his expression serious yet calm.

"George, I hope this clears any doubts about my involvement. I've worked hard to build my reputation, and I trust the police to conduct a fair investigation." He paused. "And in truth, it was your father that told me to come here today. To clear my name."

George, acknowledging Elias' sentiment, replied, "We appreciate your cooperation, Mr Marston. This will certainly aid in our investigation."

As Elias left the station, George watched him go, pondering the sudden shift in his approach. The voluntary DNA sample was a significant development, one that could potentially clear Elias' name or implicate him further in the case. George knew that the results of the DNA analysis would be pivotal in

CHAPTER THIRTY-SIX

determining the next course of action.

Returning to his office, George reflected on the morning's events. The investigation was a constantly evolving puzzle, with each piece reshaping the overall picture. Elias Marston's voluntary submission of a DNA sample was an unexpected piece, one that could either fit seamlessly into the emerging pattern or disrupt it entirely.

* * *

The Incident Room at Elland Road Station buzzed with the usual energy of an ongoing investigation as Detective Inspector George Beaumont made his way back upstairs. His mind was still processing Elias Marston's unexpected cooperation when he encountered Lindsey Yardley at the doorway to the shared office.

Lindsey, the Scene of Crime Manager, held an envelope in her hand, and her expression conveyed the importance of its contents. "George, you're going to want to see this," she said, her voice a mixture of urgency and anticipation.

"What have you got for me, Lindsey?" George asked, stepping aside to let her into the office.

Lindsey opened the envelope and pulled out a report.

"We found fibres at the scene," Lindsey began, her voice low. "They're from BEAUTECH industrial grade fabric, a specific polyester-cotton blend used in lab coats."

George's interest was piqued. "Lab coats? Do we know who uses this specific blend?"

Lindsey nodded, flipping through her notes. "It's a unique blend, mainly used by Home Office Pathologists and some in West Yorkshire. It's quite distinctive."

The team, overhearing the conversation, gathered around, their attention fixed on Lindsey. George could feel the weight of the moment; this could be the breakthrough they had been waiting for.

George leaned in, his mind racing. "Does Dr Christian Ross wear these lab coats?"

"Yes, he would," Lindsey confirmed. The simplicity of her answer belied the weight it carried.

A heavy silence hung between them. The revelation that the fibres found at a murder scene matched the type of lab coat worn by Dr Ross was a significant lead. George's thoughts raced. Was it a mere coincidence, or was there a deeper, more sinister connection?

"Thank you, Lindsey. This information could be crucial," George said, his mind already turning over the possibilities. "Any results on the unknown DNA profile yet?"

Lindsey shook her head and left.

Calling his team together in their Incident Room, he said, "Think about it. The missing light source results from Dr Ross, his defensive reaction when questioned about it, and now the lab coat fibres at the crime scene." He paused. "He wears a Tyvek suit like we all do, so we can't say it's contamination."

Jay Scott, leaning against a desk, nodded thoughtfully. "But don't forget what Jonny said about Oliver Hughes being gay, boss. He mentioned Oliver's secret lover might be involved, someone with influence."

George recalled his recent conversation with Dr Ross. "I did ask him if he wanted to bring a girlfriend to the charity event, and he said he didn't have one. It might be nothing, but it's another piece that fits."

The team, however, was not immediately convinced. Scepti-

CHAPTER THIRTY-SIX

cism was evident in their expressions. Candy Nichols crossed her arms, considering the information. "It seems a bit of a stretch, sir. We're talking about a respected pathologist here."

Tashan Blackburn, ever the analytical thinker, raised a valid point. "Plus, wouldn't we have had a hit on the CED with Dr Ross' DNA if he was involved, sir? Pathologists' DNA is typically on that database."

George hesitated, then admitted, "I've actually spoken to Dr Ross about the CED. He confirmed he's on it."

The room fell into a contemplative silence. The theory was compelling, yet the pieces weren't aligning perfectly. Doubts lingered in the air.

Tashan, his eyes fixed on George, offered, "Let me look into it, sir. I'll check the CED records and see if there's anything unusual about Dr Ross' entry. Maybe there's more to it than we're seeing."

George gave a grateful nod. "Thanks, Tashan. We need to be absolutely sure before we make any moves."

As the meeting dispersed, George remained in the Incident Room, his thoughts a tangled web of theories and possibilities. The notion that Dr Ross, a colleague and a fixture in the forensic community, could be involved in such heinous crimes was unsettling. Yet, the emerging evidence was pointing in a direction he couldn't ignore.

Jay approached George's desk, a look of concern on his face. "Boss, are you sure about this? Accusing Dr Ross is a big step."

George met Jay's gaze, his resolve clear in his eyes. "I know, Jay. But we have to follow the evidence, no matter where it leads us. If Ross is innocent, the investigation will prove it. If not, we need to be ready to face the truth."

* * *

Detective Constable Tashan Blackburn sat hunched over his computer, his eyes scanning through the digital records of the Contamination Elimination Database. The Incident Room around him buzzed with the steady rhythm of an active investigation. He was searching for any trace of Dr Christian Ross' DNA in the CED, following up on Detective Inspector George Beaumont's unsettling theory.

After hours of meticulous searching, Tashan's perseverance paid off. He found a crucial piece of information, one that could change the course of their investigation. Twenty years ago, Dr Ross had submitted his DNA for a research project unrelated to his forensic work. The submission was supposed to be a temporary measure, with the promise of deletion once the project concluded.

Tashan leaned back in his chair, processing the implications. Dr Ross' DNA was separate from the current CED records, as it had become voluntary for pathologists to submit their samples. This detail had allowed Dr Ross to escape detection in both their recent analyses and ones a decade ago.

With a sense of urgency, Tashan gathered the relevant documents and made his way to George's office. The door was ajar, and he knocked lightly before entering.

"Sir, you need to see this," Tashan said, his voice tinged with a mix of excitement and disbelief.

George looked up, his expression weary yet attentive. "What have you got, Tashan?"

Tashan laid out the documents on George's desk. "Dr Ross' DNA isn't in the current CED records. It's now voluntary for pathologists to submit their DNA. But I found something else –

CHAPTER THIRTY-SIX

he did submit his DNA twenty years ago for a research project. It was supposed to be deleted afterwards."

George's eyes narrowed as he absorbed the information. "So his DNA was in the system, just not where we expected to find it."

"Exactly," Tashan confirmed. "This could be why we didn't get a hit when we ran the DNA from the crime scenes against the CED."

George leaned back in his chair, his mind racing with the new development. "This changes everything. Dr Ross could have been at those crime scenes, and we had no way of knowing because his DNA wasn't where it should have been."

Tashan nodded, a sense of grim realization dawning on him. "We need to confront Dr Ross with this information."

George stood up, a determined look on his face. "Let's bring him in for questioning. We need to tread carefully, but we can't ignore this lead."

As Tashan left to make the arrangements, George stood by his office window, gazing out at the city. The thought of Dr Ross, a respected pathologist and a colleague, being involved in such heinous crimes was difficult to comprehend. Yet the evidence was pointing in a direction that could no longer be ignored.

* * *

The Incident Room was charged with a palpable tension, a stark contrast to the usual routine. Detective Constable Tashan Blackburn, after uncovering a crucial piece of evidence about Dr Christian Ross, coordinated with Police Sergeant Greenwood to bring the pathologist in for questioning. But what seemed like a straightforward task soon spiralled into an unexpected situation.

PS Greenwood arrived at the city morgue, the air cool and sterile, the corridors echoing with the quiet hum of diligent work. He approached the reception, his presence commanding immediate attention. "I'm here to see Dr Christian Ross," he announced, his tone professional yet firm.

The assistant, a young woman with a clipboard in hand, looked up, her expression shifting to confusion. "Dr Ross isn't here. He left early today, and he didn't mention where he was going."

Greenwood's brow furrowed. This was unusual. Pathologists like Dr Ross were creatures of routine. He pulled out his phone and dialled George Beaumont. "DI Beaumont, it's Greenwood. Ross isn't at the morgue, and no one knows where he's gone."

Back at the station, George felt a surge of alarm. He promptly tried calling Dr Ross, but each call went unanswered, ringing into the void. The lack of response was troubling. George's instincts, honed by years on the force, kicked in. He couldn't shake the feeling that Dr Ross might be attempting to evade them.

"What if he's done a runner," George muttered, his voice laced with concern. He quickly issued a Be On the Look Out (BOLO) alert with immediate circulation. His team, sensing the urgency, sprang into action, coordinating with other units and monitoring potential exits from the city.

The Incident Room became a hub of focused activity. Maps of Leeds and its surrounding areas were sprawled across tables, marked with potential routes Dr Ross could take. Officers were dispatched to key locations while others combed

CHAPTER THIRTY-SIX

through surveillance footage, looking for any sign of the pathologist. Jay and Candy were put on ANPR cameras, searching for his vehicle.

Tashan, standing beside George, couldn't help but feel the weight of the situation. "We need to find him, sir. If he's running, he knows we're onto him."

George nodded, his jaw set. "We'll find him, Tashan. He can't have gone far."

Chapter Thirty-seven

The search for Dr Christian Ross intensified. PS Greenwood dispatched a team to Dr Ross' known address, a quaint house in a quiet Leeds suburb, but the pathologist was nowhere to be found. The house, usually a place of solace, stood eerily silent, devoid of any sign of recent activity.

Recognising the need for a broader approach, George authorised financial checks on Dr Ross' current and previous addresses as per the BOLO, tasking Detective Sergeant Joshua Fry with the urgent assignment. Fry, adept at navigating the complex web of financial records, dove into the task with a sense of urgency that matched the gravity of the situation.

George, meanwhile, was on the phone with immigration, seeking any leads on Dr Ross' possible movements. As he held the phone to his ear, listening to the static-filled hold music, Josh Fry approached him with an update.

"George, Dr Ross has lived in his childhood home since his early twenties," Fry reported, his tone conveying the futility of their search. "His parents left it to him. There's no record of him owning any other property."

The revelation added another layer of complexity to the situation. George hung up the phone, his call to immigration yielding no helpful information. He took a deep breath, trying

CHAPTER THIRTY-SEVEN

to calm the storm of thoughts swirling in his mind.

"Why would he run?" George pondered aloud, more to himself than to Fry. "What's driving him? We need to understand his motivations."

Fry nodded, sharing George's confusion. "It doesn't add up. He's a respected pathologist, not some career criminal."

George walked over to the window, gazing out at the city lights beginning to twinkle in the dusk. He tried to put himself in Dr Ross' shoes, to see the world through his eyes. The man they were hunting was not a shadowy figure from the underworld but a colleague, a professional they had worked alongside.

"Could it be fear? Guilt? Or something more?" George mused, his voice barely above a whisper. The usual clarity with which he approached his cases seemed to blur when it came to Dr Ross.

The room fell silent; the team members were absorbed in their tasks yet keenly aware of the tension emanating from their leader. The search for Dr Ross was more than a manhunt; it was a journey into the unknown, delving into the psyche of a man who had hidden his true nature behind a mask of respectability.

"We keep searching," he declared, his voice firm. "Check his financial transactions, his phone records, anything that can give us a lead. We need to find him before he disappears completely."

The atmosphere in the Incident Room was tense and expectant as Hayden Wyatt, an American Scene of Crime Officer under Lindsey Yardley's command, entered with a grave expression that immediately caught everyone's attention. He held a folder tightly under his arm, its contents seemingly heavy with significance.

Detective Constable Tashan Blackburn, who had initiated this line of inquiry, stood up from his desk, his eyes fixed on Wyatt. The rest of the team paused their activities, sensing the importance of this moment.

"Hayden, what did you find?" Tashan asked, his voice a mix of anticipation and apprehension.

Wyatt took a deep breath before speaking. "The DNA on the Christmas bauble from Liam O'Sullivan's scene... it's a match for Christian Ross." He paused, letting the weight of his words sink in.

A murmur of disbelief rippled through the room. The confirmation of Dr Ross' DNA at the crime scene was a turning point in the investigation, a chilling realization that the respected pathologist was indeed involved in the murders.

But Wyatt had more to say. "There's something else," he continued, opening the folder and pulling out a sheet of paper.

The team exchanged puzzled glances. George Beaumont stepped forward, his expression intense as he processed the information. "What else, Hayden?"

A heavy silence fell as Hayden Wyatt revealed the additional finding: the DNA on the bindings at all the crime scenes, both current and from the past case, showed a familial match to George Beaumont. This revelation struck the room like a thunderbolt, sending shock waves of disbelief and apprehension.

George stood frozen, his mind grappling with the magnitude of the discovery. "A familial match? That means..." His voice trailed off, the implications dawning on him. The DNA was pointing to someone in his family, and there was only one person it could realistically be: his father, Edward Beaumont.

"Why didn't the match occur ten years ago?" George asked

CHAPTER THIRTY-SEVEN

Hayden.

The young SOCO shrugged. "DNA found at crime scenes has to be manually searched against the CED, so I guess that didn't happen last time."

It made sense, especially if either Dr Ross or Edward Beaumont were the culprit. Or both culprits. "Could it be that Dr Ross and my father were working together?" George pondered aloud, a mix of disbelief and dread in his voice. The possibility that his estranged father was involved in the murders, possibly in collusion with Dr Ross, was a twist he had never anticipated.

Before he could further contemplate this disturbing thought, Jay Scott interrupted, his voice cutting through the tense atmosphere. "Boss, we've located Christian Ross' car. ANPR cameras picked it up, heading towards Cookridge."

Without hesitation, George grabbed his phone and dialled DCI Atkinson. "Sir, we've located Ross. We need authorization for a raid team. He's heading to Cookridge."

As he spoke, the pieces began to fit together in his mind. Cookridge was where his father, Edward Beaumont, resided. The convergence of Ross' location with his father's residence was more than a coincidence—it was a sign of their potential collusion.

The phone call was brief, with DCI Atkinson quickly grasping the urgency of the situation and granting authorization for the raid. George relayed the information to the team, his voice firm and commanding.

"We move now. Jay, Tashan, Candy, you're with me. We need to intercept Ross before he reaches my father's place."

The team sprang into action, gathering their gear and heading towards the vehicles. The drive to Cookridge was tense, each member lost in their thoughts, contemplating the possible scenarios that awaited them.

George's mind was a whirlwind of emotions and questions. The thought that his father might be entwined in this web of murder and deceit was almost too much to bear. The complex relationship he had with Edward Beaumont, marked by estrangement and unresolved issues, added a deeply personal dimension to the case.

As they neared Cookridge, the reality of what they might find loomed large. The possibility of confronting both his father and Dr Ross was a scenario fraught with danger and uncertainty.

The streets of Cookridge were quiet as they approached Edward Beaumont's residence, the ANPR information guiding them with precision. The raid team, coordinated by George, took positions, ready to move on his command.

* * *

In the affluent suburb of Cookridge, Edward Beaumont sat in his study, immersed in the glow of his computer screen. The room was filled with the rich aroma of aged Scottish whisky and the soft clicking of keys. Edward, always the picture of composure, sipped his drink, his eyes scanning through financial reports with meticulous attention.

A sudden knock on the door disrupted the silence of the evening. His housekeeper had left hours ago, leaving Edward to attend to any unexpected visitors. With a slight sense of irritation, he rose from his desk and made his way to the door.

Upon opening it, he was met with a sight that wiped the smirk off his face. Standing on his doorstep was Dr Christian Ross, his expression grim, a gun firmly in his hand. For a moment, Edward's usual bravado faltered, but he quickly regained his composure.

"Christian, this is unexpected. Care to join me for a drink?" Edward asked, his voice betraying a hint of sarcasm despite the precarious situation.

Without a word, Dr Ross pressed the gun against Edward's ribs, a silent demand for compliance. Edward, sensing the gravity of the situation, slowly retreated into the study, guided by the unyielding pressure of the firearm.

Once inside, Christian directed Edward to sit behind his desk. The tension in the air was palpable as Edward complied, his usual air of authority diminishing in the face of the loaded gun. Christian found a seat for himself, the weapon still trained on Edward.

"Christian, to what do I owe the pleasure of this armed visit?" Edward asked, attempting to maintain a veneer of calm.

Dr Ross' face was a mask of cold resolve. "You know why I'm here, Edward. It's time to settle accounts."

The air in the study grew heavier, charged with unspoken accusations and years of hidden agendas. Edward leaned back in his chair, his mind racing for a way to defuse the situation.

"Is this about the murders, Christian? I assure you, I had no part in your... activities," Edward said, trying to distance himself from the implication of his involvement.

Dr Ross' expression hardened. "Don't play the innocent with me, Edward. You've been a part of this since the beginning. Your influence, your connections – they were instrumental."

Edward's facade of control began to crack. The realisation that his past actions and associations were catching up with him was inescapable. He had always been a master manipulator, but now he found himself in a game where the stakes were life and death.

"You can't pin this on me, Christian. I never asked you to kill anyone," Edward retorted, his voice laced with a mix of fear and defiance.

Dr Ross leaned forward, the gun unwavering in his hand. "But you benefited from it, didn't you? Your silence was as good as complicity."

The tension was as thick as the heavy drapes that framed the windows. Edward, seated behind his desk, raised an eyebrow at Dr Christian Ross, who stood across from him, his hand trembling slightly as he pointed the gun.

"I never told you to get rid of your lover, Christian," Edward said, his voice tinged with a blend of mockery and curiosity.

Christian's hand shook more noticeably at the mention of his lover, the gun wavering in his unsteady grip. But after a moment, he regained his composure, his face hardening into a mask of resolve. "I know. I killed him because of what he found out, not because he was my lover."

Edward's lips curled into a grin, finding a twisted amusement in Christian's turmoil. "So why are you here, Christian? What brings you to my doorstep with such dire intentions?"

Dr Ross' eyes were cold, his voice steady despite the turmoil raging within him. "It's because of your fucking son," he said, his gaze never leaving Edward. "He's on to me."

Edward's grin widened, a sense of pride evident in his expression. "I taught him well then," he remarked, a hint of smug satisfaction in his tone.

"Too well," Christian replied, his voice laced with a mixture of respect and resentment.

CHAPTER THIRTY-SEVEN

Edward leaned back in his chair, his eyes calculating. "He's probably on his way here as we speak."

Christian nodded, his decision clear in his eyes. "Which is exactly why I need to end this."

* * *

Outside, the night air was crisp and tense as Detective Inspector George Beaumont and his team approached Edward Beaumont's mansion in Cookridge. The stately home, usually a symbol of wealth and power, now loomed ominously under the cover of darkness. George's heart pounded with a mix of professional determination and personal apprehension. This was not just another operation; it was a confrontation with his own blood, his estranged father.

As they neared the mansion, George signalled his team to spread out, each moving with practised stealth. They communicated through subtle gestures, their years of training evident in their silent coordination.

In a concealed position, the team's sniper, a seasoned officer with a keen eye, had set up his rifle. He peered through the scope, his focus unwavering. Through the crosshairs, he had a clear view of Edward Beaumont and Dr Christian Ross inside the study. The tension of the situation was palpable even from his distant vantage point.

George crouched near the front of the mansion and received a message over his earpiece. "DI Beaumont, we have visuals on both targets. Ross has a gun. Clear shot confirmed," the sniper reported, his voice calm and controlled.

George's mind raced with the implications of this information. The possibility of using deadly force was always a last resort, one he hoped to avoid. "Hold your fire. We're going to try to resolve this peacefully," he whispered back, his voice barely audible.

He knew the risks involved in confronting his father and Dr Ross, especially given the latter's desperate state. The idea that his father might be involved in the murders was a bitter pill to swallow, a personal betrayal that cut deeper than any case he had worked on before.

With a hand signal, George directed his team to take positions around the mansion. They moved with precision, covering all possible exits. The goal was to contain the situation, to prevent Dr Ross from escaping and to bring both him and Edward Beaumont in without bloodshed.

* * *

Inside, the study fell silent, the only sound the ticking of the antique clock on the wall. Christian's finger tightened on the trigger, his resolve evident in the set of his jaw.

Edward, sensing the imminent danger, tried a different tactic. "Christian, think about this. You don't want to add another murder to your conscience. There's still a chance to make things right."

But Christian was beyond reasoning, his mind made up. "There's no turning back now, Edward. It's either me or him, and I'm not ready to give up my freedom."

Edward's expression darkened, a hint of fear creeping into his eyes. He knew that Christian was a man pushed to the edge, capable of anything in his desperate bid to escape justice.

The stillness of the night was shattered by the sound of a gunshot echoing through the grounds of the Beaumont

CHAPTER THIRTY-SEVEN

mansion.

Chapter Thirty-eight

As the police team secured the scene, George's focus turned to the sniper, the unexpected source of the gunshot. "Who the fuck took the shot!"

The sniper, realising the gravity of his decision, spoke into his radio, his voice tinged with regret and urgency. "DI Beaumont, I took the shot. I thought Edward was in immediate danger."

George felt a surge of frustration mixed with understanding. The sniper had acted out of a perceived threat, a split-second decision in a high-stakes situation. "Stand down," George replied firmly. "Secure your position. We're taking control of the scene."

Inside the study, the revelation of the sniper's intervention added another layer of complexity to the already tense situation. Edward Beaumont, who had been moments away from a potentially lethal confrontation with Dr Ross, now found himself inadvertently saved by the police marksman's pre-emptive action.

George, his expression a complex tapestry of shock, regret, and duty, processed the scene before him. Dr Christian Ross, the man who had been at the heart of the convoluted Santa Claus murders, lay motionless on the floor of the study, a

CHAPTER THIRTY-EIGHT

single gunshot wound marking the abrupt end of his story.

The sniper, positioned in the shadows, had made a split-second decision, believing Edward Beaumont's life to be in immediate danger. But the reality of the outcome weighed heavily on everyone present. The shot, intended to save a life, had instead taken one.

George turned to his father, his expression a mix of professional detachment and personal conflict. "Are you hurt?" he asked, scanning Edward for any signs of injury.

Edward shook his head, a wry smile touching his lips. "No, thanks to your sharpshooter. Seems I owe you one."

George approached Dr Ross' body, his mind racing with the implications of this sudden turn of events. The meticulous investigation and the pursuit of justice had culminated in this stark and unanticipated ending.

Edward Beaumont, standing a few feet away, watched the scene with a complex mix of emotions. The man who had loomed large in his life, entangled in a web of secrets and lies, was now gone, leaving behind a trail of unanswered questions and unresolved issues.

"George," Edward finally spoke, his voice a mixture of disbelief and a strange sense of relief. "After the way you left last week, I never imagined we would be reunited like this."

George, still processing the scene, looked at his father, a man he had long struggled to understand. "Neither did I," he replied, his voice low and heavy with unspoken thoughts.

As the police team secured the area and the forensic unit began their work, George stepped outside into the cool night air. The quiet of the surrounding grounds stood in stark contrast to the chaos that had unfolded within the mansion's walls.

The realisation that Dr Ross, a respected pathologist, had been the architect of such heinous crimes was a bitter pill to swallow. And now, with his sudden death, many questions would remain forever unanswered, leaving gaps in the narrative that had consumed George and his team for so long.

George knew that the sniper would face scrutiny and an investigation into the use of lethal force. It was a grim reality of their profession, the delicate balance between protecting lives and taking them in the line of duty.

As he stood there, lost in his thoughts, George's radio crackled to life. "DI Beaumont, we need you back inside," came the voice of one of his team members. There were procedures to follow, reports to write, and a case to officially close.

* * *

Detective Chief Inspector Alistair Atkinson and Detective Sergeant Yolanda Williams sat across from Edward Beaumont in the stark, fluorescent-lit interview room at Elland Road police station. The room was silent, save for the hum of the air conditioning and the faint rustle of papers. George Beaumont, observing from a separate room via a live link, watched intently, his gaze fixed on the screen that captured every nuance of the interrogation.

DCI Atkinson, his expression a mask of professionalism, initiated the questioning. "Mr Beaumont, can you tell us how you are acquainted with Dr Christian Ross?"

Edward, his usual confidence subdued, clasped his hands together on the table. "Christian and I have known each other for many years. Our paths crossed professionally and

CHAPTER THIRTY-EIGHT

socially," he replied, his voice measured.

"And what was the nature of your professional relationship?" DS Williams asked, her tone neutral yet probing.

"You don't have to answer that," Elias Marston advised.

Edward shifted slightly in his chair. "It's fine, Elias. I have nothing to hide." He paused as if trying to remember the question. "We moved in similar circles. Christian was a respected pathologist, and I had various business interests that sometimes required his expertise."

George, watching from the other room, remained stoic, but his mind was racing. He knew his father was adept at skirting the truth, presenting facts in a way that suited his narrative.

"What expertise?" asked Yolanda.

"My company, BEAUTEX, creates the polyester-cotton industrial grade blend used in Christian's lab coats." He paused. "Well, in all your lab coats in West Yorkshire. And I supply other police authorities as well as the Home Office."

DCI Atkinson leaned forward. "Did your relationship with Dr Ross extend beyond professional interactions?"

Edward hesitated, then replied, "We occasionally consulted each other on matters of mutual interest. Nothing more."

In the observation room, George frowned. He was well aware of his father's tendency to underplay his connections, especially those that could incriminate him.

DS Williams interjected, "Were you aware of Dr Ross' activities outside of his professional duties?"

Edward's eyes narrowed slightly. "If you're implying that I had knowledge of Christian's... unfortunate extracurricular activities, then you are mistaken."

DCI Atkinson's tone hardened. "We have evidence suggesting that your relationship with Dr Ross was more than just professional. Can you explain this?"

Edward's response was cautious. "In our line of work, relationships are often multifaceted. But I assure you, I had no part in Christian's... darker pursuits." He paused. "My boy upstairs is verification of that."

George's hands clenched into fists off-screen. The dance of words and half-truths was all too familiar. He knew his father was holding back, providing just enough information to appear cooperative without incriminating himself.

DCI Atkinson continued, "Mr Beaumont, where were you on the night of Oliver Hughes' death?"

Edward's answer was immediate. "That was a very long time ago."

"Answer the question, please," said Yolanda.

Elias nudged him.

"No comment."

"And during the murder of Ryan Baxter?"

"When was that?"

Atkinson told him the date.

"I'd have to consult my schedule."

"What about the night of Alex Green's murder?" asked Yolanda.

Edward shrugged. "You'd have to tell me the date because I wasn't there." He shook his head. "I haven't murdered anyone."

Elias nudged him.

"OK, so what about the night Liam O'Sullivan was murdered?"

Elias whispered in his ear.

"I was at home, alone. I had no visitors that evening."

DS Williams followed up. "Can anyone corroborate your

CHAPTER THIRTY-EIGHT

whereabouts?"

"No, I value my privacy," Edward replied, his tone bordering on defiance, but I was on a long call with Elias from 10 pm until 1 am."

The interrogation continued, with DCI Atkinson and DS Williams methodically questioning Edward, probing for inconsistencies and gaps in his story. George, watching silently, knew that breaking through his father's carefully constructed facade would be a challenge.

The atmosphere thickened with tension as DCI Alistair Atkinson broached a critical point. "Your DNA was found on the bindings used to restrain the victims, Mr. Beaumont. How do you explain that?"

Edward Beaumont, usually composed, showed a flicker of unease. He leaned forward, his voice carrying a hint of indignation mixed with calculation. "That's a perplexing detail, certainly. My theory? I believe Christian was trying to frame me."

George, observing intently from the other room, furrowed his brow. The notion of framing was plausible yet seemed too convenient an explanation coming from his father.

DCI Atkinson, not easily swayed, pressed further. "And why would Dr Ross want to frame you?"

Edward paused as if carefully choosing his words. "I wish I knew. Christian and I had our differences, but I never thought he'd resort to something so... drastic."

DS Yolanda Williams interjected, her tone sceptical. "So you're suggesting that Dr Ross somehow obtained your DNA and planted it at multiple crime scenes?"

Edward nodded, a trace of frustration in his voice. "It seems the most logical explanation. Our paths crossed often. He could have easily collected my DNA without my knowledge." Edward shrugged. "Science was his forte."

In the observation room, George's expression hardened. He knew the depths of duplicity his father was capable of. Yet, the idea of Dr Ross, a man of science and precision, engaging in such a convoluted plot to frame Edward Beaumont was both intriguing and disturbing.

DCI Atkinson leaned back, his gaze steady on Edward. "Your theory raises more questions than answers, Mr. Beaumont. Dr Ross is no longer here to confirm or deny your accusations."

Edward's response was measured. "I understand how this sounds, Detective. But you must consider the possibility. Christian was a complicated man with many secrets." He paused, and George was sure it was for dramatic effect. "For example, did you know the late pathologist was in a homosexual relationship with Oliver Hughes?"

George pondered his father's words. Was this another layer of manipulation or a genuine clue to unravelling the motivations behind the murders?

Atkinson nodded. "We did."

"And were you aware that Oliver wanted to make the relationship public?"

Atkinson said nothing, and Edward grinned. "Don't you find it rather strange that Oliver wants to make the relationship public, and then he's suddenly murdered?"

Elias nudged Edward. If either detective noticed it, they said nothing.

"Christian knew about the estranged relationship I have with my son and so sought to use it against us." Edward smiled. "Christian was a brilliant man."

DS Williams, her eyes narrowing, added, "We will, of course,

CHAPTER THIRTY-EIGHT

investigate all possibilities, Mr. Beaumont. But this doesn't absolve you from further inquiries."

Edward's expression was a mask of resigned cooperation. "Of course, I expect nothing less. I am at your disposal for any further questions."

The interrogation had provided some insights, but the true extent of his father's involvement remained shrouded in ambiguity. The complex relationship between Edward Beaumont and Dr Christian Ross was a puzzle that George was determined to solve, not just as a detective but as a son seeking the truth about his father.

* * *

Upstairs in the bustling Incident Room, the air was thick with anticipation as DCI Alistair Atkinson debriefed the team on the interview with Edward Beaumont. Officers leaned in, absorbing every detail, their expressions a mix of curiosity and scepticism.

After the briefing, Atkinson motioned George to a quieter corner of the room. His expression was serious, his voice low. "George, do you believe your father is telling the truth about Dr Ross trying to frame him?"

George, his face betraying the turmoil within, met Atkinson's gaze. "I honestly don't know, sir," he admitted, his voice tinged with a mixture of professional detachment and personal conflict. "My father... he's always been a master of keeping his true intentions hidden."

Atkinson nodded, understanding the delicacy of the situation. "It's a difficult position you're in, George. But remember, we need to follow the evidence wherever it leads."

George's response was measured, betraying none of the inner conflict he felt. "Understood, sir. I'll keep my personal feelings out of this."

As Atkinson walked away, George's mind raced with thoughts. His father's involvement in the case, whether as a perpetrator, a victim, or an innocent party, added a layer of complexity to an already intricate investigation. He knew he had to tread carefully, balancing his duty as a detective with the tumultuous history he shared with his father.

Though he didn't voice it, George was resolute in his determination to uncover the truth. The stakes were personal, but his commitment to justice was unwavering. He needed to dig deeper to unravel the web of lies and secrets that surrounded the Santa Claus murders.

George returned to his office and sat at his desk, his resolve firm. He began reviewing the case files again, looking for any clue, any piece of overlooked evidence that might shed light on his father's role in the events. The answers were there, hidden within the labyrinth of the investigation, and George Beaumont was determined to find them. The path ahead was fraught with personal challenges, but for George, the pursuit of truth was a journey he was willing to undertake, no matter the cost.

Chapter Thirty-nine

George Beaumont's car rolled to a stop in front of the imposing gates of the Beaumont estate, its grandeur stark against the twilight sky. His hands gripped the steering wheel, his knuckles white, as he stared at the mansion that held more secrets than it did memories. Taking a deep breath, he steeled himself for the confrontation ahead and drove up the long driveway.

Upon reaching the grand entrance, George stepped out, his expression a mask of resolve, tinged with the weight of familial conflict. The door opened, revealing Edward Beaumont, who stood framed in the doorway, his posture erect, yet his eyes betrayed a flicker of apprehension.

"George," Edward greeted, his voice steady but cautious.

"Edward," George replied curtly, stepping inside without waiting for an invitation.

The conversation began with palpable tension. George wasted no time. "I need to know about your involvement in the Santa Claus murders. And why would Christian Ross want to frame you?"

Edward's response was a blend of deflection and a well-practised façade of innocence. "George, I assure you, I have no involvement in these dreadful crimes. Christian's actions are a mystery to me as well."

"I find that hard to believe," George countered, his voice firm. "You've always had your hand in matters more deeply than you let on. Christian's decision to frame you must have a reason."

Edward maintained his composure, but his eyes darted away briefly. "I can't fathom why he would do such a thing. Our relationship was strictly professional."

George, his detective instincts kicking in, pressed further. "Was it? Or was there more to it — something that threatened to come to light through these murders?"

Edward sighed, a rare sign of frustration. "George, you know the business world is complex. Alliances are made and broken, but murder? That's beyond me."

George's gaze didn't waver. "I need the truth. Too many lives have been lost, too many families torn apart."

The air in Edward Beaumont's study was thick with unspoken words, the kind that shapes lives and alters relationships forever. George stood resolute, his gaze never wavering from his father, demanding honesty in a case that had become intensely personal.

Under the weight of George's unwavering pressure, Edward's defences began to crumble. "I've never spoken of this to anyone, not even your mother," Edward began, his voice a mere whisper, "but during my university years, I... I had a relationship with Christian. It was a different time, George. Choices like that had consequences."

George's expression remained stoic, but the revelation sent ripples through him. The man he had known as a figure of unyielding strength and often cold ambition was revealing a vulnerability George had never seen.

CHAPTER THIRTY-NINE

"I realized, after being with Christian, that my preferences... they leaned more towards women," Edward continued, his gaze dropping. "Then I met your mother, Marie, in Scotland. She changed everything for me. I stayed there, away from all the judgment and expectations." He paused. "And we had you, my son."

The room was silent, save for the ticking of the clock. The revelation brought a new dimension to Edward's character, a depth George had never considered.

The emotional consequences of Edward's past actions were now laid bare. George could see the weight of years of hidden truths in his father's eyes. It was a look that spoke of battles fought in silence, of a life lived under the constant shadow of unspoken truths.

They were two men, bound by blood but divided by a lifetime of choices and secrets, and George found himself reflecting on his father's legacy and its profound impact on his own life. The complex figure of Edward Beaumont, a man of influence and mystery, had shaped George in ways he was only now beginning to comprehend.

The drive back from the estate was a contemplative one for George. The city lights blurred past as he grappled with the revelations. The man he had been raised to emulate yet often found himself in conflict with had shown a side that challenged everything George thought he knew.

* * *

Detective Constable Candy Nichols strolled through the lively shopping area, the festive lights twinkling above her head, casting a warm glow on the bustling streets. The sound of laughter and chatter filled the air, mingling with the scent of roasted chestnuts and mulled wine.

As she turned a corner, Candy's ears picked up the harmonious sound of people singing. She followed the melody until she found a group of singers clad in Santa hats and holding candles, their voices rising in a chorus of a well-known Christmas carol.

The carollers stood in a semi-circle, their faces alight with the joy of the season. A small crowd had gathered, entranced by the performance. Among them were families, couples, and individuals, all united by the spirit of the holiday.

Candy paused, her investigative instincts momentarily forgotten, as she allowed herself to be drawn into the festive atmosphere. She watched as children danced along to the music, their faces aglow with excitement. Their laughter was infectious, and Candy found herself smiling, the stresses of the case momentarily lifted from her shoulders.

The melody of 'Deck the Halls' filled the air, the carollers' voices blending perfectly. Candy observed the singers, each one contributing to the harmony in their unique way. It was a reminder of the power of unity and collaboration, a parallel to the teamwork she experienced daily at the station.

As the song came to an end, the crowd erupted into applause, showing their appreciation for the carollers' performance. Candy clapped along, her heart warmed by the display of community and cheer.

For a moment, Candy reflected on the case, the complexity of which had cast a shadow over her holiday season. But here, amidst the carollers and the smiling faces, she found a respite from the darkness. It was a poignant reminder that, despite the challenges of her job, there were still moments of light

CHAPTER THIRTY-NINE

and joy to be found in the world.

As Candy turned to leave, she glanced back at the carollers, now starting a new song. Their voices, full of hope and joy, echoed in her ears as she made her way back through the bustling streets, ready to face the challenges ahead with a renewed spirit.

Candy walks away, the melody of the carollers fading into the background, but their message of hope and unity remaining in her heart.

* * *

That cold winter evening two days before Christmas, Detective Constable Jay Scott walked the frost-laden streets of Leeds, the city alive with the buzz of holiday preparations. His eyes, usually sharp and focused on the case at hand, now observed a different scene — volunteers distributing warm clothes and holiday meals to people experiencing homelessness.

Approaching a group of volunteers, Jay's natural charisma shone through. He greeted them with a smile, his demeanour a contrast to the sternness often required in his line of work. "Evening, folks. Looks like you're doing some fantastic work here," he said, his voice carrying a warmth that matched the holiday spirit.

The volunteers, momentarily taken aback by the presence of a detective, quickly warmed up to his friendly approach. "We're just trying to make the season a bit brighter for those less fortunate," one of them replied, handing out a steaming cup of soup to a shivering individual.

Jay chuckled, his humour surfacing effortlessly. "Well, I hope there's an extra cup of that soup. It's freezing out here, and I've been known to play a mean Santa when properly fuelled."

His joke elicited smiles and a few laughs from the volunteers, who were more than happy to share their warmth with someone clearly appreciative of their efforts. Jay's ability to connect with people from all walks of life was a skill he cherished, and moments like these reminded him why.

As Jay chatted with the volunteers, learning about their motivations and the people they were helping, the scene around him highlighted the spirit of giving and community support. It was a stark contrast to the harsh realities of his job, where he often witnessed the darker side of humanity.

The interaction reminded Jay of the importance of compassion and empathy, especially during the holiday season. It was a time for generosity, for reaching out to those in need, and for remembering the collective strength of the community.

Taking a moment to help one of the volunteers hand out blankets, Jay felt a sense of fulfilment. It was a small gesture, but in the grand scheme of things, every act of kindness mattered. The simple joy of giving, the smiles on people's faces, and the gratitude in their eyes were rewards in themselves.

As he bid farewell to the group, promising to drop by again, Jay took a final look at the scene. The volunteers continued their work, undeterred by the cold, their dedication a beacon of hope in the chilly night.

The encounter had been a pleasant interlude in his otherwise demanding routine. It served as a reminder that, amidst the challenges and complexities of his work, there were always opportunities to make a positive impact, however small. For Jay Scott, the spirit of the holiday season was about more than just festive celebrations; it was about the profound power of

CHAPTER THIRTY-NINE

human connection and the simple yet profound act of giving.

* * *

The evening air was crisp and refreshing as Detective Constable Tashan Blackburn strolled through a local park, transformed by the festive season. Strands of Christmas lights weaved between the trees, casting a warm, inviting glow over the area. The sound of laughter and merriment filled the air, drawing Tashan towards a lively event bustling with families and children.

As he approached, Tashan observed the various holiday-themed games and activities that had been set up. His gaze was particularly drawn to a group of children participating in a 'Find Santa's Reindeer' scavenger hunt. Their faces were lit up with excitement, each one eagerly searching the park for clues, their parents watching on with fond smiles.

Tashan leaned against a nearby tree, his usually stern demeanour softened by the infectious joy around him. He watched as the children darted back and forth, their winter coats flashing brightly under the twinkling lights. Their laughter and shrieks of delight resonated in the cool night air, bringing a rare smile to Tashan's face.

Despite the intensity of the ongoing investigation, this brief moment of respite reminded Tashan of the simpler joys of life. It was easy to get lost in the complexities of crime-solving, to be consumed by the pursuit of justice. Yet, here, in this small corner of the city, the spirit of the season was alive and thriving, a stark contrast to the darker aspects of his work.

Tashan's thoughts briefly wandered to the case, the parts yet to be solved. But he quickly pushed these thoughts aside, allowing himself to be present in the moment. It was necessary, he realised, to find balance, to remember the world they were working to protect and the innocence that still existed amidst the chaos.

As the scavenger hunt reached its climax, with children proudly showing off their found 'reindeer,' Tashan felt a sense of contentment. The laughter and happiness of the children helped combat the weariness that often accompanied his job.

Tashan slowly walked away from the festive scene, the sounds of the celebration fading into the background. He carried with him a renewed sense of purpose, a reminder of the brighter side of humanity that he often fought to defend. The challenges of his profession were many, but moments like these served as a poignant reminder of what truly mattered – the joy, innocence, and hope that prevailed even in the darkest of times.

* * *

In the tranquillity of his home office, George was immersed in a task far removed from his usual line of duty. Spread out on the desk before him was a collection of photographs, each capturing a cherished moment, a fragment of the life he shared with Isabella and their daughter, Olivia. With meticulous care, George was assembling these memories into a handmade photo album, a labour of love that reflected the depth of his feelings.

The room was quiet, save for the soft rustle of paper and the occasional click of scissors cutting through photographs. George's hands, so often accustomed to handling evidence and paperwork, now delicately placed each photo onto the pages of the album. His usual stern expression was softened by a gentle concentration, a side of him rarely seen outside the confines of his home.

Every photograph told a story. There was Isabella, laughing in the kitchen, flour dusting her nose as she baked; Olivia, her eyes wide with wonder as she played in the garden; the three of them, a family, sharing a quiet moment under the summer sun. These were the moments that mattered, the ones that brought light into George's often dark world.

As he worked, George found himself reflecting not just on the moments captured in these images but on what they represented. Each photo was a reminder of the balance he strove to find between his demanding career and his role as a husband and father. They were a testament to the love and support Isabella had given him, especially during the gruelling weeks of the investigation.

With each picture he placed, George felt a sense of renewal, a reconnection with the aspects of his life that had nothing to do with crime and everything to do with love and family. The album was more than a collection of photographs; it was a narrative of their lives together, a narrative he was determined to continue building.

The hours slipped by unnoticed as George lost himself in the task. The album slowly took shape, becoming a tangible representation of his commitment and affection. He selected captions for each photo, writing them in a neat hand and adding personal notes that conveyed his thoughts and feelings.

This project, this simple act of creating something with his own hands, offered George a sense of peace he hadn't realised he'd been missing. It was a respite from the relentless pace of his professional life, a chance to reflect on the joys and blessings of his personal life.

As he placed the final photograph in the album—a picture of Isabella and Olivia asleep, curled up together on the sofa—George allowed himself a small, satisfied smile. It was perfect, not in its craftsmanship, but in its sincerity and meaning.

Chapter Forty

Early Christmas Eve morning at Elland Road Police Station, the team gathered for a tradition that felt more meaningful this year than ever before: the Secret Santa gift exchange. The mood was decidedly festive, a welcome change from the usual intensity that filled these walls. Holiday decorations adorned the room, and in the centre of it all was Detective Inspector George Beaumont, donning a Santa hat, his usual stern demeanour softened by the spirit of the occasion.

"Merry Christmas, everyone," George greeted, his voice tinged with a warmth that mirrored the twinkling lights around the room. His team, a group of hardened detectives, smiled back, the camaraderie and relief of having closed a challenging case evident in their relaxed postures.

One by one, they exchanged gifts, the air filled with laughter, surprise, and heartfelt appreciation. The camera panned over their faces, capturing the genuine expressions of a team that had been through the darkest of times together and had emerged stronger.

Jay Scott, known for his quick wit, opened his gift to find a novelty detective's magnifying glass, comically oversized. The room erupted in laughter as he held it up, peering through it with exaggerated scrutiny. "Finally, a tool that matches my detective skills," he joked, and even George couldn't help but chuckle.

Then came a touching moment when Tashan Blackburn unwrapped a gift to find a framed photograph of the team, taken on a day they had successfully closed a difficult case. The picture, a snapshot of unity and triumph, brought a rare smile to Tashan's usually reserved face. "Didn't know we looked this good," he remarked, his voice betraying a hint of emotion.

As the gift exchange wound down, George took a moment to address his team. "I just want to say this year has been tough, but I couldn't have asked for a better team to face it with. You've all been outstanding." His words were simple but sincere, a testament to his leadership and the respect he held for each member of his team.

In this festive setting, George Beaumont, a man more accustomed to the shadows of detective work, found a moment of respite, a chance to appreciate the lighter side of life. The Santa hat he wore was more than just a holiday accessory; it was a symbol of his willingness to embrace joy and companionship, a fitting end to a year marked by darkness and light.

In the aftermath of the Secret Santa event, George stood slightly apart from his team, observing them with a contented smile. The room still hummed with the echoes of laughter and the warmth of shared camaraderie, a stark contrast to the tension and gravity that usually filled these walls.

George's gaze moved across the room, taking in the sight of his team. There was Jay Scott, still brandishing his oversized magnifying glass like a trophy, inciting chuckles from those around him. Tashan Blackburn, usually so reserved, was engaged in a light-hearted debate with Candy Nichols, both of them with smiles that reached their eyes. Yolanda Williams was sharing a story, her animated gestures drawing her listeners in.

These moments, George reflected, were the unseen threads that held them together, weaving through the fabric of their professional lives and strengthening the bonds that duty had forged. In the demanding and often harrowing world of criminal investigation, it was easy to overlook the importance of these lighter moments, the simple acts of connection and shared humanity.

The room was a microcosm of life itself, filled with a spectrum of emotions, from the depths of despair they often encountered in their cases to the peaks of joy found in moments like these. It was a reminder that despite the darkness they often faced, there was light, too, and it was worth fighting for.

George's thoughts wandered to the journey they had all been on, the challenges they had faced together. Each case they solved not only brought justice but also deepened the understanding and respect they had for one another. The trust and mutual support within this room were not just professional courtesies; they were the pillars that upheld them through the toughest of times.

As he stood there, a figure of quiet strength and leadership, George realised how much he had come to rely on these moments of reprieve, a reminder of why they did what they did beyond the call of duty and the pursuit of justice. It was about the people, the lives they touched, the community they served, and the family they had become within these walls.

This scene, set against the backdrop of holiday cheer and

festive decorations, was a poignant reminder of the resilience of the human spirit. It underscored the value of camaraderie and support in a profession that often walked the line between life and death. For George Beaumont and his team, it was these moments of unity and shared joy that made all the difference, turning a group of colleagues into a family.

* * *

Christmas Eve had descended upon the Beaumont household with a quiet yet profound sense of renewal. After the relentless intensity of the recent investigation, George found himself in the embrace of his family, the contrast between his professional turmoil and the warmth of home strikingly apparent.

The living room was aglow with soft lights, casting gentle shadows on the walls. In the centre stood the Christmas tree, previously neglected due to the demands of the case, now ready to be adorned with ornaments and decorations. Isabella, with Olivia in her arms, watched as George and Jack prepared to decorate the tree, a symbol of new beginnings and shared family moments.

Each ornament they hung held special significance, evoking memories and reflective moments. George carefully placed a crystal snowflake near the top, a reminder of their first Christmas together as a family. Isabella added a delicate angel, a memento from her childhood, her eyes reflecting the nostalgia of Christmases past.

Jack, with the help of his dad, chose a brightly coloured bauble, his tiny fingers fumbling with the delicate object. His innocent laughter filled the room, a sound that resonated deeply within George, reminding him of the simple joys of life

CHAPTER FORTY

that often got lost in the chaos of his work.

As they continued decorating, each ornament sparked a story, a memory, or a shared joke. There was the hand-painted ornament from their holiday in the Lake District, the tiny booties signalling Olivia's first Christmas ornament, and the quirky reindeer that always made Jack giggle.

The act of decorating the tree became more than just a festive tradition; it was a journey through their family's history, a tapestry of moments woven together in love and companionship. George felt a sense of contentment wash over him, a stark contrast to the adrenaline-fuelled days and nights of the investigation.

In these quiet moments, with his family gathered around the tree, George reflected on the year that had passed. The challenges, the triumphs, the losses, and the victories all seemed to fade into the background, replaced by the immediate and profound sense of being present with his loved ones.

Isabella, catching George's eye, gave him a knowing smile, one that spoke volumes of the understanding and support that had been his anchor throughout the turbulent times. Her presence, along with that of Jack and Olivia, was a reminder of what truly mattered, of what he was fighting for every time he set out to solve a case.

As George held Isabella close, with Jack and Olivia playing at their feet, they were a scene of familial bliss. In this moment, George Beaumont, the detective who had delved into the darkest corners of human nature, was simply a fiancé, a father, a man grateful for the blessings of his personal life. This Christmas Eve was more than a celebration; it was a declaration of new beginnings and a reaffirmation of the enduring power of love and family.

* * *

Later that evening, in the heart of Rothwell, the community had gathered for a Christmas event, a symbol of resilience and unity in the aftermath of the trauma that had gripped the city. Detective Inspector George Beaumont, along with his family, was among the crowd, mingling and sharing in the festive spirit that was a stark contrast to the shadows of recent weeks.

The event was a tapestry of lights, music, and laughter, with families and friends coming together under the glow of street lamps and festive decorations. At the centre of it all stood a grand Christmas tree outside the library, its lights twinkling like stars against the night sky.

George, with Olivia in his arms, and Isabella and Jack, hand in hand, joined the gathering around the tree. A temperance band played in the background, their melodies a soothing balm to the collective psyche of the community. The air was filled with the sound of carols, voices joining in unison, a chorus of hope and joy.

Amidst the singing and merriment, George found himself in a moment of reflection. He looked around at the faces in the crowd, each one representing a story, a life touched in some way by the events of the past weeks. He realized then, more than ever, the importance of community, of the bonds that held them together through the darkest of times.

The murders had cast a long shadow over Leeds, but here, in this gathering of people, George saw the light of recovery and healing. It was in the shared smiles, the warmth of a community coming together, that the true strength of the city lay.

CHAPTER FORTY

As the carols swelled around them, George felt a profound sense of gratitude. Gratitude for the resolution of the case, for the safety of his family, and for the community that had shown such resilience in the face of adversity. He squeezed Isabella's hand, feeling her squeeze back, a silent exchange of love and understanding.

Jack, wide-eyed and filled with wonder, pointed at the Christmas tree, his excitement infectious. Olivia, now nestled in Isabella's arms, clapped her tiny hands to the rhythm of the music. In these simple, pure moments, George found a sense of peace that had eluded him during the investigation. The detective, who had navigated the labyrinth of human complexity, now stood as a member of a community connected by a shared desire for peace and joy.

As the event drew to a close and the last notes of the carols faded into the night, George looked up at the Christmas tree, its lights a beacon of hope. The chapter closed with George and his family walking home, their steps light and hearts full.

The Christmas event in Rothwell was more than just a gathering; it was a testament to the city's spirit, a promise of brighter days to come.

* * *

The night had drawn in, bringing with it a peaceful serenity that blanketed the Beaumont household on this Christmas Eve. In the cosy living room, where the warmth of the fireplace contested the cold bite of the winter night, George sat in a contemplative silence, gazing out the window at the gentle snowfall that dusted the world in white.

This quiet moment was a stark contrast to the flurry of

activity and tension that had defined George's life in recent weeks. The case that had consumed him, the relentless pursuit of justice, now seemed like a distant echo as he sat there, wrapped in the tranquillity of his home.

Beside him, Isabella was curled up with a book, her presence soothing against the residual stress that lingered in George's mind. There was still a lot of work to be done back at the station.

In the flickering light of the fire, her face was a picture of contentment, a sight that filled George with an overwhelming sense of gratitude.

Reflecting on the past events, George's thoughts drifted to the challenges they had faced and the darkness they had navigated. The resolution of the case had brought relief, but it was here, in these moments of quiet normalcy, that George found true solace. It was a reminder of the importance of balancing his demanding career with the needs of his family, a balance he had struggled to maintain.

His gaze shifted to a small, neatly wrapped package that lay on the coffee table. The handmade gift he had created for Isabella was a symbol of his appreciation, love, and a promise to be more present. It was something he had neglected during the investigation, a gesture to show his growth and commitment to their life together.

"Izzy," George began, his voice soft but filled with emotion, "I have something for you."

Curiosity piqued, Isabella set her book aside, her eyes on George. He handed her the gift, his heart beating a little faster. The room was filled with a palpable anticipation as she carefully unwrapped the package.

The moment Isabella saw the handmade photo album, a

CHAPTER FORTY

compilation of memories and moments they had shared, her expression transformed. Surprise gave way to genuine joy and appreciation, her eyes lighting up as she delicately turned the pages.

"George, this is... it's beautiful," she whispered, her voice thick with emotion.

Each page of the album was a testament to their journey together, a narrative crafted with love and care. It was more than just a collection of photographs; it was a reflection of George's heart, a tangible expression of his love and dedication.

"I wanted to give you something that showed how much you and our family mean to me," George said, his voice steady but filled with a depth of feeling that seldom found expression. "I know I've been rubbish, caught up in the job, but I'm here now. I'm here for you, for us."

Isabella leaned in, her arms wrapping around George in a heartfelt embrace. "This means everything, George. You being here, with us, that's the best gift of all."

Chapter Forty-one

Christmas morning dawned bright and crisp in the Beaumont household, the air filled with an infectious excitement that only this festive day could bring. In the living room, adorned with decorations and the glow of the Christmas tree, George, Isabella, Olivia, Jack, and their dog Rex were gathered, a scene of familial bliss.

George watched with a contented smile as Jack, nearly two years old, tore into his presents with gleeful abandon, his laughter echoing through the room. Olivia, cradled in Isabella's arms, gurgled happily, her wide eyes following her brother's every move. Rex, the family dog, wagged his tail vigorously, adding to the joyful chaos.

The room was a tapestry of torn wrapping paper, scattered toys, and the warmth of the fire crackling in the hearth. George, usually so composed and serious in his role as a detective, was a different man today—a father and husband, revelling in the happiness of his family.

The doorbell rang, slicing through the sounds of merriment, and George rose to answer it. Standing on the doorstep, against the backdrop of a winter wonderland, were his mother, Marie, and close friend and colleague Luke Mason with his wife, Patricia. Their arrival was like the missing piece of a perfect picture, completing the family gathering.

Marie, with her kind eyes and warm smile, entered with open arms, embracing her son and grandchildren. Luke, a figure usually so imposing in the field of law enforcement, carried two large, clumsily wrapped gifts, his face split in a wide grin.

"Merry Christmas, everyone!" Luke boomed, his voice filling the room as Patricia laughed, shaking her head at her husband's enthusiasm.

The atmosphere in the room shifted, the joyous energy amplified by the arrival of loved ones. The value of these support networks, these bonds forged by blood and friendship, was palpable. George felt a profound sense of gratitude for the people around him, the ones who stood by him through thick and thin.

As they settled into the festivities, the room became a hub of conversation and laughter. Marie regaled the children with stories of George's childhood Christmases, much to his mock chagrin and the delight of everyone else. Luke and Patricia shared anecdotes from their own holiday experiences, creating a tapestry of shared histories and affections.

The festive atmosphere in the Beaumont household reached its peak as Isabella's grandparents, Ted and Margaret, arrived. Their entrance added another layer of warmth and tradition to the Christmas gathering. George watched with a fond smile as the elderly couple was enveloped in a flurry of greetings and embraces, their presence bringing a sense of timeless continuity to the festivities.

The dining room was a portrait of Christmas joy, the table set with a splendid array of dishes, the air filled with the aroma of roasted turkey and spiced pudding. The laughter and chatter crescendoed as everyone settled around the table, a collective of generations coming together in celebration.

As the meal progressed, George felt a profound sense of contentment. Observing the faces around him—his family, his in-laws, and his close friend Luke and his wife—he recognised the incredible journey they had all been on, particularly in the shadow of the recent challenging investigation. It was a journey marked by trials and triumphs, fears and victories.

Raising his glass, George cleared his throat, drawing the attention of the table. "I'd like to make a toast," he began, his voice steady but filled with emotion. The room quieted, all eyes turning to him.

"To family and friends," George continued, "This year has been a testament to our strength and resilience. We've faced challenges, both personal and professional, that have tested us in ways we never imagined."

He glanced at Isabella, her supportive gaze giving him strength. "But here we are, together, celebrating this special day. It's a reminder that no matter what life throws at us, we have each other, and that's what truly matters."

George's eyes swept across the table. "Christmas is more than just a festive occasion. It's a time to reflect on our blessings, to appreciate the love and support we share, and to look forward to the future with hope and optimism."

He paused, taking in the faces around him, each reflecting a mix of emotions—understanding, gratitude, and a shared sense of journeying through life's ups and downs together. "So, here's to the hardships we've overcome and to the hopeful future ahead of us. Merry Christmas to all of us."

Glasses clinked in unison, echoes of "Merry Christmas" filling the room. George's toast had encapsulated the essence

CHAPTER FORTY-ONE

of their shared experiences—the gratitude for the present and the hopeful anticipation of what lay ahead.

As the dinner resumed, George leaned back in his chair, a sense of peace washing over him. The challenges of his career and the intensity of the investigations seemed distant now, overshadowed by the joy and love that surrounded him.

This Christmas dinner, with its gathering of generations, was more than just a festive meal; it was a celebration of life's greatest gifts—love, companionship, and the promise of brighter days. For George and his family, it was a perfect culmination to a year of trials and triumphs, a testament to their unbreakable bond and the hopeful journey ahead.

* * *

The world was draped in a pristine blanket of snow, transforming the park in Morley into a winter wonderland. George, alongside Isabella, strolled through this serene landscape, their dog Rex bounding ahead, his barks echoing in the crisp air. Olivia, snug in her pram, watched the world with wide-eyed wonder while Jack, holding George's hand, skipped alongside, occasionally tossing a ball for Rex to chase.

For George, this walk was more than a simple family outing; it was a journey of reflection. The tranquillity of the park, with its snow-covered paths and frosted trees, offered a stark contrast to the tumultuous year they had endured. Each step they took was a testament to their resilience, to the strength they had found in each other amidst the chaos of his demanding career.

George glanced at Isabella, her face radiant against the backdrop of the winter scene. She had been his anchor, a constant source of support and understanding. Their relationship had weathered storms, both literal and metaphorical, and yet here they were, stronger for it.

As they walked, George thought about the challenges they had faced, the late nights and missed dinners, the worries and fears that came with his job. But through it all, Isabella had been there, steadfast and loving. She was more than his partner; she was his confidante, his co-navigator through life's complexities.

Jack's laughter, pure and unburdened, pulled George from his thoughts. He watched his son play with Rex, their joy infectious. It was moments like these, simple and unadorned, that brought clarity to George's life. They reminded him of what truly mattered, of the preciousness of the time spent with loved ones.

The park was a peaceful oasis, a place where the worries of the world seemed to dissolve. As they continued their walk, George felt a profound sense of gratitude envelop him. Gratitude for his family, for the love that surrounded him, and for the moments of calm amidst the storm.

Olivia gurgled happily, her small hands reaching out to the falling snowflakes. Isabella smiled, her eyes meeting George's. There was an unspoken understanding between them, a shared appreciation for these moments of togetherness.

The Beaumont family, against the winter landscape, were a picture of unity and peace. The snowflakes gently falling around them seemed to symbolize a fresh start, a cleansing of the past year's trials.

As they made their way back home, George's hand in Jack's, Isabella pushing the pram, and Rex trotting contentedly beside them, George knew that the journey they were on was

CHAPTER FORTY-ONE

about more than just navigating the challenges of his career. It was about cherishing these moments, finding joy in the everyday, and building a life filled with love and laughter.

Eventually, the family reached their doorstep, their faces flushed from the cold, their hearts warmed by the bond they shared. In this peaceful walk through the snow-covered park in Morley, George Beaumont, a man often caught in the complexities of crime and justice, found a moment of profound clarity and contentment, a reaffirmation of the enduring strength found in the love of family.

* * *

As twilight descended on Christmas Day, the Beaumont family gathered in their living room in Leeds, the space illuminated by the soft glow of fairy lights and the warmth of a crackling fireplace. It was a scene of tranquillity and contentment, a stark contrast to the chaotic backdrop of George's professional life.

George, with Isabella, Jack and Olivia, prepared for a family photo, a tradition that had become more poignant this year. The camera was set on a timer, perched atop a shelf, ready to capture a moment that symbolized far more than a mere holiday celebration.

As they posed, George's eyes swept over his family. Isabella, with her gentle smile and nurturing gaze, held little Olivia, who giggled in her arms. Jack, barely containing his excitement, clutched his dad's hand. It was a display of love and unity, a testament to the journey they had all undertaken together.

The camera clicked, freezing the moment in time. The

photograph it captured was more than just an image; it was a powerful visual symbol of their resilience and journey. Amidst the trials and tribulations that came with George's demanding career, this simple snapshot was a reminder of the strength and solace found in family.

George looked at the photo displayed on the camera's screen, a wave of emotions washing over him. Each smile, each pair of eyes shining with joy, told a story of overcoming hardships, of finding light in the darkest of times. It was a reflection of their collective spirit, a family that had weathered the storms together and emerged stronger.

The room echoed with laughter and chatter, the atmosphere imbued with a sense of hope and renewal. George felt a profound sense of gratitude envelop him. Gratitude for the resolution of the recent harrowing case, for the safety and happiness of his family, and for the simple pleasures that life offered.

As the evening wore on, the children played with their new toys, Isabella chatted with George about plans for the new year, and Rex lay contentedly by the fire. It was a scene of domestic bliss.

George stood and took one last look at the family photo. In that frozen moment, he saw not just the faces of his loved ones but a mirror of his own growth and priorities. It was a reminder that amidst the pursuit of justice and the complexities of crime-solving, the true essence of his life lay here, in these moments of togetherness and love.

This Christmas photo, a snapshot in time, encapsulated the essence of George Beaumont's journey—a man who, while dedicated to his duty, had come to realise the invaluable importance of the time spent with those he cherished most.

CHAPTER FORTY-ONE

It was a powerful testament to the balance he sought to achieve, a balance between the rigours of his profession and the nurturing of the relationships that defined his personal life.

And so, George turned to his family and smiled, seeing a lasting impression of resilience, love, and the enduring strength of family.

About the Author

From Middleton in Leeds, Lee is an author who now lives in Rothwell, West Yorkshire, England with his wife and three children. He spends most of his days writing about the places he loves, watching sports, or reading. He has a soft spot for Pokemon Trading Cards, Japanese manga and anime, comic books, and video games. He's also rather partial to a cup of strong tea.

You can connect with me on:
- https://www.leebrookauthor.com
- https://www.facebook.com/LBrookAuthor

Subscribe to my newsletter:
- https://leebrookauthor.aweb.page/p/cfff8220-7312-4e37-b61a-b1c6c2d15fc2

Also by Lee Brook

The Detective George Beaumont West Yorkshire Crime Thriller series in order:

The Miss Murderer

The Bone Saw Ripper

The Blonde Delilah

The Cross Flatts Snatcher

The Middleton Woods Stalker

The Naughty List

The Footballer and the Wife

The New Forest Village Book Club

Missing: Michelle Cromack novella

The Killer in the Family

The Stourton Stone Circle

A Halloween to Remember: The Leeds Vampire novella

Shadows of the Ripper: The Long Shadow novella

The West Yorkshire Ripper

The Shadows of Yuletide

More titles coming soon.

Printed in Great Britain
by Amazon